D0849173

# Vassily Aksyonov

# *SURPLUSSED BARRELWARE*

Edited & Translated by
Joel Wilkinson & Slava Yastremski

*Ardis, Ann Arbor*

Translated from the original Russian

Ardis Publishers
2901 Heatherway
Ann Arbor, Michigan 48104


ISBN 0-88233-904-4 (cloth)




Library of Congress Cataloging in Publication Data

Aksenov, Vasilii Pavlovich, 1932-
       Surplussed Barrelware.

       Translation of: Zatovarennaia bochkotara and other stories.
       Contents: Surplussed Barrelware—Poem of ecstasy—
Rendezvous—[etc.]
       I. Title.
PG3478.K7A28       1984       891.73'44       84-6348
ISBN 0-88233-904-4

photo: S. Gitman, "Window Display on Lenin Square." Tbilisi, 1982.

# Contents

# Introduction

This anthology is the second volume of Vassily Aksyonov's stories to be published in English by Ardis; the first, entitled *The Steel Bird and Other Stories,* appeared in 1979 and presented readers with translations of works that had been written (but not, in all cases, published) prior to 1968. The present anthology, which contains five stories composed during the twelve years that elapsed between 1968 and 1979, will bring Aksyonov's English-speaking audience up-to-date and give it an opportunity to examine some of the thematic and stylistic experiments which culminated in the author's two recent novels, *The Burn* (1980) and *The Island of Crimea* (1981).

The stories translated here differ in genre. The two longest works, *Surplussed Barrelware (Yunost',* August 1968) and *Rendezvous (Avrora,* May 1971) are called novellas (*povesti*). The first belongs to the narrative tradition of picaresque fiction and it also resembles a parable in the form of a modern fairytale. We have named our anthology after this work because we consider it to be the central story in our selection and one of the major documents which reveals Aksyonov's maturation as a writer in the late 1960s. The second is a fantastic tale with strong elements of satire or, vice versa, a satire constructed as a nightmarish gothic tale. "A Poem of Ecstasy" *(Literaturnaia gazeta,* January 1968) takes the form of an interior monologue or self-styled "interview" provided by the story's protagonist, Gennady Mabukin, a boxer who becomes an intellectual. Appearing as it did on the pages of *Literaturnaia gazeta* which featured writers in the "Twelve Chairs Club," "A Poem of Ecstasy" is a humorous parody on facile and pretentious sports heroes but, like *Rendezvous,* it is not altogether a sociological spoof since Mabukin's development is transforming him, as it does all of Aksyonov's positive characters, into a creative, artistic person. Much is left unsaid and unresolved in these three stories; their exaggerations, dreams, and narrative twists and turns both amuse and delight the reader and require that he or she interpret what moral is to be drawn. By 1978, when "Super-Deluxe" appeared in *Literaturnaia Rossiia,* Aksyonov had begun to involve his readers to an even greater extent in the act of engaging a work of fiction. "Super-Deluxe" is a short story about writing and reading short stories, a work which bares its own devices and breaks down the traditional barriers and distinctions between narrators and readers. "Destruction of Pompeii" (written in 1979 and published in *Vremia i my,* No. 56, 1980) is a political allegory and literary parable, a fictional by-product of Aksyonov's involvement with editing and issuing the controversial literary almanac "Metropole" (1979). Partially because the present is recast as the past and because the narrator in "Destruction of Pompeii" plays a secondary role to that of the character of Arabella, this last story requires that the narrator adopt a reflective stance to convey some details. There is a certain *apologia pro vita sua* flavor to this story which reminds us that shortly after it was written Aksyonov left the Soviet Union (1980) and was stripped of his citizenship.

Shortly after Aksyonov took up residence in the United States as an emigre, Ardis published four of his novels in Russian *(Zolotaia nasha zhelezka,* 1980 and *Bumazhny peizazh,* 1983, in addition to the two mentioned previously) and several major short-fiction pieces. In the West Aksyonov has also published his plays in Russian and had a number of his stories reissued, often with the parts deleted by Soviet censors reinstated. To this last category of works belong the novella *Rendezvous* and the story "Super-Deluxe." Our translation of *Rendezvous* is based on the un-expurgated text which the emigre firm "Silver Age" published in its anthology of Aksyonov's fiction entitled *Zatovarennaia bochkotara, Randevu, Povesti* (1981) and that of "Super-Deluxe" on the authorized version which appeared in one of the May 1982 issues of the Californian emigre newspaper *Panorama.* A small but central passage in our rendering of *Surplussed Barrelware* likewise restores to this work, thanks to the author's cooperation, a segment not found in the version published in *Yunost'.* For the text of "Destruction of Pompeii" we relied upon the one found in *Vremia i my,* and for "A Poem of Ecstasy" we used the *Literaturnaia gazeta* version which has been reprinted at least twice in Russian with no changes.[1]

All of these details and differences might suggest that the works assembled here have little in common. However, we chose them not only because in the aggregate they are illustrative of major trends evident in Aksyonov's works from 1968 to 1979, but also because we detect certain thematic, structural, and stylistic threads which bind these stories together.

In all five stories, for example, one finds two plot elements—travel adventure and a personal quest—combined in a way that may seem traditional to readers of nineteenth- and twentieth-century American fiction, but which has characterized only a small number of works (from the 1920s and 1960s) in modern Russian literature. The classic, nineteenth-century Russian literary masterpiece which builds on these two plot elements is Nikolai Gogol's *Dead Souls*; Aksyonov does not imitate Gogol (no one has very successfully), but he has been one of the authors who revived and revitalized the Gogolian tradition in Russian letters during the past two decades. Although verbal pyrotechnics and exaggerated satirical caricatures supply much of the liveliness, charm and appeal of these stories for contemporary readers, it is the theme of a search for the meaning of life, for spiritual self-fulfillment which really unites them and reveals how

8

extensively and diversely Aksyonov explored the theme of "physicists versus lyricists" once he began to people his fictional works with more individuals experiencing mid-life crises than young adolescents who represented a new lifestyle. This change took place in almost precisely the same year as the Soviet suppression of Czech liberals who were styling their own independent version of socialism under Dubček's leadership.

The characters in *Surplussed Barrelware* grope to discover their own personal identity. At the beginning of the story, they are not distinct personalities but rather literary versions of certain sociological stereotypes. Volodya Teleskopov represents the workers and self-educated philosophizers, Irina is a pedagogue—an attractive but not very bright schoolmarm, Gleb Shustikov is a handsome Romeo who serves in the military as a sailor, old Mochenkin is a disgruntled informer and pensioner, Vadim Drozhzhinin epitomizes the political activist and successful, but highly specialized, bureaucrat, and Stepanida (who joins the travellers later) is a superstitious, but congenial peasant woman who has found work as a scientific lab-technician. As the story develops, the characters shed more and more of the sociological labels which define them and become real human beings. This change can be seen clearly by comparing the four sequences of dreams and examining what manifestation of Good Person appears to all six of them.

In the first dream Drozhzhinin envisions Good Person as a ploughman, a peasant who is carrying a compass and a T-square. He appears in this form after Vadim has completed an imaginary trip to his beloved Haligalia, which is described as a "country of suffering." Consequently, Vadim's first dream portends that Good Person represents in some meaningful way all people who suffer hardships and are oppressed. In Gleb Shustikov's initial dream, the sailor introduces himself to us by means of flashbacks to events that reveal the hardships of military service and his longing for some romantic adventure; Good Person first appears to him as a beautiful woman, a sex object which he can use to find relief from his tough life in the marines. Old Mochenkin's first dream also transports him to a world rather similar to that of his regular sphere of activity—the meeting of some investigative committee. His Good Person is a personification of his scheme for achieving retribution which he calls Alamoney. Irina Valentinova returns in her first dream to her days as a college student and tries to come to grips with her sexual libido. Her Good Person is a sailor, apparently Gleb Shustikov, to whom she feels a strong attraction. Finally, Volodya Teleskopov's first dream encapsulates a number of episodes from his life before the onset of the trip he is on with the other people to the city of Koryazhsk, where he is supposed to redeem his cargo of empty barrels, like pop bottles, for their cash value. His dream begins in a police office where his stomach is being pumped to remedy his overindulgence in alcoholic beverages, then it shifts to his place of work where he is awarded a trip to the southern resort of Tskhaltubo. Tskhaltubo fades into a snowy, northern location to where Serafima (his lover) follows him. Subsequently, the dream turns to a recollection of a football match and then to Sima's entrusting him with the task at hand. As the dream ends, the truck crashes and Volodya has a vision of Good Person who, to his mind, appears to be Sergei Esenin.

In between the first and second sequence of dreams by the main characters the pilot Vanya Kulachenko, who joins the group briefly, has a dream. He appears in the story as an answer to Irina's question about what else she needs to have complete happiness. Yet his image of Good Person is a projection of his commander into a guardian angel who can intercede for him in courting Irina and winning her love.

The second group of dreams develops further the notion of Good Person. For Volodya he takes on some of the attributes of Vadim Drozhzhinin, with whom he has made friends on the basis of mutual care and concern about the barrelware. Old Mochenkin doesn't see Good Person in any physical form, he just hears his steps; this is because Mochenkin is slow to understand such simple but elemental emotions as friendship and love. Irina and Gleb have complementary dreams in which Good Person arrives at the moment their sexual fantasies become united in the act of an orgasm.

A peculiarity of the third set of dreams is that individuals who have appeared earlier in one character's dreams start to move into the dream world of other characters making the journey to Koryazhsk. This takes place in accord with the conversion of the travellers into a collective, a group whose identity is based on a pool of shared experiences. All of these dreams are nightmares and Good Person, who comes to the rescue, is identified in three incidences with one of the travellers or with the barrelware they are transporting. To Irina he appears as Gleb coming to save her from would-be seducers and to Gleb as the warm and loveable Irina who rescues him from the clutches of a grotesque and female False-Science. In Vadim Afanasevich's dream his beloved Haligalia is transformed into the barrelware which is floating down a river. He envisions Good Person as a qualified cooper who can mend these suffering rejects and restore to them their social and symbolic value. For the remaining three main characters—Volodya, old Mochenkin, and Stepanida—Good Person in this sequence of dreams symbolizes someone who alleviates their suffering and provides a means of escape from the nightmares which they have.

Finally, in the last dream which they all share, everyone sets once more upon a quest with the barrelware being in control of where they go. They are now travelling on a symbolic Ocean, drifting inside the barrels, towards the island where Good Person is to be found. If their journey is timeless, that is of no consequence since Good Person always is waiting for them.

Thus, it is possible to say that Good Person is the personification of every traveller who sheds his or her confining sociological shell and is capable of manifesting elemental human emotions. In the process of maturation which takes place during the journey, the barrelware plays the role of a guide, a leader that directs them on the road to a fundamental but necessary spiritual rebirth. In this regard, it is noteworthy that the transformation from stereotype to real human being takes place at a rate of speed which is commensurate with the time it takes the journeyers to develop a close relationship with the barrelware. For example, from the very start of the novella Volodya is very closely tied to the barrelware emotionally. His nearness stems from his basic honesty and goodness, because his status as a déclassé worker and his eye for true craftsmanship allow him to identify with the abused, but poetically beautiful wooden casks. Another person who does not have to undergo the agony of stripping off the mask of convention is Stepanida Yefimovna. She is a simple person and has no need to acquire spiritual values since she already possesses them. Irina and Gleb come to a fuller understanding of their identities when they give themselves to one another in a private sexual act which takes the graphic form of the barrelware's "cellbellies." Vadim Drozhzhinin's conversion is perhaps the most enigmatic. Volodya's friendship serves as one catalyst in Vadim's reformation but maybe it is Vadim's own idealistic interpretation of materialism, his penchant to see revolution as a liberating force, and his delusions of sexual prowess which motivate him from very early on to feel very close to the barrelware, to rebuke the other travellers for neglecting its welfare. Old Mochenkin has the most difficult time of all, principally because he is the one who has been retarded the most by the pressures of Party propaganda, bureaucratic insensitivity, and his own selfishness. He bears some resemblance to Gogol's Akaky Akakievich; this parallel is clearly evident in old Mochenkin's second dream, where he imagines that the whole country is sewing him a coat.

The barrelware is a magical object, similar to the magical caps or carpets found in fairytales. It breaks out into a yellow-flower bloom and rescues travellers so they can continue their quest just when they need it the most: once they have decided not to board the train, which we can view as the locomotive of history, especially when we note its arrival time as 19:17—the same numbers as those in the date of the decisive Russian Revolution.

The Russian word for "barrelware" is *bochkotara*; it is a collective noun and feminine in gender. Due to the importance of these grammatical categories in Aksyonov's use of the word, we created the collective noun "barrelware" (analogous to "software" or "hardware") for our translation instead of using simply the noun "barrels" or the more cumbersome and outdated collective in English for wooden containers—the technical term "tare." Emotional bonds established by the travellers with the barrels can be described as analogous to that between mother and child or between a man and a woman, and it is in keeping with this that our translation retains the feminine pronoun "she" and possessive adjective "her" of the original. "Cellbellies," or *iacheiki* in Russian, are the most important attribute of the barrelware for the passengers riding on the truck. We invented the term "cellbelly" because the meaning of the *iacheiki* is open to interpretation. Their symbolic value extends beyond the lexical definition of this word as "cell," whether we interpret them to be the biological cells in the womb of a woman, socio-political cells at the grass roots level of an organizational infrastructure, or as a kind of nesting place in some special beehive where human emotions are hatched in a cocoon-like atmosphere.

Aksyonov has used the word *bochkotara* in other works, too, both before and after *Surplussed Barrelware* was written. One comes upon it, for example, in the novella "Halfway to the Moon" (1962), the humorous satirical sketch "Happiness on the Shore of a Polluted Ocean" (*Literaturnaia gazeta,* 34, September 13, 1970), and his recent long novel *The Burn* (1980). The satirical sketch is not very well known, but it sheds some light on certain difficult passages in *Surplussed Barrelware*. "Happiness on the Shore of a Polluted Ocean" can be viewed as a low-keyed polemic with Stanislaw Lem, the Polish fantasist and science fiction author; in the sketch Memozov, Aksyonov's anti-author figure who grew to full stature in "Around the Clock Non-Stop" (the memoirs of a trip to America in 1975), rides along the seashore on a fantastic machine (a "video-sound-phono-organ-guitar-moped") known by the generic name of "Galaxy-Lazha" while he composes, records, listens to, and watches this impromptu song of his which he entitles "Ocean's Smile":

> We'll leave to Gramps Kruzo
> The Fish, the crab, and the medusa!
> We'll take out our mini-maxi
> While riding around on our "Galaxy"!
> Let our exchange premium (*lazha*) glisten
> Along this oil-slicked coastline region!
> How nice those dreams on a guitar
> Make sounds about some barrelware!
> Spreading our telewings far out,
> Let's concentrate our efforts
> And Ocean will bring to us
> Products from various countries!
> Ocean, Ocean, give us a smile!
> Ocean, Ocean, don't skimp at all![2]

Aksyonov's "Ocean" is not the frightening environment and organic-like substance found on Lem's planet of Solaris, but rather it is comparable to a god of Greek mythology—both immortal and mortal, capable of interacting with humans and revealing to them their fate. For example, in this sketch the narrator's spouse Aglaya becomes fascinated with the exotic foreign-made goods which Ocean tosses onto its shore in order to improve the quality of human life and begins to conceive herself primarily as a sex object, a statuesque but plastic "sculpture." Via telepathy and telekinesis, Memozov—the form which the narrator's jealousy takes—conveys his wishes to the Ocean and Ocean receives Aglaya's body into its waves one stormy night, transforms it and returns it to the beach at dawn in a "perfected" form with this "label of quality" attached to a rosy spot on her body: "Fifty centuries a gennädige Frau. Our greetings and compliments, the 'Universal' Firm."

With these thoughts in mind we can interpret the water imagery and allusions to Poland in the second orgasmic dreams of Irina and Gleb as referring to an Ocean every bit as fantastic and mysterious as that found in Stanislaw Lem's *Solaris,* but one which is also an anthropomorphized god of love who unites human beings and reshapes their elemental passions into tender, caring emotions in the process of transporting them inside barrels to an island on which Good Person is waiting. Just like the Ocean which encloses and unites disparate elements of the Greek world depicted on the shield of Homer's Achilles in the *Iliad,* Aksyonov's oceans and seas are life-giving and life-unifying forces—they are beneficent images of a *deus ex machina* whose resolutions to human problems cannot be dismissed as mere artistic devices. This is all the more true since the seemingly inconsequential or unclear classical allusions in Aksyonov's stories often provide the reader with the keys for interpreting enigmas and fantasies. For example, in the same dream mentioned just above, Gleb exclaims "O, Alcinous!" at one point, and in so doing appropriates for a second the guise of Odysseus, that famous sailor of antiquity who in Homer's *Odyssey* is cast by the waves of the ocean onto shore in the foreign land of the Phaeacians. The naked and travel-weary Odysseus is greeted in this strange land by the beautiful Nausicaa, daughter of the Phaeacian king Alcinous. Homer's Odysseus and Nausicaa are obviously attracted to one another physically even though they do not become romantically involved; after he has been provided with safe conduct to the Phaeacian capital and the two individuals part ways, Odysseus thanks Nausicaa and calls her his "guardian angel" because she has saved him. Gleb and Irina are sexually liberated strangers who meet on a symbolically foreign shore—at the threshold of experiencing basic human emotions in their rite of passage— and they become romantically involved while simultaneously raising their image of each other to the "guardian angel" status of Good Person.

To the extent that such classical allusions occur in those of Aksyonov's stories which are set in the Crimea or along the northern and eastern shores of the Black Sea, we can understand that they not only contribute to the mythopoeic and fantasy elements in a story and imbed directional signals for interpreting events and characters, but also highlight certain real landmarks which are to be found in this region of the Soviet Union to which Greek and Roman culture once extended. Yet in this same environment a surname like Teleskopov takes on an ideational meaning which is much more weighty than the humorous or ironic sound quickly heard by our modern, jaded ears; Teleskopov's eyes are directed at the stars, his soul is troubled by age-old philosophical problems. There is a Greek bent to his romantic idealism. Stepanida's quest is for an elusive beetle—a "Sire Photoplexirus" (*batiushka fotopleksirus'*); this strange name sounds like a slightly distorted epithet for Zeus ("lord of lightning"), and her Tempter (*Igrets*) is a Germanic barbarian who vaguely resembles Hades, one of the other sons of Chronos. Such word play becomes very complicated in Aksyonov's prose at times, and it can include puns involving the sounds and meanings of several words in two or more languages or even become a kind of jabberwocky which, even though it sounds nonsensical, echoes thematic and phonetic patterns in the work at hand.[3]

A specific example which merits discussion here is the way in which Aksyonov refashions clichés or uses them in an ironic way so that the character who mouths them gives no thought to their meaning. Yet, they take on some of their original metaphorical freshness when the reader considers how they highlight a motif or theme which is being developed or how they serve as an important part of the subtextual meaning of the story. Such is the case with the term "surplussed barrelware" (*zatovarennaia bochkotara*)—a totally fresh metaphor that restyles two time-worn figures of speech in Russian which concern legends about the Greek philosopher Diogenes, the epitome of the Cynics of antiquity: "Diogenes' barrel" (*bochka diogena*) and "Diogenes' lantern" (*fonar' diogena*). These epithets derive from apocryphal stories about Diogenes—that he lived in a tub in order to demonstrate his distaste for the artificial dwellings which humans inhabit (instead of living like animals) and that he lit a lantern one afternoon when the sun was shining and walked around saying, "I am searching for a man." Aksyonov seemingly draws our attention to these everyday expressions in modern Russian by purposely emphasizing that his barrels are used, second-hand, rusting, and surplus goods. Neverthelesss, these old flimsy casks retain their monetary value (at least, temporarily) and take on a symbolic value which is exactly the converse of the tub Diogenes used. The travellers in Aksyonov's novel develop a symbiotic relationship with the barrelware and by riding in them their minds and hearts are opened to new, fresh and life-affirming perspectives on how life can be lived more fully. At the end of Aksyonov's barrelware fantasy the reader should take note that the barrels burst out into yellow-flower blooms. This phenomenon is comparable to the legend involving Diogenes' lantern, but mocks the import of Diogenes' search: barrelware seeks out people, not the reverse, and lights the way to a better future in a poetic way which has nothing of Diogenes' crass and sarcastic use of a lantern on a sunny afternoon. Moreover, the symbolic value of the barrelware causes a chain reaction whereby clichés or epithets other than those about Diogenes become more than casually uttered phrases or hackneyed allusions. Two examples will suffice to illustrate what takes place in *Surplussed Barrelware*. The title of Nikolai Dobrolyubov's critical essay, "A Ray of Light in the Kingdom of Darkness," familiar to every Russian schoolchild, becomes a kind of shorthand which indicates that an individual needs to undergo a spiritual transformation but is not aware that the need exists. In some of the dreams, rays of light represent a kind of structural principle whereby the narrative builds toward the appearance of Good Person at the end of the dream; that is, the light imagery occurs sporadically, like flickering signals, but intensifies toward the end of the dream. As a result the dreamers seem to be trying, haltingly and subconsciously, to bring under control the jumbled or chaotic world of their dreams and, in so doing, they naively create the right environment for the appearance of Good Person, the symbol of hope. As a literary device, of course, this kind of light imagery is not the result of mere coincidence or sheer intuition on the part of an author; it happens because the author knows how to use words and images to achieve certain effects.

The first of the functions which Aksyonov assigns to the phrase "A Ray of Light in the Kingdom of Darkness" can be found in other stories in this anthology, too. The allusions in *Surplussed Barrelware* to the legend about the Roman soldier Scaevola are also a part of the light imagery in this novella. In addition, a negative value is placed by Aksyonov on blind loyalty such as Scaevola demonstrated, for when Gleb burns his right hand in his dream he is not only committing an act whereby he loses his right hand— the symbol of power and authority—but summoning False-Science, who frightens him terribly (presumably, so that he won't ever try to act out a legend again which leads to the destruction of part of his body or symbolic control over himself).

There is only one classical allusion in the short story "A Poem of Ecstasy"; it comes at the point when Gennady Mabukin recites the first poem he has penned in which he says of himself that he is no "Narcissus" even though he is in love (presumably with himself). Thus, the boxer's upward mobility into the ranks of the intelligentsia is not self-destructive, even though it is characterized by an egotistical drive to become a cultural hero. Through the medium of Ilya Slonov and Ilya Ehrenburg, Mabukin's horizons are expanded and his transformation into an intellectual actually takes place in conjunction with his travel abroad to win the Syracuzers boxing trophy. After he wins the match against Jorge Luis Barracuda, he withdraws to his dressing room where he shows his newly developed taste for the "classics" by reading from the poetry of Innokenty Annensky, a renowned expert on classical studies, and demonstrates his recently acquired taste for emotional experiences by immersing himself in Rachmaninov's music and Morandi's paintings. Perhaps it is only retrospectively that Mabukin strikes us as being more than a caricature, but we note that Syracuzers is an archetypal villain, a capitalist exploiter, in the first three stories of this anthology and Mabukin's brilliant victory of the Syracuzers Cup not only made him acceptable to the proponents of socialist realism but puts a positive interpretation on his metamorphosis from "physical-ist" into a "lyricist."

The main hero of *Rendezvous* is a young Soviet cultural hero and a modern renaissance man named Lyova Malakhitov; he is simultaneously a scholar, a poet, a sportsman, a film producer, a Party activist, an amiable socialite, a jazz musician, and a good and loyal friend. The union of so many personalities and talents in one person is one method of stereotyping a fictional character and it is noteworthy that in Aksyonov's novel, *The Burn,* also set in the metropolis of Moscow, we find the converse method for structuring the portrait of a fictional hero: to split and diffuse his personality into the identities of other people (5 individuals in the case of *The Burn*). Lyova's search is for a Beautiful Lady; it begins once the question is raised as to why no one loves him. This quest is tied, thematically, with motifs derived from Alexander Blok's plays "The Rose and the Cross" and "The Song of Fate": a snowstorm, a Beautiful Lady, and Mephistopheles. It ends with the rendezvous Lyova has with all that is false in the world of the "Nashsharabi" restaurant, where there is only pseudo-romance, vulgarity, aesthetic shabbiness. The physical body is glorified in this incongruous national shrine ("Nashsharabi" sounds rather like "Our Arabia"); there is no spirituality evident there at all. It is the watering hole of the vacuous people who make up the crême-de-la-crême of society and these same individuals bear the brunt of responsibility for lionizing and denegrating their cultural hero, Lyova Malakhitov.

The rendezvous also turns out to be a rendezvous with death to which Smelldishchev, a black angel of death who has some of Mephistopheles' traditional traits, leads Lyova. On the deserted construction site where the confrontation with death (in the form of Stinking Lady) takes place, Lyova dies as a cultural hero (i.e., as a stereotypical figure) and is reborn as a human being. Or, at least, Lyova's vision implies that such a transformation is conceivable, for even if we view this dream as revealing a truth at death's door, it is no less meaningful in what it tells us about Lyova's search for his true identity. Malakhitov sees an angel in this vision; in all likelihood, she is his wife Nina. Almost precisely the same resolution occurs in Blok's play "The Song of Fate," which dramatizes the spiritual quests engaged in by the Russian intelligentsia at the beginning of the twentieth century.

Dreams are an important structural element in Aksyonov's works. They usually conclude on an optimistic note, but this resolution should not be interpreted to mean that the author is thereby saying, in effect, that we should ignore or place less significance on the grotesque and frightening elements in his characters' dream world. Neither art nor life is that simple. The recurring appearance of Good Person in the dreams found in *Surplussed Barrelware* is a signal that a solitary vision of happiness or goodness is not sufficient to produce a "happy ending." The novella does not end, therefore, with the arrival of the travellers on the island where Good Person awaits, even though it is clear that eventually they should reach that destination, for they are voyagers who are at home in the bright sunshine of a southern clime and this colors their outlook on life. In contrast, whenever dreams of alcohol-induced hallucinations turn nightmarish for Aksyonov's characters, as a rule the world of the dream will be that of a bustling and threatening metropolis. Such dreams also frequently contain literary allusions to the fantastic Petersburg world which is found in the works of Gogol and Dostoevsky. The nightmarish rendezvous with Stinking Lady takes up more space in the narrative and is much more forcefully presented than the "happy ending," when Lyova has his vision of his wife Nina as his guardian angel, his savior. In coming to an understanding of what this signifies, the reader needs to pay close attention to the literary allusions made by Lyova Malakhitov because they provide us with important clues about how he views himself.

In addition to the fact that he identifies himself as a kind of Blokian mystic who is searching for a Beautiful Lady, he also quotes from the Symbolist poet Vyacheslav Ivanov and the Futurist Velimir Khlebnikov. His literary tastes are an integral part of his personality, just as significant as the fact that the two shady characters in the novella are parodies of fairytale villains and castigate Lyova because he doesn't fit the mold of inane stereotypes about cultural heroes which they have picked up from contemporary poetry. When Lyova expounds his philosophical ideas at the gathering in the "Nashsharabi," therefore, it is important that the reader understand that his quote from Vyacheslav Ivanov's poetry does not mean that he no longer places much value on youthful innocence and dreams of the "golden apples of the magical Hesperides." On the contrary, this is a clue that at heart he is an idealist, that he believes certain legends can and do shape our lives in positive ways.

In passing we note that the cultural model for innocence, beauty, and youthful ebullience in Aksyonov's works is very often that provided by the ancient Greeks. Similarly, but to opposite effect, Aksyonov often associates negative cultural values and inappropriate role models with Roman civilization. Thus, if his characters live in a Roman-like world, they are doomed if they cannot find a means of escape, a fantasy or dream to believe in which will, symbolically if not figuratively, transport them backwards in time to the world of classical Greece.

Vladislav Ivanovich Vetryakov, the protagonist of the story "Super-Deluxe" is one such individual. The dark blackmarket affairs in which he is involved are not the dominant theme of this work, but rather Vladislav's search for total happiness. The definitive trait in his personality is his optimism. He is optimistic because he can enjoy the good life and indulge himself in eating and drinking sumptuously, dressing in the latest fashions, and having an active sexual life, but likewise because above all this kind of life enables him to give others an opportunity to have access to some of the luxuries of life. In return, the people on whom he has bestowed gifts are made happy and this uplifts Vladislav's soul and brings him joy. In "Super-Deluxe" these people include the "art people" and the cabin attendant Lyuda. Of the "art people" Razdvoilov plays the most important role in the story since it is he who mentions Aristotle and thereby provides the impetus for the Roman "feast of Lucullus" to be changed into Vetryakov's personal search for the quest of Aristotle's spiritual soul. Razdvoilov is a medium like the surplussed barrelware for propelling an individual in the right direction; he provides Vetryakov with the Aristotelian definition of happiness—the activity of a soul in harmony with virtue—and this idea, which is connected with the concept of freedom, grips Vladislav Ivanovich. He has defined himself up to this time as a lever in the system of redistributing material goods in Soviet society and the only freedom he has known has been economically based. He can purchase the best cabin on the cruise liner "Caravan" but he is not truly free to act as he wishes. The agony of this limitation is induced by the appearance of the "bogdykhan," rather like Malakhitov's Smelldishchev but also a Mephistopheles of Asiatic origin, not by introspection. Like Smelldishchev, the "bogdykhan" seems to have some tenuous but nonetheless close ties with the police, but more importantly he is also one of the individuals aboard the "Caravan" who engages in the shadier and more illegal aspects of the "system of redistribution." Bogdykhan is a black marketeer with the status comparable to that of a godfather in the Mafia; thus, he outranks Vetryakov, has more clout, and experiences no spiritual joy from bestowing favors on others. He lives by the code of thieves and he does not believe in the nobility of human life or the feasibility of happiness. The only Aristotle whom he can acknowledge and accept is the man who educated a future "bandit," Alexander the Great. Since he has the insight to know that Vetryakov couldn't do that (a role which many intellectuals in the Stalinist forced labor camps had to assume vis-à-vis the true criminal types in order to survive) and because he is either aware of or has helped to

18

bring about the collapse of Vladislav's network of friends, he advises Vetryakov to move on and hide out somewhere so that the authorities won't find him.

Vetryakov does not follow the bogdykhan's advice. At the moment when he makes his decision to stay he is standing alone on the quay in the rain and pondering whether or not to re-board the "Caravan." He catches sight of his acquaintances on the ship and envisions the figure of the Greek philosopher. This motivates him to return to the ship and to follow in whatever direction the winds of fate blow him.

Aksyonov offers three variants as to how the story develops beyond this point. The first possibility is Vetryakov's arrest, which is described in a passage that relies upon the painting *Life is Everywhere* by the artist Yaroshenko for most of the details it refashions into a "literary cliché." The second ending likewise culminates in Vetryakov's arrest, but it focuses upon a declaration and celebration of friendship which is founded on the cliché "I will wait." In this version, Vetryakov admits his guilt, Valentina Sokolova makes a declaration of her love, and his friends speak of legal efforts to try and reverse his misfortunate victimization as a scapegoat. The final choice of a resolution, which is in fact the most satisfactory since it is truly open-minded, is based upon the literary cliché which Aksyonov calls the rebellion of individualism. Vetryakov acknowledges he has sought to undermine the social system in which he has lived and succeeds miraculously in abandoning the ship, which a storm has blown off course into the Aegean Sea, to float on the waves toward an island where philosophers of the Lyceum School established by Aristotle will judge him. Ultimately, for Vetryakov and many other male protagonists in Aksyonov's fiction from the 1970s, love—especially eros—does not play as decisive a role in their spiritual search as it did for his fictional heroes of the 1960s.

The story "Destruction of Pompeii" which rounds out the selection of works in this anthology is a political allegory linked with events that brought about the publication of the almanac "Metropole." However, our principal interest here is the thematic bond between this story and those discussed above.

We discern two main characters in this story: one is the narrator who functions on two levels, as a red-headed giant vacationing in Pompeii who participates in the events surrounding the destruction of Pompeii and as an eye-witness reporter who at some time subsequent to the events has recorded his version of what happened and dedicated it to the second main character, the songstress Arabella.

The main body of the story recounts the destruction of the Sicilian city of Pompeii, but if we read this in allegorical terms, the location is probably a small city in the Crimea. Initially, Aksyonov's Pompeii is described as a "little niche of paradise" and when you view the shorelined city from the mountains behind it you don't notice the crowded living quarters of its people, all of its drunks, prostitutes, or murderers. The destruction of this city begins from the time two lovers of the local prostitute Svetka die—one murders the other and then takes his own life. Or, perhaps, it is the other way around—the destruction begins with the threatening signs of a volcanic eruption and the murders are but one manifestation that this city is a den of iniquity which deserves to be destroyed. At any rate, it is important to note that the destruction of Aksyonov's Pompeii does not bring about the termination of the town's inhabitants. All of the townspeople and vacationers escape alive and, what's more, Svetka's dead lovers are resurrected; everyone climbs up the Hill of Glory following the lead of Arabella, and cleansed by rain and fire, continue on their way through the mountains on a narrow path behind their guide who now takes the form of a she-goat.

During the course of the story the red-headed giant undergoes a number of changes. Initially, he appears as a writer who has come to Pompeii to conclude his scholarly but literary work "Repercussions on a Quasi-Discrete Level." This is a physics treatise which can be read as a political commentary about events taking place in the country at large (the Roman Empire-cum-Soviet Union). Therefore, it is not surprising that outside the window of his hotel room no one less than Historic Titan should turn up, i.e., a fictional character patterned after the founder of the Soviet state, Vladimir Ilyich Lenin. Later, after this author has witnessed the bloody deaths of Svetka's lovers, he becomes "sucked" into the decadent life of the city; he forgets about his identity as an author and refers to himself simply as the red-headed giant. The red-headed giant makes love to the prostitute beautician Svetka on the beach and their orgasm coincides with the eruption of the volcano. Subsequently, his body swells up and he becomes a piece of meat (Aristotle's nutritive soul) and loses all of his spiritual attributes. He would have perished in a telephone booth trying to call Moscow to report the catastrophe if not for Arabella. She appears with her friends and with a yellow-belly snake wrapped around her shoulders, drags him out of the booth and draws him into the procession she is leading. Around the procession all of the statues of the idols of the "Roman" state topple over, including the main statue of Historic Titan. There remains only the personal historical Titan situated outside the hotel room of the author of "Repercussions," who joins the procession behind Arabella. In following Arabella, the narrator becomes a new person, much younger and oriented towards matters of the spirit, not the flesh.

Arabella's symbolic role in the story is that of a New Eve, who tempts people to "prop up their existence" by kissing the snake on her shoulders and joining the merry band of people from all walks of life who find her non-conformist music refreshing and inspiring. She is the Beautiful Lady which Lyova Malakhitov sought and she is a female guide like the barrelware for the passengers riding on Volodya Teleskopov's truck. She hails from the Caucasian republic of Georgia and is a legendary figure who attracts people to come to her in their search for happiness just as the mythical Golden Fleece brought Jason and the argonauts to Colchis, the Greek word for the land now known as Georgia.

The later half of the story, in particular, contains Biblical motifs. The Hill of Glory is a Golgotha where the spirit is resurrected after being subjected to a symbolic death, the carrying of the sturgeon beam suggests the carrying of the cross to Golgotha (but it can also be read as a parody on the free work extracted by the Soviet state from its citizens on the so-called subbotniki—Saturdays on the job for no pay), and the appearance of a she-goat at the end of the story suggests that Arabella is to become a scapegoat who is punished for her role in leading suffering people out of the little niche of paradise that has turned into a veritable Sodom and Gomorrah.

Although the narrator of "Destruction of Pompeii" is a participant in the events which he describes, he ultimately puts more distance between himself and the story he tells than the narrators of any of the other works in this anthology. His dedication of the story to "Bella" casts him in the role of a disciple eulogizing the deeds of his teacher; his story becomes a testament to the secret power which Arabella possesses to transform ordinary people into a vibrant and spiritually oriented community—one which knows the real meaning of life.

We have attempted to make our translations both accurate and lively. The further we became immersed in our project, the more we came to respect and admire Aksyonov as a consummate stylist. Occasionally, we judged it necessary to render some of the lightning-quick reverses in tense which are characteristic of Aksyonov's narrative style into a smoother flowing, single-tense version in English. More often, we had to make decisions about how to handle colloquialisms, nicknames, plays on words, allusions to facets of Russian culture, etc. We were not always consistent in our practice, mainly because we set ourselves the goal of translating into a prose which would be fun to read, especially aloud, like the original, without simplifying or smoothing over difficult passages in Aksyonov's works. Early on we also came to view our anthology as a kind of cultural reader for American students with a particular interest in the Soviet Union during the decades of the 1960s and 1970s. Therefore, we decided to make generous use of footnotes for our translations and some of the notes are rather lengthy because Aksyonov constructs long lists of prominent figures in Soviet culture who are little known in the West, ticks off series of historical or legendary figures familiar to most Russians but not necessarily to Americans, and demonstrates a penchant for complex allusions with more than one level of meaning. We hope that we have made notes which will assist rather than impede the reader; in some places we chose not to footnote because we were unable to cite the proper documentation (for example, some lyrics taken from popular Soviet tunes) and there may be some things we have failed to comment upon and should have. The poems which are set off in the text and are not referred to in a note can be presumed to come from Aksyonov's own pen, although one or two of them sound very much like stylistic parodies directed at one of his peers.

We consulted very closely about every detail in the translations and they represent an equal division of time and labor between us to bring this anthology to publication.

*Joel L. Wilkinson and Slava Yastremski*

## Notes

1. The Russian text with footnotes to difficult passages was published in P[eter] Henry, ed., *Modern Soviet Satire,* Vol. 2 (London & Wellingborough: Collet's Pub. Ltd., 1974), pp. 50-57 and the Russian text alone in the new emigre magazine of satire, *Petukh* (No. 1, October 1982), pp. 4-9.

2. The translation is ours. For Russian text see *Literaturnaia gazeta,* 34 (September 13, 1970), p. 16.

3. For a concise and accurate description of Aksyonov's prose style, see Deming Brown, *Soviet Russian Literature since Stalin* (London, New York: Cambridge University Press, 1979 paperback), pp. 197-204 and for a general overview of Aksyonov's works see the introduction by John J. Johnson, Jr. in *The Steel Bird and Other Stories* (Ann Arbor: Ardis, 1979), pp. ix-xxvii.

# Surplussed Barrelware

# Surplussed Barrelware

## (A Novella with Exaggerations and Dreams)

*Having surplussed and surfaced herself in yellow-flower bloom, the barrelware surged and surgeoned at her hoopseams and went sauntering off.*

—From newspapers—

Towards evening. A swarm of bees in the small, front garden. Buzzing. Working. Latticed flights—from dahlias to sunflowers, from tobacco plants to black-eyed susans. Inspections: potted plants indoors, wallflowers at the open windows. Labor, arduous labor! In the sultry atmosphere of a regional center.

An invasion: insolent foreign bodies—fat horseflies—gorge themselves on the compost heap.

Fluttering, swooping and darting—like a tango—a sombre-hued butterfly draws near to death. A red admiral, almost a Baron Wrangel.[1]

On the road beyond the garden, dust is still settling down from a truck which passed half an hour ago.

The resident is a pensioner from a working family. Comfortably and quietly ensconced on a bench, with a hand-rolled cigarette clutched tightly between his yellow-stained fingers, he is telling a friend, almost his double, about his son's escapades:

"I've atrophied all my fatherly feelings toward him. We Teleskopovs, as you know—Peter Ilyich—are on the mechanical side; we serve industry, usually in the product test shops. For four generations, as you know, Peter Ilyich. We return here, to the idiocy of village life, for our earned rest, but only when the creaks in our joints hamper our ability to work, as is the case with you, Peter Ilyich. But my oldest, Vladimir, he sowed his wild oats god knows where for a full seven-year term after the army. Then, he returned to Piter[2] in a thoroughly reprehensible state—a walking vodka bottle, with a rebellious look.[3] I set him up in the shop. He's got Teleskopov talent, Teleskopov hands, and our Teleskopov head—flaxen and agile. His eye became truly artistic. My heart would sing, Peter Ilyich, when Vladimir and I made our way home from work ... But then, aach, ... off he went carousing again. And what's to become of him!! I myself will never understand. He's turned up now at my place, expecting to share my pension. A shame and a disgrace. 'It's the call of the earth,' he says, 'here's my ancestral home.' "

"Does he work anywhere or just strike up deals for cash?" asks Peter Ilyich.

"Two days ago he signed on as a driver at the village general store ... A shame and a disgrace ... But since then he's been on a binge over at Simka's hole-in-the-wall. There are no orders to fill and he won't sober up."

"Have you heard what's happening in China?" Peter Ilyich interrupts, in order to switch the subject. "The Hun-wei-ping are fooliganizing."[4]

Vladimir Teleskopov is, in fact, now on a binge at the hole-in-the-wall tended by Sima, a resolute widow. He is perched on a rather ominously squeaking box, even though he could have picked a more suitable seat for himself. Together with his new friend, Gleb Shustikov—a marine in the Black Sea Fleet—he's treating himself to some home-made mandarin orange liqueur. Their shadow and the shadows of the glasses with tangerine light inside them are visible against the pale pink, plastic curtain. Gleb Shustikov's profile is sharply etched, like a poster silhouette. One can tell right away that he's a man who'll become a commander. But Vladimir's profile reveals him to be a shaggy-haired, snub-nosed, and unreliable fellow.[5] He wobbles unsteadily, lurches over the glass, and then moves away from it.

Near the counter, Sima is counting her earnings; she can hear, behind her, the slurred revelations of her man.

"...and he, the S.O.B. director, calls me into his office at the factory, but I tell him I'm drunk, and he says to me, I'll take you to our medical station and they'll get you back to norm there. But I'm not going to tell you, Gleb, what my labor skill is..."[6]

"...Volodka, stop glazing your eyeballs with that stuff," says Sima. "Tomorrow you're supposed to transport the containers to the station."

She draws the curtain aside and, smiling, looks at the fellows. She stretches her large, sweet body.

"The barrelware has really built up round here, boys," she says languidly, with a subtle, but vague suggestiveness, "she's really stacked up, surplussed, and surfaced herself in yellow-flower bloom ... as they say in the newspapers."

"Well, then, Serafima Ignatyevna, take care of your robust health," says Shustikov Gleb, springing up and straightening his uniform. "Tomorrow I depart for my duty station. And Volodya here'll drop me off at the train station."

"That means you're leaving us, Gleb Ivanovich," Sima comments, as she makes some unnecessary movements around the storeroom and flashes smiling glances at the marine from behind her magnificent shoulders. "Oh, mercy, the gals will certainly grieve when you're gone."

"That's a gross exaggeration, Serafima Ignatyevna," smiles Shustikov Gleb.

A delicate mutual understanding exists between them and it might have been something more, but Sima, after all, is not at fault because she fell in love with the self-destructive Teleskopov prior to the arrival of this splendid marine on furlough. Such is the game of nature, of fate, and life's secrets.

Vladimir Teleskopov, the cause of this foul-up, doesn't notice any concealed meanings in their talk. He's melancholically engulfed in his thoughts, in a tin of fish in tomato sauce that he's eating.[7]

He sees the marine off a short way. Then, he stands on the porch for a long time, looking at the endlessly darkening fields, at the strips of steaming fog, at the wing-like sweeps atop the water well, at the thin crescent moon which hangs in the green sky like a lonely sea horse.

"Oh, Seryozha Esenin, Seryozha Esenin," he mumbles to the moon, "do you see me, Volodya Teleskopov?"[8]

And the Junior Petty Officer Shustikov, Gleb, heads for the club with firm strides. He knows that the (kolkhoz) tractor drivers organized something against him at the last meeting; nevertheless, he walks—crisply and self-confidently—to meet the dangers.

It grows darker and darker. The dust settles down; insects calm down; animals stamp drowsily—dreaming about tomorrow's fresh grass; and people stomp in dances, near stoves or under the windows of their own or neighbors' homes, whisper something to one another—words like "scoundrel," "dear," "drunkard," "damn you," and "darling mine."

Darkness set in, and then at once it began to grow light again.

Vadim Afanasyevich Drozhzhinin, a refined intellectual, likewise readied himself to return to his place of work, that is, to one of the foreign but unprepossessing cultural institutes in Moscow where he'd become a staff consultant.

On this summer morning he sat on the porch of a forester's hut in a gray, lightweight-tweed suit and waited for the vehicle which was supposed to take him to the Koryazhsk station. Around a large table sat his village relatives who had come to see him off. They eyed him reverently, quietly . . . not able to make up their minds to take a sip of the tea or a bite of the dumplings and potato pancakes. Only papa Drozhzhinin, the forester, noisily ate his daily portion of shchi, and mama, for etiquette's sake, joined him. She barely moved her austere lips.

"They've got a strange habit, nonetheless—eating out of one bowl," thought Vadim Afanasyevich, even though he had long ago, one might say from birth, known about this habit.

With his eyes, Vadim surveyed the forest shimmering idyllically in the morning light, the black-currant bushes bordering the porch, the leaves covered with dew, and his shy and silent parents: pop's pointy beard fell into his field of vision, of course, and the comb in mum's thin hair. He smiled warmly. He was sorry to be leaving his idyll, this quiet. Yet, of course, this sorrow meant little to him by comparison with the charms of that always rich and full life which a refined and bachelor intellectual leads in Moscow.

After all, all that he had achieved—this "Fitzgerald & Sons, Ready-Made Clothes" suit, the "Hunt" shoes, the little brush moustache under his nose, and the perfect, absolutely irreproachable "stiff upper lip," the irreproachable manners—all this marvelous English-ness—he had achieved himself.

A-a-ch, whither had vanished that long, long ago time when Vadim Afanasyevich had showed up in Moscow dressed in a velveteen suit and carrying a wooden trunk?

Vadim Afanasyevich had no intentions of setting the world on fire, but he was proud, justifiably, of his specialty, his knowledge in one narrow field.

Let's lay out the cards: he was a unique specialist, the only one on the small Latin American country of Haligalia.

No one else took such a lively interest in Haligalia as did Vadim Afanasyevich. Well, with the exception of one Frenchman, the vicar of the Swiss canton Helvetia. Religio-philosophical questions, of course, had more appeal for the vicar, whereas Vadim Afanasyevich's circle of interests embraced all aspects of Haligalian life. He knew all the dialects in this country—of which there were 28—the folklore, the history, the economy, all the streets and back alleyways of the capital of this country, the city of Polis, and of the other three large cities, all the stores and shops on these streets, the names of their owners and members of their families, the nicknames and habits of all domestic animals there. Even though he'd never been to the country! The ruling junta in Haligalia wouldn't give Vadim Afanasyevich an entry visa, but all of the ordinary Haligalians knew and liked him. He corresponded with about half of them, gave advice on family matters and mediated all sorts of conflicts.

This all began with the normal sort of zeal. Vadim Afanasyevich had simply wanted to become a knowledgeable specialist on Haligalia. That's what he became, and more—the best and only specialist in the world.

With time his zeal turned to passion. Hardly anyone, in fact practically no one, would suppose that a sinewy fellow in an austere gray (or brown) three-piece suit, who daily had his coffee and apple pie in the cafe of the "Nationale" hotel,[9] could be gripped by a passionate love for such a sultry, humid and almost unknown country.

As a matter of fact, Vadim Afanasyevich lived a double life. And it was his second life, the Haligalian one, which was most important. Every minute of both his professional and personal life he thought about the aspirations of the Haligalian people . . . about how to wed the bicycle-shop worker Luis with Rosita, the daughter of the restaurant manager Kublitski. He grieved about the slightest rise of inflation in Haligalia, the corruption and unemployment there. He gave considerable thought to the under-handed machinations of the junta, to the ceaseless struggle of the people with the Argentine cattle magnate Syracuzers, who had inundated defenseless little Haligalia with his tinned meats, patés, beefsteaks, sirloins and julienne of game.

Only the outer veneer remained of Vadim Afanasyevich's first, seemingly main life. That is, this irreproachable English-ness: the pipe in a pouch, lawn tennis, coffee and tea at the "Nationale," faultless crossings of Arbat Street and Kalinin Prospect.[10] He was single and dispassionate. Only Haligalia, oh, yes, Haligalia...

Now, as usual after a fortnight of papa's exhortations and mum's dumplings, after all this idyllic life and secret, soul-gratifying longings to have been born an aristocrat, he already felt drawn back to Haligalia, to his two outposts of Haligalia: the Haligalian literature and ethnographic rarities in his one-room apartment and the sign "Haligalia Sector, Consultant V. A. Drozhzhinin" on his office door at the institute.

He was joyous now about the forthcoming departure. The only causes for any unpleasantness were those numerous jars of jam—strawberry, cherry, and black currant—which his relatives had brought to see him off with.

"What am I to do with this huge quantity of preserves?"

Old Mochenkin, gramps Ivan,[11] had cussed and haggled with his son and daughter-in-law a whole hour. Once again, the insensitive youths had offended him: they hadn't heated up the steambath and hadn't brought the kvass as had been the case earlier when old Mochenkin still wheeled around as the Colorado Beetle inspector, when he pedalled a bicycle around and toted a new attaché case trimmed with fake-crocodile skin. Old Mochenkin had never seen a Colorado beetle in all his long life—'cept in some portraits.[12] However, he had spent a long time in hot, but vain pursuit of it all over the region's vegetable warehouses, collective farms and private-garden plots.

In those days there'd been a steambath with kvass, his own special and favorite drinking mug decorated with roosters,[13] an embroidered hand towel, a glass or two of vodka, and a seat of honor in the house under his Certificate of Meritorious Labor.

To this let us add that old Mochenkin, gramps Ivan, passed on a true profession to his son: he taught him to castrate sheep and pigs. Yes, he gave his apolitical son a very lucrative trade. One could say he provided him with security for his whole life. Essentially, the "Ural" radio-grammophone, the chest of drawers, and the motorcycle (even if it didn't have a motor)—all these things—were the profits reaped from old Mochenkin's hands.

But everything turns out topsy-turvy, with no bright prospects. His

29

son and daughter-in-law gave birth to a pack of hooligan schoolkids who had absolutely zilch respect for granddad...an unending lack of deference. There was no "Hello, dear grandfather, Ivan Alexandrovich" for you; no "please allow us to sit down dear grandfather, Ivan Alexandrovich," for you, either. And he no longer had the strength to tolerate their disrespect.

For a while he tried writing complaints: a letter to the Pioneer organization about the hooligan schoolkids; another concerning his son to the assembly-shop (for cowsheds) authorities; and a third against the daughter-in-law to the magazine "Peasant Woman"—but the bureaucracy, which the family had "in its pocket," paid the complaints no attention.

Now, old Mochenkin had concocted a new idea and the name of this captivating idea was Alamoney. Old Mochenkin hadn't accumulated enough service for a pension because, if one were to tell the truth, he had been clever enough to avoid a laborer's life in our worker's society. He'd spent all his time castrating the small Artiodactyla animals[14] or drinking away the prime of his life at tea counters where he could observe various types of people. For example, he could conjure up in his mind's eye a whole kaleidoscope of just barmaids alone. Thus it was that he now fantasized about his idea of Alamoney.

The ungrateful son, with whom old Mochenkin now lived in constant turmoil, was a talker. His other three sons weren't loquacious, but they were extremely active, hardworking and skilled. They had long ago flown their father's coop and now, in various parts of the country, were nailing down their own personal interests by becoming self-supporting. These— the non-talkers and unseen—old Mochenkin respected greatly even though it was on them also that he planned to dump his idea of retribution, the Alamoney.

So, on this quiet summer day old Mochenkin was in a thoroughly cross mood—not having found a drop of steam or kvass in the bathhouse, nor any bathhouse for that matter. He and his son (yes, the talker) and the squabbler daughter-in-law barked at one another. He scared off the hooligan schoolkids with his crutch and loaded his briefcase, which had floated along the African Nile as a fake crocodile, for confrontations with the various authorities in the *oblast*.[15]

For the last time he cast a fiery eye around his own, worker's izba, built by his deceased grandmother but now seized by an impudent descendant (no "Allow us to take another morsel, dear grandfather, Ivan Alexandrovich" for you, no chance to expound on the homework topic "A Ray of Light in the Kingdom of Darkness").[16] He grinned maliciously—"I'll ignite them with Alamoney, from all four sides." And he set off for the village general store, where he knew that a vehicle was supposed to depart for the Koryazhsk station.

Irina Valentinovna Seleznyeva, a geography teacher in an eight-year school,[17] was packing for a vacation in the sub-tropical Black Sea resort area. Her initial decision had been to head for the shores of the short, but deep Neva which, flowing through the museum city of Leningrad, empties into the Finnish Gulf of the Baltic Sea. But this had been changed when she conjured up the thought of that southern tan which graces a stupendous figure and recalled the cardinal principle—"don't bury, Irina, your treasures."

A year had already passed since she, after graduation, had dug a pit for her treasures here ... in the boondocks of this regional center. She visited the House of Culture only with geographical interests at heart, but she never danced, no not under any circumstances, because she was *the* representative of the intelligentsia.

With a sigh, Irina Valentinovna glanced out the window: near the telegraph pole, in the full blaze of the morning sun, stood the amazing seventh-grader, Borya Kurochkin, in a new dark-blue suit that hung tightly on his petite, athletic figure. He had on a green tie and a red kerchief in his breastpocket. His long hair had been slicked down into a part with generous gobs of brilliantine. He stood under the pole in the midst of cow paddies like a fugitive from another world and he disturbed Irina Valentinovna's entire being with his chic look and penetrating glance locked into an idée fixe.

About a year ago Irina Valentinovna, going through her class list, gave the amazing seventh-grader Borya Kurochkin, the son of the chief agronomist, a fairly simple question from the conspectus: "Tell me, Kurochkin, how the silt of the Mozambique River affects the economic development of the Indonesian peoples?"—or some such nonsense. There was no answer. "Sketch for me, please, the contours of the Western Hindu Kush, or, uh, let's say those of Eastern Kara-bagh."[18] Silence.

Irina Valentinovna, astonished, looked at his very broad shoulders and his typically masculine smile which always disturbed her whole being.

"Her eyes are blue," the amazing seventh-grader intoned in a bass voice.

"An 'F'. Take your seat!" Irina Valentinovna burst out. Then she jumped up and removed her "treasures" far from the classroom.

"Hey, guys!" the amazing seventh-grader yelled from the corridor, "teach has a crush on me."

Since then it had gotten worse. Western and Eastern Hindu Kush began to blur into one another, Eastern Kara-bagh merged together with Lake Erie into one economic cartel-carousel of the neo-colonialist elements of all the Guianas and the forest-steppe zone.

Even in college Irina Valentinovna had been a very low achiever, but now everything was really mixed up in her head: the amazing seventh-grader Borya Kurochkin answered even the most difficult questions with a "compliment."

Irina Valentinovna, pursing her lips, showered him with 'D's and 'F's. The situation was almost catastrophic—ones and twos (fence-posts and swans) for all four terms of the year.[19] It was with great difficulty that Irina Valentinovna succeeded in giving Kurochkin an 'A' for the year.

During the course of the whole school year the amazing seventh-grader had disturbed the very being of this pedagogue, who, toward spring, had dreamed up the trip to the subtropics.

Frothing and swelling up into bubbles, there flew into the suitcase powder-blue, pink and sexy black lace undies; perlon and nylon stockings; a tight-fitting, ready-made dress; elastic garters; fancy duds; inexpensive jewelry; and, on top, like a relief map of the Gobi plateau, laid a neatly creased and splendorous décolleté flounce for evening foxtrots. The locks snapped shut.

"The mute tête-á-tête of eyes are forgotten so quickly, are forgotten so quickly," the radio station intoned as a farewell.

Irina Valentinovna ran out into the street and marched to the village general store. Bored hens flew out from under her legs that ached for the sub-tropical foxtrots, insulting any sort of spiritual advancement with their fat, dirty rumps and idiotic clucking.

"Just a moment, Irina Valentinovna!" the amazing seventh-grader Borya Kurochkin shouted to his teacher.

In full view of the whole town he followed her along the plank footpath to the very general store, glancing sideways with the bloodshot eyes of a clever little lion.

A side-board truck loaded with empty barrelware already stood near the porch of the village general store. The barrelware was in pitiful shape on account of being treated inhumanely and because her needs and desires had long gone unattended. She'd really surged and surgeoned at her hoop-seams, surfaced herself in yellow-flower bloom . . . as if begging for retirement.

The monumental Shustikov, Gleb, the marine, stood near the truck—bracing himself picturesquely against the hood. His unmarked face bore no traces of last night's talk with the tractor drivers, for Gleb's military specialty was amphibious landing force attacks and he was well able to defend his handsome face.

He watched Irina Valentinovna approaching, almost in a run. He eyed her with such exceedingly enormous astonishment that he completely failed to notice the amazing seventh-grader Borya Kurochkin.

"Doesn't it appear we're fellow travellers as far as Koryazhsk?" the marine kindly asked the teach as he took hold of her little suitcase.

"Precisely so," Irina Valentinovna replied gaily and saucily, quite happy with the way their conversation had begun, and glanced disparagingly over her shoulders at the amazing seventh-grader.

"And where, my dear miss, are you bound for beyond there?"

"I'm travelling to the Black Sea subtropical zone. And you?"

"Almost precisely to that same zone," said the marine, voicing surprise at his good fortune.

"What weather do you think there is now in the subtropics?" the teach asked, continuing their conversation primarily to denigrate the amazing seventh-grader.

"I believe the weather there is favorably disposed to . . . to . . . to vacationers," the marine answered with a smile.

Having caught this smile and grasped its intent, Borya Kurochkin's childish lips burst out with a noisy "booph," his childish nose snorted a "hmrfmph."

"Well, I'll be off," he said.

He left, stirring up the dust with his mod bell-bottom trousers. Hunched in dejection, he spat vigorously in all directions. Thus, for the first time, life had clouted the amazing seventh-grader on the head with a sandbag.

The sailor helped the teach climb onto the truck (and was once again surprised, as he lifted her up, at his good luck) and, then, hopped onto the truck himself. Having settled themselves cosily on the barrelware, they continued their conversation and didn't even notice how a third passenger, old Mochenkin—gramps Ivan, had scrambled up onto the barrelware like a hungry lynx.

From habit old Mochenkin quickly examined the barrelware concerning any Colorado beetle. But, having found no such, he situated himself near the cabin and right away began writing one of his complaint letters to the authorities about the teach Seleznyeva who was captivating men in the armed forces with her naked knees. And you don't need any imagination to wonder what she's teaching the rising generation!

Sima, yawning with delight, appeared on the porch.

"Hey there, Gleb Ivanovich, you've made the accommodations fit you nicely," she drawled out, "Oh, that's you, is it, Irina Valentinovna? Pardon the improper inference," she sang out in languorous perfidy as she exchanged knowing smiles with the marine. "And where are you off to, gramps Ivan, eh?"

"What's that you say? I didn't sleep atop the stove with your granny," old Mochenkin hissed out angrily. "You'd best drop this letter in the mailbox." And he handed the waitress his denunciation of the teach.[20]

His mug all covered with egg, the nutty Volodya Teleskopov darted out onto the porch.

"Everything's O.K., nobody's drunk!" he pronounced. "Hey, Serafima, where's my fancy cap and kid gloves?[21] And where's my favorite book, the collection of fairy tales? Gimme a ten-rouble note, Serafima, I'll buy you a gift in Koryazhsk. I'll buy you some rare treat, other than food, and you'll be happy."

"Listen here, you go pick up the forester's son," Sima said, "and straight on to Koryazhsk. I won't give you ten roubles; you'll manage to get yourself a half-liter bottle somehow. Make sure that white lightning doesn't zap you in jail for fifteen days, cause my love for you might dry up."[22]

And right then and there, with no shame, she kissed Teleskopov smack on his dirty lips, as if she were his wife.

Volodya climbed up behind the wheel, revved up the motor and tore off down the road. The barrelware clattered and crackled, knocking the passengers over before she settled down.

Ten minutes later this insane truck, taking a jaunty little curve on its right wheels alone, flew into the forester's courtyard.

Vadim Afanasyevich would have absconded with just his elegant suitcase, or, more precisely, his carry-all, but his relatives, groaning and sobbing in unison, had skillfully mounted a huge rucksack loaded with jams onto his shoulders. Haligalia almost lost its best friend in the process, for the rucksack nearly split the consultant in half.

Vadim Afanasyevich had already made himself comfortable in the cabin when he spied a person of the opposite sex on the barrelware in the back. He offered her a place in the cabin, but Irina Valentinovna categorically refused. The wind on the lengthy journey didn't frighten her at all. In fact, it exhilarated her.

Old Mochenkin likewise rejected the intellectual's pestering offers; he didn't want to abandon his observer's post. Vadim Afanasyevich, already quite up to his ears in gentlemanliness, even offered Shustikov, Gleb, as a member of the armed forces, his place in the cabin.

"Knock it off, pal. Sit down and stop screwing around," Gleb interrupted him rather angrily, and Vadim Afanasyevich, flustered by the word "pal,"[23] took his seat in the cabin.

Finally, they took off, terrorizing the whole regional center as they roared past the agronomist's house, near which a small figure stood with his face to the wall—his broad shoulders convulsing from sobs; past the House of Culture, whose entire contingent of active male supporters saluted the travellers from its porch; past the Mochenkin house that had no presentiment of the punitive Alamoney; past the glowing mandarin orange infusion which highlighted the condescendingly polite and cunning Sima; past the small garden with dahlias across which old Teleskopov lovingly arched his eyebrows at the familiar truck; and beyond—through the open fields. It was about 65 kilometers to Koryazhsk, or a two hour drive if you take into consideration the condition of local roads and ignore the peculiarities of Volodya's personality.

These peculiarites began to manifest themselves right away. At first

Volodya chatted animatedly with Vadim Afanasyevich. To be more exact, he actually just blathered on, shocking his intellectual companion with the tale of his unbelievable life...

"... In short Edik and I ran into the hire-and-fire office where one six-by-six mug shoots us off to the Regional Office of the Road Workers Union and together with us there was a I don't exactly recall his name—Ovanesian, Petrosian, Oganesian—a blonde fellow who used to play in the "Water Transport Workers" forward line for Krasnovodsk... well, someone slammed his shoulder against the counter and all hell broke loose I he says will see you get sent to the penitentiary, but who wants to it's good I had a friend on an excavation crew he says Volodya listen to me and put some piss and vinegar into your petition to work it off... of course we just leg, leg, legged it so then Edik and I poled timber down the Amur from rafts let's go he says to Komsomol Lake... we dug it ourselves so we'll go boating on it with our chicks we turned the skiff over and the old fart says I'll file charges against you unless you ply me with vodka Vitka Ivashchenko just shuffled along to join up with us this guy was a right stout ox who played the tuba and I the drums in a funeral band in Poti but the plan's been hanging around his neck two years already so he's walking around gloomily like a tomcat Yegorka and Burkin came tippling along with us, too, a young lieutenant took down all our names to check out... to the girls he says I'll pack you off but such cocky stuff didn't mean a damn to us so we took the train to Kemerovo in the baggage compartment and there leg, leg, legged it on Do you like to fish?..."[24]

He suddenly fell silent, became as gloomy as a dark cloud, and snorted threateningly through his nostrils. Vadim Afanasyevich was frightened at first and leaned back hard against the seat. However, he then realized that the fellow was suffering for some reason.

In the back end life was becoming difficult, entangled as it was with the barrelware. On account of Volodya's unbelievable driving and the ruts in the country roads, the barrelware was also suffering: she creaked, crackled, rolled around and out into little pieces... losing her identity.

The passengers kept on falling off her onto the loose staves, bruising their noggins and cutting themselves. Soon, however, Shustikov Gleb the marine found a solution to the problem: having turned the barrelware on her head, he proposed that each passenger occupy the barrelware's "cellbellies."[25]

The barrelware steadied herself and settled down. The passengers, for their part, found cozy bunks for themselves in the "cellbellies" and resumed their activities.

Old Mochenkin went on writing complaints about Sima's surplussed barrelware, about Volodya Teleskopov's ties to Sima, about Vadim Afanasyevich's wholesale shipments of private garden plot jams,[26] and also continued to pile up material against Gleb and Irina Valentinovna.

Having blushed a bright red, the happy Irina Valentinovna went on and on with her prattle about the subtropics. She kept pushing her fantastic wind-blown hair back, glancing from time to time at the marine's laconic, masculine features and glowing warmly inside. The marine nodded—smiling and gazing deeply into her eyes.

Suddenly the truck came to an abrupt stop. The barrelware wailed in fright, shifting her cellbellies around. Consequently, Irina Valentinovna unexpectedly turned up next to old Mochenkin, who seized her in a clenching embrace.

Volodya Teleskopov, gloomier than a storm cloud, crawled out of the cabin.

"Hey, Gleb, hop down here for a minute," he said, gazing at the endless fields, not at the marine.

Puzzled, Gleb shrugged his shoulders and vaulted over the side of the truck.

"Let's walk off aways," Teleskopov said.

They walked off a short distance down the dirt road.

"Tell me, Gleb,...be...honest...you hear," Volodya pausingly stammered. He frowned, then stuck out his pathetic chin in defiance and whined threateningly. "Tell me the truth, now, you got me? Was there anything between you and Simka?"

Shustikov Gleb smiled broadly and flung his arm around Volodya's shoulders to show his friendship.

"Honestly, Volodya, there wasn't anything at all."

"You had your eye on her though, didn't you, eh?" Volodya quipped excitedly. "It came to me—I understood—it just hit me, sitting there at the wheel."

"Do you know the song?" Gleb asked and immediately broke out into song with his fine, clear voice: "If I find out my friend's in love, that his girl and mine are the same. Then, I'll step aside—that's the rule of the game: the odd man out has got to leave."

"You going to honor those words?" Volodya asked calmly.

"Honest—I'd burn my hands, like Scaevola,[27] to prove it," the marine replied.

"Yes, I believe you. Let's get going again," Volodya yelled and burst out in a guffaw.

The rest of the trip went smoothly, with no complications. They drove past pale-green fields where mowing machines were at work; past blue groves; past villages with windmills, water-well sweeps, and pillaged churches; past high-tension wire pylons. The landscape was pleasant, soporifically level and flat; it had a grandeur, like soft music wafting through the air. Trails of jet vapor drifted idyllically across the sky.

On and on down the road they travelled. Then, they fell asleep.

## Vadim Afanasyevich's First Dream

A large puppy, the size of a cow, was walking properly along Florida de Maestra Avenue. Dogs in dreams are a good omen.

"Hi, Carabanchelle!" Vadim Afanasyevich greeted it in accord with the rights of a long-term friendship. "How's your mother these days?"

Carabanchelle's mother—auntie Gusta, a perennial favorite in the national races—was a bewhiskered dog with a glossy coat the color of copper tubing. She appeared with some rouge-pink meat patties on the second floor of the trattoria "My Haligalia."

"Señor Drozhzhinin!"

The street was teeming with simple Haligalians. A crowd of thousands sat on their haunches in the shadow of agave and cactus plants. Vadim Afanasyevich or, almost he—no, don't worry, we're just ignoring the driver and the little old man; papa and mamma don't count—he, in person, scampered up a plum tree and discussed with the simple Haligalians the vital issues of friendly relations with foreign countries.[28]

Junta appeared, twisting her pale lips in a diplomatic smile. She wore stiletto high heels and a threadbare fox-fur stole around her neck. Everything else on her dripped and oozed dark-blue. Weak little clay feet trembled under the weight of her huge body.[29]

"Oh, I had thought that our friend, señor Syracuzers, had come, but it's only you, monsieur Drozhzhinin. What a pleasant disappointment."

Vadim Afanasyevich spent the night in the swampy lowland of Cuccofuega. Bloodthirsty Haligalian roosters and poisonous geese scurried all around him. Yet, nevertheless, the sun still rose over this country of great suffering.[30]

Vadim Afanasyevich rubbed his eyes. Good Person, a simple ploughman with compasses and a T-square, came walking toward him across the dew-covered grass.


## Marine Shustikov Gleb's First Dream

Boatswain Dopekailo[31] blew a sharp note on his silver pipe.

"Up and at 'em! You cream of wheat."

The cream of wheat, shuffling their boots, passed out the firearms among themselves.

"Junior Petty Officer Shustikov, Gleb, who was it you were with yesterday?"

"A chemical engineer, Comrade Boatswain of the guard, Sir."

"Congratulations! You'll get 'Serenade' cigarettes for your decoration. Cookie, give 'doughnuts' to Shustikov."

With "doughnuts" clenched in our teeth, it's straight down into the underwater kingdom. We swim with aqualungs—tasty "doughnut" mouthpieces—and beside me Guliamov is blowing bubbles: a rehearsal for operation "Lily." Greetings from bright sunny May! The next number on our program is the parachute jump.[32]

Who's that there suspended on the lines, grinning like mommy's pancakes? Why... it's Shustikov, Gleb, the model and aspiring marine. Right, right. I saw him in the mirror at the cafe "Lily."[33] The problem is what he ought to do—go to graduate school or to the military academy.

Down below, under his boots, is the botanical garden's greenhouse. Or is it just a bunch of motley colored umbrellas? The umbrellas collapse to reveal the familiar faces of a chemical engineer, an inspection officer in the regional office of the Education Ministry, a soil scientist, a linguist—the girlfriends of his bleak days.[34] Like a stone, released from a slingshot, boatswain Dopekailo whizzes past.

"If you miss the mark, Shustikov, you'll have to clean the heads."

There's a ten-knot wind, so try not to miss the mark. It carries you off the target, off the target.

I plunked down on a hayrick, slept about 600 minutes,[35] awoke, took my position from the stars, and caught another couple of hours of sleep—no one ever died from oversleeping. Next morning I see Good Person walking across the dew-covered grass and bearing treasures, visible under the translucent dress.


### Old Mochenkin's First Dream

Then he caught sight of sumptuous palaces with ornate stucco moulding and wreaths.[36] O ye saints above, Most Holy Virgin Mother... as granny used to say, still clinging to phrases mouthed as a child under the yoke of serfdom.

A committee has been formed and authorized to examine and evaluate the reports of what follows below from the above explicated.

He is led into the bathhouse ante-room and given sour kvass... already in the ante-room, mind you, not the steamroom itself.

... They hand him an extraordinary gift of plain, dry rations. And here you got shixteen kilos of lard, here's your shixteen kilos of dry apricots and shixteen kilos of sugar for the home-brewed hootch.[37]

They then lead him into a room painted two colors and trimmed with red velvet. They push him to his knees, anoint his tresses with sunflower oil from roasted and pressed seeds, and part his hair straight down the middle.[38]

The authoritative commission and its chairman are in the presidium. The chairman in and of himself is stout, very familiar and anthropodal looking[39] —ye saints above, a Colorado beetle! On his left and his right are frantic, little syncophant baby beetles.

"Your reports have been examined thoroughly in a favorable disposition," the chairman says in an imposing voice.

"Allow me to make a statement as a point of order," squeaked a small beetle.

Old Mochenkin's blood ran cold—they'll unmask me, unmask me!

"Take a careful look at him, respectful committee, for indeed this is a genuine potato. We've scoured the whole world over, but haven't found one. And here before our very eyes, is a high quality tuber."

Judgment was pronounced. You yourselves know the kind of verdict.

He barely managed to squeeze into an underground crevice, and then he lept out into the freedom of the great outdoors. Through the window, with his own eyes, he watched as the beetles tore the huge tuber into pieces.

He spent the night at Kvass Way-Station, in darkness and grief. A false crocodile came along, snapped him from behind with locks on his legs and tickled him.

But in the morning he sees Good Alamoney, his young defender, come walking lambently across the dew-covered grass.


### Teach Irina Valentinovna Seleznyeva's First Dream

For some time now she had had suspicions about the existence of that chapter "Elastic-Majestic-CeMagnifique," which wasn't included in the program.

Gooli-goolishki-goolyu, I love you . . . At the carnival, under the cover of night, you whispered in my ear . . . I love you a lot. . . .

It's the red-head Somov, the leader of Group One who took her in tow as an underachiever.

"Do you remember the passage in Hemingway? Don't you recall the place in Druon? As Zhukhovitsky said . . . , you remember, don't you?"[40] Goodness me! What impudent rogues—I'm supposed to recall everything just because they bought me a "Kamikaze Mind-Blower" cocktail.[41]

But the Polish magazines from countries all over the world came flying down from up above, from up above.[42]

"Rise, children!"

The tiny lion cubs with cunning eyes stood up.

Oh, she could recall that one of them was a lion of Pirosmanishvili. If you're a complex individual, you're supposed to like primitives.[43] Or at least that's what the practice-teaching supervisor Genrikh Anatolyevich Reinvolf used to tell her. They said damn near anything and everything to her and still got a 'C' grade.

But, then once again: the-gooli-goolyushki-goolyu-I-love-you-at-the-carnival-under-cover-of-night handsome men went round and round, half-naked, on the dance floor of the Gel'-G'yu train station. Irochka, my pet, come here, I'll give you the ball. But grandma, why do you have such big hands? To embrace you. And why've you got those shovels? Take one, dig a pit, and give up your treasures!

> By the edge of green, green cliffs
> On a meadow near the woods,
> Little bad wolf caught a good whiff
> Of a tough, little, sexy broad.

Bid farewell, raise your lovely head with pride. Don't give up your treasures. Stop, you're saved. Across the dew-covered grass Good Person is approaching you and his bell-bottoms are wet to the knees.


### Volodya Teleskopov's First Dream

At the first-aid station they spent hours over treating him: they gave him a transfusion of special consciousness through a rubber tube—oh, you parasite doctors!—and pumped out his seething organism from below.

However, it made him feel better—he got up inspired.

The director climbed down off the stove, walked around in soft felt boots and suddenly gave a loud "oooff."

"Give Comrade Teleskopov the very best machine, the one as big as a mountain."

"Oh, no," I say, "you calculate the piece-work scale on it for me first."

The director goes on his knees before him.

"Don't be like that, Volodya, we'll knock ourselves flat as a pancake for you. We'll treat you to a free trip to Tskhaltubo."[44]

Screw you, you and your Tskhaltubo. This Tskhaltubo of yours is now all covered with snow, up to the neck.

A tractor is running. Simka is in tow; she looks really big on the trailing sled.

> Volodyenka, Volodyenka,
> Come to me in winter,
> Love me, while I'm young and spry,
> My gorgeous hunk of splendor.

Of course, the poet's soul couldn't tolerate the shame of trivial offenses[45]—being totally drowned in down pillows, lost in a red blanket; his whole mug splattered with marinated sprats and his paws covered with kippers tinned in tomato sauce. However, they don't gag him; they just fill him up to the brim.

Edyulya, Stepan, and that, what's his name, I don't recall just now, turn up in the morning.

"Shake a leg, Volodya, there's a football match."

The rolling ball was huge, like one of those bulls at the VDNKh.[46] Boban, you bow-legged ballerina, how we rooted for you, what spirit we cheered you with; you hooked an "inslinger" off a corner kick, but muffed it.[47] Ivan Sergeyich right then and there took him off under escort—to jail for fifteen days. I remember it well, as if it had just happened . . . it was on a Tuesday.

So Simka kept on throwing her weight around: Volodyenka, Volodyenka, my dear fellow, haul the barrelware to Koryazhsk. She's my nervous and capricious one—I'm responsible for her before the Central Consumers' Cooperatives Council.

So, I'm hauling her. Looks like I'm going to smash into a pole now. I'm pumping the brake and wrenching the steering wheel round. Where are we flying off to? Into the ditch? The lights suddenly went out, we lost consciousness and then came to. We look up and see Good Person coming toward us across the dew-covered grass. Seems he's got a cap tilted back on his head. Seems he's got kid gloves on his slim hands. Seems he's Seryozhka Esenin.

* * *

The blow, fortunately, wasn't severe. Only two or three component parts of the barrelware went flying off, but even these small casualties caused her, sensitive as she is, untold suffering.

The truck, totally intact, lay on its side in the ditch.

Marine and teach, sitting on the ground at the edge of the field, looked at one another in astonishment—seized by a steadily escalating mutual feeling.

Old Mochenkin was already running across the field, grabbing his reports, cassations and appeals in mid-air.

Vadim Afanasyevich, always inwardly prepared for catastrophes, was unperturbably tamping his pipe according to the rules of English-ness.

Since a half minute after the accident, Volodya Teleskopov had been sound asleep, with his head on the steering wheel as if it were a soft pillow. He had a blissful smile on his face, as though he'd just met an old friend. Then, he jumped down from the cabin and rushed to examine the barrelware. Having found her to be in a satisfactory condition, he beamed and took to seeing after the passengers.

"Well, then, is our community all assembled?"

He went around to each person, asking, "How do you personally feel?"

41

Everyone, personally, felt just fine and smiled approvingly at Volodya with the exception of old Mochenkin, who bellowed something inarticulately. But even he was generally satisfied: he'd retrieved all his papers, counted them and appended them to his file.

Having conferred, they next decided to have a bite to eat. They made a little campfire on the berm and brewed tea. Vadim Afanasyevich opened a jar of cherry preseves.

Volodya offered his favorite food for general consumption—a case of sardelles packed in their own juice.

Shustikov Gleb, somewhat ill at ease, contributed some of his mother's curd pancakes and Irina Valentinovna a container of processed cheese called "Novelty," the consolation of her maidenly solitude.

Even old Mochenkin, having rooted a bit in his briefcase, pulled out a pretzel.

They sat down around the fire and a conversation was soon underway.

"What's this then if not a joke?" Volodya Teleskopov asked. "Why, I recall from my days at the Ust'-Kasimov quarry[48] how a generator tractor thumped off the highest terrace. Four dumptrucks—flat as a pancake. We hauled it out with tanks. That evening we cooked some macaroni and one guy in the artel fixed up some meatballs. And, as required, we got drunk as skunks."

"It stands to reason that accidents more serious than ours do occur in the world," Vadim Afanasyevich assented. "I remember how in 1964 in Puerto, this little oil-tanker port in...." He hemmed and hawed in embarrassment and lowered his eyes. "...in a certain Latin American country. Well, there, in Puerto, a Panamanian tanker caught fire near the loading docks. If it hadn't been for the resourcefulness of Miguel Marinado,[49] a forty-three-year-old greasemonkey, whose daughter... hmm... uh... yes, well, it'd have been all over."

"I remember, I remember," Volodya nodded to him.

"Well, once we had," Shustikov Gleb said, "a hydraulic boiler burst in the galley. It might seem a trivial thing, but the whole Guards' crew was wild with rumors. Honest to goodness, comrades, we thought it had started."

"Negligence... not... yet... as... to lead... to that," old Mochenkin managed to squeak out in between bites, as he tucked in heartily the curd pancakes, sardelles in natural juice, cherry preserves, "Novelty" cheese and sipped tea with a vigilant eye on the pretzel. "Negligence can cause fires, too, where whole institutions go up in flames. In '33 in Koryazhsk-the-Second[50] the negligence of instructor Monakhova—my sister, by the way—caused a "Lick Illiteracy School," the local MOPR and OSOA-VIAKHIM offices to go up in flames.[51] That produced a sabotage indictment against her."

"Well, I've never had anything like that happen to me and that's wonderful!" Irina Valentinovna exclaimed and glanced over at the marine with her light-blue, searchlight eyes.

Woe is you, Gleb! Gleb, what's happening to you? For indeed you knew well, you did, handsome Gleb, the chemical engineer—Marina the technician—and lots of women with only an eight-year-school education. Now what's happening to you here, in the midst of your native, black-soil fields?

To tell the truth, something unusual is also happening to Irina Valentinovna. The fact is that Shustikov Gleb has been the first male who didn't elicit an inner rebellion and protest in her heart. Rather, to the contrary, he made her heart flutter with a certain stupendous, tango-like musical beat.

Her happiness at this moment was so complete that she couldn't even understand what she might still be lacking. Indeed, could it be that plane in the sky with a handsome pilot at the wheel?!

She glanced at the light-blue, gorgeous sky which was pierced by beams of sunlight and caught sight of a plane plummeting from the heights. It fell just like a feather, not like a rock. Just like a little piece of silver foil. But closer to earth it began to toss round and round, just like a gymnast on the horizontal bar.

Then, they all caught sight of it.

"If my sight does not deceive me, that is a plane," Vadim Afanasyevich proposed.

"Aha, it's Vanya Kulachenko falling," Volodya affirmed.

"For some reason I feel afraid for him," Irina Valentinovna commented.

"Kulachenko has got what's coming to him, he's been making a nuisance of himself long enough" old Mochenkin summarized.

He recalled now how the day before yesterday he had been wandering in the vicinity of the regional center, counting hayricks so no one could be caught stealing. And Vanka Kulachenko, flying along the hedgerows, had flipped him a finger.

The plane fell to the earth, made a couple of hops and came to rest. Vanya Kulachenko jumped down from the cockpit, removed his pilot's jacket made of dark-blue cheviot that had a most remarkable gold chevron on it, and began to extinguish the flame which had engulfed the motor. Having put the flames out, turned around towards the people running to greet him, and flashed his gold-capped tooth as large as an acorn, he said: "A rare instance in the history of aviation, comrades!"

"I don't understand myself, comrades, how the dive occurred," he said with a knowing smile as if he nonetheless understood something. "I was calmly gliding at the height of two thousand meters, on the look out for the place to scatter the chemical fertilizer. I clarify: the superphosphates. And here I'm gliding calmly when something mystifying happens to me. It was as if a certain pair of large eyes were looking at me from below, as if a certain summons—he quickly stared at Irina Valentinovna—as if the call, pardon me, of a swan. Then and there I lost control and here I am in your midst."

"Discipline comes to an end where aviation begins," Shustikov Gleb said angrily. To clarify matters, he flexed his biceps and led Irina Valentinovna off aways.

Volodya Teleskopov, meanwhile, examined the airplane and consoled Vanya Kulachenko.

"It'll be seven roubles and a few kopecks for the repairs. You will still log some flights, Vanya, on your kerosene 'chine. I worked on a thing like this in Karakum;[52] it's a reliable plane. There were days I catapulted head first into the dunes—that really raised the dust!"

"That's right, you'll fly again, citizen Kulachenko, in about ten to fifteen years you'll certainly fly again," old Mochenkin said maliciously.[53]

"Listen, this is what we're going to do," Shustikov Gleb said as he approached with vigorous steps. "First we pull our mechanism from the ditch and then we attach a towline to the machine of this unlucky, hee-hee, ha-ha, aviator. Is that O.K., Volodya?"

"By the way, comrades, I must register a complaint with all of you," Vadim Afanasyevich suddenly spoke out excitedly. "At some point, to take a broad view of the matter, we behaved inhumanely concerning the barrelware. Pardon me, friends, but we drank tea and observed the rare sight of a falling airplane while the barrelware, meantime, lay totally forgotten by all of us. She lost several of her components. I would like for this not to be repeated in the future."

"It's for precisely that, Vadik, that I'll love you for the rest of your life!" Volodya Teleskopov proclaimed and gave Drozhzhinin a kiss.

Flustered by the kiss, but even more by the "Vadik," Vadim Afanasyevich strode over to the barrelware.

Soon, they were on their way again, in previous fashion, but with the addition that the airplane was in tow. The pilot, Vanya Kulachenko, sat in the plane's cockpit and read the book loaned to him by Volodya Teleskopov—"Anthology of Himalayan Fairytales."[54] But he didn't feel like reading. The golden hair of the teach, Seleznyeva, bothered him as it fluttered in the air. She'd already been noticed by him in the midst of the region's intelligentsia; her hair would not let him immerse himself in the fantastic poetry of the Himalayan people.

Indeed, how many times had Vanya Kulachenko flown past the teach's house, just above the roof, as he was skirting the hedgerows! And how many times over her house had he tossed out little bunches of wild or hothouse flowers! Vanya wasn't aware that the majority of these little bouquets had fallen into the neighboring courtyard, auntie Niusha's place, and that she'd given them to her she-goat.

At dusk, in the crimson sunlight, the Koryazhsk water tower loomed ahead of them. The huge poplar trees of the city park drew closer, and closer, the site of the rooks' twilight bacchanalia.

It would seem that their group's journey was approaching its end, but no—upon drawing closer the water tower turned out to be the cupola of a half-destroyed cathedral and the poplars checked out to be oaks. Now that's a nasty fix to have got yourself into—where's Koryazhsk, then?

Old Mochenkin glanced out from his cellbelly, gasped in surprise and began to beat on the cabin window with tense blows of his fisticuffs.

"Whare've you brought us to, you cruel bastard! This is Myshkin! It's a hundred versts from here to Koryazhsk!"

Vadim Afanasyevich glanced out of the cabin.

"What a nice little patriarchal settlement! Almost as quiet a place as Grande Caballeros."

"Precisely, they're very similar," Volodya Teleskopov assented as if he knew, too.

In the pink twilight along Myshkin's main street there wandered cows who mooed contentedly and alongside them ran their sprite herders, young girls with twigs in their hands. Youths cigaretted on the steps of the club, waiting for the travelling film operator to show up. The pride of Myshkin was lit up—the neon sign "Book Dealer."[55]

"I'll send Simka a letter from here," Volodya Teleskopov said.

### Volodya Teleskopov's Letter to His Friend Sima

*Greetings, honorable Serafima Ignatyevna! Your correspondent is the perhaps not forgotten Teleskopov, Vladimir. In any case I report on our arrival in the town of Myshkin where we are to spend the night. Do not be grieved or sorrowful of countenance.[56] The barrelware is in complete shape. Vadik and I have covered her with a tarpaulin as well as with his checked plaid, if only we had such ourselves, and now she voices no complaints or personal desires.*

*As for me, Serafima Ignatyevna, do not grieve yourself cause for concern. In the first place, I am wholly in control of my own emotional stimula and, secondly, the Myshkin policeman, Sergeant Major Borodkin, Viktor Ilyich, acquainted with you before our love, is now a guest in Gusyatin of his hoodlum brother, Junior-Lieutenant Borodkin, who is also known to you.*

*May this evening's unspeakable light stream over your little izba, too.[57]*

*By the way, tell the parents of pilot Kulachenko that he is alive and well and wishes them the same.*

*Remember, Sima, how we used to go together to a restaurant and pour wines into a sparkling goblet and the saxophone would sing to us about happiness, but if I find out something now ... then ... watch out!!*

*Dear sir, rest assured of my total respect for you.*

*Take a pound of that creamy butter and dash over to my old man's with it ... to be paid in cash.*

*Kisses like wine, sweetie mine.*

*Vladimir*

\* \* \*

Just imagine a grove of birch trees that rises to the top of a knoll. Pretend that it is the simple and transparent scenery for an unsophisticated drama about beautiful human passions. And, now, to make the setting complete, the exaggeratedly large moon rises over the knoll and hangs suspended beyond the birch trees; the birds who sing at night and witness our secret deeds begin to warble; the smell of mint fills the air; Gleb Shustikov, the marine, spreads his peacoat that has seen everything on the hillock with a deft touch and teach Seleznyeva—both trepid and pensive—sits down on it.

Panting, Gleb fell down next to her and buried his nose in the mint. Romance, that clever forest sprite whose body is covered with fluffy, fox fur and who is as wiley as a Fagan or a wolverine at stealthily dogging every uncertain step we make, suddenly clouted the breath out of Gleb, poisoned him with s sweet-smelling gas, and hypnotized him with her enlarged and pseudo-sorrowful eyes.

Trying to rescue himself, Gleb pressed his nose to mother earth.

"Isn't it true that there is a particular charm unique to the black-soil region, to the forest-steppe zone?" Irina Valentinova asked wearily, "Don't you think so, Gleb? Gleb? Gleb, darling?"

Exultant, Romance wandered among the birch trees with either a balalaika or a mandolin in her hands.

Gleb crawled a bit closer to Irina Valentinovna. Having "ooh'ed" in alarm, Romance unceremoniously plopped down on the ferns and began to wail a divertissement.

Gleb, on the other hand, struggled in agony; his entire armored body shook like the deck of a destroyer under full steam.

Howling mournfully, Romance was already sitting above them, on a bough of a tree, like a gigantic wood-grouse.[58]

"On the whole ... generally ... it's like this, Irina," said Shustikov

Gleb, "to tell the truth . . . I was planning . . . to make a short visit to a friend in Berdyansk[59] before returning to the place where I am engaged in service, but now, as you yourself understand, I'm no longer up for seeing this friend."

They were walking back to Myshkin through watery meadows. Above them, in the clear night sky, were flying bitterns. Romance was following at a safe distance, camouflaging herself as an ordinary entertainer and trying to lure them with her accordion:[60]

"One can never forget those first dates, those first embraces, those years of one's Komsomol youth . . ."

"Leave me alone!" Gleb roared, "I'll catch you and rip out your guts."

Then and there Romance came to an abrupt stop, ready to retire back into the birch grove.

"Let her be, Gleb," Irina Valentinovna murmured softly, "Let her go her way. She's got to be understood, too."

Upon hearing this, Romance began to stride off gaily, flouncing jauntily with her fur.

" . . . untouched with an affectionate sun-tan your uncovered hands. . . "

Meanwhile: on the square of the town of Myshkin, the cropduster pilot, Vanya Kulachenko, slept in his uncoupled airplane.


### Dream of the Pilot, Vanya Kulachenko

Undesirable insects circled above the earth like motley colored stormclouds.

"From above I can see everything, as you well know![61] Now I'm going to spray!"

Above a region of Europe he caught an imposing-looking dragonfly (lady) by the tail, at the perigee of his flight.

From all the tracking stations, he heard a warm and hearty greeting and this question: "God visible up there, comrade Kulachenko?"

"God I don't see. Greetings to the struggling peoples of Oceania!"[62]

On all the tracking stations: "Hurrah! God doesn't exist! Our prognoses have been confirmed. Do you see any angels, comrade Kulachenko?"

"As a matter of fact, I do see some angels."

Angel was flying pompously toward his spaceship, like a large swan.

"What is your normal occupation in life, comrade Kulachenko?"

"I spread fertilizers from a plane; I adorn our mother planet with superphosphates."

"That's a good thing. We can approve of that," the Angel clapped his hands in a gentle applause. "Do you have any personal requests to make?"

"The teacher does not love me, dear guardian uncle Angel."

"We know, we know. We shall ventilate this situation thoroughly. We shall bring it up before comrade Shustikov. While you go in for the landing."

Smack! I'd come to earth. Hard! I look up to see Good Person coming across the dew-covered grass; seems to be either the school teacher or the detachment commander Zhukov.[63]

\* \* \*

Meanwhile: Vadim Afanasyevich Drozhzhinin was sitting on the protective mound of earth that encircled the Myshkin House for Itinerants and was leisurely puffing on his pipe.

By the way, this pipe has quite a history. At the Yalta Conference it had been smoked by Lord Beverly-Brahms,[64] Churchill's personal advisor on matters concerning the re-treading of automobile tires; it had come into his hands by inheritance, from his grandfather Brahms—an Admiral and devotee of music, who for many years served as Keeper of the Seal at the court of the king of the Maldive Islands. His grandfather, in turn, obtained it from his grandmum, the mistress of Sir Elvis Crosby, Her Majesty's most enterprising buccaneer and friend of Sir Francis Drake, who owned the sea-chest in which the pipe was discovered. Thus, it is apparent, that the (hi)story of the pipe extends back into Great Britain's cloudy past.[65]

When he was in Moscow, Lord Beverly-Brahms who was also a devotee of Brahms' music, burned all his notes up (in bankruptcy) and let it go for a fantastic sum to our composer Krasnogorsky-Fish,[66] who, in turn, having burned his notes up, too, pawned it at one of Moscow's pawn shops, where it was acquired for the same fantastic sum by Vadim Afanasyevich's current neighbor, Arkady Pomidorov,[67] a great lover of horse racing and a frequenter of the Moscow Hippodrome.

Once, when he was in an excellent and expansive mood, Arkady Pomidorov let this historical English pipe go to his neighbor, that is, to Vadim Afanasyevich, for a purely nominal sum of 2 roubles 87 kopecks. As, of course, a gesture of friendship.

Thus, Vadim Afanasyevich was sitting on the mound of earth and guarding, as Volodya had directed, the barrelware coiled up comfortably under his plaid mohair.[68]

He was fond of this quiet Myshkin, so much like Grande-Caballeros. Yes, in general, he even liked sitting on the mound of earth and guarding the barrelware that had become so near and dear to him.

Yes, if it hadn't been for that damned Junta, Vadim Afanasyevich would have long ago have made a quick trip to Haligalia for a fiancée, the dark-complexioned Maria Rokho or the beautiful Silvia Chesterton

(English blood!), he would long ago have put an order in for a cooperative apartment in Khoroshevo-Mnevniki,[69] since there had accumulated a sufficient sum, the weal from years of moderate living, but . . .

While waiting for Teleskopov, Vadim Afanasyevich indulged himself in such peaceful, dreamy reveries as these, occasionally getting up to twitch at the plaid blanket on the barrelware.

Suddenly, Teleskopov's voice rang out behind the cathedral at the end of the street. He was ambling towards the House for Itinerants, belting out a song which caused Vadim Afanasyevich to shudder as he listened:

> Yea, yea, yea, Hully-Gully!
> Yea, yea, yea, our stills' hootch!
> Yea, yea, yea, we brewed bubbly!
> Yea, yea, yea, let's drink, lads!
> For who's concerned now, anyhow,
> With where or how the yeast was had . . .[70]

Volodya sang this Haligalian song which was unknown to anyone except Vadim Afanasyevich. Was this a miracle? Or just a delirium? Gallucinations can't be heard nowadays, can they?[71]

Volodya walked along the street, raking up dust with his feet.

"Hi, Vaddy buddy!" he boomed out as he approached. "That old auntie Nastya is really a low-down skunk! Can you believe she rips people off for four bits a glass?!! Now when I was working in Yalta at the canning plant, I could get a liter of wine for four bits at the "May Day" kolkhoz and that wine, mind you, was the bubbly, champagne sort of stuff . . . take an eyedropper, add about as much cologne as there'd be in half of one of those little flasks and you'll be bombed out of your mind all evening."

"Have a seat, Volodya, here," Vadim requested, "I need to have a chat with you."

"In general, if you wish, Vadim, take a swig," Teleskopov said, extending the glass jar to him as he sat down.

"Yes, yes, of course," Drozhzhinin muttered and began to gulp down zestfully the strong-smelling, fizzy, hydrogenated, vinegary-meaty-and-yeasty carbonated, more-than-culture cultured, refreshing tipsyfying beverage.

"That's fastastic, Vadim," Teleskopov praised, "You're the kind of guy I'd even be willing to go on a spying mission with."

"Tell me, Volodya," Vadim pleaded in hushed tones, "How is it you know that Haligalian folksong?"

"Why I was there," Volodya answered, "I've been to Haligalia-Maligalia."

"My apologies, Volodya, but what you've said just now calls into question, to my mind, everything you've stated previously. It would seem

we've already managed to become pretty good friends and we've acknowledged our respect for one another in the liquid custom with which you're
familiar. So why are you transforming the information you've obtained
indirectly into a gibe at my expense? I know every Soviet citizen who has
ever been to Haligalia. After all, there aren't very many of them. But more
than that, I am also acquainted with all foreigners who have been to that
country and carry on a correspondence with them. You, however, you
personally were never there."

"You want to wager on that, do yah?" Volodya asked.

"Wager? How's that?" Drozhzhinin asked in disbelief.

"Want to bet a bottle of 'Backwoods Oak'?[72] Cause, Vaddy, my friend,
I really was there, in that precise place. In '64 by sheer chance I signed on as
a carpenter with the liner "Baskunchak"[73] that was sent to Haligalia. If you
get my drift?"

"It was the only European liner to call at Haligalia during the last forty
years," Vadim Afanasyevich whispered.

"Precisely," confided Volodya, "We shipped them supplies on account
of the earthquake."

"That's correct," Vadim Afanasyevich said in a barely audible whisper
as he began to be wracked with an unheard of excitement. "You wouldn't
happen to recall your exact cargo, would you?"

"Oh, there was lots of stuff—medicines, bandages, children's toys,
condensed and evaporated dairy products; so much that it made your eyes
water just to look at part of it—enough goodies to handle three
earthquakes and, for the hospitals, four paintings by the artist Kalenkin."

With amazing vividness Vadim Afanasyevich recalled the happy
moments associated with transporting these huge, sturdily encased paintings; he recalled the massive exultation on the docks occasioned by the
disappearance of the paintings into the holds of the "Baskunchak."

"But allow me, Volodya," he exclaimed, "to . . . For, indeed, I knew the
entire crew of the "Baskunchak" very well. I was on board ship on the
second day after it docked upon returning from Haligalia, but you . . ."

"But I, Vadik, was dismissed the first day in port," Teleskopov
explained confidently. "As soon as we had moored, Yevgeny Sergeyevich
Pompyezov immediately gave me talons for rouble certificates. Go buy
yourself some goodies, Teleskopov, he says,[74] and don't set foot ever again
in our steamship line offices, you bird-brained carpenter. So you see what
the matter was, my dear friend? Somehow, I just sort of made a mess there
with my contacts."

"Volodya, my dear Volodya! I'd like to know the details. It is
extremely important for me."

"There's nothing special to say," Volodya dismissed the matter with a
wave of his delicate hand. "I was hanging about one day in Puerto, quite

bored. I chuggalugged a Coca-cola and was full of gas; got no satisfaction. I looked up and saw a sympatico hombre coming my way. We got acquainted, Miguel Marinado and I. Then, along came another work-horse, Jose Luis..."

"The bicycle dealer?" Drozhzhinin gasped.

"Yep. We laced our ties of friendship by knocking off a bottle between the three of us,[75] and then there was a second. We went over to Miguel's house and a bunch of girls ran in right away to get a closer look at me. You'd have thought I was one of those Caucasus peacocks in the Murmansk zoo that Grishka Ofstein plucked a feather from last year."

"Which of the girls were there?" Vadim Afanasyevich asked in a tremulous voice.

"There was Sonka Marinadova, Miguel's daughter,[76] but I didn't lay a hand on her, honest, Vadik, that's the truth and then there were Marishka Rokho and Silvia whose surname I don't recall and, well, Jose Luis pedalled his bicycle off to fetch his fiancée, Rosita. He returned with a humongous shiner on his mug. So, Vadik, you got the picture? The gals had on short skirts and they kept showing off their bare knees. After all, I'm not made of stone, now, am I? I fell in love for real with Silvia and she with me. If you don't believe me, I can show you a snapshot. I'm hiding it from Simka, at the pad of one of my chums."

"Do you write each other?" Drozhzhinin asked.

"Yeah, we still write, but Simka tears up her letters out of jealousy. Now, jealousy, my dear Simochka, demeans a person... as William Shakespeare long ago stated as solidly as stone. An individual, Serafima Ignatyevna, is the master of his own 'I'. And I assure you, dear counter attendant, that there was almost nothing at all platonic between Silvia and me and even if there was, well, only when we lost control over ourselves. Maybe my love, Simochka, was really the strolls along the avenidas of theirs with the girl and the pup Carabanchelle. I love beasts of that sort like they were our lesser brothers, so likewise, Serafima, you ought to love birds—the source of knowledge."[77]

With these words Volodya Teleskopov broke off entirely, plopped down on the mound of earth and began to snore.

Trained in the art of gentlemanly conduct, Vadim Afanasyevich had no difficulty in carrying the lightweight body of his friend (yes—friend, because he was now, once and for all, a friend) into the House for Itinerants. He sat a while on the end of his companion's cot, silently moving his lips as he thought about the deceitful Silvia Chesterton and how she had not informed him of her affair with Teleskopov, choosing to report only on all sorts of girlish nonsense. He likewise gave some basic thought to the strange and charming character of the frivolous Haligalian girls, to the periodic earthquakes which rock the sleepy Haligalian towns like a Fandango.

## Volodya Teleskopov's Second Dream

Serafima Ignatyevna has a birthday today, but you've got a shiner under your eye. I began to dig in my pockets—I pulled out my gas coupons, the certification of my psychological inferiority complex which I keep for emergencies, a nail, a lock, a piece of fir-scented soap, a beautiful bird— source of knowledge, and eight kopecks in change.

He began to shake out his suit and his jacket. Out flew about 3 meters of tariff grid charted graph-paper with a fish in it as a bonus—a cod, one-of-those-what-do-you-want, old man? kind;[78] returnable containers— sixty kopecks worth of bottles, twenty of jars (we'll make do!); a songbook entitled "Travelling time, my friends, lands distant and foreign"; a bill of lading for the barrelware; a comb; and an ashtray. Finally, the sought-for object was discovered: he shook out a little worthless lie from under the concealed lining.

"I've had this thing since I was in Daugavpils.[79] I caught my foot in the coil of a hawser and fell smack on my eye against a crate."

The guests—all the bigshots from the Regional Consumers' Co-operatives Council—rode past astride white cows.

Dressed in a red, velvet dress, Simka is standing there and smiling like a Kuzbass blast-furnace.[80]

Of course, they won't let him past. He had chuckled away his mangy little lie as unwanted trash.

"The others' lies are normal lies, but your lie's just a louse."

However, the lie—very unlike a louse, but quite like a frog—caught little skeeters on the jump as it splashed merrily into a puddle.

"Thieves, besmirchers, I'll scatter you in a jiffy, all of you." They dragged me out right away, as a vigilante group walked past.

"Drag the thug back to the DLT department store[81] or toss him under a cabbage in the garden patch."

One of me got hauled off to the store by an armed vigilante and the other me was tossed under a cabbage.

I looked out from behind the cabbage head. Good Person is coming, coming across the dew-covered grass, seems like he's a caballero, seems like he's Vadik Drozhzhinin.

"Hey, Good Person, let's go save Serafima—fix the books, oh, honest, I'm afraid she's into embezzlement."


## Vadim Afanasyevich's Second Dream

The golden lands of distant Alpukhara[82] fade away as I crawl across the tile roofs of Haligalia. Ahead of me, in the distance, is a house with a facade which looks like a narrow and damaged cliff. It is wholly bathed in moonlight. On its top floor is a balcony, a shadow enshrouded niche.

Having arched my back, I creep like a snow-moon leopard[83] along the roof ridge. Before the decisive leap I tug at my shirt and pants—is everything here? Hurrah, all is here!

I leap across the street, fly up past the fire-wall and here I am on the balcony, in the niche. And then I'm in the boudoir, and there's an alcove in the boudoir, and an eighteenth-century bed in the alcove, and on the bed the reclining young body of Silvia Chesterton, offspring of the Spanish conquistadors and Her Majesty's buccaneers. I leapt onto the bed. A struggle ensued and a dagger seized from under the pillow glistened. I search for Silvia's lips.

SILVIA: "Vadim!"

HE: "It's I, my darling."

The dagger flies onto the carpet. The night sighs with the ecstasy of passion...

"My darling, where're you going?"

"Now I'm off to Maria Rokho. It's but one night..."

His legs were wrapped in iron, his coat was made of steel plates. The teddy boys, of course, dispersed in a run—like goats, brandishing their long locks.[84]

Maria Rokho trembled like a doe when he entered.

"Vadim!"

The spring flowers in the garden are nice... But this is something else, where's it from?

I continue walking through the moonlit squares, through the light blue streets paved with wooden blocks. Somewhere my disgraced foe, Diego the Instantaneous, attempts to lay hands on himself. Window frames creak noisily as windows everywhere are thrown open and they—the beautiful women of Haligalia—plead:

"Vadim!"

"Restrain yourselves, my beauties, one at a..."

Like a whirlwind, in one window and out the chimney, then in another window and out, again, by the chimney... Gabriella Sanchez, Rosita Kublitski, auntie Gustya, Concordia Moro, Stephania Sandrelli... solemn promises, daydreamy plans, whispering, bated breath[85] ... An insane thought: isn't Junta a woman, too? Woke up again in Cunco-fuega full of grief... How to bind my life with those darlings? After all, I'm not a degenerate or a frivolous fly-by-night.

Through the smoky beams of sunlight Good Person approached across the dew-covered grass.

"I have arranged a rendezvous for you, Vadik, with the barrelware under your patronage."

Old Mochenkin, gramps Ivan, did not do himself powerfully proud on
this night in Myshkin, before his croney and hostess, Nastasya:[86] firstly, he
wolfed down an omelette made of ten eggs; secondly, he gulped down
almost three liters of home-made beer; thirdly, of course, he switched on
the radiola and listened to a program about fire-resistant clay and a
"Mademoiselle Nitouche" concert[87] straight through, nodding his head
pompously in agreement from time to time.

All this time croney Nastasya stood by the stove, hands under her
apron, and looked reverentially at old Mochenkin. Just once in a while she
would move off, making bows and begging his pardon—when youths
jangled their four bits under the windows. The respect for old Mochenkin
which she cultivated was the ancient and traditional sort that started up
years and years ago from over indulgence. To tell the truth, old Mochenkin
was even glad that he had ended up in the town of Myshkin; yes, it was only
unfortunate that it had been unexpected. If he had just known earlier, well,
he would have found the coryphaeus of all times and peoples—fishpie with
pike—awaiting him now on the table. In former years croney Nastasya had
always baked a whole pike in thick batter for his arrival. The pie turned out
very marvelously—on the top a ruddy crust and inside the thoroughly
baked reptile, the imperialist predator.[88]

"Dowse me, croney, with some more beer," old Mochenkin commanded.

"It's my pleasure, Ivan Alexandrovich."

"Right here, croney," old Mochenkin said as he whacked the palm of
his hand across his fake-crocodile briefcase, "right here I gat 'em all—the
dumb and the talkers."

"Your strapping boys, Ivan Alexandrovich?"

"Not only..." old Mochenkin threatened the croney harshly with his
finger, "by no means just the sons. Atsit!" he proclaimed suddenly, stood
up and headed wobbily for the bed. "Atsit! Oopla! Oompha!" he
threatened someone again, prodded someone with his index finger and fell
into bed asleep.

### Old Mochenkin's Second Dream

A vision seized him: our entire large country had decided to construct
him a coat.

No sooner said than done. Excavation was done for the foundation,
the work was in full swing. Mochenkincoatconstruction![89]

The thick, navy-blue cloth of the overcoat was laid out and marked,
like a battleship; its lapels were of horse-hair, its bounteous breastfronts

were projected to be agrogargantuan—like those of Andron Lukich Fefyolov. How's that for you!

One ought to stuff the lining of such a coat with the crème-de-la-crème. I'll get a medical release from comrade Teleskopov, our driver, and then I'll import to my stomach crème-brûlé, jellied meats, duck-yellow egg noodles, scrambled eggs. -00-percent results; access to the goodies is lacking, even if you wail! The family greases the palms of scoundrels, the scoundrels grease the palm of the family, so whom can you write reports to, before whom can you bow low with petitions? You squeal and squeal, but can't squeal yourself in anywhere. The coat rose up over the fields and wooded groves like an elevator; its collar is like the wispy rings in the clouds. And here I am going for a fitting.

But in the center of the field is a ram—uncastrated and huge; a commodity, a commodity... And you're walking, mister-comrade, somewhat by the side, somewhat by the way.

So I'm walking along and the ram just paws the ground—thanks, kind people. There's the coat, but there's a door in the coat and in the doorway is Andron Lukich Fefyolov.

"Where are you headed, good citizen?"

"To the fitting, Andron Lukich."

"Now even though I'm a Lukich, don't you go and get palsy-ish. There'll no longer be any fitting citizen. It's been a long time since a regional history museum was set up in your coat. For four bits, if you so desire, you can whet your curiosity on the exhibit. Here's a commodity-ram, natural mutton... and here's a quality diagram with abcissa and ordinate... and here's an old man marinated in a jar. He's neither a candle for God, nor a stoker for the Devil—you recognize him?"

Howling in horror, he leapt out of the pocket and plopped onto the grass.

"Where are you, where are you, my dear Protectress? Where are you, Jurisprudencia, maiden virgin, aromatic mint, unbribeable one?"

The dew-covered grass rustled; there was a big squeaky crunching, as if from the weight of heavy steps.

* * *[90] [see poem on next page]

The joyful sun soon rose over the town of Myshkin and all our travellers woke up feeling happy. Volodya Teleskopov turned on the ignition, lifted the hood, and began to look at the running motor. He was very fond of looking at running mechanisms. Occasionally he makes a stop somewhere, looks at his running engine... looks at it for several minutes, comprehends everything about it, smiles quietly, and without any hustle or bustle, walks off as happy as if he'd washed up with warm and clean water.

Harp

      O Sea!
Scram you boors
Why should I
  Know all
    All now
    Of love     ooooooo     Twixt
   By love
O sky O'diamonds             Heaven
Dreams of Poland    And earth
Where is my pole    A nightingale
O grannie-dearie    Sings
And dance in whirlwind
Swirls me on, on
O upto, upto
  Hindu
Kush, Kush    Brief-coursing
  Gleb
My love    but deep, affluvial
Yes Milk
And Barrelware    Neva-Neva-Neva
   Dear
      Silence
      Silence

Prepare for the assault    Night
Up and at 'em!
    Cream
    O' wheat
      Scaevola, here!    Whack!
      You lubbers
      Lips O' lyre
      We stride through Poland
Desdemona    And to the pole
    Whose is bigger
    Fiddle-faddle
Coda    Claptraps
    O Alcinous
+++++    I won't give up
    Barrelware, love
    We are swimming
A grandeur    In tandem
the sea    Poland—the pole
Most holy    Sailor's whim
Baikal    And doughnuts
    Filled with cream
    You with the ammo
    Now open fire!

Good Person comes strolling across the dew-covered grass.

Meanwhile Vadim Afanasyevich was luxuriating the barrelware with soap and scrubbrush, treating her to a morning toilette. He scrubbed her brown sides to a sheen and she cooingly basked and wheezed under the sun's rays and the soapy water. They hadn't had it so good in a long time and it had been a long time since Vadim Afanasyevich had felt so good. For him things were always generally okay, always arranged and laid out flat, but he hadn't had it so good as now since, well, maybe since childhood.

Old Mochenkin returned from croney's. Standing to one side, he frowned and observed everything with a critical eye. It would be difficult to say why he had not taken the bus to Koryazhsk. Perhaps, he had some thoughts of economizing because he had decided, after all, to pay Teleskopov no more than fifteen kopecks for his escapades. Or, perhaps, he like all the other passengers, already felt some sort of spiritual ties with this sim-eye, with the grubby and self-destructive Teleskopov, and with the thoroughly damnable barrelware that was so tender and delicate.

Meanwhile, Irina Valentinovna was serving up breakfast in the front garden: eggs and potatoes. Her loyal friend—Shustikov Gleb—was cutting up some cucumbers.

"Please come to the table, comrades!" Irina Valentinovna invited in a happy voice. Everyone sat down to breakfast, not excluding by any means old Mochenkin, who had tanked up nicely at croney's but wasn't one who could let an extra opportunity pass, of course, to do a little parasitical lubricating for nothing. He pulled out his pretzel once more and placed it on the table near his elbow.

The passengers were already finishing their breakfast, when a friendly voice hailed them from beyond the fence that stood along the road: "Enjoy your meal, good comrades!"

Beyond the fence stood an attractive old woman dressed in a neat, ivy-colored jacket. She was carrying a little suitcase, a bundle tied in knots, and a net like the one children use to catch butterflies.

"Greetings," she said as she bowed low, "Is it you, citizens, who are transporting barrelware to Koryazhsk?"

"That's us, granny!" Volodya said gruffly, "but what business of yours is our barrelware?"

"Why, I'm requesting you to take me on as a fellow traveller, dearie. Who's the senior in your patrol?"

The passengers looked at one another in amusement. They had not known that they were a "patrol."

Old Mochenkin gave a grunt, flicked the crumbs off his coarsely colored cotton jacket, and assumed a dignified pose, but Shustikov Gleb said, winking slyly to his girl:

"Little momma, we don't have any administrators here. We are just simple people, little momma, with different views and jobs. We linked up voluntarily on the basis of our love and respect for our barrelware. And where may you be bound for, dear and kind little old momma?"

"On a trip, sonny; I'm travelling to the town of Khveodosija.[91] The institute is sending me to the Crimean steppe for the final capture of the photoplexirus."

"That's a beetle, isn't it, granny? A horny beetle?" Volodya shouted.

"The same, sonny. It's very difficult to capture once and for all, this sire photoplexirus, and so they've sent me."

It turned out that Stepanida Yefimovna (thus the old woman was called) had been serving for five years already as a lab-techinican in one of Moscow's scientific institutes and received a monthly wage of forty roubles, plus bonus pay, from the institute.

"For the bonuses, my dearies, I catch field grasshoppers, dragonflies, butterflies, various kinds of maggots, and the silkworms which they especially value," she said in a sing-song voice, "they are very satisfied with me and so they're sending me to the Crimean steppe for the final capture of the photoplexirus, the horned beetle that is yet to be caught but is so needed for scientific research."

"Just imagine that, Gleb," Irina Valentinovna said, "such an ordinary and modest granny, but she is a servant of science! Let's devote ourselves to science also, Gleb, let's give ourselves up to it totally without any reservations."

Irina Valentinovna somewhat constrained her flush of excitement, but she still trembled slightly on account of her inspiration. Gleb embraced her by the shoulders.

"A good idea, Irinka, and we'll give it some flesh and blood, bring it to life."

"This is, nevertheless, strange, Volodya," Vadim Afanasyevich whispered to Teleskopov. "Did you notice that they've already switched to using the familiar form of address? The tempo is truly Mach One! And then this old woman here . . . can she really be going to capture a photoplexirus? What a strange world . . ."

"Nothing strange about it, Vadim," Volodya said. "Gleb took teachie for a stroll through the birch grove yesterday. And the little old momma catches beetles. Nothing to worry about. You can bet on my trained eye: little old momma here will nab the photoplexirus."[92]

Stunned and hurt by Stepanida Yefimovna's tale, old Mochenkin remained silent. "How is it now, comrade buddies, that things turn out like this?" He—the renowned specialist on insects who had devoted so many years to the struggle against the Colorado beetle—he, the educated but politically tread-upon man, wasn't even remembered at the scientific institute. But little momma, Stepanida, who just weeds out goose-foot . . . Why, make her a lab-technician, if you please! They don't take care of the cadres; they just squander a valuable cadre. They don't provide financial support; they just suppress initiative. They'll get their just rewards in the end—the bastards, destroying the people's kopecks, the economy.

"Climb aboard, gang, let's be off!" Volodya began to shout. "You climb aboard, too, little old momma," he said to Stepanida Yefimovna, "but just be careful with our barrelware."

"Gracious me, dearies, your barrelware is so good looking; she is so cute and uplifting," Stepanida Yefimovna sang out, "my she is a right first-rate wife for a merchant, a first-rate plump doe-elk. And such a pla-a-ayful disposition, my la-ad-dies."

Then and there everyone fell in love with the old woman lab-technician for the relationship she made manifest towards the barrelware. Even old Mochenkin was placated more easily than might be expected.

Everyone crawled into their own cellbellies and they took off—rocking along the humpbacked streets of Myshkin.

"We'll drop by the square first and hitch up Vanka Kulachenko," Volodya said.

But neither Vanka Kulachenko nor the airplane were visible on the square. Pilot Kulachenko was already soaring through the blue skies, soaring along in his reliable machine with loving patches of sunlight on its aerodynamic surfaces. As it turns out, Vanya had already repaired his tried-and-true machine and once again taken off in it to fertilize the mother planet.

No further than the city limits, the travellers caught sight of a biplane diving right at them. This time pilot Kulachenko maneuvered precisely and tossed a little bouquet of heavenly daffodils straight into Irina Valentinov-na's barrelware cellbelly.

"Toss 'em away, right now!" Shustikov Gleb commanded and lifted his eyes, like a paired ack-ack gun, to the sky. "Phooey," he thought, "it's a shame I didn't have a chat with that fly-boy on esoteric literary topics!"

In addition, Gleb noticed that the damned Romance was sort of swirling along the road behind them, or, maybe, it was just a cloud of dust. He suddenly felt his love threatened. So, having summoned up all his iron fortitude, he pulled himself together and asked:

"You thrown it away or not?"

"Oh my, Gleb!" Irina Valentinovna exclaimed with some vexation. "I threw them away long ago."

As a matter of fact, she had hid one heavenly daffodil in a secluded place and also managed to cast a furtive glance at the plane as it receded from view and turned into a mere speck . . . and to inspire its motor. What woman doesn't cherish the memory of such a rousing episode in her life?

And so—once again—they set off along the drowsy fields and rustling groves. Volodya Teleskopov gunned the gas pedal, looked at everything but the road ahead, took forks right and left at full speed—without the slightest consideration of traffic rules. He sucked on lollypops, lifted some "Capstain" tobacco from Vadim Afanasyevich's pocket, rolled himself a few smokes, and regaled his fellow traveller with vignettes from his fascinating life.

"That summer, Vaddy-laddy, I worked as a go-fer in the crew filming the Southwest Blazes Eternally a first-class film on life abroad we got there a sky-blue lake, white mountains dear old momma a factory there rolls out champagne for export aroma with Appeal all the strapping women washing dishes in the mess you wouldn't believe how they sing all sort of riff-raff cooling themselves with champagne mash Vovik Dyachenko and I took some sailor jackets some hats and tassels from props and beat it we shoot the breeze lovetalking in French gooli-mooli and in the morning on Wednesday that is Bushkanets, Nina Nikolayevna, chucked me out of the crew on my ears an ad hoc court of comrades vindicated Vovik and I set myself up as a tasting specialist at the factory and they, yeah, they came to me the pups but I (you vagrant soul less and less)[93] really took off in the amateur theatrical performances the main bookkeeper cried honest I got so tired there, Vadik."

Meanwhile, Vadim Afanasyevich, who was no longer surprised at anything, kept sucking on his pipe, glancing at the fields and groves in an elegiacal mood and listening to the squeaking of his beloved barrelware. He spoke nary a word to his friend, even when he noticed that they had sped right past the turnoff to Koryazhsk.

Old Mochenkin: like-a-wise. He'd gone soft from piling up his arguments. He'd sapped his strength in his own cellbelly, what with exercising his nostrils to devour the smell, so dear to his heart, of pickle brine mixed with beer. And only occasionally, recalling things, would he get angry—"and when I reach the OBLSOBES,[94] how I'll seeeze upon, how I'll..."—but then, again, he'd go slack and limp.

Stepanida Yefimovna had set up house nicely in her cellbelly: she'd spread out her shawl and nodded off to sleep under the little rosy pennant of her net. For the most part, her sleep was calm and relaxed, but every once in a while she would suddenly spring up in a fright, with her light-blue eyes almost bursting out of their sockets: "Make the sign of the cross, Devil, make the sign of the cross!" She would cross herself as if by reflex or by instinct and fall back asleep.

"What's got you in such a panic, little old momma?" Shustikov Gleb called out several times to her.

"I've seen the Tempter, dearie. I dreamed about the Tempter, my apologies," Stepanida Yefimovna said in embarrassment and fell as silent as a mouse.

And so they travelled along, each and every one in his or her own cellbelly.

Once, along the berm on a sloping hill, the travellers spotted an old man with an upraised finger. The finger was huge, twisted and gnarled, like a branch. Volodya slammed on the brakes and gawked at the old man from the truck cabin.

The old man groaned weakly.

"Why are you groaning, pops?" Volodya asked.

"Can't you see how my finger here's swollen up?" the old man retorted. "About tin days ago, I was agathering mushrooms, good people, 'mongst the pines and firs when this dark green viper just cropped up from nowhere. That there viper fanged me good on the finger, hissed sumpin awful and crawled off. It's tin days now since I've had any shut-eye..."

"Whew, pop, you've noshed on the mushrooms, you have!" Volodya Teleskopov suddenly guffawed in a wild voice, as if he'd never heard anything more amusing than this tale in all his life. "You did a little munching on the mushrooms, eh, pops! Were the things tasty, then, or not? Well, gang, ain't that a side-splitter—pops here got greedy for some fungi!"

"What's with you, Volodya?" Vadim Afanasyevich dryly asked. Why is it you find this cause for amusement? I wouldn't have expected that of you."

Volodya became so choked up with laughter that his face flushed a bright red.

"As a matter of fact, why am I neighing like a jinny? Pardon my stupid laughter, gramps. You need medical treatment to fix up your fingy. You oughta drink a half-liter of vodka, pappy, or maybe at least 700 grams."

"That's O.K., the pain is still tolerable," the old man said as he groaned.

"Dear fellow, you must take some crushed brick..." Stepanida Yefimovna intoned, "...some stewed wheat-germ, dried goose-foot and tobacco sprigs. Add a copper five-kopeck piece and bring everything to a boil. Let the new moon view your concoction and when the cock starts to crow thrice, immerse your finger and..."

"That's O.K., the pain is still tolerable," the old man groaned.

"What superstitions you have, Stepanida Yefimovna, and you a scientific lab-technician!" old Mochenkin hissed out maliciously. "Heed my advice, brother! Take your wound to the VTEK,[95] where you'll be granted status as a 'first-class' invalid. That'll bring you quick relief."

"That's O.K., the pain is still tolerable," the old man said, sticking to his guns... "I can still endure it, good people..."

"Well, in my opinion, the best antidote is pork fat!" Irina Valentinovna exclaimed. "The natives near Kilimanjaro, when a poisonous python bites them, always slaughter a hefty sow," she said, letting her knowledge sparkle.

"Never mind, never mind, my tolerance still hasn't busted yet," the old man suddenly began to wail in falsetto.

"The finger ought to be amputated, oi-weh, right away," Shustikov Gleb advised sympathetically. "The fellow is on in years, but he'll hold out somehow without his finger."

"Now that's a healthy thought," the old man enunciated very clearly and suddenly, as he glanced quickly at his horrible finger as though it were some total stranger.

"Comrades, how can you blather such nonsense—comrades!" Vadim Afanasyevich uttered suddenly, jumping into the foray. "What's this ignoble advice you proffer? At the closest aid-station they'll just slit the comrade's finger lengthwise to drain it and pump him full of antibiotics and more antibiotics."

"That's correct," Volodya shouted out. "This finger's gotta be saved. If we toss our fingers around with abandon, we'll have no fingers to line our pockets with. Well, then, climb up onto the barrelware, pops!"

"That's O.K., that's O.K. I can still tolerate the pain," once again grumbled the old man who had been bitten by a viper. But everyone else, quite agitated, suddenly began to raise a racket and Shustikov, Gleb, who just a few seconds ago had proposed his attack plan, jumped down onto the ground, lifted the featherweight wanderer and sat him in a free cellbelly by way of demonstrating that he wouldn't insist on an amputation.

"Seems once again we're about to hang a detour," old Mochenkin said feigning disgruntlement.

"What sort of detours can you have in mind, Ivan Alexandrovich!" Vadim Afanasyevich dismissed the comment with a sweeping gesture of his hands. And hearing him speak these words, Volodya Teleskopov gunned the gas, knifed the gearshift into third and began to climb up the sloping hill. Then, raising huge clouds of dust, he sped along the side road towards the little white houses of a state grain farm.

"I apologize, brother," old Mochenkin said, unable to contain his curiosity as his squinty eyes groped to examine this moaning peer of his. "Might one say you simply went off awandering with your finger, or was it someplace specific you were trekking to?"

"I was on my way to my sister's, good citizens, to the city of Tuapse,"[96] the old man groaned.

"To where?" Shustikov Gleb burst out in amazement, recalling immediately that aromatic southern port so distant from them now, the dark night and the glistening islands of tankers on a foreign raid.

"Onto Tuapse I go, bright laddie, to my one-and-only sister. I want to bid farewell before I die."

"Now here's a real character, Irina, take careful note. He's nothing short of a modern day Scaevola," Gleb said, addressing himself to his girlfriend.

"Tell me, Gleb, whether you could, like Scaevola, ignite everything which you pay obeisance to and pay obeisance to everything that you ignite?" Irina asked.

Thoroughly shaken by this question Gleb began coughing. Meanwhile, old Mochenkin had already sharpened his pencil and directed its point towards the oblast courts.

## Old Mochenkin's Request
## To Liquidate the Dark Green Snake

*For many years already, regional agencies have been developing a successful campaign to liquidate a dark-green, ugly phenomenon which has coiled up a comfortable snake lair for itself in our forests.*

*However, side by side with the accomplished success, many comrades do not get an ear of anything excepting oink-oink empty words. There ain't no posted bills anywhere.*

*It is necessary to fully develop in all places visible propaganda against the grovelling beasties which bite our fingers, to arm the populace with literature concerning the question at hand, and, contrariwise to expectoration, to establish a regional inspector of snakes with a basic pay scale of 18 roubles 76 kopecks and a milk ration.*

*I request you not to reject this request.*

*Mochenkin, I. A., former Colorado Beetle Inspector, currently non-employed.*

And thus it was they kept travelling. Teleskopov and Drozhzhinin in the cabin; the others in the barrelware, each in his or her own cellbelly.

However, they did reach the state grain farm and there deposited the ever patient old man at the aid-station.

The old man raised quite a ruckus at the aid-station and demanded an amputation. But they just staggered him with antibiotics and his finger soon healed. Of course, the whole state grain farm, to a person, ran to check out the disturbance and, in their midst, there turned up the "one-and-only sister," who hadn't lived in Tuapse at all—only here, precisely on this state grain farm from where the old man himself also hailed. The ever patient old man had made a mess of things here. Probably, on account of the pain.

\* \* \*

They once spent the night in an open field. The field was rather queer looking on account of its curved hillock. They sat on this hillock, by a campfire, under the stars—as if they were perched on the Earth's curvature. There were the smells of semi-withered grass, flowers, smoke and celestial picklebrine. Crickets were chirping.

"Chirp away, lovelies," Stepanida Yefimovna sang out tenderly. "Chirp and chirp—I've already fulfilled my quarterly quota of crickets. If I could just demonstrate some signs of catching brother photoplexirus nowadays, why I'd be a satisfied woman."

Her tiny face began to fade, like the flames, into the darkness, but her teeny light-blue eyes started to gleam slyly. Her petite hand gently, gently—"Oh, our sins are burdensome"—passed across her yawning little mouth and the old woman dozed off.

"Now little old momma's going to see the Tempter again," proposed Gleb.

"Ai, ai, ai," the old woman cried out in her sleep, "cross thyself, Satan, cross thyself."

"I'd like to catch sight of this Tempter of hers," Vadim Afanasyevich said. "It'd be interesting to know what sort of fellow he is, this so-called Tempter."

"He's very handsome," Stepanida Yefimovna replied, having re-awakened immediately. "His cap is a pretty little thing, his boots are the height of fashion, his tummy's nice and round and virry intresting."

"So why are you so afraid of him granny?" Irina Valentinovna asked out of surprise and naivete.

"How can I do anything other than fear him, my pretty little dove, for Mary's sake?" the old woman asked with a sigh. "Why he'd start to tickle me and sweep me off my feet to dance and begin flirting with his fiery peepers! Oh, he's clever, this Tempter, and bad..."

"Little old momma, you've got to reform yourself," Shustikov Gleb said severely, "reform yourself in a most decisive way."

"As a matter of fact, granny," Teleskopov said, "tell your own fortune and you'll see how a good person..."

"...approaches across the dew-covered grass," everyone suddenly echoed in a chorus and then shuddered, as they glanced at one another in confusion.

"A Knaight?" the shrewd old woman asked as she clasped her hands.

"Not really. Just a friend prepared to come to your aid," Vadim Afanasyevich said. "Well, for instance, a simple ploughman with a compass..."

"Precisely," Volodya agreed with a nod, "a handsome dude wearing kid gloves."

"An arm of the law, authoritative," old Mochenkin began to drawl out plaintively.

"An authority?" the old woman gasped. "Cross thyself, cross thyself! My Tempter is likewise an authority."

"No, no—little old woman—what a slow wit you have," Gleb said with annoyance, "he's simply got a handsome face, nice clothes, and interior fortitude. For him all fiddle-faddle claptrap on wheels are no big deal."

"And he's manly," Irina Valentinovna exclaimed, "heroic, like Scaevola..."

"I've got it, my dearies, I've got it!" Stepanida Yefimovna lit up and gleamed with her sly eyes. "A blessed person is approaching across the dew-covered grass—oh, how grand!"

And with that she immediately fell asleep with her mouth open.

"The little old momma was just getting herself programmed nicely," Shustikov Gleb began guffawing, but stopped short out of embarrassment. Indeed, all were very embarrassed and didn't look at one another, for the common secret of their dreams had just been revealed.

Flames from the campfire flickered across their embarrassed faces and the forced silence dragged on and became as thick as a migraine. Then, however, the barrelware wrapped in kerchiefs and plaids gave a cozy little squeak in her sleep and everyone forgot their discomfiture right away and calmed down.

Shustikov Gleb offered Irina Valentinovna "to go awandering, to trample goose-foot in the crimson fields,"[97] and they set off ceremoniously.

As vast flashes of lightning lit up for a few seconds the endless hilly plain and the receding figures of the marine and teach, old Mochenkin suddenly had a thought: "The beauty of love adorns our lives by the vanguard you—uh—u—th." So he thought, became frightened, and—for his own piece of mind—drafted yet another entry for his files on the low and amoral level of conduct.

Vadim Afanasyevich and Volodya lay on their backs next to one another, enjoying their tobacco for a while at day's end and blowing smoke up at the starry sky.

"How insignificant we are, Vadik," Teleskopov suddenly said, "who in this universe needs us, eh? After all, everything in the universe moves, rumbles, cooks on its own—the universe is busy with its own chemistry and we are just fiddle-faddle to it."

"The idea of universal solitude? Lots of minds are taxed by that," Vadim Afanasyevich pronounced and recalled his opponent, the vicar and famous grasshopper from Helvetia.

"But what does it cook and what does it move and what will happen in the final result? Yes, and what does that mean—'the final result'? Honestly, Vadik, a fear-and-trembling chills me to the bone when I ponder the words—'In the Final Result'; I fear for myself, I feel like howling due to lack of understanding. I fear for everyone whose got hands, legs, and a numbskull atop their shoulders. I feel like hightailing it somewhere with results to boot, like knocking me off for good, no fooling around! After all, I didn't used to exist and I won't then . . . so why did I materialize at all?"

"Man continues to live through his deeds," Vadim Afanasyevich uttered indistinctly, to spite his vicar.

"Old Mochenkin, granny Stepanida, and I, God's unlucky harrumph. By what sort of deeds are we to continue to live?" Volodya continued: "Earlier, now, the guileless masses knew God, Heaven, Hell, and the Devil and they lived under the law of those forces. But now, indeed, there's none of all that—as they'll tell you at any public lecture. Right? As a consequence, I am to depart whole hog, dissolve into a zero. And even right this moment I'm supposed to carry on with no details, just like someone expecting, eh? Right or not? We had a Yurka Zvonkov at the Ust'-Kasimov quarry. He had a one-track mind—how to bum a fiver (for booze) "'til payday,' to strut around (bragging about it) like a peacock, and to go sneaking into the girls' dorm. Every night the babes would pound him soundly. Oh, it made us laugh. Once, a crane hoist fell on Yurka and we carted him to the cemetery; I banged the brass cymbals. I'd look back and see: Yurka was lying there looking stern and important, as if he knew something special. I had never seen him look like that before. So I went to the aid-station and asked Semyon Borisovich why Yurka's face was like that. And he said the muscles of a dead man go slack and that's why the face was like that. You understand that, Teleskopov? It's clear to me; as concerns muscles it's clear..."

"Man continues through love..." Vadim Afanasyevich mumbled indistinctly.

Volodya became silent. Now, only the crackle of the campfire and a light dreamy squeaking of the barrelware broke the silence.

"I understand you, Vaddyuk!" Volodya suddenly shouted. "Where there's love, there's also human kind and where there's non-love, that's where there's this damn chemistry, chemistry—all that dark and black-and-blue mask of a mug. Is that right? Is that it? That is why people seek love and get into mischief and fool around. But it's in everyone, even if just a jot or a tittle of it. Is that right? Isn't it? Eh?"

"I don't know, Volodya, whether it's in everyone. I don't know, I just don't know," Vadim Afanasyevich muttered in an almost inaudible whisper.

"Well, whoever doesn't have it has got only chemistry instead. Chemistry, physics, and no residue...Something like that? Is that correct?"

"Go to sleep, Volodya," said Vadim Afanasyevich.

"I'm already asleep," replied Volodya and began to snore.

Vadim Afanasyevich lay for a long time with his eyes open and gazed at the flickering lightning which lit up the peaceful fields. He thought about his friend snoring away next to him, about his revelations; he recalled his beloved work (it's no sin to reveal that he sometimes jumped up in the middle of the night in a cold sweat), which dampened any such similar thoughts. He thought about Gleb and Irina Valentinovna, about Stepanida Yefimovna and old Mochenkin, about the pilot Kulachenko, the ever patient old man, his mother and father, the world famous vicar hopping around to different countries and defending the intellectual elite all the time with stunning Catholic, Buddhist or Dionysian concepts and returning each time to his canton in Helvetia in order to prepare the next intellectual brouhaha—what new thing is he readying now for blissful, pants-down defenseless and unsuspecting Haligalia?

With these thoughts and in this uneasy state of mind, Vadim Afanasyevich also dropped off to sleep.

\* \* \*

Like the queen of Eastern Hindu Kush, Irina Valentinovna was sleeping under a sailor's peacoat on a distant hill covered with wormwood. The whole world lay at her feet and in that world her faithful Gleb was running through the bushes scaring away the she-goat Romance.

The she-goat kept on harrumphing as she went crackling through the bushes, and then she was fidgeting around in the roadside ditches and howling like a bittern from the nearby swamp. Gleb had completely exhausted himself, when everything suddenly came to a hush, a dead calm; a deceptive tranquility enveloped the earth and Gleb, expecting a new dirty trick, grew as taut as a spring.

And sure enough... he soon heard a low droning as slowly along the road, like silhouettes on transparent wheels, some fiddle-faddle claptraps came riding by.

There's a good one for you, now! If I were to tell this story, they wouldn't believe me. Gleb leapt across the ditch and tautened himself in preparation for active resistance.

With one trembling flicker of sheet-lightning, the figure of their leader flashed before Gleb's eyes: a child's unfurrowed brow, beady little eyes, and broad (let's be frank) athletic shoulders.

Almost without thinking Gleb rushed forward, roaring like a terrible wild beast. Then it was that something really broke loose, began to flash and squeal... and, as a result, the marine nabbed all four of them.

"Ho," Gleb said as he had an absolutely clear thought: "Now if I tell this story, they surely won't believe it."

He shook down the fiddle-faddle claptraps—they were clean.

"Well," he said magnanimously, "one could say you've got yourselves into a mess, comrades fiddle-faddle claptrapping on wheels."

"Let us go, uncle Gleb," whined one of the fiddle-faddle claptrap creatures.

Surprised, Gleb freed all of them right away, but he got an even bigger surprise then: in front of him stood four schoolboys from his native regional center.

"What's going on?" the young marine asked in confusion.

"It's the 'Do You Know Your Country' bicycle race,"[98] one of the schoolboys said in a trembling bass voice.

"Come on, now, uncle Gleb, you know us," squealed another. "I'm Kolya Tyutyushkin, he's Fedya Zhilkin, he's Yura Mamochkin, and this is Borya Kurochkin.[99] He was the one who instigated it. He came running up to us like some loony and organized us as a geography club. Do you know your country, he asked. Forwards, he said, in pursuit of her..."

"In whose pursuit, whose?" Gleb asked insinuatingly and, just in case, took Borya Kurochkin by his amazingly strong hand.

"In pursuit of Romance, don't you know?" muttered the amazing seventh-grader, and he pointed with his free hand somewhere off into the distance.

Another flash of sheet-lightning lit up the horizon, and Gleb saw plump Romance riding a lady's bicycle in the distance, raising up dust.

"This is a good deed, guys," he said, having cheered up. "Good and useful. May the happiness of hard roads be with you."

With that he let the schoolboys go completely and, absolutely calm and in a most excellent mood, he returned to his queen atop the hill covered with wormwood.

### Teach Irina Valentinovna Seleznyeva's Third Dream

Oh, to live quietly, to live carelessly, to fly eternally in a whirlwind dance! Eternally! Oh, Gleb, the floor is so slippery! Oh, Gleb, where... where are you?

Irochka, let me introduce you to my friend, the Physics prof Genrikh Anatolyevich Dopekailo.

Genrikh Anatolyevich, no old man at all, came flying up to her—gliding across the floor on his satyr's hooves at the height of a whirlwind waltz: "Do you recognize me, Seleznyeva?"

He had an anode on one shoulder and a cathode on the other. Well, how's my poor head to understand this?

"Tell me, dear heart, why should the square of the cathetuses of a hypoteneuse equal the regional conferences of underdeveloped countries in the atomic pool system?"

Another man is dashing up to her, constantly gaining speed. This is the world champion, Diego Instantaneous. He has a bouquet of examination-question tickets. Oh, yes, this is my solo.

> With card 15 you'll get both an "A" and love, with card 16 you'll smash your nosie so it bleeds lots of blood. With card 17 you've the prize of a smoked-sprat's tail, and with this card your question's hard as hell.

World champions, men and women, kept waltzing round and round—these instructors and examiners were pestering her. Everybody was waiting for a legal advisor from OBLSOBES. It was his duty to sum up things.

And here the old man is. Having spread his hands so he glides in inclined like a bouncing spring, the fiery-red redhead has flown into the room. Everybody stepped aside as the old man, drawing his circles narrower and narrower, bellowed: "Have you prepared your application for retirement with full pension?"

There was ice everywhere, smooth ice, decorated with some weird ornamentation. And only there, somewhere in the boundless distance, Good Person was walking across damp, royal meadows. He was walking, blowing his nose and coughing, and little marble lion cubs (each one smaller than the next) were trudging behind him on a little chain.

### Marine Shustikov Gleb's Third Dream

In the morning I noticed a certain flab in my *musculus deltoideus,* so I took some measures immediately.

So, I'm standing near my bunk and giving my *musculus deltoideus* an extra bunch of exercises. The guys are working out, too, each one as he sees fit. Some are working on triceps, others on biceps or quadraceps. Seva Antonov is pumping up his *musculus gluteus.* I can understand why.

Our favorite midshipman, Reinvolf—Kozma Yelistratovich, comes in. "At ease! At ease! Today, you cream of wheat, is the final tug-a-war competition with the submariners. Everybody gets a double portion of butter and meat, a triple portion of compote."

"Will we get some doughnuts, comrade shipman?"

"Atten-tion!"

And then the battle here is in full swing. Right in front of me an elusively familiar submariner has strained all his brawn. He struggles skillfully to win. The admiration he receives is deserved and the envy's not begrudged, either.

As a result: an unbelievable precedent in the history of the Russian fleet since the time of Peter's boat.[100] Namely, a draw. The cable broke, so everybody's contented.

I am satisfied with myself, too, and go strolling in my best bib and tucker along the shady parklanes. The elusively familiar submariner comes up to me and says, "Listen, friend, I propose we get acquainted."

"It seems to me that we're not exactly strangers."

"And I thought you didn't recognize me," the submariner smiles.

"Volodya Teleskopov?"

"Cold, cold," he smiles.

"Drozhzhinin? Is that right?" I ask.

"Warm, warm," he laughs.

I look intently. "Irinka, is it you?"

"You've almost guessed, but not quite. My name is Scaevola."

"Ah, so it's you!" I exclaimed. "Wait, both your hands are whole and in place. So, it turns out this is all just myth, rubbish, and legend?"

"Disappointed?" Scaevola asks, then says, "Kid's stuff! Big deal, to burn your hand!"

At this moment Scaevola flicks his lighter and the sleeve of his flannel shirt begins to burn.

He raises his burning hand like an Olympian torch and runs along a dark parklane. "Come on, Gleb, do like I do!"

To set my hand on fire was so easy and quick. I am running after Scaevola. My hand crackles above my head; it burns fine.

Scaevola ducks into a little black tunnel. I follow him. Pitchblack darkness. Only here and there do mugs of imperialists light up and bare their teeth. On the run, I shove my burning hand into their aggressive traps. They howl.

I run out of the tunnel. Everything is clean, quiet, and deserted.

The elusively familiar voice comes over the radio: "Are you, young and handsome Gleb, ready to dedicate yourself to science, to give yourself to her completely to the last drop of blood?"

I look and see: Science is lying, plaintively squeaking, groaning, and singing something in a thin, tender, and nervous voice. Some kind people have wrapped her in tarpaulin and plaid blankets.

I shout, "Ready!"

And here for your pleasure: out of a funhouse comes False-Science. She is immense in size and reminiscent of some Junta from a certain hot country. She holds a whip in one hand and a can of fish and a bottle of "Backwoods Oak" in the other. Yeah, we know these political tactics![101]

I automatically shift gear to combat alert... I come closer to her and address her in the manner of foreigners: "Do you have a light?"

False-Science stares at my burning hand with her shameless peepers. She swings her whip. Oh, we know this! I kick her in the shin with the toe of my shoe, then in the *periosteum*. And, immediately, also a punch straight in the nose, in order to blind her! With two hooks I finish up the tottering colossus. False-Science vanishes into thin air.

A tropical downpour is gushing down. It's poisonous. I cough and blow my nose. My hand is extinguished. I run through the funhouse; I'm handsome, but wet, in all the mirrors. It's not funny at all. I make my way through the plywood wall and see...

... beyond the meadows, beyond the seas, the blue mountains, the sun is rising, and straight out of the sun, my beloved is coming towards me, wearing a silk mask. Good Person is coming through the dew.

# Vladimir Teleskopov's Third Dream

With life there's pain, make no mistake: it's bread you want, but you're eating cake. I overheard what seems a rumor: our Vanya's riding, Popelnukha. And S. Tarasov, master jockey?—He's sure to come, and that's no joshing.[102]

I shouldn't even set eyes on the damn racetrack, but here I am. I drag myself, shame on me, to the 80-kopeck window. But as I enter the hall, why is everything so quiet? It's so quiet, like in an empty church. But, as typical, everybody is elbowing one another as they watch Volodya Teleskopov entering. And I am also looking at him, as if in the mirror, as is typical, too.

And, as typical, Volodya is walking in the void all white, as if he had a hangover. And, as typical, he is going straight to Andryusha.

Andryusha is standing by a column. And, as typical, he is also all white, like a plain teapot.

"Andryusha, the odds are for Botany and Be-Fast. Will you go halves with me on a stake of a rouble?"

Gloom-doom Andryusha looks around fearfully, as is typical, and silently moves his lips.

"Wha-atsa matter?"

"Do you believe, Volodya, we're betting on them? They, the nags, are betting on us."[103]

They've turned on the PA. Applause. Guffaws. The 46th District Militia orchestra has started to play.

Andryusha proudly has cocked his head back and is kicking up one of his hooves. I also kick up a hoof and snort. They've come up, bridled us and led us to the ring. I am in an excellent mood. I need to learn this new profession.

I've got a nice guy for a jockey. Andryusha's got a small, grey one that's like a cricket, and, as is typical, the guy wears glasses, so he's probably from the clergy. The bell! We're off the wire and running!

We are galloping head to head. My native stable where I read an anthology in my colthood flashes past us. There's my stable, there's my native home and there I am—pulling sleds with millet cereal. From marker to marker we run head to head. Andryusha is covered all in lather, but he's cheerful.

The stands are getting closer and closer. The crowds in the stand are all white, they're enthralled. Aha, it's angels that are packed in there everywhere. They beat their wings, they whistle.

The finish. The bell! But Andryusha and I press on. The jockeys fell off, but we keep at it, and how, oo-lah-lah!

We notice that under a tulip Serafima Ignatyevna and Silvia are drinking tea and eating meatballs.

"Join us, guys!"

71

We want to join them very much, but it's impossible. We run through a swamp, where our feet stick in the mud. In front of us something has bloated up and started to stink: immense, Chemistry has risen to the surface. It gapes with a toothless mouth, blinks its ginger eyes, and issues us an invitation with its drooping ears.

I have mounted Andryusha and we've got through.

We are running along the rails. Behind there's knocking, whistling, and hot panting and puffing. It's Physics catching up with us. Andryusha mounts me and we break away.

We're so beat down and bled dry. Our resistance is over. We're lying down now. Take us; we're baked!

There is grass all around. Crickets chirr and it smells of camomile. Andryusha raises his shnozzle. "Hey," he says, "look Volodka!"

I look and see: through the dew comes Good Person, the cook, carrying two bowls of fresh fish stew. There's beer, too!

### Vadim Afanasyevich's Third Dream

To solve the cardinal questions here on neutral ground three knights have gathered: the cattle magnate Syracuzers from Argentina, the learned vicar from canton Helvetia, and Vadim Afanasyevich Drozhzhinin from the Arbat.

Blue and gold hopes and expectations were flourishing in this neutral ground. A three-legged table stood in the middle of it. A bottle of "Backwoods Oak" and a can of fish in tomato sauce were on the table. A map of Haligalia served as a table cloth.

"As for me," Syracuzers says, "well, I'm not going to give up my habits. I have always inundated underdeveloped countries, and I'll inundate this one again."

"You lean on Junta for support, señor Syracuzers," I said in a voice quivering with indignation.

Syracuzers began to grunt, to giggle, and to toss and turn his beefy neck—in pretended embarrassment.

"I own up, sometimes I do a bit of leaning."

The abbott, that dirty sneaker, also smiled scabrously.

"Well, what about you, you learned man?" I addressed myself to him. "What are you preparing for my country? Do you know how many children were born there yesterday, and how they were christened?"

That damn judaspriest immediately reads a prepared note: "Nine individuals male, seven female. All the girls, without exception, were named Azalia; five boys—Diego, four—Vadim, in your honor. As you can see, Diego has taken the lead."

The choking cuts my breath short. I am choking with rage, seething

72

with anguish. "But what does it matter to you? After all, you couldn't give a damn!"

He smiles. "Quite right. My friend, you are too late. Soon Haligalia will wake up from her lethargy. She will become the epicenter of a new intellectual storm. There's a new phenomenon in philosophy being born into the world—haligalithet."

"In its own juice or with spices?" Syracuzers asked in a business-like, but curious manner.

"With spices, my colleague, with spices," the vicar giggled.

I get up. "You double-dealing, shameless fleecers! I'm going to belt your face with just my left hand alone."

Both jumped up holding blades in their hands.

"Come! Help me! Volodya! Gleb Ivanovich! Gramps Mochenkin!"

There was silence. Rocking back and forth, the neutral ground was moving swiftly in the ocean of a people's tears.

"To each his own Haligalia, but give me mine!" the vicar squealed and slashed the map with his blade.

"And I'll take mine!" roared Syracuzers, and he also brandished a knife.

"And where is mine?" Vadim Afanasyevich shouted.

"Yours? There it is! Be my guest, look and admire!"

I looked and saw my dear one floating atop a quiet, azure body of water. Her brown cheeks were softly shining in the sunlight. She was floating, squeaking very quietly and singing something vague and tender. She was covered with my Scottish plaid, with Volodya's quilted jacket, and with the handkerchief of old Mochenkin.

"This is really my Haligalia," I whispered, "I don't want any other."

I jump into the water and swim. I don't look back, but I see that Syracuzers and the vicar are emptying the bottle of "Backwoods Oak." I swim up to my dear one, kiss her cheeks and take her in tow.

We swim for a long time, singing softly. Finally, we see that Good Person, a qualified cooper, is coming towards us, carrying new hoops.


### Old Mochenkin's Third Dream

And there he saw his Resume. She was walking in the middle of the field, howling in a low voice.

"—he-is-diligent-in-work-he-is-decent-in-his-private-life-"

Fefyolov, Andron Lukich, and I are strolling in the field, like friends do, stroking the ears of wheat.

"You, brother Ivan Alexandrovich, present me to your Resume," Andron Lukich winks at me with his right eye, "and I will requisition shixteen kilos of raisins for you."

73

"Here she comes, my Resume. Please, make her acquaintance, Andron Lukich."

Fefyolov looks sternly at her as she is approaching us and I tremble all over, thinking, "What will happen if he doesn't laik her?"

"So-o-o, this is your Resume?"

"Yes, it's her, Andron Lukich. Please, don't take anything amiss."

"We-e-ll . . ."

She could have at least painted her lips, damn her, and I won't mention the permanent she needs. She is walking along, sweeping her skirt back and forth and tearing my soul into pieces.

"he-is-politically-educated-he-is-punctilious-with-state-property-. . ."

"We-e-ll, Ivan Alexandrovich, to tell the truth, I'm disappointed. I thought your Resume would be a tasty young morsel, but this one—we-e-ll, she's like a year-old beet."

"Oh, you're being fastidious, Andron Lukich! Oh, you're underestimating her . . ." I say this in a low voice, but in fact I am really quivering like a lonely, pint-size trifler. I want the raisins real bad.

"Well, it's O.K.," Andron Lukich resigned himself. "She'll do, but she is still a broad."

He went back on his haunches, puffed out his chest and bellowed; how he'll throw his whole body into the running charge at her, my Resume!

"Ai-ia-ia," Resume shouted and took to her heels, the stupid popeyed thing.

She ran to the river and Andron Lukich's legs are pumping hard in pursuit and he's hooting like a train: lo-ove you-u-u. Well, I also started to run. I thought I could intercept the stupid broad.

"No!" shouts Resume, "it'll never be! I'd rather jump into the river!"

And sure enough, whammo, right from the cliff into the river. Then she surfaced, opened her eyes wide and howled,

"-he-is-a-man-of-principle-with-his-colleagues-!!! . . ."

And, like a stone, she went to the bottom.

Andron Lukich just stands there, meditating and rubbing an ear of wheat in his hand.

"It's been a good year for wheat, Ivan Alexandrovich, but we have a shortage of raisins."

And he went away from me a proud, but sad man. Of course, from the purely human point of view I could understand him, but it didn't do me any good.

And for the first time in his life the former inspector Mochenkin started to cry bitterly. And I felt pity for someone, maybe for myself, maybe for raisins, and, maybe, for Resume.

"Where can I go now? What can I hope for?"

I don't know how long I was sitting there. I wiped my eyes and saw that on the other side of the river, standing in the dew-covered grass, was Good Person, the tasty young and juicy Resume.

### Dream of the Free-Lance Lab-Technician, Stepanida Yefimovna

Oo-lah, dearies, of Persian thread the little psalteries! Oo-lah, laddies, bulbous the onions and sweet the carrot roots... Rootie-tootie, cheep-cheep-cheep...

Oh, the Tempter seized me by the hem—that gay young buck, that round tummy tuck. Oh, he grabbed my tresses, my maiden tresses.

"Give me leave, Tempter, to hie to Ant Mountain!"

"I'll not consent."

"Give me leave, Tempter, to hie to Dragonfly forest!"

"I'll not consent."

"And whither art thou drawing me, into what accursed temptation?"

"Ach, granny-my pretty, you free-lance lab-technician, Thou lackest understanding *in toto!* I shall twirl you, nanny-baby, sweet-roll, eggs-milk-bread-and-butterer in a dance, in a foreign-to-most-grams reel! You'll be a right bun, you dear young Grossmutter! Voi-lá!"

The Tempter began his wiles: he whipped up his fashionable hooves, he shook his succulent limbs. He pokes me on the forehead with his bony finger and tickles—like he wants me to die laughing—ai! Phew, phew!

"Cross thyself, Devil, cross thyself!"

He doesn't cross himself. He whirls me through the potato patch leaves in otherunderworldly dances.

Oh, in the forest the sward is aromatic. Ach, it's narcotic... And whither thou with me, whither thou goest with me, oh—whither thou goest with me... pretzels-shmétzels...

I take heed: my Tempter has sat down by the campfire—he of the brunette hair, mischievous eyes and tummy so fair.

"Well, now, nanny-my-pretty, you old rogue—cook me some soup! My hotel desireth to eat zuppa 'dritte Nachtigall'.[104] Cook me some soup, foaming hot so the bones pop!"

"Soup?"

"Soup!"

"Soup?"

"Soup!"

"Soup?"

"Soup!"

"Ah, my laddies! Nachtigall, dearies, is our nightingale, only in their tongue it's called Nachtigall and it's enchanted. Oi, I go awandering, wretched sinner of an old woman, through the blades of sward. I hunt down baked eggs, I pluck sorrel, jerk up some dill, drown them all with bitter tears, and bid farewell to my gentle barrelware and to you—yes, to you, too, my midnight doves."

Goo-tyen', Fee-son', vitriolic squanderer!

"But the darkness is so pitchblack and endless, laddies, as if there were no electricity in the world! And from behind there the cock crows, the owl hoots, and the Tempter guffaws with a leer."

And here it is: an abundant stillness began to reign, a festive and idle quiet. Above the stubble field there hung an oily icon lamp. And here it is— I see: across the dew-covered grass, dearies, the Blessed Knaight ambles. He's scientific and pensive. And by the hand he is leading, holy holy Marys... he is leading like a swaddling babe a horned beetle, that most desirous beetle: sire-photoplexirus.


### Volodya Teleskopov's Second Letter to His Friend Sima

*Your Honor, Serafima Ignatyevna,*

*How are you?*

*Business first. I inform You that Your barrelware is safe and sound, and she wishes You the same.*

*Sima, do you remember Sochi, those days and nights the inspired words of the sacred oath you paced the room in agitation throwing into my face like something sharp and I missed you very much although I am very pleased with my trip you said it's time for us to part I am very frightening in my rage.*

*There is no overexpenditure of gas because we've been driving on empty how many days already and this of course is an innovative initiative so I'm even surprised.*

*Perhaps you think, Serafima Ignatyevna, that I do not inform You correctly, that I crashed myself into 15 days jail. But that would be a big mistake on Your part.*

*Take 1 (one) kg. of homemade pork sausage to my father for payment in cash.*

*Simka, you want the truth? I don't know when we'll see each other again, because we go not where we want to but where our dear barrelware wants us to go. Understand?*

*Thanks for your love and food.*

*Your perhaps still unforgotten,*

*Teleskopov, Vladimir*

## Volodya Teleskopov's Letter to Silvia Chesterton

*How do you do, honorable Silvia, whose surname I don't remember.
I've heard form our mutual friends that you've joined the organi-
zation "Maidens' Honor." Heartily congratulate you, but tell Gutik
Rosenblum that I am going to feed him a knuckle sandwich in any case.*

*Silvia, do you remember that magic southern night when we . . . Let's
put the subject on ice to be crystal clear about it. Do you remember or not?*

*Now I'll tell you about my achievements. I head up a convoy. The
salary is modest—15 hundred, but it's enough. I read a lot. I've read Jules
Verne's* The Children of Captain Grant, *this year's number 7 issue of the
journal "Knowledge is Power," and* The Anthology of Himalayan
Fairytales.[105] *It was very interesting. Right now I'm completing a
responsible mission. You want to know what kind? The more you know,
the faster you age! But I can trust you. I'm accompanying barrelware. I
don't know how to say that in your Haligalian language. She is very
nervous and if you knew her, Silvochka, you'd of course fall in love with
her.*

*Long live the friendship of young people of all countries and of all
colors of skin. Inform me regularly about your achievements in studies and
sports. What do you read?*

*Your maybe you still remember, Volodya*

*Teleskopov (Sputnik)*[106]

\* \* \* \*

Spitting onto his indelible pencil, Volodya wrote both these letters on
a torn pack of "Belomor" cigarettes; the one to Sima was written on the side
with the map, and the one to Silvia on the reverse side. [107] Sniffling sadly in
the dusty rays of the sun, he was sitting on a wooden bench (penknifed with
indecent words), in the detention room of the Gusyatin militia office.
Here's how that came about . . . .

One day they arrived at the little town of Gusyatin, where on a hill in
front of an ancient merchants' arcade there stood a magnificent Ferriswheel called "Flight Into the Unknown."[108]

Volodya stopped the truck near the Ferriswheel and suggested to his
passengers that they spend the rest of the day and the night in the curious
town of Gusyatin.

Everybody gladly agreed and got out of their cellbellies. Each took off
on his own. Old Mochenkin went to the local med-center to test his gastric
juice because the record for the VTeK of his terrible gastric juice was lost

somewhere. Shustikov Gleb and Irina Valentinovna set off to look for a library with a reading room. They needed to do literature for a while, to raise their intellectual level slightly, to grow brainier. As for Stepanida Yefimovna, she saw a poster for the movie "Bela" on a fence near the clubhouse and on the poster she saw Pechorin.[109] With impatient curiosity she exclaimed "ah-ah" and, immediately, bought a ticket. There seemed to be something elusively familiar to her in the face of the young officer with pink cheeks and a trim moustache.

Volodya Teleskopov could not tear his eyes away from the wondrous Ferriswheel which looked like some gigantic, ominous pop-art sculpture.

"Vadik! Just look at it! Well, isn't it the tops! Isn't that it? Let's go for a ride!"

"What are you saying?" winced Vadim Afanasyevich, "I don't want to ride that contraption at all."

"Either you're my friend, or I'm garbage to you. Let's go for a spin for sure—what's a bloody nose; the last night out will have painted the town red," Volodya shouted.

Vadim Afanasyevich sighed, liked a man condemned. "What's the source of this infantilism of yours, Volodya?"

"What do you mean, Vadik, it's not infantilism, word of honor!" Volodya put his hand on his chest, opened his eyes wide, and breathed hard at Vadim Afanasyevich "You see? Haven't had a drop. I swear on my honor I didn't drink even a gram. You believe me or not? You my friend or not?"

Vadim Afanasyevich, dismissing it with a gesture of his hand, said "O.K., O.K."

They came up to the base of the Ferriswheel, where rusted legs rose from thickets of stinging nettle, goose-foot and burdock. It was obvious that the inhabitants of Gusyatin did not enjoy the "Flight Into the Unknown" very often. They woke up some bum who was sleeping under an elderberry bush.

"Turn on your machine, child of nature!" Volodya ordered him.

"There's no current and there won't be any," the bum said, as was his habit.

Vadim Afanasyevich sighed in relief. Volodya flashed his angry eyes, bit his lip, and flicked the knifeswitch on towards himself. Reluctantly, the Ferriswheel began creaking, as some gearwheel slowly began to move.

"A miracle!" the guy flabbily expressed his surprise. "There's never been any electricity in it, but now it up and creaks. Please, gentlemen, take your seats according to the number on the tickets you buy. 15 kopecks for three turns."

The friends took their seats in the compartments. The bum pushed some buttons and ran off a safe distance, away from the Ferriswheel. A series of explosions was heard and about two dozen curious inhabitants and five or six goats gathered at Gusyatin's sunbaked square.

Finally—tossed up, pressed down, and deafened—they slowly began to turn in sweeping revolutions.

With his teeth clenched ready for any and everything, Vadim Afanasyevich soared over the houses of Gusyatin, over the merchants' arcade. And somewhere, laughing happily, Volodya was flying in an orbit which sometimes intersected with Vadim Afanasyevich's line of vision.

The revolutions became faster and faster. Planets and stars flashed by: the plump, fissured Venus; the blue-nosed clod, Mars; Saturn, with the ring; and nameless other ugly ones with tails.

"Stop the machine!" shouted Vadim Afanasyevich, feeling dizzy. "That's enough! We aren't children!"

The square was empty. The curious spectators had already left. The bum was also nowhere to be seen. There was only a lonely goat still staring at the buzzing and creaking Ferriswheel, and two robust men who were sitting on a bench, with their butts sticking out, and playing chess.

"What a move, are you stupid or something?" Volodya shouted as he flew by above the chessplayers. "Take it with your bishop, E-8! You don't know how to play!"

"Volodya, I'm bored!" shouted Vadim Afanasyevich, "where's the attendant? Let him stop this thing!"

"What are you saying!" yelled Volodya, "I gave him a fiver! He's sitting in a cafeteria right now!"

Vadim Afanasyevich fainted and, in this unconcious state—stiff, pale, and holding his pipe in his mouth—he circled over sleepy Gusyatin.

It was getting dark. The sun which had been hanging over the belltower for a long time finally plopped down beyond the river. The streets came to life. A herd passed by and motorcycles rattled past. A tired Shustikov Gleb and Irina Valentinovna were coming back to the town. They hadn't succeeded in finding the Gusyatin reading room for all their day of searching.

Old Mochenkin was raising a ruckus at Gusyatin's med-center. "I can't believe your gastric juice!" he shouted, waving a document on which there was only the boring notation "normal" instead of the previous, terrifying data.

For the third time in a row Stepanida Yefimovna was watching the film "Bela," scrutinizing the rosy face and ribald eyes of the young officer and shouting, "No, it's not him! It looks like him, but it's not him! Oh, my God, not him!"

Vadim Afanasyevich regained consciousness. Above him there circled stars, not Gusyatin's, but real ones. "How all this reminds me of an ordinary starry sky," he thought, "I always thought that beyond that terrible borderline everything would be quite different. There would be no stars, or anything which was before. However, here are the stars and here, just the same, is my pipe."

In the starry night, something wild and hairy rushed past, above Vadim Afanasyevich, and yelled, "Have you had enough of the ride, Vadik?"

Startled, Vadim Afanasyevich caught sight of Teleskopov, who was flying off along his own orbit. Volodya was standing up in his compartment, waving a familiar bottle with a thoroughly soppy stopper.

"Either I am again here or he is already there, that is—here, and I'm not there, but here, that is—there, and we both are there, that is—here, but not there, that is—not here," Vadim Afanasyevich thought in a complicated manner and finally had the sense to look down.

He caught sight of the little truck situated not far from the Ferriswheel's steel leg and in it his beloved barrelware, slightly offended and annoyed with her strange solitude.

"Hurrah!" thought Vadim Afanasyevich, "if she is here, then I'm here, too, and not there, that is ... Well, that's O.K.," and his heart sank from this ordinary earthly agitation of his.

"Vadim, have you had enough of the ride?" Teleskopov suddenly yelled from below. "Let's go play chess! Hey, child of nature, cut the motor off!"

The bum was standing below now, dressed in somber evening garb and with his hair parted to one side.

"Throw down some money, and I'll let you ride more!" he shouted.

"Do you hear, Vadim?" cried Volodka, "what's your suggestion?"

"Quite enough for today, thank you!" Vadim Afanasyevich shouted, having gathered all his strength.

The Ferriswheel emitted a monstrous gnashing howl, similar to the cry of the earth's last surviving dinosaur, and came to a stop. This time forever.

Vadim Afanasyevich, pressed against the floor of his compartment, fainted again, but this time not for long. When he regained consciousness, he came out of the compartment, cleaned himself up, lit his pipe, threw back his head ...

... oh, spring without-end-or-limit, without-an-end-or-limit dream ...[110]

after all, if there weren't all this terror, this terrible Ferriswheel, I wouldn't have grasped anew with such sharp emotion the beauty of life, its eternal spring ...

and he started to walk towards the truck. When he approached the barrelware and put his hand on her side, she purred anxiously.

Meanwhile, with unsteady steps, Volodya Teleskopov headed towards the chessplayers, not less than a dozen of whom had gathered around the bench.

"Fishers!" he shouted, "Petrosians! Tigrans![111] You don't know how to play! You don't know a thing about the midgame! As for the endgame you don't know your ass from a hole in the ground![112] I saw everything from up there! You have no right to play this clever game!"

He went along the length of the bench, brushing the chessmen off onto the dusty ground. The chessplayers jumped up and waved their hands, appealing to an elder, sly and thickset man wearing striped pyjamas and a green velour hat. An "Izvestiya" newspaper was hanging from under the hat to protect the back of his head and neck from the sun, the flies, and from other unhealthy outside influences.

"Why does it come to this, Viktor Ilyich?" the chessplayers shouted, "they walk up, scatter pieces, and bandy about offensive names. What should we do? You tell us!"

"You should be submissive," the man wearing the striped pyjamas told the chessplayers and, with a gesture, invited Volodya to the board.

"Hey, man, I see you want to play with me!" Volodya laughed.

"You are not mistaken, young man," the man wearing pyjamas uttered with certain marked inflections characteristic of the voice of a man possessing power, not of just a common man.

In spite of his craziness, Volodya caught that inflection so familiar to him and his heart skipped a beat. However, showing off his fearlessness and strutting like a bantam rooster and, more importantly, firmly believing in his extraordinary prowess at chess (after all, he had won quite a few pints of vodka with the help of this clever ancient game), he sat down at the board and said, "I'll give you ten moves, my dear friend, but don't count on more."

And he moved forward with his secret pawn. Pyjamas, having propped up his head with his hands, plunged into serious thought.

The circle of chessplayers, wobbling like a sensitive grovelling organism, began giggling.

"Get him with the slammer, Viktor Ilyich, in the mug, in the mug... Entice him into a corner and then lash him with your doublet."[113]

One must say that Gusyatin had its own special chess theories.

"Ga-att out of here, smallfry!" Volodya roared at the fans, "Scat when the masters are playing."

"Such hooligans. They won't let you and me play," he said to the pyjamas. He was also somewhat toadying to Viktor Ilyich, feeling that he'd got into something of a mess. However, temptation was stronger that his will, stronger than any wariness. Therefore, with innocent-looking fingers and whistling peacefully, Volodya constructed the so-called "Kid's checkmate"[114] for Viktor Ilyich.

He had already lifted his queen off the board to make the final blow when he suddenly noticed on Viktor Ilyich's meaty hand the dark-blue tatoo "SIMA REMEM..."

The rest of the inscription was hidden under his pyjama sleeve.

"Sima! What other Sima can it be if not mine? Maybe this snout, this buttonnose bussed my Serafima! Maybe, this is the Borodkin Viktor Ilyich? Well, I'll show him!":—and jealousy, fuelled with kerosene, crude- and refined-oil, started to burn Volodya's insides.

"It's checkmate to you, pal!" he roared at his opponent, whom he ogled closely, having moved his hot face close to him.

With his brains grinding slowly, Viktor Ilyich was having difficulty trying to figure out the situation. Where could he move his king to? There was no place to move. It would be nice to take the queen, but he didn't have the right pieces. Force him into a corner? Lash him with the slammer? No, it won't work. There weren't sufficient grounds for that.

Then, suddenly, on the thin, ordinary arm of this offender he saw the little blue letters SIMA, REMEMBER YOU...—the rest was hidden, almost in the armpit.

"Serafima, can it be possible that you've forgotten me on account of this retard? Yes, maybe, this is that very Teleskopov, the offender...the offender of chessplayers of all times and all countries, the wandering hooligan, the paragon of an unmoored labor force?" Viktor Ilyich arched his neck; his little nose started to glow like a flashing signal on top of a police car.

"Teleskopov?" he asked in a pushy tone.

"Borodkin?" Volodya asked with the same pushiness.

"Come with me!" said Borodkin and got up.

"You're off duty," Volodya began to chuckle. "And secondly, you're in checkmate, and thirdly, you're wearing pyjamas."

"Checkmate?"

"Checkmate!"

"Checkmate?"

"Checkmate!"

"Are you sure?"

Viktor Ilyich extracted a whistle from under his pyjamas and began to fill the air with colorful, inspired roulades whose trills matched the trembling of his offended soul.

"Run, run," thought Volodya, but he couldn't move. He, too, was whistling, with two fingers in his mouth.[115] It was important for him to have the last word in the argument with Viktor Ilyich: he needed a moral victory.

And Volodya got what he'd been waiting for. The elder brother, Junior-Lieutenant Borodkin, appeared in front of him in full-dress uniform and on duty.

"Get him with the slammer, comrades Borodkin!" the fans bleated merrily. "Sack him in the corner and lash him with a doublet."

Apparently they now put some other meaning into this chess terminology.

So that's how Volodya Teleskopov got a night to view captivity. They led him by the arm past the stunned Vadim Afanasyevich; past the barrelware which cried out painfully; sat him down in the detention room; brought him pea soup, borsch, noodles, steamed meatballs, stewed goose-meat,[116] and kissel; and locked him up. All night long Volodya ate, smoked, sang, recollected details of his life, cried with bitter tears, blew his nose, expressed his indignation, and, towards daybreak, began to write letters.

All night long the brothers Borodkin argued between themselves. The younger brother thumbed the pages of the Criminal Code looking for the most terrible articles with punishments for Volodya. The elder brother, whose spiritual wounds inflicted by Serafima Ignatyevna had already healed with the passage of time, offered administrative solutions. "Let's shave him bald, Vityok, and give him a broom for fifteen days. Then I bet Simka will understand who she's traded you in for."

At these words of his elder brother, Viktor Ilyich threw away the Criminal Code, fell flat onto the ottoman and burst into bitter tears. "I wanted to wipe myself out," he muttered feverishly, "I left, dunked myself into chess, didn't remember ... Now this retard appears who stole ... Sima ... my love ..." he gnashed his teeth.

Should I tell in what agitation Volodya's fellow travellers and friends spent the night? None of them slept a wink. All night long they discussed various means for his salvation.

With proudly raised head and her hair waving, Irina Valentinovna expressed her readiness to talk about Volodya with the brothers Borodkin—personally, directly, tête-à-tête, cherchez la femme. Recently, she had finally started firmly to believe in the power and strength of her beauty.

"No, Irinka, no! I'd best talk with the brothers myself," Shustikov Gleb categorically cut short her noble impulse, "I'll talk with them privately, and that'll put an end to the matter."

"No, no, friends," Vadim Afanasyevich impassionedly exclaimed. "I'll submit an official request to the Gusyatin public court. I'm sure ... we ... our institution ... our entire community ... will bail Volodya out. If it becomes necessary, I'll adopt him!"

With these words Vadim Afanasyevich had a fit of coughing, took a deep drag on his pipe, and let out a smokescreen in order to hide his bemoistened eyes.

Stepanida Yefimovna spent half of the night rushing around the square in confusion, catching moths and lamenting. Then, she ran over to her Gusyatin friend's place (a lab-assistant at the Leningrad Research Institute),[117] brought back from there a black rooster, laid cards out, and began to tell fortunes with "ah's," "oh's," and tearful sobs. From time to time whe would untie her bag and, doing a dance step, show the black rooster to the new moon, and mutter something.

All night long old Mochenkin wrote a positive resume on Volodya Teleskopov. It was a difficult, dreary and unusual task for him: you want to write "politically educated," but your hand writes "uneducated"; you want to write "moral," but your hand writes "amoral."

And the whole night their beloved barrelware creaked plaintively and hummed something with hidden passion, entreaty, and hope.

In the morning Gleb drove the truck right under the windows of the detention room, which had a porch where there stood Junior-Lieutenant Borodkin, holding a bunch of keys, and Sergeant Major Borodkin, holding a little volume of the Criminal Code.[118]

By that time Volodya had finished his correspondence with the friends of his heart and was now singing in a dramatic tenor voice:

> On northbound convoys, we all have sentences
> No matter who's asked, we're lifers all.
> Look hard, look hard at my face, so stern it is,
> Look now or never, no time to stall.

Stepanida Yefimovna crossed herself. With a deep sigh Irina Valentinovna squeezed Gleb's hand. "Gleb it sounds like Cavaradossi's aria.[119] Darling, free our dear Volodya. After all, it's thanks to him that you and I got to know each other so well."

Gleb stepped forward. "Hullo, friends, put an end to this farce. Volodya is an unkempt thing, of course, but in general, he's one of us—a sane fellow, a participant in great construction projects. Anyone can drink to excess, that's no secret to you."

"People've got too smart for their own good," muttered the Sergeant Major.

"And who do you represent, mister?" asked the Junior-Lieutenant, "the arrested person's relatives or colleagues?"

"We are representatives of the public. Here are my documents."

The brothers Borodkin, with scarcely concealed surprise, scrutinized the lean gentleman whose external appearance made him look almost like a foreigner. With no less surprise, they familiarized themselves with a whole pile of blue and red identification books which were presented to them.

"People've got too smart for their own good," the younger Borodkin repeated.

Old Mochenkin lept forward, rapaciously bared his teeth, shook his canvas cap at the brothers Borodkin, pointing a bony digit and squealing: "You'll answer yet for this excess of prerogatives and authority, for your blood ties and nepotism."[120]

The brothers Borodkin got a little bit scared, but, of course, they didn't show it—being under the protection of their uniforms, which everyone respected.

"People've got too smart for their own good," the younger Borodkin roared in fright.

"Goo-ten', Fee-son', vitriolic squanderer," Stepanida Yefimovna harrumphed and suddenly showed the brothers the black rooster which, in her opinion, was Volodya's main savior.[121]

Irina Valentinovna Seleznyeva stepped forward, in the brilliance of all her unforgettable treasures.

"Listen, friends, let's speak seriously. I am a woman and you are men..."

Younger Borodkin dropped the Criminal Code.

The elder wheezed soundly and took himself in hand. "You, comrade, made a very precise remark about the seriousness of the situation. Teleskopov, Vladimir, who was detained in a state of intoxication, upset the chess tournament which was to decide the champion of our amusement park. What's that? you question. The answer: it's at least malicious hooliganism. Certain comrades recommend criminal charges be brought against Teleskopov, and you know what that smacks of for him, don't you? But we, comrade very-beautiful-lady-unfortunately-don't-know-your-name-in-the-hope-for-a-future-with-blue-eyes, we are not beasts, but humanists, and we'll undertake only administrative measures to punish Teleskopov. Let him swing the broom for fifteen days, and then he'll be free."

Having moved his bulging eyes closer to her, the Junior-Lieutenant explained it to Irina Valentinovna intimately, personally. And she, flattered by the rumble of his voice, heard him out thoughtfully, inclining her head slightly to one side. However, when Borodkin finished, Volodya's face, as pale as that of the Count de Monte Cristo, appeared behind the bars.

"I've perished, brothers, perished!" Volodya howled. "There is nothing more terrible for me than the fifteen-day sentence! Better to throw the book at me than just the 15 days! Simka will stop loving me, if I do fifteen, but Simka, brothers, is the last island of my life!"

After this wail of one soul, a strange silence that tormented all their souls fell over the porch which led to the detention room.

The elder looked at his younger brother off and on and, perplexed, twirled his keys around his finger.

"What will happen to the barrelware?" shouted Volodya. "What did she do wrong?"

"I cannot stand it!" the younger Borodkin exclaimed, pressing the Criminal Code to his chest. "I cannot breathe. It's so hard."

"What do you mean 'ware? What 'ware? Where?" the elder Borodkin became nervous.

Vadim Afanasyevich silently raised the tarpaulin. The brothers Borodkin saw the tarnished and sad barrelware, furrowed with embittered wrinkles.

With his face frozen in a fixed look, the younger Borodkin went up to her.

"A fine," elder Borodkin said in a trembling voice, "we'll substitute the fifteen days for a fine. A fine of 30 roubles. Or, more precisely, 5."

"Hurrah!" exclaimed Irina Valentinovna and, having flown onto the porch, she kissed the elder Borodkin right on the lips. "Five roubles. That's nonsense in comparison with love!"

"Hurray!" old Mochenkin exclaimed and threw up his cherished 15-kopeck coin.

"Pass the hat!" Gleb shouted, pulling from his tight bell-bottoms the last three-rouble bill which he had been saving to buy fruit flavored lollypops for his assault team.

"Will you take eggs instead of money, dearie?" Stepandia Yefimovna squeaked.

Following Irina's kiss, Borodkin-Senior came unglued and went flailing wobbily across the porch like a "groggy" boxer.

"There will be no fine, brother," Borodkin-Junior, Viktor Ilyich said, looking right in front of him into the dark and warm depths of the barrelware. "Is it really Volodya's fault that Serafima fell in love with him? It's my fault that I wanted to vent my arrogance upon him. Please forgive me for this if you can, friends."

Reflections of sun rays began to bound back and forth across the cheeks of the barrleware. Her wrinkles smoothed out; beautiful, heavenly balalaika music wafted through the air.

Borodkin-Senior nabbed old Mochenkin and kissed him right on his garlicky lips. Gleb gave Stepanida Yefimovna a big buss; Vadim Afan-asyevich kissed Irina Valentinovna three times (in a brotherly manner); Borodkin-Junior, Viktor Ilyich, without worrying what anyone might think, climbed onto a wheel of the truck and kissed a warm cheek of the barrelware.

Sniffling, Volodya Teleskopov kissed his cellbars and, of course, in thought Serafima Ignatyevna and, likewise, Silvia Chesterton and the entire human race.

* * * *

And so they drove on past lands of plenty. And the slanted rain was behind them. And the sun kept swirling on its rays like the eye of a theodolite on its tripod, and at night the moon would take their pictures using silent flashbulbs of lightning, and the seventh-graders, those fiddle-faddle claptraps, would encircle their encampments sitting on transparent radii that seemed nothing but a soapfilm coating. And the dreamy cropduster pilot wove silver loops in the sky over their head. And they peacefully drove on, sitting in the cellbellies of their dear barrelware, each in his own or her own.

Once, a strange and cumbersome structure loomed on the horizon.

Sensing something bad, Volodya wanted to turn off the main road onto a country road, but the steering wheel would no longer obey him, so the truck slowly rolled forward along the straight and cushiony road. The structure was receding from the horizon, coming closer, and growing; soon, all doubts and hopes faded—in front of them there stood the tower of the Koryazhsk train station, with a spire and monumental granite figures of representatives from all spheres of labor and defense. [122]

Soon, along the road, there stretched the small houses and doleful storage sheds of Koryazhsk. Suddenly, the motor which had been working so many days without gas died right in front of a filling station.

Volodya and Vadim Afanasyevich got out of the cabin.

"Holy Fathers, where have we landed today?" Stepanida Yefimovna asked in her affected voice.

"The station Get Off, grandma Stepanida!" Volodya shouted and gave a wild laugh in order to hide his confusion and anxiety.

"Holy Virginnie, is it really Koryazhsk?"

"Yes, little old momma, it's Koryazhsk," said Gleb.

"Already?" Irina Valentinovna sighed sadly.

"Twist it this way or that; you can't get out of it," screeched old Mochenkin. "Koryazhsk is Koryazhsk, and from here each of us will take his or her own road."

"Yes, friends, this is Koryazhsk, and soon the express train will probably arrive," Vadim Afanasyevich said quietly.

"At 19:17," Gleb made things precise. [123]

"Well, comrades, fellow-travellers, comrade wanderers, I congratulate you on the successful completion of our trip. Forgive my company. Wish you success in your work and private life," Volodya wagged his tongue, but at the same time he was absent-mindedly looking to one side, and his soul had the jitters.

The passengers got out of their cellbellies and gathered their own luggage. The gloomy tower of the Koryazhsk train station was looming above them. Saucers of sunlight were shining above the heads of the granite figures.

The passengers didn't look at one another. The moment of distressing silence had come, the time to say goodbye. Each of them painfully felt that the ties which had bound them together were becoming tensile-thin and that now just one last very thin string was stretched between them, and then...

"What will happen to her, Volodya?" Vadim Afanasyevich asked in a quavering voice.

"To who?" Volodya asked as if he didn't understand.

"To her," Vadim Afanasyevich said, pointing with his chin at the barrelware, and everybody looked at her with consternation, but she was silent.

"Oh, to the barrels? Nothing special. I'll deliver them according to the order, and that's that," Volodya spat to one side and

...and then the string burst and the last farewell sound climbed upward...

...and Volodya started to cry.

The Koryazhsk train station was equipped with the latest novelties of technology: automatic information booths and lockers with a personal secret; cologne-dispensing machines which, for two kopecks, would spurt a thick stream of fragrant "Shipr"[124] which certain irresponsible transients were letting squirt into their mouths; but, the prize installation was an electric electronic clock which displayed the month, day of the week, date, and precise time.

Thus, it specified: August, Wednesday, 15, 1907. Ten minutes to go before the arrival of the express.

Vadim Afanasyevich, Irina Valentinovna, Shustikov Gleb, Stepanida Yefimovna, and old Mochenkin were standing on the platform.

Irina Valentinovna trembled for her love.

Shustikov Gleb trembled for his love.

Vadim Afanasyevich trembled for his love.

Stepanida Yefimovna trembled for her love.

Old Mochenkin trembled for his love.

Burnished steel rails stretched out in front of them. Further, on the slope beyond the railway embankment, in sharp contrast to the station's automats, there crooked the lopsided little houses of Koryazhsk, and, still further, fields were becoming a rosy pink and the forest a thick, dark blue. The feathered sun was hanging over the forest like a rooster on a fence with its head lopped off.

Minute after minute went by. On the slope beyond the railway embankment, Volodya Teleskopov appeared with his hair dishevelled and his collar torn.

He clambered up the embankment, stood up with his legs apart and, rubbing tears all over his dirty face with his fist, shouted:

"Comrades, think, what a scandal! They didn't accept her! They didn't accept her, comrades!"

"It cannot be!" Vadim Afanasyevich began shouting and, stomping his feet on the cement platform, "I can't believe it!"

"It cannot be! What's this? Why didn't they accept her?" we all shouted.

"She surplussed, they said, surfaced herself in yellow-flower bloom, they said, surged and surgeoned herself! They spurned her, the damned bureaucrats!" Volodya shouted in a high pitched, sobbing voice.

From behind the warehouse there appeared the yellow head, blue moustache, and huge blinkers of the express.

"So where is she, Volodenka? Where is she? Where?"

"In a ravine! I dumped her into a ravine! I don't want to live anymore! Farewell!"

With a whistle, the express foreshortened the distance and came to a stop.

Transients of all kinds rushed to the compartments. A radio began to growl like an animal. The smell of the romance of distant roads was suddenly in the air.

Two minutes later the famous "North-South" express started up. It began to move past us slowly. Past us there moved the windows of an international, nylon, copper, suede-leather, and fragrant car. At one of the windows stood a nice gentleman wearing a crimson vest and holding a cigar. He glanced at us with a slightly spiteful curiosity, took off his cap and gave a snappy and playful salute of farewell.

"It's him," Stepanida Yefimovna whispered to herself, swallowing an exclamatory "ah." "He himself, the Tempter."

"Midshipman Dopekailo? Or, maybe, Scaevola in the flesh?" thought Gleb.

"It's him, the deceiver, him, him. Reinvolf, Genrikh Anatolyevich," guessed Irina Valentinovna.

"None other than Fefyolov, Andron Lukich, has set off on a business trip abroad. Good riddance. Let him go to . . . ," hemmed old Mochenkin in annoyance.

"So that's the type you are, señor Syracuzers," whispered Vadim Afanasyevich, "goodbye, forever!"

Thus it was the mysterious passenger snatched up by the express disappeared from our view.

The express had gone; its whistle had died away in the non-existence, the non-existent space, and we were left in silence on the hot and stinking platform.

Volodya Teleskopov was sitting on the embankment, with his head hung between his knees, and we were looking at him. Volodya raised his head, gave us a look, and wiped his face with his shirttail.

"Let's go, eh, friends," he said quietly and we didn't recognize the former rowdy in him.

"Let's go," we said, and jumped down one by one from the platform. One of us, old Mochenkin by name, managed before he jumped to drop this letter addressed to all institutions into a mailbox: "I ask all my reports and denunciations to return in back."

We followed Volodya along a narrow path on the bottom of a ravine, through a carpet of buttercups, ferns, and burdock; at eye-level, tall lilac candles of willow herb were swaying in the glassy twilight.

Then we caught sight of our truck, which had found shelter under a sandy precipice, and in it we saw our misfortunate, desecrated, surplussed barrelware. Our hearts sank on account of her alluring tenderness which was dissipating itself with the sunset, at dusk.

And then she saw us. She purred, poured forth some special song, pearled herself with light under the early morning stars, and proffered her little yellow flowers to us, which were now already the size of sunflowers.

"Well, let's hit the road, friends," Volodya Teleskopov said quietly, and we climbed into the cellbellies of the barrelware, each into his or her own.

### Last Common Dream

Through Russia flows a river. Along the river drifts the barrelware, singing. In the river swim annulated, emerald eels, pink loaches, irridescent flounder...

The barrelware drifts to distant seas; her journey is endless.

And in the distant seas, merry and calm in the dewy grass on a meadowed island, Good Person awaits the barrelware.

He always waits.

## Notes

1. The Russian word for this butterfuly is 'admiral', which refers to the "red admiral" butterfly (*Vanessa atalanta*), not the "white admiral" variety (*Limenitis camilla*). Nevertheless, the correlation between the butterfly's flight of death and Baron Wrangel alludes to one of the leaders of the "White" army in the Civil War of 1918-21: Admiral Alexander Kolchak (1874-1920). The allusion here to Admiral Kolchak and Baron Wrangel is a telling detail since it implies that the fictional setting of *Surplussed Barrelware* bears some resemblance to the region of the Crimea (one of Aksyonov's favorite settings and a locale imbued with special political overtones in the writer's recent novel *The Island of Crimea.*

2. "Piter" is a fairly common (sometimes affectionate, sometimes ironic) epithet for the city of Leningrad. The word is a folksy rendition of the name Peter (i.e., Peter the Great—founder of St. Petersburg/Petrograd/Leningrad).

3. In the elder Teleskopov's encapsulated biography of his son and in Aksyonov's description of this pensioner there are some curious "telescopic" references to personages and events in Russian history. If Peter Ilyich is the pensioner's double (*dvoinik*) in name as well as looks, then Volodya Teleskopov's given name and patronymic would be Vladimir Ilyich, the same as Lenin's. This veiled allusion to Lenin is further suggested by the parroting of one of Lenin's famous statements ("the idiocy of village life"—*idiotizm selskoi zhizni*) by Volodya's father. One may also view Volodya's return to "Piter" with a "rebellious look" (*vozmush-chennye glaza*) as a kind of tongue-in-cheek and comical comparison of Volodya to V. I.Lenin, who returned to Petrograd from abroad in 1917 to lead the "rebellion" which became a revolution. There is good humor in such allusions, but not much narrative substance since

Volodya Teleskopov is clearly a youth of the 1960s. His sowing of wild oats for a full "seven-year term" (*semiletka*) marks him at least as a product of the Soviet educational system (seven-year school) and perhaps, also, as an individual "rebel" on whom history has left an indelible mark (his dissipation is roughly concurrent with the seven-year plan from 1959 to 1965 which Khrushchev created and was distinguishable from all preceding and subsequent five-year plans). As the reader will learn in due course, Volodya's stargazing and simultaneous philosophizing are an adequate explanation for his surname, but there may well be another explanation. Perhaps, the Teleskopov family's "four generations" of service to industry (i.e., roughly 120 years) is to be understood, when read as an allegorical statement in Aesopian language, as having started when the famous literary-political journal *Teleskop* (1831-36), published by I. I. Nadezhdin, was closed for printing the first of Peter Chaadaev's famous "Philosophical Letters."

4. The Hun-wei-ping, better known to Americans as the "Red Guards," were created in 1966 by Mao-Tse-Tung in order to help him suppress his opponents during the "Cultural Revolution." The Russian text here contains a linguistic pun: the word for "fooliganizing" (*fuliganiat*) is a corruption of the word for "hooliganizing" (*khuliganiat*).

5. Aksyonov puns on the dual meaning of the Russian word "profile" (*profil'*) in this paragraph: 1) a side-view of an individual and 2) an official record book of a person's work references which supervisors or bosses compile and the worker must show when applying for a new or different job. Vladimir is therefore to be understood as an "unreliable" person only for prospective employers and not necessarily by his travel companions or the reader.

6. The word "norm" has two basic meanings in modern Russian which are alluded to here: 1) that which is normal or commonplace and 2) whatever is required to fulfill the norm or quota of work which is set by the government in its all-embracing economic plan.

7. The specific fish referred to here is called *riapushka* in Russian. Tinned in tomato sauce, this fish is a favorite snack to accompany the drinking of alcoholic beverages, especially vodka.

8. Seryozha (Sergei Alexandrovich) Esenin (1985-1925) is known to Americans as the Russian poet who married the dancer Isadora Duncan. Volodya Teleskopov appears to identify rather closely with both Esenin's debauched lifestyle and the sentiment of much of Esenin's verse. Perhaps this is partially explained by Esenin's simple origin—he was born a peasant youth in the town of Ryazan—as well as by the poet's reputation as a dandy and heavy drinker (see, for example, his famous poem "Confession of a Rowdy"—"Ispoved' khuli-gana"). In the 1960s Esenin was viewed as a kind of secular patron saint by many young Russian males and, thus, Volodya's fascination with the poet marks him as belonging to this kind of "social" rebel. The moon is a recurring image in Esenin's poetry and it serves here as a kind of personification of the poet for Volodya.

9. The "Nationale" hotel, located on Karl Marx Prospect at the lower end of Gorky Street, was built in 1903 and underwent several renovations in the 1960s. Muscovites still consider the hotel's restaurant a fashionable place to eat, although for the most part the hotel and its restaurant accommodate foreign tourists.

10. Kalinin Prospect—a wide avenue constructed in the 1960s as a showpiece of modern Soviet architecture; it is situated adjacent to the old merchant quarter called the Arbat (hence, Arbat Street) which symbolizes the Moscow of old and, for some, is the epitome of Moscow itself. Arbat Street and Kalinin Prospect intersect at the point of a triangle on which stands the "Prague" hotel.

11. Mochenkin's surname is derived from the noun 'mocha' (urine) so it might be rendered into English as "Pisser," especially since this old man seems to have an ample amount of "piss and vinegar" in his character. As Aksyonov uses the epithet "gramps" to describe Mochenkin, the word emphasizes more the man's age than his status as a grandfather; occasionally, however, Aksyonov plays on the ambiguous connotations of this epithet (the word 'ded' in Russian).

91

12. Colorado Potato Beetles (*Leptinotarasa decemlineata*) are insects which cause great damage to crops and, to a certain significant degree, were responsible for poor harvests of potatoes in the USSR from the 1940s through the 1960s. These beetles were apparently carried to the Soviet Union by American planes or ships, but some of the more virulent Soviet propagandists ascribe their arrival to an espionage plot hatched by the American government or the CIA. Special administrative offices were created to carry out efforts to exterminate this pest. That the struggle was taken seriously is attested to by the existence of several serious treatises in Russian on the Colorado Beetle which were published in the late 1950s and early 1960s and by the collective memory of former young Pioneers and members of the Komsomol who, as children, were organized to attack the beetles in the fields as one would attack a foreign aggressor invading the country.

13. The rooster is a favorite motif in Russian folk art. This detail, as well as the "embroidered hand towel," contributes to the characterization of Mochenkin as a man of the people. Gramps Ivan is not, however, an idealized peasant; rather, he is a retired minor bureaucrat of peasant stock.

14. Aksyonov's training as a physician is sometimes evident in his choice of vocabulary, as here, where he uses the technical term "Artiodactyla" (any of various hooved mammals which have an even number of toes—two or four—on each foot).

15. An oblast is a geopolitical and administrative unit which is sometimes translated as "district" or "region." The oblast is larger in size than a 'raion' (also, "region" as in "regional center" in this translation).

16. "A Ray of Light in the Kingdom of Darkness" was first used by Nikolai A. Dobrolyubov (1836-61) as the title for one of two critiques he wrote of Alexander Nikolaevich Ostrovsky's dramas. Dobrolyubov's "ray of light" was the character Katerina in Ostrovsky's play "The Thunderstorm"; his "kingdom of darkness" was the bleak milieu and society in which she lived. As a literary critic and publicist, Dobrolyubov distinguished himself not for his critical insights into a literary work per se, but rather by his wide-ranging thoughts on how well or poorly an author constructed "realistic" plots and/or characters worthy of emulation.

Soviet school children are required to copy Dobrolyubov's methodology in reading and writing about literature. They are assigned to write compositions about individuals in pre-revolutionary Russia who, as "rays of light," were forerunners or prototypes of Communists in an age of "darkness." Some of their discoveries are as fanciful as those of Dobrolyubov even though the students are taught to believe that the assignment is based on a scientifically and pedagogically sound critical methodology.

17. Irina Valentinovna would be considered a secondary-school teacher in the United States. Eight-year schools are common in country areas of the USSR and formal education begins at the age of 7. The subject of geography is taught from the 5th to 8th grades.

18. Kara-bagh is a purely fictional mountain range in this novella. However, there is a particular mountain in the Caucasus region of the Soviet Union which is named "Kara-bagh."

19. "Fenceposts and swans" (*koly i lebedi*) are euphemistic terms for "F" and "D" grades (just like "ones" and "twos"), but in the USSR both these grades are failing marks. It is rare for a student there to receive a "one."

20. Mochenkin becomes a literalist here, interpreting Simka's remark as an insinuation of kinship rather than as a jocular term of endearment for an older man who approximates the age of one's grandfather. Sleeping atop a traditional Russian stove is in no way dangerous or unusual. These stoves are constructed in such a way that there is a good deal of plaster or plaster-enclosed bricks between the oven and the top of the stove. Stovetops were the warmest place in the peasant houses and the prize bed on which to sleep on cold winter nights.

21. The Russian words for "fancy cap and kid gloves" (*kepi, laikovye perchatki*) suggest that Volodya's consciousness of clothes was shaped by two of the sartorial symbols which Russians associate with the dress of Sergei Esenin (or, more generally, with the attire of Russian dandies in the first two decades of this century). As in the United States, some of the

fashion trends in Russia during the 1960s aped the dress of the 1920s.

22. The normal sentence for drunkenness in the Soviet Union has been 15 days since the early 1960s.

23. The word "pal" is used here for the Russian word 'koresh', an appellation for a young male which belongs to the slang lexicon of Russian youths, even though the word "pal" is not used by speakers of American English in the same way or on the same occasions when a Russian might address a young man as his 'koresh'. Attention is drawn to this Russian slang word because its usage here is a concrete example of how Aksyonov's literary style is illustrative of the so-called "youth prose" or "youth literature" of the 1960s (in other words, literature about the lives of young people which makes use of the speech mannerisms of these youths as well as focusing upon issues and experiences central to their experience). Many of the writers identified with this type of literature either got their start or achieved noteworthiness as a result of the works they published in the journal "Youth" (*Yunost'*).

24. Volodya's rambling thoughts are even more incoherent in the original, where there are no marks of punctuation. The names "Ovanesian, Petrosian, Oganesian" indicate that the individual being talked about is of Armenian descent. Krasnovodsk is a port town on the Eastern shore of the Caspian Sea, in the Turkmen Republic; Krasnovodsk means "red water(s)" and this probably explains how its fictional soccer team got its name. The Amur is one of the longest rivers in the Soviet Union; it serves as a boundary between Russia and China for much of its length. The Komsomol Lake referred to here is probably to be associated with the lake constructed by Soviet youths at the town of Komsomolsk-on-Amur (one of the first gigantic building projects of Stalin's first five-year plan). Poti is a Black Sea port in the Georgian Republic situated at the mouth of the Rioni River; it is an ancient settlement which is known today mostly as a resort. Kemerovo is a real town, located on the Tom' River south of the city of Tomsk. Volodya's sojourn in Poti is rather confusing, but otherwise his ramblings suggest that his journey was from far eastern Siberia towards European Russia.

25. We invented the word "cellbelly" to translate the Russian word 'iacheika', which is not used here in either of its standard meanings (a biological cell or the primary, ground-level political unit of the Communist Party's organizational structure). The word "cell" sounded too ominous and foreboding, the word "belly" too physical and jocular. "Cellbelly" had the sound we wanted in order to convey the symbolic, almost womb-like, relationship of the travellers to the barrelware. It is also sufficiently ambiguous so as to allow for the possibility of interpreting these "cellbellies" to be unorthodox but politicized *iacheiki*.

26. Private garden plots were not sanctioned or encouraged by the Soviet government at the time this novella was written to the degree that they are today.

27. Gaius Mucius Scaevola (Scaevola = "lefty") was a legendary hero of ancient Rome (end of the sixth century to the beginning of the fifth century B.C.). According to legend, the young Gaius Mucius had to sneak into the camp of the Etruscan enemies and kill king Porsenna. He was caught and Porsenna threatened him with tortures if he did not reveal the names of his helpers. Wishing to show his fearlessness in the face of pain and death, Gaius Mucius put his right hand into a fire and did not utter a sound while his hand was burning up.

28. Vadim Afanasyevich's dream has him acting out the duties of a Soviet envoy or propagandist in Latin America. Such phrases as "vital issues of friendly relations with foreign countries" occur over and over in Soviet newspapers and often mask in ideological rhetoric an appeal for the "unliberated masses" to revolt and join the socialist bloc. The fictional country of Haligalia derives its name from a popular dance tune of the early 1960s, the "Hully Gully" (see note 70).

29. With the transformation of "junta" into "Junta" at this point in the novella, physical features of the personified ruler become an embodiment of the figures of speech which appear in the Soviet press and Communist Party literature to describe cruel, despotic, and capitalistic dictatorships.

30. The words to describe the sun and the fictional country of Haligalia are metaphorical variants of the homework topic "A Ray of Light in the Kingdom of Darkness." If repetition is the "mother of learning" (as a Russian proverb asserts), it is not surprising that the politically savvy Vadim Afanasyevich "structures" his dreams on the same principle he used to write essays on as a schoolchild.

31. Although Dopekailo serves in the navy, he has a legendary prototype in the person of the dull-witted, brawny, and irksome Red Army sergeant (often, too, of Ukrainian descent, like Dopekailo). At least, such is the case in many Russian jokes. The sergeant of the jokes is a careerist who rarely rises in the ranks because he lacks both savvy and brains. "Dopekailo" is a surname which is associated with Russian words that mean "half-baked" and "pestering."

32. The last two sentences in this paragraph as well as in the next paragraph appear to be realized metaphors on the theme of "A Ray of Light in the Kingdom of Darkness." As such, these metaphors revitalize a hackneyed idea and serve as a kind of artistic device for propelling the narrative in this first sequence of dreams forward to the point when Good Person appears on the scene in the various individuals' dreams.

33. The Moscow cafe "Lira" may be the prototype for the fictional cafe "Lily" in this novella, but operation "Lily" is most likely just a convenient coincidence which allows for distinctions between acts of war and love trysts to be blurred.

34. "Girlfriends of his bleak days" is an adaptation from the first line of A. S. Pushkin's poem "To Nanny" ("Niane," 1826).

35. In the slang of Soviet military personnel serving in the lower ranks periods of sleep are often referred to by the number of minutes one's eyes are shut. This custom may follow from the military's use of a twenty-four-hour clock, but it also suggests that soldiers are allotted little time for sleeping.

36. In this dream old Mochenkin appears to find himself in Moscow. The "sumptuous palaces with ornate stucco moulding and wreaths" suggest the seven wedding-cake skyscrapers in Moscow which were erected during Stalin's reign and were repudiated by Khrushchev.

37. Old Mochenkin is being received as if he were an emissary to a Tartar khan. The "extraordinary gift of plain, dry rations" sounds like a puzzling sort of present (in both English and Russian), but it is probably comparable to the last meal served a person who is condemned to die. The word for "shixteen" in Russian is an orthographical form which marks the uneducated speech of country bumpkins.

38. The anointment ceremony described here derives from ancient Russian folk customs for dressing up a groom for his wedding or for making a male presentable for a festive, public ceremony or celebration.

39. The Russian word for "anthropodal" is 'chlenistonogii', which would amuse native speakers of the language because the noun 'chlen' (member), which is one of the basic roots of this adjective, designates either a member of an organization such as the Communist Party or the male sex organ. In off-color jokes there are a lot of puns on these two meanings of the noun 'chlen'.

40. Ernest Hemingway, Maurice Druon (b. 1918-    ), and Leonid A. Zhukhovitsky (b. 1932-    ) have little in common except that Russian youths of the late 1950s and the 1960s admired them all. Druon is known mostly for his historical novels about fourteenth-century France and Zhukhovitsky, the same age as Aksyonov, for his stories, articles and plays on problematical aspects of daily life in the Soviet Union.

41. There is a cocktail drink in the United States called a "Kamikaze," but this is not true of the analogous word in the Russian original: 'taran'. A 'taran' is a heroic pilot who sacrifices his life and plane by ramming into an enemy plane when there is no ammunition left in his guns and little gasoline in his tank. Such sacrifices occurred during World War II, which gave rise to the special word. Unlike the Japanese, the Soviets did not organize suicide "kamikaze" units; the sacrifice of a taran was an act of patriotism performed by well-intentioned

individuals. The metaphorical association of heavy drinking and dangerous flying requires no explanation, but such comparisons are noteworthy here because they do occur rather frequently in Aksyonov's prose and, in general, in the Russian "youth literature" of the 1960s.

42. The phrase "Polish magazines from countries all over the world" sounds nonsensical in both English and Russian. However the expression becomes meaningful when one realizes that it was via Polish art magazines that young Soviet males first learned of the sexual revolution of the 1960s and got their first look at naked female bodies. More explicit "sex" magazines, such as the American *Playboy,* were and are banned in the USSR and although copies do get through, they rarely reach the hands of such "country boys" as Irina's school children.

43. Niko Pirosmanishvili (1862-1960) was a Georgian painter born in the small village of Mirasaani in the region of Kakhetia. His paintings are in the tradition of "primitive" art and one of his most famous canvases is entitled "Lion." Pirosmanishvili became very popular among the young Soviet intelligentsia during the 1960s, largely because his works were perceived to be more lively and artistic than the dull products of socialist realism.

44. Tskhaltubo is a tourist resort in the Georgian Republic, located about 40 kilometers to the northwest of Kutaisi. It is noted for its mineral springs.

45. The phrase "the poet's soul couldn't tolerate the shame of trivial offenses" is a literary allusion. M. Yu. Lermontov used these words in his poem "Death of a Poet," which commemorated A. S. Pushkin's death by duel in 1837.

46. VDNKh is the Russian acronym for the (permanent) Exhibit of Achievements of the National Economy in Moscow. Bulls displayed at this exhibit site are, indeed, huge and in no way typify those to be found "down on the farms."

47. "Inslinger" in Russian soccer terminology is, literally, a "dry leaf" (*sukhoi list*). The phrase "bow-legged ballerina" is not a common designation in Russian sports terminology; it is used here, apparently, for comic effect.

48. Ust'-Kasimovsk, where the quarry is located, exists only as a fictional town. There is, however, a Soviet city named Ust'-Kamenogorsk in the Eastern Kazakhstan oblast of the RSFSR, where a large hydro-electric power station was built. This fact and the charactaronym Kamenogorsk ("rock mountain") suggest that Ust'-Kamenogorsk might be the real-life prototype for the fictional Ust'-Kasimovsk and its quarry.

49. Miguel Marinado is a humorous name. The surname sounds like the English word "marinated" and, as such, carries associations with drinking alcoholic beverages to excess. In colloquial Russian there is a similar word which can mean as a verb "to get drunk" and as an adjective "drunken." As a "drunkard" with a daughter named Sonya, Miguel Marinado reminds Russians of the famous Marmeladov of Dostoevsky's *Crime and Punishment.*

50. The town of Koryazhsk mentioned in this novella cannot be more than a medium-sized town, so the name Koryazhsk-the-Second is truly humorous. It is possible that the name "Koryazhsk-the-Second" was suggested by an actual locale where a second railway station was built (hence, the name) for transferring convoys of prisoners on their way to Siberian camps during the Stalinist era.

51. MOPR is an acronym for *Mezhdunarodnaia organizatsiia pomoshchi bortsam revolutsii* (International Organization to Aid Soldiers of the Revolution) and OSO-VIAKHIM for *Obshchestvo sodeistviia oborone i aviatsionno-khimicheskomu stroitel'stvu SSSR* (Civic Society to Aid Defense and Aviation Chemical Works Construction in the USSR.) The latter existed from 1927 to 1948. In a small place like Koryazhsk-the-Second, the fire of which Mochenkin speaks need not have been very large since the offices of these societies and the "Lick Illiteracy School" would not have taken up much space. Russians would understand that there might well have been no real question of a political conspiracy even if the woman actually set the fire.

52. Karakum is the name of a desert in the Turkmen Republic; the name translates as "black sand." On the basis of Volodya Teleskopov's references to other places in the Soviet

Union where he has been, he is probably speaking here about a mechanic's job that was funded by allocations for the Karakum-Canal building project (begun in 1954) which was a means for reclaiming arid wastes in the Central-Asian republics.

53. Mochenkin's comment implies that Vanya Kulachenko is going to receive a ten- or fifteen-year prison sentence for his misconduct.

54. The "Anthology of Himalayan Fairytales" is to be understood as a totally imaginary booktitle.

55. The second sequence of dreams in this novella takes place in the small town of Myshkin, which, judging by the character of the dreams, is one of the exaggerations in this work to which Aksyonov alludes in his subtitle. That is, Myshkin functions as a composite of Russia's two cultural centers, Moscow and Leningrad. Vadim Afanasyevich's comparison of Myshkin to "Grande Caballeros" (Great Gentlemen) suggests that the town is a microcosm of a macrocosm. The name of the town recalls the surname of the hero of Dostoevsky's novel *The Idiot* and this coincidence may explain why the pride of the town is a neon sign which reads "Book Dealer" (*knizhnyi kollektor*), i.e., a place where a used copy of a book not readily available in most Soviet bookstores might be found. The "House for Itinerants" (*Dom priezzhikh*) may sound like a Soviet equivalent for our Salvation Army shelters, but it actually finds no parallel in Soviet reality except, perhaps, the organizational headquarters of such professional associations as the Writers' Union "House of Writers" or the Architects' Union "House of Architects."

56. "Do not be grieved or sorrowful of countenance" ("Ne grusti i ne pechal' brovei") is a line of verse from Sergei Esenin's last poem, composed on the day of his suicide (December 27, 1925).

57. "May this evening's unspeakable light stream over your little izba, too" ("Pust' struitsia nad tvoei izbushkoi tot vechernii neskazannyi svet") is a line from S. Esenin's poem "Letter to My Mother," first published in 1924.

58. The wood grouse (*glukhar', Tetrao urogallus*) is noted for being deaf during its mating call because its ear passages are blocked off. This fact is connoted by the Russian name for the bird (deaf = 'glukhoi').

59. Berdyansk is a city on the Kharkhov-Simferopol railway line and a port on the Azov Sea.

60. The entertaining which Romance performs here resembles the way amateur or professional artists amuse guests at wedding receptions in contemporary Russian (Soviet) life. These performances are patterned on ancient folk customs but the revival of these customs in recent years has been characterized by as much (or more) nostalgic sentimentality than artistic vitality. The "de-mythologized" Romance of this novella demonstrates her own lack of artistic taste or cultural refinement by failing to find her identity with any single musical instrument. Her refusal to acknowledge the physical aspects of love also makes of her an ineffectual Cupid, a Party puritan.

61. These words are taken from a popular song in the movie "Slowly Moving War Plane" (*Nebesnyi tikhokhod*), released in 1946. The music for the song was composed by Solovyov-Sedoi and the lyrics by Fingelson.

62. In the original the word "God" appears at the beginning of the sentences here in which it is used. Possibly, this was an intentional positioning of this word, since Soviet editorial policy would otherwise cause it to appear in lower-case letters. This explains our choice of word order in English.

63. Zhukov is a fairly common Russian surname. Recently, the most famous "Zhukov" to pursue a military career was not a detachment commander (as here), but Marshal Georgy Konstantinovich Zhukov (1896-1974), whom Khrushchev dismissed as Minister of Defense in 1957. Aksyonov may be engaging in a sophisticated pun on names here. That is, Vanya's image of Good Person is colored by his patriotism and his ability to distinguish between insects which he should spray (cockchafer beetles, 'khrushchi', analogous to Khrushchev) and those

96

he need not or dare not exterminate (common variety of beetles, 'zhuki', analogous to Zhukov).

64. Lord Beverly-Brahms is certainly just as fictional a character as Sir Elvis Crosby (see below in text), however his surname and association with Churchill call to mind the famous newspaper magnate and Churchill advisor, Lord Beaverbrook, who did make a couple of trips to Moscow although he was not present at the Yalta Conference.

65. This passage in the novella has a distinctly allegorical flavor to it, but the allegory eludes us. The style is very reminiscent of that found in Lawrence Sterne's *Tristram Shandy* (cf. Uncle Toby's pipes) and Nikolai Gogol's *Dead Souls,* but no substantive textuals parallels or analogues substantiate this comparison.

66. Pipe-smoking is a status symbol for Russians; it is a more expensive habit than cigarette smoking and good pipe tobacco is often hard to obtain in the Soviet Union. There is a hint in this passage that the bankruptcy of both Lord Beverly-Brahms and Krasnogorsky-Fish probably resulted from heavy drinking. It is a custom for Russian males to drink in threesomes and three people are mentioned here as having owned the pipe before it came into Vadim Afanasyevich's possession.

67. The linguistical complexity to the humor in this passage as well as the name Arkady Pomidorov would call to most Russians' minds the monologues of the famous Leningrad comedian Arkady Raikin. Raikin was at the height of his popularity in the 1960s; he achieved fame largely on account of his satirical sketches of Soviet life.

68. Mohair is the wool from an Angora goat. In the Soviet Union of the 1960s it was the most popular wool for knitting. There was almost a national craze to have a sweater made of mohair at that time. This kind of wool was smuggled into the USSR (where it was not readily available), so the mohair sweaters and jumpers cost people a fortune.

69. A Moscow suburb which was considered a very desirable address at the time *Surplussed Barrelware* was written.

70. The song "Hully Gully" which popularized a dance in the USA in the early 1960s was known in the Soviet Union by a recording made by Cuban musicians. This fact explains the correlation between the music and the fictional Latin American country of Haligalia.

71. In Russian the word "hallucinations" is spelled with an initial "g." We retained this feature of the original in order to reinforce Aksyonov's word-play association between "Hully Gully" (rendered phonetically in Russian), Haligalia, and hallucinations.

72. "Backwoods Oak" in Russian is, literally, "Mountain Oak" (*gornyi dubniak*). However, this translation would be misleading as the name for an alcoholic beverage. In the Soviet Union one can buy an alcoholic beverage with a vodka base which is called "oak" (*dubniak*), so the adjective "mountain" suggests a kind of "moonshine" or illegally distilled "white lightning."

73. The proper name "Baskunchak" has a negative connotation in Russian which is rather similar to the idea conveyed by the English expression "salt mines." There is a Lake Baskunchak in the Astrakhan oblast of the RSFSR, to the east of the Volga River and near Mt. Bogdo. Salt is extracted from the lake and at least one dissident writer has written a poem about the desolation of this region, presumably in allusion to the existence of one or more hard labor camps nearby.

74. Some Soviet citizens who work or travel abroad are accorded the privilege of receiving their pay or "perks" in the form of so-called "rouble certificates" which allow them to purchase luxuries in special hard currency stores.

75. It is common practice for Russian males to drink vodka in groups of three (here, this custom is transferred to Latin America). The number of people who share a bottle is determined, to a large extent, by the cost of the beverage that is being drunk. When the price of vodka was relatively stable at 3.62 roubles for a half-liter, three men could share the cost evenly.

76. Sonka Marinadova's name and questionable reputation (hinted at here) will remind

students of nineteenth-century Russian literature of Sonya Marmeladova in Dostoevsky's *Crime and Punishment*.

77. In colloquial Russian the epithet "source of knowledge" refers to a book, apparently thanks to a phrase coined by V. I. Lenin. Therefore, to love "birds—the source of knowledge" means to like books. As will become clear as the story progresses, Volodya Teleskopov has obviously read a lot and has a genuine appreciation for books.

78. Volodya uses words from A. S. Pushkin's fairytale "The Golden Fish" to describe his unexpected find. The fish of the fairytale could grant wishes and it is for this reason that Russian readers would be amused to read of Volodya's discovery of something to eat in the work-chart grids (which are called a "net," *setka* in Russian).

79. Daugavpils is a Latvian town established by the Livonian Order and known as Dvinsk from 1893 to 1917. The town is located on the Daugava River in the southeastern part of the Latvian Republic; it is a river port, not a seaport.

80. Kuzbass is a Russian acronym for Kuznetskii ugol'nyi bassein (Kuznets Coal Basin), where coal is mined and fed to the blast-furnaces of steel plants in the area.

81. The DLT Department Store is located in Leningrad. The acronym DLT stands for Dvorets Leningradskoi torgovli (Palace of Leningrad Trade). The close proximity of this department store to one of Leningrad's OViR offices (Visa and Registration Department) may explain why the vigilantes refer to the department store here.

82. Alpukhara is an old name for Spain. One can presume that for Vadim Afanasyevich the term "Alpukhara" is a code word for "Soviet Union."

83. This animal is called a "snow leopard" in English and a "white leopard" in Russian. Aksyonov, however, uses the adjective "moon," so we decided to render his unusual choice of words as "snow-moon leopard." There is a strong possibility that Aksyonov's choice of words was motivated by a desire to parody the language of romantic poetry (say, in particular, that of Lermontov or Fet) in this scene where sexuality is described much more explicitly than it is in much "Romantic" verse.

84. The teddy-boys (i.e., "English" toughs dressed foppishly) appear to be the bodyguards of Silvia Chesterton (English descent) and of other women in Haligalia.

85. The phrase "solemn promises, daydreamy plans, whispering, bated breath" contains no verbs, just like the poem of 1850 by Afanasy Afanasyevich Fet (1820-92), to which it alludes by repeating the two words of the first line in Fet's poem (specifically, "whispering, bated breath").

86. The word "croney" is used here to translate the Russian kinship term 'kuma' (literally, "godmother"). Nastasya may have been a godmother to Mochenkin's boys, but that is not the role which she plays in this narrative so we adjusted our translation accordingly.

87. *Mam'zelle Nitouche* is an operetta by the French composer Houdain Herve (pseudonym of Florimond Ronger, 1825-92). This comic operetta was premiered in Paris on December 26, 1883. It was very popular in Russia at the turn of the century and, later, in the Soviet Union. Since 1955 it has been a part of the repertoire of the Moscow Operetta Theater.

88. The pike is an ugly, predator fish. Here, once caught, it is cooked, as a capitalist enemy (or spy) might be punished once he is captured. A former Colorado Beetle Inspector might be expected to relish such an analogy, particularly if he were, like old Mochenkin, a gourmand.

89. The Russian word for this construction company is an acronym which parodies the long unwieldy abbreviations created by the Soviet bureaucracy to designate various socialist construction projects. The Russian term is *Pal'tomochenkinstroi*. In general, the language, stylistic devices and content of Mochenkin's second dream call to mind Nikolai Gogol's famous story "The Overcoat."

90. This concrete poem was not included in the text printed in the Soviet magazine *Yunost'* in 1968 nor in the reprint of this work in the United States by the publishing firm "Serebriannyi Vek" in 1981. The French translation of *Surplussed Barrelware* does contain a rendering of this poem, but our translation relied upon the author's reconstruction of his

unpublished Russian text. Aksyonov has referred to this poem as a "circle."

Lake Baikal is the deepest lake in the world and is located in Siberia, near the town of Irkutsk; the lines about Lake Baikhal quoted here come from a famous Russian folksong about prisoners escaping from pre-revolutionary Siberian prison camps. The Neva River flows through the city of Leningrad in its short course from Lake Ladoga to the Finnish Gulf. In Greek mythology Alcinous was the king of the Phaeacians and father of Nausicaa; he entertained Odysseus and the Argonauts on their return voyage.

91. **Khveodosiia** is Stepanida Yefimovna's corruption of "Feodosiia" (or, Theodosia), a seaport on the Crimean peninsula.

92. The photoplexirus is a variety of beetle known to exist only in this novella.

93. The parenthesis does not appear in the Russian text here, but the words are used by Volodya as a kind of interior monolgue. Russians hear in these words ("dukh brodiazhnyi ty vse rezhe i rezhe") a literary echo of a line of verse in Sergei Esenin' poem "I Neither Pity, Nor Call, Nor Cry..." (1922). In context the line reads in our translation:

> Spirit of wandering, you less and less
> Stir up the flame of my lips,
> Where are you, my lost freshness,
> Turbulence of eyes, and flood of feelings?

94. OBLSOBES is an acronym for Oblastnoi otdel sotsial'nogo obespecheniia (District Social Welfare Office).

95. VTEK or VTek, is the acronym for Vneocherednaia trudovaia kommissiia (Special Commission to Determine Working Ability), with the vowel "E" or "e" inserted to make the acronym more pronounceable as a word.

96. Tuapse is a seaport on the Black Sea, located to the northwest of the town and port of Sochi.

97. These words in Russian (*pobrodit', pomjat' v stepiakh begrianykh lebedy*) appear in quotation marks in the original. They allude to lines in one of Esenin's untitled poems ("I won't wander,/I won't trample the goose-foot/in the crimson bushes,/and I won't look for footprints...") written in 1915-16 and first published in 1918 in the collection of Esenin's poetry entitled *Goluben'*.

98. This bicycle race is fictional, but art here imitates life. Pioneer and Komsomol youth in the USSR participate in a variety of activities which always have some slogan or motto that identifies the purpose of what is going on. A bicycle rally organized under the motto "Do You Know Your Own Country?" shows how enamored the schoolboys (especially, Borya Kurochkin) are with their geography teacher.

99. The boys' surnames have a humorous ring to them in Russian: Tyutyushkin = "he's had it" ('tyu-tyu'); Zhilkin = "ribs are showing" ('zhilka' is a rib or vein); Mamochkin = momma's boy; Kurochin = chicken or pullet ('kura', 'kurochka' = hen, pullet).

100. The euphemistic phrase "Peter's boat" refers both to Peter the Great's love for and involvement with shipbuilding. It is a popular belief that the Russian navy was founded in the eighteenth century, when Peter the Great himself built a boat at a shipyard in Voronezh.

· 101. These political tactics are known to Americans as the "carrot and stick" (i.e., promises of privileges or rewards on the one hand and threats of unpleasant consequences or reprisals on the other).

102. This dream begins with three sentences in rhyme, with the first statement about "bread and cake" being rather reminiscent of Marie Antoinette's response to the dilemma of the French peasants ("They have no bread."): "Let them eat cake!" The poetry here is a hint that this dream represents an allegorical reworking of and statement about the scandalous event of March 7, 1963, when Nikita Khrushchev lost his temper and attacked young writers viciously, especially the poet Andrei Voznesensky. The occasion was a gathering of intellectuals and members of government in the Sverdlov Hall of the Kremlin.

103. Andryusha's words here in Russian ("Ty dumaesh', Volodia, my na nikh stavim? Oni, kobyly, staviat na nas") are a formulaic reworking of the following lines from Andrei

Voznesensky's poem "Moroznyi ippodrom" ("Winter Racetrack," 1967): "Ty dumaesh', Vasia, my na nikh stavim? Oni, kobyly, postavili na nas." Voznesensky dedicated this poem to Vasily Aksyonov and the poem itself is, like Volodya's dream, an allegorical statement about the scandalous event of March 7, 1963 mentioned in the previous note.

104. "Dritte Nachtigall" is included in the original text in Russian transcription and means "third nightingale" in German. Such words might be viewed as the kind of jibberish and confused (sometimes macaronic) speech heard in dreams, but they also appear to serve here to underline the identification of Stepanida's Tempter as being German or Germanic in origin. Possibly, the reference to a nightingale is also meant to suggest that the Tempter is asking Stepanida to render him services which are similar to, but also more intimate than, those of the famous "free-lance lab-technician" of the Crimean War, Florence Nightingale.

105. Jules Verne's tale *The Children of Captain Grant* is read by almost every generation of Russian children and teenagers and it is often mentioned by Aksyonov's heroes as being one of the books they best remember and cherish. The journal *Knowledge is Power (Znanie—sila)* is a Soviet popular-science magazine with a large circulation. As mentioned previously, "The Anthology of Himalayan Fairytales" is a purely made-up book title.

106. Volodya's association of himself with "Sputnik" (the first space satellite) is probably motivated, psychologically, by his uncertainty as to whether Silvia Chesterton remembers him and by his concommitant desire to jog her memory by identifying himself with a particular object which everyone in the world associates with Soviet citizenship and Russian nationality. Thus, if Silvia cannot recall his name, she will recall him as being her Russian lover. The word "sputnik" is also sometimes used to mean a "fellow traveller" and if Aksyonov had that in mind in choosing this word we can deduce that by this he is attributing some of Vadim Afanasyevich's character traits to Volodya in this third dream. Such a reference would be in keeping with the general confusion perpetrated by the third set of dreams, where one person dreams about people who earlier in the story occupied the dream world of a different travelling companion or where at least the reader is aware that the dreams in the third sequence represent a kind of pool of the "collective" (rather than "individual") subconscious reworking of real life experiences and aspirations.

107. On one side of the package of "Belomor" cigarettes there is a map of the Belomor Canal. These are the traditional Russian-type cigarettes called *papirosy*, which have long empty filters in order to make the tobacco smoke less harsh. The word "Belomor" is contracted from the words 'Beloe more' (White Sea). A canal was built during the 1930s to link the White Sea in the North with the Black Sea in the South via the Volga River and its tributaries as well as dregging a canal wherever necessary. Much of the canal was constructed by prisoners from forced labor camps and this fact may color Aksyonov's characterization of Volodya as a "Belomor" smoker since his truck-driver appears to know underground, camp songs. However, in general, the "Belomor" cigarettes are one of the most popular brands smoked by Russians and the light, white cardboard of their container could be used for writing a short message or letter.

108. Both Aksyonov and Volodya Teleskopov can be said to share a certain affinity for using metaphors associated with the technology of space travel and sometimes these metaphors link space travel or, more broadly, aviation with the heavy consumption of alcoholic beverages. Given this proclivity on the part of both the author and character of this novella, it is curious that Volodya is identified with an unmanned space satellite ("sputnik") before he climbs aboard the Ferriswheel "Flight into the Unknown" and experiences, metaphorically, a space flight of his own (NB: the Russian word for "flight" is the same used to speak of a manned spaceflight). Perhaps, it is not a coincidence that Volodya's fictional flight into the unknown (1968) occurred in the same year that the first Soviet cosmonaut Yury A. Gagarin died. Gagarin was aboard the "Vostok" rocketship launched in 1961.

109. "Bela" is the title of one of the sections of M. Yu. Lermontov's novel *A Hero of Our Time* (1841) and also the name of the main female character in that segment of the novel (she is the daughter of a chief of one of the mountain tribes in the Caucasus). The main protagonist in

Lermontov's novel is a Russian army officer named Pechorin, who suffers from an acute and self-perpetuated case of ennui. Pechorin kidnaps the beautiful, exotic Bela and tries to woo her. She is attracted to Pechorin but rejects his overtures because she has an abiding fear that her people will take revenge (either by murdering her or both her and Pechorin). It seems in character for the superstitious and highly impressionable Stepanida Yefimovna to be attracted to such a tale, which epitomizes the strains of Romanticism in nineteenth-century Russian literature and was made into a film in the Soviet Union in the 1960s.

110. These words (in Russian: "O, vesna bez kontsa i bez kraia,/bez kontsa i bez kraia mechta") are a literary echo. They first appeared in the initial poem of a group of verses by Alexander Blok (1880-1912) entitled "Oath Sworn by Fire and Darkness" (Zakliatie ognem i mrakom," 1908). These poems were dedicated to N. N. Volokhovaya, whom Blok considered to be a woman "poisoned by her own beauty." In keeping with the reference to Lermontov's Bela and Pechorin, it is perhaps significant that Aksyonov quoted precisely from one of Blok's works which is prefaced by the following lines from M. Yu. Lermontov's poem "Gratitude" ("Blagodarnost' ")provided in our translation:

> I thank you for everything, everything:
> For these secretly tortuous passions,
> For the bitter tears, the poisoned kisses,
> For my friends' betrayal, my enemies' revenge;
> For the ardor of my soul having evaporated in a desert.

111. Volodya alludes to two famous chessplayers, Bobby Fisher (1943-    ) and Tigran Vartanovich Petrosian (1929-    ). Fisher earned the rank of grandmaster in 1958, was USA Champion from 1957 to 1970, and became World Champion in 1972 (to 1975). Petrosian has held the following titles: International Grandmaster (1952...); World Champion (1963-68); and USSR Champion (1959, 1961, 1969, and 1975). Volodya's use of Petrosian's given name as a plural noun is amusing since it suggests the Russian word for "tiger cubs" (i.e., teenage chessplayers who aspire to greatness, but lack the skill).

112. The derogatory analogy is, literally, between people who don't know how to play according to a respected strategy and chickens that peck for seeds on a manure pile ("...kak kury v navoze").

113. Neither the Russian word "zhgentel' " ("slammer") nor "duplet" ("doublet") is commonly used in speaking of chess moves or chess strategy. The word for "doublet" is used by Russians when playing billiards or dominoes and it here refers, apparently, to the chess move or chess piece which produces double-check. "Zhgentel' " is a more obscure word; we have not been able to establish its origin.

114. "Kid's Checkmate" is a particular chess strategy which can produce a victory in just three moves from the beginning of the match.

115. Russian youth have a way of whistling that imitates the way thieves send each other warning signals. They place the forefinger of each hand just inside the corner of the mouth and, drawing the lips tightly, produce a high, shrill and loud whistle.

116. This sumptuous feast finds no parallel with the way incarcerated or imprisoned individuals are fed in the USSR (or anywhere else, for that matter). However, it is worth noting that the stewed goose-meat on the menu ("tushenaia gusiatina") is in keeping with or, perhaps even the explanation for, the town's name (Gusyatin < "gusiatina").

117. Stepanida's friend is employed as a local specimen-hunter by a Leningrad research institute. She might be expected to travel to Leningrad once or twice a year to deposit whatever she has collected.

118. The Criminal Code of the RSFSR is a weighty and thick tome, not a "little volume" as the Russian text speaks of here. By reducing the size of the book in which the Criminal code is to be found, Aksyonov creates two humorous effects: 1) Sergeant-Major Borodkin is holding it as one might a volume of poetry and 2) as if the book has little relevance to the way criminal justice is administered in the USSR.

119. The tenor lead in Puccini's opera *Tosca* is sung by a painter named Mario Cavaradossi. The famous aria he sings just before he dies is entitled, in Italian, "E lucevan le steele" ("Stars were shining"); this is the aria which Irina Valentinovna appears to have in mind.

120. On Southern beaches of the Soviet Union a "canvas cap" ("pestriadinovaia tat'ia") is used to shade one's head from the sun. Such caps are usually white, made of canvas, and have the shape of an air force pilot's regulation headware. Mochenkin's cry for justice comes from allegedly expert knowledge of how small bureaucrats abuse their legal rights. His is a complex mind, sometimes almost "Stalinist" in orientation and at other times, as here, wholeheartedly in support of the reforms which began under Khrushchev.

121. The phrase "Goo-ten', Fee-son', vitriolic squanderer" ("Guten', fison', mot'va kuporosnaia"), though largely "nonsensical," has the sound in Russian of an incantation or magical charm spoken to ward off evil. Although the first two words of the charm are untranslatable, they bear a certain relationship to the identity of Stepanida's Tempter as a German. For example, the word "goo-ten'" sounds like the German word "guten" (good) in combination with the Russian explicative "gu!" (boo!) and the Russian word "ten'" (shadow). Similarly, the word "fison'" sounds like oxymoronic nonsense based on the German word "Fee" (fairy, sprite) and the Russian "son" (dream). Aksyonov's prose style makes fairly frequent use of such phrases which rely on the reader's knowledge of several languages in order to create a humorous effect.

122. The gargoyles on this railroad station suggest that the building was built according to the grandiose "wedding-cake" designs popularized by Stalin's architects.

123. The time on the clock corresponds to the date of the revolution of 1917, which brought about the formation of the USSR as a state.

124. "Shipr" is the name of a men's cologne which has a strong alcoholic base and, consequently, is used by some heavy drinkers as a cheap and readily available substitute for alcoholic beverages.

# A Poem of Ecstasy

From age twelve I very rapidly began to develop physically and my physical growth began to frighten my parents. They took me to the doctor, and the doctor, a middle-aged woman with light-blue eyes, even shuddered when I pulled the sweater off over my head.

"A phenomenal boy," she said in a very beautiful voice.

For some reason I didn't want to leave the physician's office, but my dad took me by the arm and led me away.

Dad was already half a head shorter than me, and with each passing year he was becoming still smaller and smaller. Yet, all the same, I respected and loved him and never laid a finger on him even though I had really surpassed him in physical development. By the way, such is precisely the kind of relationship to one's parents which I recommend to all beginning athletes.

My intellectual developments lagged significantly behind my physical growth. In general, I was absolutely on a level with my classmates; I didn't, of course, worm my way up to the head of the class—why bother?—but as concerns the Pythagorean theorem or Newton's binominal theorem or that there "Who can live happily in Russia,"[1] why my teeth just popped those subtleties out of their shells like sunflower seeds.[2] However, compared to my intellectual advancement, my physical growth had gone far out ahead. Sometimes, when I'd glance at my peers, laughter would seize hold of me, but of course I held back the laughs . . . tried as far as possible not to make myself stand out. It's stupid to strut out your physical development. I don't recommend this to beginning athletes.

When I turned fourteen, I started to engage in a little monkey business, sort of. I busted all the dynamometers in the phys ed office and blew into the spirometer once or twice—it came unsoldered, and words just won't do to talk about those test-your-strength contraptions in the park. But once without realizing it, I lifted up the principal Valerian Sergeyevich in the school corridor, sat him on my shoulders and, like that, with the principal on my shoulders, walked into class. Result: they expelled me from school for ten days.

Well, I didn't lag, of course, behind my class. Every day I studied five hours on the assignments, consulted with Misha Gurfinkel on the phone about all the unclear questions. Can't neglect the studies or otherwise it'll turn out that you're walking around in circles while everyone has already moved far out ahead.

The strange incident with the principal taught me a lot. I began to give thoughts to my life in the future. And there was something to think about: the unbelievable development of my muscles and inner organs had made a completely different man of me. Think about it yourselves: there's quite a lot of boys, after all, who want to put the principal on their shoulders, but by far not all can do it, and I went and got the urge—and did it. Given such physical development, notions acquired by a lot of boys, or maybe even all of them, have led me and others around to undesirable consequences.

Once I'd weighed all the "pros" and "cons," I decided to resort to sports. I shared my plans with the parents. Dad said:

"That is the right decision. Once you've directed your excess energy into sports, Gennady, you will avoid confrontations with society."

And so the decision was taken. The only question left was what sport to pick. It was a joke, of course, for me to do track and field when during the sixth grade in phys ed classes I'd already highjumped 2.16 meters, ran a 10.3 hundred, and shotput 19 meters. All this without any effort whatsoever, and if I'm to be honest about it, without any sort of satisfaction either. Maybe, swimming? I didn't know how to swim and I wasn't prepared to learn. Why bother?

Lapsing into deep thoughts about this choice of a way of life for me, I went walking through the streets and looking at passersby. I selected a fellow on the healthy side, introduced myself, shook his hand, glanced into his eyes that were paralyzed with pain, nudged him once or twice with my shoulder and then, ashamed, ran away. I no longer know how all this would have ended up if I hadn't happened into boxing.

I recall my first sparring partner—a massive Master of Sport about 40 years old.

"Don't be afraid, sonnie, I tap lightly," he whispered to me before the start of our session. For approximately a minute he hammered away as he wanted, but his hooks and uppercuts affected me like B-Bs would an elephant. By the second minute I'd figured out all the subtleties of this sport. I feinted, and, well, gave him one straight from the shoulder—the old guy fell down. That's how my ticket to life got written for me.

I've liked boxing a lot. I've really enjoyed standing in my corner a second before the bell—with my long luxuriant eyelashes and a blush on my soft cheeks—and then at the bell to toss my luxuriant eyelashes up, open my large light-blue eyes, smile a sparkling smile, glance into my opponent's eyes which have drawn narrow out of fear, and rain down a squall of blows on him. Usually it's never gone to the second round.

Fame has come to my doorstep. I daily receive from 50 to 60 letters from young people. I answer all letters neatly and thoroughly. Question: "How can one become as strong as you?" Answer: "Only by means of diligent effort." Question: "How were you able to achieve such success in sports?" Answer: "Only by means of diligent effort." A girl's question: "Why are you so beautiful?" Answer to the girl: "Only by means of diligent effort."

It would be appropriate to say that I've combined sports with learning successfully; I didn't lag behind the class. I used every free minute to do the scheduled assignments.

Once before a fight I was sitting in the dressing room in my shorts and gloves and memorizing quotes from "A Ray of Light in the Kingdom of Darkness"[3] for a composition, when in walked Ilya Slonov the journalist, with a photographer. The camera guy circled around me, clicking away.

"Scram, Edyula," Slonov said to him and, having sat down nearby, to me: "I like your boxing, Mabukin."

I even blushed. I was always modest before and I'm modest now, too. In this sense I am also an example for beginning athletes.

"I like it, but not altogether," Slonov said.

Well right then and there I started worrying.

"You've got everything," Slonov continued, "Strength, instinct, and skills—they're all high class. Only you don't have an artistic soul."

"How so not?" I asked.

"Take, for example, Cassius Clay..." said Ilya Slonov.

At the mention of Cassius Clay's name my spleen even began to quiver. Oh, how I'd like to meet this comrade, to work out with him to my heart's content.

"...undisputed champion of the world and at the same time a refined lyric poet," Slonov continued. "I assure you that above all he floored Sonny Liston with his intellect."

"A modern boxer is above all a creative person, an artist," Slonov went on. "And boxing's a poem. A poem of ecstasy. Boxing's a symphony or, if you wish, a jazz symphony. Boxing's a Surrealist canvas. Boxing's sheer inspiration, noble impulse, a supple fugue, assonance or dissonance."

Having said this he glanced up at the ceiling and specks of twinkling light flittered past in his dark velvet eyes.

"In general, Mabukin, do you read books?" he asked.

"In general, yes—I read. See, here's..."A Ray of Light in the Kingdom of Darkness." I showed him.

"Well, but other than the condensed, humdrum anthologies? Have you read Kafka's *The Trial?* Are you familiar with the poetry of Velimir Khlebnikov?"[4]

Thus our friendship began, and it's continued to the present day.

Soon, my portrait appeared on the cover of *Ogonyok.*[5] With me in boxing gloves and holding an anthology. The caption read: "Gennady Mabukin. Master of Sport & Avid Booklover."

At that time our team was preparing for the Syracuzers Cup tournament in Latin America. Slonov travelled to our training camp in the country every day, bringing books, records, and albums with reproductions of art works. In a short time under his guidance I conquered Kafka's *The Trial,* Bulgakov's *Master and Margarita,* and Kataev's *Grass of Oblivion;* read Updike's *The Centaur,* Jules Verne's *The Children of Captain Grant* (now there's a real book for you!); got a firm intellectual grasp of the French anti-novel; and, of course, became up-to-date on Sartre (nowadays one can't get by without that).[6] I memorized by heart several verses by Apollinaire and Velimir Khlebnikov—"A country villa by night Chengiskhan!...but the sky is dark blue, Rops!..."[7]—listened with tremendous satisfaction to Bach, Mahler, Prokofiev, the Modern Jazz Quartet; became conversant with the works of Vasily Kandinsky, Salvador Dali, Giacometti and many others. I especially like Morandi's still lifes. As Ehrenburg said, "for all their philosophical depth, there's no intellectualization or dryness in them—they harken to the world of emotions."[8] Gradually, the true character of modern boxing became thoroughly clear to me.

On walks through the forests, woods, copses, and glades in the countryside near Moscow or up the hillocks and down the gullies I composed verses. I recall my first poem:

> My face gazes
>> Out of a swampy darkness;
> It's tired and lonely,
>> but it looks adamant.
> The bulwark of my love
>> are the eyes and forehead...
> I'm not Narcissus,
>> but all the same I'm still in love.

Our head trainer once said to Slonov, "Why are you messing with the fellow's head? He may have to work on Jorge Luis Barracuda in the finals and you know what a right he's got!"[9]

Slonov countered right away: "How can you fail to understand? Gena is practically unbeatable. He's got the Syracuzers Cup in the bag as well as all the other world trophies, but I want to fashion out of him a new type of boxer, a creative person, an artist!"

"Maybe you're a spy, Slonov, eh?" asked the trainer gloomily.

And so we arrived in South America at a very large city. I can no longer recall now whether it was Buenos Aires or Rio de Janiero. The bouts for the Syracuzers Cup began. What a to-do there was! From fifty to sixty reporters photographed my training sessions. From morning to night I was featured on all twelve TV channels. Every day fifty to sixty letters were delivered from Latin American youths. "How can I become as strong as you?"—"Only by means of diligent effort." "How can I become as good looking as you?"—"Only by means of diligent effort." "Is it true that you're a poet?"—"It's true."

In an elimination match, when there were thirty-two contenders, I was supposed to do a job on a Hungarian. His trainer forfeited. "He's our country's hope for the Olympics and we can't risk him," the trainer announced to the newspapers. In the bouts between the last sixteen contenders, an Englishman also refused to fight me. "I am the father of five children, why in the hell should I go and get bashed up?" he announced to the newspapers. In the quarterfinals an Italian also didn't enter the ring: "Life is dearer." And in the semifinals a Japanese boxer spared himself: "The bronze is mine, that's good enough."

I had a lot of free time and spent it with Ilya at art exhibits and symphony concerts, in the underground hangouts of local Bohemians.[10] That way we continued to shape my personality as the new type of boxer. Meanwhile my chief opponent, Jorge Luis Barracuda, slugged it out in grueling fights to reach the finals.

And then the time came for the championship. Before the fight Adolphus Celestine Syracuzers himself, the millionaire cattle-magnate, dropped by my dressing room. A huge middle-aged fellow with the neck of a bull and with a grey-hair crewcut on his pointy head as bristly as a porcupine. He was dressed in a crimson waistcoat, with a diamond ring on one finger and a ruby in one of his ears. Gazing at me with pleasure, he said to representatives of the press:

"I recognize it now. I recognize my youth in him."

And then I went to the ring and for the first time caught sight of Barracuda: a very large, very black and very aging fellow—about thirty years old. He stood in the corner opposite me. He was extremely worried, it seemed, for even his knees were trembling. But having lowered my luxuriant eyelashes, I stood unassumingly in my corner. And as I looked at him through my long luxuriant eyelashes, I smiled affectionately.

"His hands are long. Force him to fight in close. Watch out for the right," my trainer whispered to me.

A real card, my trainer. He didn't even know that I'd decided to conduct this fight like a symphonic poem, like a supple fugue in a Surrealist key of assonances and dissonances. Fighting in close or fighting out at a distance—what nonsense! Boxing is a poem of ecstasy!

I played it all out as if it were a musical score. With his despair and obstinancy, Barracuda was an excellent instrument in my hands, exactly like a *Stradivarius* violin. This fight, for the first time, gave me a truly genuine aesthetic pleasure, because by now I had already become the new type of boxer: a boxer intellectual.

In the third round Barracuda knocked me against the ropes with a sudden uppercut. In the solitude and silence a ringing, divine pain was piercing its way through me. Gasping with inspiration I looked at Barracuda's face drawing near, at his quivering jaw and sparkling-diamond eyes. The moment of truth was approaching. The last stroke, the last tremulous note. Barracuda's head, just like a bowling pin, went thump against the mat.

Once I'd answered fifty or sixty questions I asked the journalists to leave me in peace. Also, I asked my friend Ilya to clear the place out. When everyone had gone I turned on my taperecorder and listened to a recording of a Rachmaninov concert, opened an album of Morandi's prints and a volume of Innokenty Annensky's poems.[11]

Deep into the night, when silence reigned, I left the Sports Palace. On the steps sat Jorge Luis Barracuda. He was crying.

"Why are you crying, Barracuda? Not really because of the defeat, is it?" I asked.

"Yeah, on account of what else would I?" he answered.

"In general, Barracuda, do you read books?"

"Yes, I read, I read."

"It follows you don't read enough. You've got to read more, listen to music, look at paintings."

"Yeah, I know, I know. I know everything about you. I imitate what you do, but what's the use?"

"Do you like Morandi, Barracuda?"

"Yes, I like him, I like him."

"And the Modern Jazz Quartet?"

"Of course."

"Then the future's yours, Barracuda. Don't cry. Ciao."

"Leave while you're still one piece," he growled.

I didn't get into an argument with him.

What can I say about my diet? In the mornings I drink a can of juice and eat two eggs. For lunch a little piece of herring, a half bowl of bouillon... chicken. For afternoon snacks a glass of milk and a muffin. At dinner I let my soul take its own way: caviar, salmon, sturgeon fillets, mushrooms in sour cream. A sirloin on a skewer, a couple of portions of shishkebab, crème-brûlée, strawberries in cream, cake, ice cream, etc. I recommend this regimen to all beginning athletes.

Who was I earlier? A steam hammer.

Who am I now? An attack artist.

(1970)

## Notes

1. "Who Can Live Happily in Russia?" is the title of the Russian poet Nikolai Nekrasov's satirical but optimistic masterpiece written in the years from 1873 to 1876. The poem tells the story of seven peasants who travel over Russia in search of a happy man (cf. *Surplussed Barrelware*), and in spite of the fact that they do not find one the poem ends on an optimistic note about Russia's future.

2. Sunflower seeds are not mentioned in the Russian original, but the verb used here

alludes to the widespread practice of noshing on sunflower seeds and spitting out the hulls.

3. "A Ray of Light in the Kingdom of Darkness"—see note 16 to *Surplussed Barrelware*.

4. Franz Kafka's unfinished novel *The Trial* was published in 1925/26. Kafka's works were totally blacklisted by Soviet authorities and publishers until the thaw periods of the 1960s. For information about Velimir Khlebnikov see note 42 to *Rendezvous*.

5. *Ogonyok* is an illustrated weekly which has been published in the Soviet Union since 1923.

6. Mikhail Bulgakov's novel *Master and Margarita* was completed in 1940, shortly before Bulgakov died, but it was not published until 1966/67 (in the journal *Moskva*). Valentin Kataev's book *The Grass of Oblivion* was published in 1967 (in *Novy Mir*) and John Updike's novel *The Centaur* appeared in print in 1964 (the Russian translation in *Inostrannaia literatura* in 1967). Jules Verne's tale is very widely read by Russian adolescents. The "French anti-novel" is a nontraditional kind of narrative also called the *roman nouveau*; it was popularized by such authors as Robbe-Grillet and Sarraute.

7. These lines come from one of Khlebnikov's untitled poems which is commonly referred to by the opening words of the first line, "Villa at Night..." The poem first appeared in the poet's collection called *Four Birds (Chetyre ptitsy)* in 1916 although it was written at least two years before this date. Critics have commented on Khlebnikov's conversion of proper names into imperatives in this work (e.g., Chengiskhan!—from the name of the Tartar ruler—and Rops!, the surname of a decadent Belgian and fin de siècle artist). Mabukin cites the first and sixth lines of this work (albeit with different punctuation marks).

8. Vasily Kandinsky (1866-1944)—Famous modern painter of Russian birth who left Russia in 1922 to live permanently in the West. He founded a number of groups of artists and was a leading figure of the cultural revival in Germany during the Weimar period. Salvador Dali (1904-    )—Spanish Surrealist painter, sculptor and illustrator. Alberto Giacometti (1901-   )—A Swiss-born artist, sculptor, painter and poet who became famous after 1945 for his elongated sculptures of solitary figures. Giorgio Morandi (1890-1964)—Italian painter and etcher who influenced developments in Italian graphic art. Ilya Ehrenburg (1891-1967)— Soviet novelist and memoirist who lived abroad during much of Stalin's reign and who was an important figure in the cultural thaws of the 1960s. He commented on Morandi in the last volume of his memoirs, *People, Years, Life* [see English translation by T. Shebunina in Ilya Ehrenburg, *Post-War Years: 1945-54* (Cleveland & New York: World Publishing Co., 1967), p. 77].

9. Mabukin's opponent has curious names. Students of Latin American literature cannot help but be struck by their similarity to those of the erudite and world-famous Argentinian writer, Jorge Luis Borges (b. 1899-  ). Moreover, since Aksyonov visited Argentina in 1963 as a member of a delegation from the USSR when the film of his first novel, *The Colleagues,* was being shown at Mar-del-Plata, one wonders whether there is anything more than playful humor in the author's choice of names for his Latin American boxer.

10. The Bohemian establishments mentioned here are nightclubs located in cellars or basements. "Bohemians" gather in the Soviet Union in cellars and basements, too, but this practice is not sanctioned by the government (although in good times it may be tolerated). In "Destruction of Pompeii" the Russian "Bohemians" are referred to as the "basement elite."

11. Innokenty Fyodorovich Annensky (1856-1909) was a poet of the early twentieth century and an outstanding teacher and scholar of classical studies. Mabukin is reading Annensky presumably out of an affinity for the poet's favorite theme: the weariness and futility of life which only love or art can overcome. The volume of poetry referred to here is probably that published in the USSR in 1959.

# Rendezvous*

It was a very long time ago, in the mid-sixties . . .

He had the recognition of everyone belonging to the intelligentsia. The young women from the intelligentsia acknowledged their recognition of him timorously, but the most intelligent ones greeted him with an all-understanding smile. Young experts with rhomboid-shaped pins who came to town on special work assignments made a real public show of their unabashed and enthusiastic recognition of him. They sent bottles of champagne to his table, trying whenever possible to present him with the "Brut" label, but if that wasn't available, at least a "Dry" label: *"Now then, comrade waiter, you be sure to say that it's from the fellows at Box 14789 Security-Plant."*[1] There was a certain haughtiness evident in the recognition of the older specialists, followed later by a serious attempt to establish closer contact so that matters of importance could be discussed in detail. As for the foreigners with any degree of intelligence at all, they were always, all of them, profuse with their respects. Foreign professors flocked to see him—tugging nervously at their tweed jackets and tottering, obsequiously but helplessly, in the labyrinths of our powerful Russian tongue; their purpose in consulting with him was to clarify some vitally important question, which they would then develop with all due attention to its importance into articles for scholarly journals and thereby make their contribution to solving the enigma of the Russian soul.

He was recognized, as well, by a lot of individuals in other spheres of society. All those who kept up-to-date on trends and events in contemporary life nodded respectfully to him. Regular policemen and traffic cops from the GAI Traffic Control Department knew him, too.[2] And even the doorman at the "Nashsharabi" restaurant remembered his face.

Some half-baked Salieris,[3] spiteful people, put on airs of not recognizing him or, if they did acknowledge him in some way, it was by showing disgust. They'd say that they were already boored-tooo-death with him, that to mention him was offensive and ohh-soo baa-nnal. They'd persist in talking on and on about him, repeating how offensive and banal it was to discuss him, and then they'd launch into such malicious gossip and fantastic anecdotes about him that in due course it became clear what a truly important figure he was for them and their shrivelled- and dried-up lives.

But, right now, he was trucking along in his walrus-skin ski-boots purchased last fall in Reykjavik and the coat that was popular for Moscow's gray and white winters, along a soft muddy surface—Gorky Street on New Year's Eve.[4] At this moment, walking in a dense crowd and

111

rarely recognized—only by occasional shouts of greeting—this pensively lanky fellow had suddenly fallen into a melancholic trance.

And, suddenly, publicistic journalism struck him as boring and unnecessary and, equally suddenly, his soul began to pine for the still distant spring, for the encounter which he'd been waiting for all his thunderous life.

You see, he had never given much thought to himself. It had been fights, clashes, refutations, speculations, advancements, and tears of reconciliation in everybody's eyes, but where oh where is there now a teardrop for me, a little one of my own, where are you then?

That Tahitian girl at the poetry reading who, with her softly sparkling Tahitian eyes, had cast frequent glances at him from the third row... He had seized the opportunity then to shout to her: "You're a Tahitian flower, you're a lotus! And I'm a Russian juniper! Got it? I'm a Russian juniper! Do you understand what a juniper is?" She had nodded to him from within a whirlpool of faces and stretched her slender arm out to him, but the crowd was already carrying him off in the opposite direction.

Here, near a gift shop and with the snow falling hard, verses about the Tahitian girl began to take shape and, suddenly, right then and there, having become totally oblivious of his presence before a nation-wide crowd that was awed by the sight of him, Lyova Malakhitov, the thirty-three-year-old darling *of the people,* composed a poem about a Russian juniper:

> I'm a juniper tree, a juniper tree small in stature,
> And you—a tiny, scarlet, Tahitian flower...
> I'm a little juniper tree, up to my neck in snow:
> My berries profit bears who venture where they grow.
> But you, there on some Tahitian shore, must know!
> Don't believe the press, its lies and vanity!

"He's composing!" the crowd whispers.
"Soon he'll let it rip!"
"Lyova, let's hear it!"
"Lyova, quick, strike while the iron's hot!"

Having finished the verses and felt a tremulous shudder, he spied the large number of shining faces all around him. His heart skipped a beat and his blood, pulsing with rapture, started to clamor like bells; he threw open his coat, removed his flap-eared Urals' style winter hat he'd bought in Montreal, and began to read...

The big uproar quite recently was the "match of the century." Lyova defended the goal of our country's national hockey team. His defense of the goal was daring and decisive against the attacks of vicious Canadian and American professionals, the all-star team of the "Star League." One trio of the stars' horsemen-forwards was captained by Maurice Richard himself,[5] hockey player numero uno, and an old friend of Lyova's since that emergency landing on the island of Curaçao.

Here's what had happened: at the end of the third period Richard was awarded a "bullet" penalty-shot, that is, a one-on-one duel with our team's goalie, Lyova Malakhitov, *the people's darling.*

There stood Richard, bent over, with his frightful hockey stick thrust forward. And there stood Lyova, in his goalie's mask, looking like a clown. There they both stood, in a sound vacuum which was unexpected after fifty-nine minutes of tumultuous roaring.

The score's 2-2. Richard's "bullet" will be the last chance for the "stars" to win. It's a sure thing, 100 percent odds.

Now the terrifying Richard has started skating towards Lyova. Richard the terrifying and powerful, flashing his platinum teeth, with a pirate's earring in his disfigured ear and a chromium-plated head: he moves to the attack slowly, his muscles bulging like those of the armored Lancelot—Richard the Terrifying, the world's leading gladiator. By no means is he just some Kelowna Packers amateur or other.[6]

"You're coming at me, Maurice," thought Lyova, "you're coming at me, you shaggy red Canadian bison, as Semyon Isaakovich said. O teammates of mine—Loktyev, Almyetov and Alexandrov, Maiorov brothers and Vyacheslav Starshinov,[7] o momma dear, my modest librarian, and you my gray-haired Urals and my nursemaiden Volga, o Nina, my saintly and inaccessible wife, and dear comrades from all sections of society, here I am, standing here before him, a skinny clown, a wretched Pierrot, a simple little shepherd boy from the Urals. Maurice, there's no mercy in you, you've forgotten about everything, Maurice. Do you recall at this second that emergency landing in Curaçao? Do you remember how our "Boeing" tossed and turned as it fell towards the ocean, and all my gals, my beloved stewardesses, heroically combated against our queasiness, and how we leveled out just above the ocean and barely held out to reach Curaçao, and how you and I that night went to a bar with those brave gals from the *KLM* airline, and, in the bar, how we were recognized and given an ovation, and I played Paganini on my miniature "Stradivarius" and you, Maurice, shared your expertise in wrestling, and the proprietor, deeply moved, presented the two of us with little triangular watches for which there's no equal on this earth. Where's your watch, Maurice? Mine's in the dressing room. And where's your momma, Maurice, the little cashier for the Salvation Army in your native Quebec? Ah-ha-ha, Maurice, you're about to make a feint and then you're going to hurl that puck as if it were a chunk of your own ruthless soul, but I, the skinny clown, will nab it ruthlessly and it will throb in my glove until it stops zinging, yes, I will nab all 100 of your hopes and we will go our separate ways in peace."

Then, the following took place: suddenly, Lyova lunged forward and fell onto the puck. Richard skated through him splendidly, gliding brilliantly over the ice. The puck flew off against the sideboards behind the goal. Lev shot after it like a rocket and with his lean, trim stomach pressed Richard's bisony buttocks against the boards. Together, they both slammed down on the ice and the puck, like a top, spun off a short distance. Afraid to stand up on their legs, they both maneuvered their stomachs around and, suddenly, our Lyova swirled halfway around impetuously and covered the puck. Scattering sparks, the chromo-horrific Richard slowly skated up to Lyova, now back on his feet, gave him a tap on those pale Ural eyes with his stick, heaved a sob in an apparent recollection of Curaçao, and clasped him in a bear hug. They both began to cry. The picture of the kiss they gave each other was printed in all newspapers of the world; even the *Jen min jih pao* published it, *although it's true, under the rubric "Their Morals."*[8]

A thickening twilight altered the day's coloration. The light began to turn dark-blue, with streaks of white, and then grew to be whiter and whiter; snow fell in flakes the size of a handkerchief. Distinctly, one by one, the kerchiefs glided down and the dark-blue sky, already almost black, barely peeped out between them here and there, only peeped, and Lyova had turned white all over, and even wobbly like Father Frost.[9]

He ran up to a snow-covered telephone booth, tore open the door and hid from view. This was an ordinary glass and snow wrapper, but inside it was gloomily warm and comfortable, and there was a smell like that of innocent sin (a thousand memories!), and here everything rose up before him in the little holes of the telephone receiver—beginning with the childhood stuff ("Is this the zoo? No? Well, why's there a monkey on the phone, then?") and ending with that of the adult male of today (a call home to my wife Nina, the saintly and inaccessible).

"Nina?"

"What's the matter?"

"It's me, Lyova."

"What's wrong?"

"Uh-h-h...well...I...don't think...Ninochka, it's just Mishka Tal' and Tigran...we were glued to our chairs, you understand? Ninok, Nitush...we were analyzing Bobby's last game."[10]

"Why should I care?"

"Well, of course, you're thinking..."

"I'm not thinking ('...that I've been with some chicks...') anything! ('...Athenian nights, I know...') I'm not thinking anything ('...you don't believe me, you...')! I'm not thinking anything! ('...you think that...')

"...I'm a scoundrel, a cut-loose ('...When at last...') type, but I really love ('...when, at last...') you, you're saintly, but I'm a pitiful sort ('...when, at last...will these sobs end?')."

Silence...

"Ninok, what are you doing?"

114

"Reading."

"What?"

" 'Stavrogin's Confession'."[11]

"Why the ooh?"

"That's interesting."

"Have you read it?"

"Ninochka!"

"You're lying!"

...silence, in the booth an aside in an almost inaudible whisper: "No prophet in his own country..."

"You have your glasses on...?"

"Yes."

"That's my sweet **Bubo Bubo**."[12]

...silence...

I'll use this third pause to tell the story of their love and union.

It's been seven or eight years since they met on a distant Siberian construction site, to which Lyova Malakhitov, at that time a truly young youth activist, had come with some undefined goal.

Lyova, then a fly-by-night progressive, was strolling along a viaduct and saying the kinds of things one was supposed to: "Well, then, guys, how's it going? Say, gals, how are things?"—sometimes he would also turn cold, freeze in his tracks, and strike a serious pose—he had caught a vision of Yermak's campfires on Siberia's immense horizon. And soon after his arrival, things started going well at the construction site with the education of the masses in political and social-work activities.

*After he'd spent a night conferring with the engineers, Lyova managed to move off dead center one of the crews working on a most important section of the dam.*

On one occasion, as he was standing with pole in hand on a wildly tossing raft and racing down the wildly impetuous river, as he was standing with his pole thrust among the breakers and the boulders, as he was standing with his pole in a thundercloud of spray, in the rainbows—drunk with happiness, not booze—as he was standing with his pole on the raft, he suddenly caught a glimpse of a complicatedly lonely gantry crane on the riverbank. It seemed at first that blue searchlights had been installed on the cabin roof, but it was just Nina's eyes. Nina, a minimally educated but dreamy girl, was then working on a tower-crane isolated in the taiga. How often she had dreamed, screwing up her eyes at the river, of the arrival in a cloud of spray of a fairytale-beautiful and young-looking *Komsomol member,* and here he goes and appears, Lyova Malakhitov!

For Lyova, it was a matter of but a single minute to maneuver abruptly in between the cliffs, to beach the boat at the base of the steel giant, and to prostrate himself at the feet of searchlight-eyes Nina.

They remained, just the two of them, in the cabin of the crane until nightfall, yackety-yakking and heave-hoing, loading and moving the boulders from one place to another in order not to just sit there without doing some work.

*Now it was already after the brightly shining day had changed into a flaming red sunset that Nina and Lyova turned up alongside the future hydroelectric power station. And there, inside a turbine rotor, they made love for the first time.*

Long afterwards, a number of tales about their wedding circulated far and wide across the vast expanses of Siberia.

Well, for example, it was said that . . .

In Moscow Nina spent her time educating herself. Unexpectedly, she manifested exceptional or, to speak more simply, fantastic capabilities. Nina gulped down book after book. No matter what time of night he happened to rouse, Lyova would see her reading, her forehead propped up against the table lamp. First, she went through the classics, then, contemporary foreign literature. Simultaneously, she mastered three European languages. And with that achievement she gained entry into the company of the most serious people in Moscow and in this circle she passed judgment, with the proper condescension, on contemporary Russian literature. Then came philosophy—Hegel, Kant, the study of Zen Buddhism, a return to Christianity, and then a new breaking away from it, nighttime tears on the pillow next to the tranquilly snoring Lyova, night-time tears over the fate of humankind, early-morning seriousness with glasses on her puffed-up face (my sweet Bubo Bubo), attempts to read out loud and the criticisms of her world-famous husband.

In the circle of serious people they talked about Nina's husband with a kindhearted little smile: What do you expect? He's a student idol, fate's spoiled child, poet, hockey and soccer player, musician, construction designer, and, what else? Leonardo da Vinci, hee-hee-hee? Nina suffered and criticized poor Lyova because he led such a flash in the pan life. Lyova's pillow was perpetually flying from the bed onto the sofa. And Lyova would sit in darkness, on the sofa, tug his ears reddened by champagne—no words, o my friend, no signs—and cry.

The reading skills which he possessed were no less than those Nina had and, what's more, he possessed a photographic memory and could, like V. B. Shklovsky,[13] recall everything he had read by heart. But he couldn't devote himself wholly to reading, to immersing himself in philosophy, to sitting at home nights when calls were coming in right and left—Lyova, play . . , Lyova, write a . . , perform a . . , Lyova, design this or that, make a quicky flight here or there, help with this, come to the rescue of . . . , chew 'em out good . . . Lyova!

Yes, Ninochka criticized her Lyova for his lack of seriousness, but not at all from jealousy of some imagined crowd of blondes, brunettes, or redheads who, it goes without saying, hang around fellows such as Lyova.

116

These supposed hordes, legions of profligate women, didn't disturb her at night, didn't cause her to grit her teeth at all or to be tormented by insomnia; all that was just nonsense, beneath contempt. She was a person with a solid education and a philosophical mind. Lyova's lack of seriousness—now that's what distressed her!

"Did Oistrakh call, Ninochka?"

"No."

"Well, who did?"

"Stravinsky called from Paris."[14]

"What did he have to say?"

"For Christ's sake!" (Sometimes, something like that just popped out—memory of days in the taiga.)

"Ninok, I beg you, what did Igor have to say?"

"Oh, he's writing a bass solo for you. Do you really sing bass?"

"Nina!"

"You always sang tenor."

"You're having your fun again, eh, Nina? Why are you making fun of my bass voice? After all, that's what God gave me and He alone will take away"...(A plaintive sobbing)

...Silence to the sound of bu-bu-bu, an elephantine rumble of contrebasses (the love of contre-basses for all other instruments is well known), the honeyed flow of a flute and a strained **forte piano** in 2/4 time.

"Where are you off to now, Lev?"

"A New Year's party."

"Ahh-khh!"

"What's that, Ninochka, darling?"

"No strength left to say."

"You've got to understand, they asked as a special favor...the kiddies are expecting it...kids from the Philharmonic, Zoya Avgustinovna... well..."

"Aww, to the devil with all of you!"

Siberian woman: telephone receiver bangs on the hook at the other end of the line in Izmailovo![15] Siberian woman: a running leap and her face buries into the pillow! Siberian tears on "Stavrogin's Confession," and to the devil with 'em all!

As for Lyova, he left the telephone booth and ducked behind a corner onto a relatively quiet square where there were patches of unblemished powdery snow; he and a fellow walking four excellent Boxers on a leash exchanged bows, then he ducked under the archway to the courtyard of a gloomy apartment building, and reappeared from there with the courtyard attendant's shovel.

At the rear of the square, about one hundred meters from the memorial statue, there was a hill of snow that reached shoulder height. Lyova cheerfully went at it with the shovel. Scoops with the shovel uncovered a light-blue "Moskvich," purchased last year in Rome.[16] The courtyard attendant, a woman, rushed out of the gloomy building.

"Oh, I was wondering what scoundrel swiped my shovel. But it's just you, Lyova, eh?"

"Console me, Marfa Nikitichna!" Lyova exclaimed and pressed his face against her immensely padded shoulder. He had a short cry.

"Here, here, Lyova, why're you, come now...why're you!" the attendant began to squirm as if she were being tickled.

"Thanks, mommy, o mommy mine," he shouted, making no sense at all.

"My second mommy," he thought, gazing at the attendant's back as she walked away with the shovel. "No, the third," he corrected himself as someone else came to mind. "My third mommy: a Russian woman!"

"Marfa Posadnitsa!" he shouted, making even less sense than before.[17]

He turned on the ignition and the little "Mosvich" began to tremble feebly.

"My dearest, my true friend," Lyova whispered, kissing his "Mosvich" on the windshield, steering wheel, speedometer and ashtray. "My kittie-cat, puss-puss," and the car zoomed forwards.

*Inspector Major Khrapchenko bowed to the pale-blue "Moskvich" from his sentry box near the Telegraph Office, Inspector Lieutenant-Colonel Polupanchenko waved to him on Manezh Square, and Inspector Lieutenant-General Fesenko shook hands with Lyova at the entry to the Kremlin's Bronnivitski Gate.*[18]

*Lyova parked his "puss-puss" alongside Bronnivitski Gate and entered the Kremlin on foot.*

*At Bronnivitski Gate there is a constant wind current of unusual force and under the gate's archway the whistling and roaring is like that in an aerodynamic wind tunnel. And the snow which falls into its zone sticks together and flies like a solid mass; in it human figures, pelted in the face and in the back, gyrate helplessly.*

*Thus, the wind and snow pelted against Lyova, under his "popular" coat and thermal sweater. Having overcome the resistance with difficulty, having fallen down flat several times onto the cobblestones, and yet forced his way into the Kremlin, Lyova swerved around the corner of the tower— to catch his breath.*

*Right beside him the wind was howling and moaning, but just above his head the snow was twirling peacefully.*

*Lyova pressed his back up against the ancient brick and turned rigid as he suddenly heard Blokian music:*

> *Hurricane squalls,*
> *Ocean song trawls,*

118

*Snow swirls and swirls,*
*Instantaneous century whirls,*
*And dreams of blessed lee-shore world.*[19]

*In a gap in the dark clouds—my God!—a star suddenly flickered;*
*it winked encouragingly.*

Through the glass-marble facade of the Palace of Congresses there shone a candled fairytale world: gigantic fir trees in pendulant silver filaments; red, yellow, and light-blue balls and pointed ornaments, bonbonneries, huge fluffs of completely white cotton, and, yes, everything else you might or might not imagine!

Here, right from the start, representatives of Moscow's kiddies fell into the solicitous hands of masked entertainers—buffoons, grey-wolves, Red-Riding Hoods, bunny rabbits and baby foxes, Barmaleis, Crocodiles, Aibolits, Buratinos, and Behemoths—*the leaders of the Young Pioneer organization in the capital and artists from the Central Children's Theater.*[20]

The whole atmosphere was charged with anticipation—they were waiting for Father Frost. Zoya Avgustinovna immediately led Lyova off to the dressing room, rushing him along the hallway and chastising him mildly for his tardiness. There was a conversation between them. This is what it was:

"Zoya Avgustinovna, do you remember...once...in the Crimea...I...I'm possessed...you'll understand..."

"Lyova, doll, put the beard on, right away. The kiddies are waiting."

"Strike up your shaggy sail..."[21] Give me a kiss on the cheek...motherly like...right away, I'll..."

"Lyova, doll, the coat and boots..."

"Aim your stalwart armor with the sign of the cross on your breastplate..."[22] Zoya Avgustovna, I'm possessed...for I, too, am a human being...Do you remember, there was a storm?"

"Oh, you forgot the padding! Lyova, doll, unbutton the coat and put on the padding. Hee-hee-hee, that'd be an act now—a skinny Father Frost!"

"You know my Nina, don't you, Zoya Avgustovna...saintly, inaccessible...she's castigating me for a lack of seriousness...I'm anxious about it...I...I..."

"Straighten the beard. That's right. Marvelous. Your sheepskin. The bag. Your trumpet. C'est magnifique."

Massive, rosy-cheeked and with a nose like a potato, Father Frost stood at the threshold of the dressing room and sighed.

"Is it really my life or did you just appear to me in a dream..."[23]

"Lyova, doll, bless you, man!" Zoya Avgustovna began to shout, her eyes goggling in horror, "Bless you! Don't think about anything now! Put yourself into it!"

Puffing obediently and good naturedly, putting himself into the role, Lyova Malakhitov—Father Frost—ambled along the corridor.

Bear cubs—activists of the Central Young Pioneers' Palace—in bells and ribbons, hopped all around Father Frost.

> Children, children, form a circle,
> Form a circle, form a circle,
> We are friends, yes, you and I are,
> And I love you!—ecstatically shouted Lyova.

> Quickly, children, wipe your nose.
> Wipe your nose, oh, wipe your nose,
> He's brought presents, our good host,
> Lyova, jolly Father Frost!—the children shouted

beside themselves with joy.

Dancing jauntily around the circle, Father Frost took in tow a multi-racial band of kiddies, *among whom a fair number were little Laotian and Cambodian princes.*

Soon the gold trumpet was snatched from his bosom and Lyova began to make it sing in such a way that Armstrong himself would have been envious. Indeed, the great Satchmo had already envied Lyova—at last year's Newport Jazz Festival when he alone had vindicated the honor of our music. Louie turned absolutely green on that occasion, and then all gray before he once again blossomed with happiness and returned to being a kindhearted-brown Louisianian; the heavenly Ella Fitzgerald dashed on stage and gave Lyova an expansive kiss, and Duke also exuded with kisses, and then they all four played together. And how!—such that several hundred people in the Newport crowd were carried from the field with heart attacks.

Lyova pranced around the tree with his trumpet, his beard and locks flipped and flopped, his padding fell out, and wide pleats of the baggy Father Frost suit flapped lightly and freely in the air. Gifts flew out of his voluminous bag—Eastern sweets, fruits, experimental mechanical toys. The children clambered onto his shoulders; a pair of tots had been sitting on his head for some time already, hanging on by his ears.

Zoya Avgustovna and the Palace Manager were in tears. The tree-trimming party had been a success.

"They criticize him in vain," the manager said, "the critics, paralytics, gnash their molars on him in vain..."

"You think so?" asked Zoya Avgustinovna, drying her eyes with light flicks of her lace kerchief.

"I had in mind the caustic lashings, the overkill," the manager corrected himself. "Criticism, of course, is necessary, *but not with such voluntarism, mark my words, that's how it'll be.*"[24]

"In the Philharmonic we keep an eye on everyone," Zoya Avgustinovna icily ended the conversation.

Aside from the general gaiety and commotion there stood two mummers—the Buzzard from "Tale of Tsar Sultan" and the witch Baba Yaga.[25] They were talking in husky masculine voices, talking and glaring intently in Lyova's direction.

"What in the deuce is he jumping around here for, like an idiot, like a hypocrite?" asked Baba Yaga. "What in the deuce is he shaming our whole generation for?"

"And you, in what deuce?" Buzzard sniggered unpleasantly.

"I? In the deuce of Pollitrovich and Zakusonsky!"[26] Baba Yaga exclaimed. "But as for him, he's got everything going for him!"

"Don't get excited," Buzzard rasped, "I see you have some scores to settle with him."

"My score with him is on behalf of our generation!" Baba Yaga cried out fervently, even frightening himself somewhat with the vastness of this idea, but he continued once he'd clenched the bit between his teeth:

"A personal score, too! You remember what the poet once said: 'the best of our generation, take me for your trumpeter!'[27] Who else could be our trumpeter if not this Levka with his talents, but he just clowns around. Our generation is strict, 'fellows with upturned collars,' as the poet said . . ."

Baba Yaga kept talking in this vein for quite some time, but Buzzard, having crossed the wing-hands over his chest, followed Lyova's movements with his flaming eyes.

"Let's get out of here," he finally said. "They no longer need us here. The forces of evil ought to withdraw."

They left the Palace proudly and majestically—like sad demons, exiled spirits—and for some time they strolled together through the square that crackled with frost.

At about this time the snow stopped falling and a small lake formed an intricate shape in the dark clouds in which the moon appeared, *its reflection lackluster on the frost-rimmed cobblestones, the cupolas of the Ivan-the-Great, Archangel, and other cathedrals, the cupolas of the little Church of the Enrobement.* Baba Yaga continued to develop his views, but Buzzard kept his silence.

"An amazing individual," said Baba Yaga, "Ghiaurov's bass, *Yehudi Menuhin's* bow, Konovalenko's reactions, Yevtushenko's pen, Popenchenko's fist, a gifted weaver of verses, and talented in everything, absolutely everything.[28] No matter where you go, he's there—everywhere, Lyova Malakhitov—the star attraction." "Exactly right," thought Buzzard.

"But this clowning around, these ah-s and oh-s, this exaltation," continued Baba Yaga, "sometimes I think, just imagine, it's not a game, maybe, not a bitching state of affairs, perhaps it's because of a pure heart or something god-like, eh?"

"Exactly right," thought Buzzard and a trifle internally he gnashed his internal teeth.[29]

"Seems it's time," he said, "the party's ended."

*They set out together for Bronnivitski Gate. Buzzard shot a look at Tsar Cannon, and with a sly and malicious joy recalled previous years and the nights he'd spent in the muzzle of this gigantic weapon.*

"Time for what?" asked Baba Yaga, "what do you have in mind?"

"Well, haven't you been dreaming of currying Lyova's favor?" Buzzard laughed loudly, "dreaming of basking in his rays, dreaming of getting on familiar terms with him, of sassing him around a bit, dreaming that a few more of your acquaintances will see you together with him? Isn't that right?"

"And just what are you dreaming about?" the barb-tongued Baba Yaga shouted, "isn't it exactly the same?"

Buzzard burst out in a roar of internal laughter with his deep vocal cords.

Happy, red-cheeked, and panting, Lyova strolled towards his car with *travesti* from the Central Children's Theater surrounding him. These tiny actresses--perpetual bunny rabbits and baby foxes—usually return to their feminine selves with difficulty, and by no means do all of them totally return: they peck like fledgling birds; they buzz like a swarm of bees; they smell sweet like flowers; they twist and fidget like their heroes—the bunny rabbits and baby foxes.

"Ai-ai-ai! How little you are," the surprised Lyova cried, "tell me girls, it's probably marvelous, eh, living on the verge of absolute Lilliputianism?"

"Lyova, take us with you! We want to go with you!" the actresses shouted.

"I'll take all of you with me! How many are there? Seven, eight? Everyone crawl into the 'Moskvich'! I'll take you all home."

Near the car two men were waiting for him: one was a ruddy-faced, blue-eyed, and self-searching type; the other a sardonically quiet individual with eyes like dark tunnels, where there shine the yellow lights of a locomotive.

"Hello," the men said.

"Greetings," Lyova replied politely. "I hope you recognize me. Do you? In any event, I'll inform you that I'm Malakhitov. I myself was a volunteer militia man and not a bad one, either, you can believe me. As you see, I'm not doing anything reprehensible. The girls? They're my comrades from work."

"Hey, Levka, don't you recognize us?" the ruddy-faced one said. "Gotten conceited, eh?"

This little word "conceited" was a genuine curse for Lyova. Once he heard it used, our public's darling began to fidget and babble, stuff like "Aw, dammit, forgive me old man, it's my damn visual memory, old man, say, old boy, gettin' what you can?" et cetera. At such times he was rescued by the words "old man" or, depending upon the circumstances, other derivative phrases which he'd mouth, like "old boy," "old buddy," and "old buddy boy." So it was that Lyova began to mumble now:

"Aw, damn it, old men, it's my damn visual memory—old boys, say, old buddies, gettin' what you can?" In reserve there was still "old buddy boys."

"That's it, gramps," the ruddy-faced one rejoiced. "It's not nice of you to forget old pals. Our generation must support one another, pops."

"True, old buddy boy!" Lyova proclaimed, deeply touched by this simple thought. "Here, let me kiss you!" He bussed the powdery cheek of the ruddy-faced one and turned impetuously to the gloomy one. "And a kiss for you, too, allow me!" He kissed the steely cheek and his lips stuck to it, like what happens in childhood when you kiss a sled runner and your mouth becomes frozen to it.

The situation turned rather bizarre: Lyova tried, but could not pull his lips off the steely cheek; the gloomy owner of the cheek stood still, smiling sardonically. Finally, with an abrupt twist of his head, he set Lyova free.

" 'ell, then," Lyova muttered in embarrassment. Little drops of blood came to the surface on his lips, but that was of no consequence. The main thing was a feeling of friendship, which unlocked Lyova's soul and left it wide open as he watched the little actresses skipping along and the two people of his own "generation," that rosy-cheeked old friend and the gloomy but likeable Mephistopheles. What a pity not to be able to spend the evening with these fellows, he thought, but I really must go home to Nina, beg her forgiveness, immerse myself in her stern intellectual life.

"My friends, our union is beautiful!" he exclaimed. "Some time or other let's spend an evening all together."

"Okay, let's do it right now," Gloomy pronounced in a squeaky, but surprisingly tender metallic voice and, with equally surprising sincerity, gazed into Lyova's eyes.

And once again a bizarre phenomenon took place: Lyova's pupils seemed to freeze, stuck on the cold and yellow train lights immobilized in the two tunnels.

"What a brilliant artistic personality," thought Lyova as he tried hard to wrench his intent stare away from the lights, "what a pity we can't do that right away . . . have a serious chat right now, open our souls to one another, become of one mind. Verily, verily, one life's not enough for a person . . ."

The snow maidens, bunny rabbits and baby foxes danced in a circle and sang in their thin voices:

> Our kind Lyova Malakhitov,
> Yoŭ have a soul that's candid!
> Malakhitov, Lyova, you are kind,
> You're a sacred cow of kine...

Ruddy-faced, having taken him by the shoulder, hooted into his ear:

"But do you, Lyova, remember Kolka Ksenokratov, the one who sat in the back row and chewed paper? Just imagine, he's a laureate now! And Kuzya, remember him? How about his riding into class on the back of the principal, no less... you remember? Just imagine, he's a book reviewer... on his sixth wife already!... No, brother, our generation..."

Lyova jerked his head, trying in vain to tear his eyes away from the yellow flames. "There's a real nuisance for you," he thought, "I don't even remember the last names of these most distinguished fellows of my generation. Have I really gone and got conceited? Shame, shame..."

"As a matter of fact, why couldn't we set off somewhere right now?" he exclaimed. "Let's whip over to 'Nashsharabi', watcha say, old buddies, old pals?!"

The yellow lights backed off with a jerk and shifted into faintly discernible dots. Lyova freed himself and jumped into the "Moskvich." Chirping raucously, the travesties found themselves places in the back seat, and Lyova's peers took seats next to him. Already overwhelmed with a stimulating wave of joy, Malakhitov switched on the ignition.

"Won't take," "Moskvich" suddenly pronounced with a cough.

"Don't shame me, don't shame me, don't shame me, pet," Lyova mumbled heatedly and rapidly as he fawningly but unobtrusively stroked the steering wheel with his tongue.

"Won't take; that's that!" "Moskvich" turned stubborn. "I'm no tank or tractor that's fit to haul such freight. Let one of 'em get out..."

"But who, who?" Lyova asked.

"He'll know himself..."

It stands to reason that this dialogue wasn't heard by anyone in that honorable company, but Gloomy Peer just happened to guffaw loudly and climb out of the car.

"Don't want to cramp anyone, fellers, so I think I'll just get there on my own. Ciao!"

With these words he dashed off towards the nearest churning eddy of the snow storm and disappeared. Immediately, the "Moskvich" started up and drove off to the world-famous "Nashsharabi" restaurant along well-beaten paths.

O "Nashsharabi," "Nashsharabi," you've eclipsed "Maxim's" and the "Waldorf Astoria"!![30] O, you Mecca of our century's sixties! Is there a heart—whether from Moscow, Leningrad, Siberia, the Urals, or, yes, of any human being, even a Dane—which doesn't flutter when entering through this archway with tiger faces and ox-eyed beauties, through this archway which retains and blabs out so many secrets, which has heard so many oaths and toasts and has even been embarrassed by bragging lies, through this archway where the "wild melody of the clarinet" and the biological howl of the saxophone swing,[31] where the stupefying scent of the house speciality—"Seywha" (calf ears and chicken rumps in a sauce made with a "Caruso" cocktail)—drives even the experienced gourmets of Barbizon to distraction, is there a heart that doesn't flutter?

It's not at all known what means of transport Gloomy Peer used, but he was already awaiting Malakhitov's company near the restaurant, standing a bit to one side of the line left over from last year, in which people were caked with snow.

"This one with you, Levka?" the doorman Murat Andrianych asked.

Andrianych was such a hefty fellow that he thought nothing at all of addressing even the most respected citizens informally, though he would exchange polite, reciprocal niceties only with those whom he didn't let in, that is, with practically all humankind.

"With me, with me, Andrianych!" Lyova exclaimed. "Greetings to you, Andrianych, from Thor Heyerdahl!"[32]

"Notify Thor I reciprocate, my regards," Andrianych whistled.

Such greetings, I tell you—the warm signs of human concern—were more dear to the old man than the most generous of tips. For is the meaning of life really in the tips one gives? Ponder that one yourself!

With little travesties clinging to him, Lyova entered the vestibule of the restaurant, arm-in-arm with his peers.

"Malakhitov with his children," the line whispered respectfully, "seven daughters..."

"And those two, who are they, his brothers?"

"Friends. One's a boxer from the GDR and the other's Cosmonaut 10."

"Cut it out, comrade. They're Malakhitov's colleagues."

"Think you know more than anyone else, eh?"

"Can you imagine it? I do. My wife's sister..."

The evening hadn't turned out to be a failure for the people in line after all.

"There we were, chewing the cud and not wasting our time. We saw for ourselves how Lyova Malakhitov made his entry with seven Japanese girls. What a sight—handsome, shapely, in a thermal sweater made of semi-conductors. Ooo-eee, Lyova's sweater was made to order by Levi Strauss himself at the 'Philips' plant, and it's permeated throughout with platinum wires that heat you up or cool you off, whenya wanna, depending upon the outside temperature..."

125

Reserved, yet with dramatic flair, Lyova walked through the buzzing crowd.

"Oh gals, Malakhitov's shown up!"

"So maybe it's even trite, but I like him. Son of a bitch he's good looking!"

"Salute, Lyova, doll! Doesn't see me! Got conceited, the rattler!"

"Pardon me, but now there's a genuine walking anachronism, a fossil! All that super-gifted talent of his, his exaltation... No doubt about it, his time has passed... He's a pterodactyl, a mammoth..."

"They say he's become a sozzler."

"Hell, no! He's married a fifth time! Got married in Latin America!"

"Gotta ask, think maybe he'll do a song?"

"Mister Syracuzers, Malakhitov's shown up. Do you want to be photographed with him?"

"What do you think, would it be acceptable if I, a proper lady, were to invite Lyova to dance? Oh, I'm just joking, joking!"

"Good fellow, a box of 'Claret' for Malakhitov's table! And keep the change!"

"Have you seen his new sculpture?"

"Primitive!"

"You're a snob! Personally I always reread his marvelous 'Discourse on Cooking Salt...' before going to bed."

*"Oh, girls, I'd give myself to him with my eyes shut, only it's frightening..."*

"Mister Malakhitov! Oi, sorry—Levka. I just let my tongue absolutely run off awagging. I'm Shurik, from the Society for Cultural Relations. We've met. Remember, in Damascus?! You asked me for a light. Hey, listen, the Argentine cattle magnate Syracuzers and his girlfriend, the daughter of Maharajah Adzharagam, want to drink a toast to you and have their picture taken with you. Professor Willington from Cambridge has plans to present you with his all-weather cap... Of course, you understand how important it all is."

"Comrade Malakhitov, Jean-Luc Godard and Marina Vlady[33] have been asking for you."

"An anachronism, a walking fossil..."

"Hello, hello, hello, friends—ladies and gentlemen! Hello Tanya, Natasha, Claudine! I remember, I remember everything, it can't be forgotten, Marisya..."

With these words Lyova conducted his retinue to a free table. Fifteen minutes hadn't even gone by when the stately waiter Leon rose up beside the table.

"Seywha?" he asked with his customary sullenness.

"Good memory, Leon!" Lyova grinned fawningly. "Seywha for

everyone, à la Malakhitov, with vegetable oil, dill, vinegar, and that Japanese 'sooi' sauce. The chef knows."

"That won't wash," Leon snapped curtly.

"What?!" Lyova shouted, glancing at everyone in his retinue one by one. "You see? It's the beginning of the end!" Then, having propped his head on his fist, he pronounced bitterly: "It's falling, my popularity's falling..."

"Your popularity, comrade Malakhitov, is in no way falling," Leon said sullenly. "We don't have any vegetable oil in the kitchen."

"Well, then, serve us... serve us your Seywha," Lyova said tiredly. "See here how mine is already standing on end, in a tuft?" he asked, pointing with his finger to a triplet of crow's-tail tufts on the back of his head...[34]

Having placed the order and tossed a crafty green glance at the dining room, and having convinced himself that everyone was looking at him, Lyova knitted his brow seriously and started up a conversation about the fate of members of his generation and about life in general.

"Everything returns full circle, old men, but life—that's a serious matter. You agree? Our lifespan is short, but we still complicate it with all kinds of stupid actions. True? Take Ortega y Gasset, who writes that a new reality has risen up, different from both natural inorganic and natural organic reality;[35] however, we find in Engels' works that 'Life is a form of essence of albuminous bodies,'[36] and the thought is full circle. But recall now our youth—'And whither does the azure Nereids' songful sorrow beckon us? Where is she, the magical Hesperides' goldening distance?'[37] Well, that's from Vyacheslav Ivanov... Yess-ss, old pals, but humans are free beings and they can create a better life. That's my own contribution, though. But maybe it's not mine after all, no matter. I remember how we conversed with Sartre in Las Vegas..."

Rosy-cheeked Peer, whose surname turned out to be Babintsev, was enjoying himself. Lyova Malakhitov in the flesh, Lyova Malakhitov himself, had braced his elbows on the table and furrowed his famous forehead into a grid of wrinkles and was conducting a conversation with him, and what a conversation—a conversation about the meaning of life! And the eyes of prominent individuals were directed at them, including even at him, Seryoga Babintsev, who very recently, for the sum of 6 roubles 54 kopecks had been hooting at a children's party as Baba Yaga.

Gloomy Peer, the owner of an extremely strange calling card which identified him as "Yu. F. Smelldishchev,[38] Modern dances," listened to Lyova very attentively, trying to catch the thread of his thought; he looked with a frozen grin at the tablecloth and, after every spiral in Lyova's speech, clicked peculiarly—it seems, with his tongue, as if he were counting off something.

And as for the baby foxes, bunny rabbits and kitties—they were at the pinnacle of bliss. With quivering little noses they were snaring the smell of Seywha, with their entire skin they were feeling the looks of great men; they were also bobbing up and down, fidgeting, doing pirouettes, whispering in giggles, and only occasionally would the more serious little faces, recalling the historicity of the moment, turn towards Lyova, nod at the word "Sartre," and restrain their effervescence with all their strength of will.

It had to be said that even Lyova was pleased with the start of this evening.

There he sat with sympatico contemporaries, people of exceptional acumen, and conducted a pleasant and serious conversation with them, without carrying on disgracefully, or guzzling champagne, or kissing everyone who happened along—they were sitting and conversing like your ordinary intellectuals.

Alas, this didn't continue for long. Soon, under the pressure of universal love, general understanding, a hail-fellow-well-met attitude, and even effrontery, Lyova could not restrain himself and, as usual, plunged into dissipation. He made the round of tables, surrounded himself with bosom buddies, guzzled down a bottle of cognac and about a half a case of champagne, sang, of course, his favorite song—"Don't put out the fire in your soul, put out the fire of war and lies"—improvised, of course, on the saxophone to the melody of "How High the Moon," danced the lezgin by himself, taunted the cattle magnate Syracuzers with anti-bourgeois innuendoes, accepted the all-weather cap from Willington, returned that gift with one of his own—the thermal sweater, accidentally fell headlong into a bowl of "Spearchucker" soup[39] on the table of his polite hosts from the Caucasus, and, to all-around raucous laughter, told the Princess Adzharagam that women like her were once thrown into the "appropriate waves" in Russia, reached an agreement with the wizards of the leather ball about the next day's practice, *and promised the builders of a box-numbered oil refinery to catch a flight tomorrow to Tiksi*[40] so as to investigate the complications there. In a word, it all resulted in the most ordinary of chaotic "Nashsharabi" drunken muddles. At times Lyova went icy, turned cold, or was covered with goosebumps as he pictured to himself how, at this moment, "my sweet Bubo Bubo" is rustling pages, meditating on the humble words of Tikhon and on Stavrogin's bravado,[41] but . . . once more, from all sides glasses were handed him and shouts were heard: everyone wanted something from him.

Suddenly, that evil little word "anachronism" reached his ear and he froze as if caught in a lasso, in the middle of making an impetuous movement.

"How's that? Me, it's me that's an anachronism? Me, Malakhitov, I've outlived my time? I'm a pterodactyl? Is that what you've said, friends?"

Light blue eyes blinked in assent, but a pointy little beard cocked itself straight up:

"Yes, namely you. But we're no friends of yours. Don't you love the truth, Malakhitov?"

"Hey, how can that be? Hey, what's going on here?" Lyova surveyed the dining room again with his eyes. It was all astir and, in places, stormily seethed. Everything spun round and round before him.

At this moment, Charlie Willington, having been driven nuts by freedom, was putting on a bizarre exhibition in the center of the room as he poetically thumbed his nose:

> I, Professor Willington,
> Despise the Pentagon
> For its wadded purse,
> And bubonic-plague curse!
> Why spill people's blood?
> Better to "Make Love!"
> I totter, as with the flu,
> My kids are hippies, too,
> But I myself—a handsome beast!
> Russhians, brothers, all zee best!
> *Who gives a spit we've got gray hair,*
> *Peace will conquer, will conquer war!*

At another time Lyova might have kissed the professor for such a marvelous song, but right now the shaken "anachronism" only superficially applauded this daredevil from Cambridge and surveyed the dining room again with his eyes, searching for salvation. And suddenly, it seemed to him that it was there!

Two pairs of huge, affectionately calm eyes looked at him from a marble corner. In his head flashed Khlebnikov's words: "As waters of distant lakes behind the dark boughs of a willow, the sisters' eyes were silent, but they were beautiful."[42]

Lyova wasn't mistaken: directly at him, darkening with affection, shone the eyes of two sisters, two scholars, Alissa and Larissa. Beautifully planted heads swayed back and forth, *and the sisters' breasts fluttered, just like the Gulf of Joy and Tranquility* in the midst of the whipped up sea of "Nashsharabi." Lyova dashed off. "Can a little spot be found here for a walking anachronism, pterodactyl, mammothsaur?" he babbled in faltering speech.

"Sit down, Lev," the sisters answered simply.

*"Girls of Russia!"* the idol mumbled through his teeth,[43] dunking a small tuft of his forelock into the "Rkatsiteli" wine[44] in the glass before him—"they will not spurn you or deceive you... Maybe, you... you are the feminine ideal of which Blok, Tsiolkovsky,[45] and I have dreamed all

our lives... Maybe, you both... you are personifications of the Beautiful Lady, you... I love you. And words like that aren't spoken in vain!"

Meanwhile, the next incident took place in the restaurant. Syracuzers and his girlfriend replaced Professor Willington in the limelight. Princess Adzharagam, dressed in a sari that was iridescent like a spot of crude oil, was swimming like a peahen, that is, just like a Georgian woman, and was manufacturing purely enigmatic, Indian movements with her arms. Meanwhile, the bull of the meat industry, having thrust out his stony belly which was strapped in a raspberry-colored vest, was acting silly as he smoked his forty-dollar cigar. The sight would have been tolerable if the multi-millionaire hadn't suddenly begun to sing:

> Hardly anyone here will say, I dare,
> He seriously knows about billionaires.
> Yet, meanwhile, right here's Odessa's grandson
> Who's a master, wheeler-dealer businessman.
> I like gobbling up the little nations,
> Without any foolish hallucinations.
> And I innundate the continents
> At exactly the right moments!
> With their bitter groans, Papuan lieges
> Eat up only pseudo-sausages;
> The English people gulp down neat,
> But despairingly, pseudo-meat...
> I just love the cataclysms
> And the paroxysms of capitalism!
> I have dreams of profits with my eyes shut;
> No, not of any losses—I despise their guts!!

On another occasion, Lyova would have given the high-handed shark a worthy rebuke, but now he only growled: "There you have it, the morals of a yellow devil! No matter how much caviar you feed them, they've still got greedy appetites."[46]

Having said this, he once again turned to the sisters:

"Alissa, Larissa, would you be able to love me?"

"Oh, stop it, what nonsense!" the sisters broke out laughing. "How can we love you, Lyova? We're writing dissertations about you. Now I'm the philologist and I'm writing a study called 'From Sumarokov to Malakhitov,' and I'm the chemist writing a study on 'Certain Problems of Coagulation in Light of 'Discourse on Cooking Salt'...' Would you be able to answer a series of questions for us?"

"But what about love?!" Lyova asked, perplexed. "And what about the idea of the Majestic Eternal Feminine?"

130

"Oh, stop it," the sisters began giggling. "How can you love your dissertation topic?"

"How so?" Lyova uttered longingly. "And why not? I mean, hey, ain't I a human being, too?"

He got up, wobbly. Princess Adzharagam swam past. Lyova, half exhausted mentally and physically, swam after her.

"Madame, my dame, am I not really a human being? Couldn't you, tired of the luxury and whimsies of a multi-millionaire, love me—a simple, poor, prominent fellow? However you like—carnivorously or platonically—just love me!"

"In general I don't have anything to do with men, especially during the first week of a full moon," the princess answered in Hindu.

"Oh why, oh why don't women love me?" the public idol cried, stopping in the middle of the room.

A burst of laughter was his answer. The baby foxes and bunny rabbits, having already dispersed throughout the dining room, roared with laughter together with all the rest.

"Oi, no more or we'll die laughing! The women don't love Malakhitov!"

*"Gals, I'd give myself to him with my eyes shut, only it's frightening— it's Malakhitov, after all!"*

"The women don't love him! I'll die!"

A creampuff-bodied lady, the director of the Photographic Studio in Stoleshnikov Lane, hooted:

"Comrade Malakhitov, would you be surprised if I were to invite you to dance?"

"Invite! Invite me!" Lyova begged.

"No, I could never dare do that! I do have a favor to ask, though, comrade Malakhitov: Come to our studio with your championship medals!"

Lyova flung himself to one side, searching within the guffawing dining room for an empathetic, deeply touched face. In vain. The whole "Nashsharabi" thundered, the night was a success! The joke that "women don't love Lyova Malakhitov" whizzed around the room like ball-lightning, smiting everyone out right. And as for the confidant of school-day sheenanigans, Seryoga Babintsev, he was bathing in the rays of his own fame already and telling inspired lies to the young specialists who sat around him: "Lyova and I clambered all over the Caucasus, old man. Once, at Klukhorsky Pass we drank ourselves blotto."[47]

And only one person, Yuf Smelldishchev, having crossed his hands over his chest, was standing next to the serving table; in his mesopotamian eyes Lyova again spotted the approaching yellow flares. Responding unconsciously and uncontrollably to their call, Lyova began to draw near, but he was seized by the hand by an elder comrade—his longtime instructor in billiards, horse-racing, and descriptive geometry—Helmut Osipovich Lygern, now director of one of the film studios. They embraced with a kiss.

"Helmut Osipovich, I've had a frightful day today," Lyova said bitterly. "I learned that I've become a walking anachronism and that women definitely do not love me. You, as an old comrade of mine, ought to have some understanding..."

"That's ashes and smoke," Lygern brushed it aside, "your 'Large Swings' received the grand-prix in Acapulco. Have you heard? Now that's hot stuff! And you're grieving about women! Listen, Levka, you have any new ideas along our line, about cinematography? We've waited a long time."

"New ideas?" Lyova laughed ironically. "Everyone demands new ideas from me, and you're no exception, Helmut Osipovich." He laughed again, this time mischievously. "Here's a new idea for your enterprise. You ought to set fire to Studio 6."

"Set fire, how so?" Lygern asked matter of factly, already scribbling the "idea" into his notebook.

"Soak it in kerosene and put a match to it."

"Sensible," Lygern mumbled, "sensible, sensible..."

Two bleached blondes ambled past them and gazed intently at Lyova, with perhaps more than a look of business interest.

"But why, why! don't women love me, Helmut Osipovich?!" Lyova cried out, in genuine despair.

"That's nonsense, I'll arrange it for you," Lygern mumbled, developing Lyova's idea in his notebook.

Lyova jumped up again and tore off through the length of the dining room into the buffet, to Roza Naumovna, whom he always held live in his memory as a lady of pleasant exterior and kind personality, even though Roza Naumovna was already, at least partially, an old woman.

"Women don't love me, Rozochka, little momma," Lyova cried, being crowded by the shapely "Nashsharabi" waitresses. "No one loves me except an unattainable Tahitian girl... You say I've got a wife, Rozochka? Not a word about Nina, she's saintly... She's perpetually chastising me and there's cause to do so! Take, for example, today—instead of quietly drinking tea with her and having a conversation about Dostoevsky, I'm here again and everyone wants something from me... everyone is laughing... but the women don't love me..."

"You ought to take off for the Volga, Levchik, for the Yenisei, to the rafts," his snackbar attendant admonished him sincerely, "nearer to the sources..."

"And you, do you love me, little momma—Rozochka?"

Roza Naumovna smiled at her recollections.

"I love you, Levchik, but now I'm already like a mother to you. Or, more exactly, like an auntie..."

"I know, Lyova, why the women don't love you," came a familiar gritty voice behind Lyova's back which sounded like a knife scraping across a skillet. Smelldishchev, yes, it was he who took Malakhitov by the elbow and led him into the restaurant's cambric-velour "changing room" and sat him in an armchair and bent over him.

"Okay, why?" Lyova mumbled and tried hard to laugh it off. "Just why, Yuf, old puddy, don't women love me?"

"Because you are not handsome!" Smelldishchev bellowed out quietly.

Lyova screeched, like a wounded gull.

"What did you say? Yuf, you mean that seriously? Malakhitov is not handsome?"

"Yes, if one must look truth in the eyes, you are very unattractive," Smelldishchev axed away cruelly. "Women love thick wavy hair, but you, Lev, have got a scrubbrush on top. Women adore black or light-blue languishing eyes, but yours, Malakhitov, are buttons, not eyes. Women, of course, like short Roman noses, but your shnozzle, admit it, is even beneath criticism."

Not saying a word more, Lyova dashed out of the "changing room" towards the toilet. Smelldishchev, having grinned with satisfaction, sat down in an armchair and began to wait.

*Meanwhile, the joke of the century had already spread to the kitchen and auxiliary rooms of the "Nashsharabi." Forgotten, the "seywha" boiled and boiled—the cooks were rolling on the floor from laughing so hard.*

*"Whaaat? Is he really having bad luck with the broads?" the chef, Chibar, asked as he poured half a pail of water onto the parched dry "seywha." "But there's been talk that he exchanged four thousand for hard currency."*[48]

*"In general, now, he's got broads hanging everywhere," the waiter Leon said, sucking at his bad tooth, "each is more frightful than the next and the jabber that comes from them—just rotten philosophy. Such 'sophy that your bald patch would corrode before you could figure it out... Yuck, I hate it!" he ended, with unexpected passion.*

Fifteen minutes later Malakhitov reappeared in the "changing room." He was walking with his head lowered, with the face of a clearly unhandsome man.

"You were right, Yuf, old puddy," he blabbed thickly. "I examined myself from all angles. All true—the straw brush, the buttons, and the nose—nothing special... No wonder women don't love me. What the hell, it's never too late to discover bitter truths. Yes, Malakhitov's an unattractive man."

"But meanwhile, through me, a certain lady has arranged a rendez-vous with you," Smelldishchev said, his voice vibrating with tension.

"That's all in the past now," Lyova said. "How could I possibly go to a rendezvous with such a mug as mine?"

Weakened, he lowered himself onto the canopy bed of pile velvet; his head began to spin, his eyeballs were filled with lead, the surrounding reality began to be transformed into fog, and out of this dreamy fog the vibrating voice of Smelldishchev once again floated to his ears.

"And meanwhile this lady picked you out from among hundreds of others! Let's go!"

. . . . . . . . . . . . . . . . . . . . . . . . . . . . . . . . . . . . . . . . . . . . . . . . . . . . . . . . . . . . . . . . . . . . . .

He pitched the popular coat onto Lyova's shoulders, pulled the "flap-ears" on over his head, and shoved him out into the whistling, storming Moscow night. Like mudded yellow spots, occasional lamplights lit the way in the whitish fog. Wildly and incoherently, the trees on the boulevard creaked and creaked.

"Where in hell are we going?" Lyova asked. "What district does she live in? Hey, wait up, Yuf, old puddy, why are you grabbing me like that? Where's my puss-puss then, eh?"

He eyed the line of snowbanks, trying to guess under which one of them his "Moskvich" was sleeping. Yuf held him in steely embraces. A police patrol car rode past, noiselessly. Lyova suddenly felt, for some reason, like calling for help, but he just marveled at the absurdity of this thought.

"There's my 'Moskvich'!" he cried out. "There's my joy!"

"That beasty won't take us anywhere," Smelldishchev gnashed his teeth. "Let's search for some other transportation."

He suddenly grabbed Lyova and raced him through the blizzard, yes, so rapidly and forcefully that no transportation, seemingly, was necessary. Lyova barely succeeded in shifting his almost unnecessary legs and kept muttering something about the rush being in vain—say, is it worth it, for me to rush, with this external appearance?—but the wind whistled and howled.

Yuf gave him no reply, but he somehow did growl strangely and frighteningly in a voice boiling with anger. Then he twisted his head around and flashed his right eye—behind them loomed the headlight of a police motorcycle. Yuf impetuously crossed the square, leapt behind a corner, and having straight away saddled an asphalt roller left by workers for the night, pulled Lyova to him with a jerk. The roller moved off slowly, then built up to a speed which was abnormal for its build, and accelerated along the axial thruway—under the automatic traffic lights. Patrol cars encountered this strange crew twice, but it didn't even enter the policemen's minds to stop it. Once they'd noticed Lyova's lanky figure on the roller, the officers only laughed kindheartedly: Malakhitov's clowning around again...

"Yuf, old puddy, where oh where're we, hee-hee, rolling off to? Now where's this lady of yours? Pulling my leg, eh?"

"There'll be a lady, there'll be one," Smelldishchev uttered as if forcing himself, and glanced at Lyova with one of his mesopotamian eyes and laughed internally.

*An almost forgotten foundation pit from a construction project closed down at some point has existed at the outskirts of Moscow since time immemorial. For several decades all kinds of legends circulated about this foundation pit and the construction project, but then the tales came to bore Muscovites and were forgotten. However, one was preserved. It reads:*

> *In a remote epoch there lived in Moscow maybe a merchant, maybe a prince, maybe a bandit from the high road, or, in short, a well-to-do man. This man had a love—maybe a German, maybe a Tartar, maybe an Egyptian—who passed on to eternal peace with God. The merchant decided to immortalize theese madaamie, and namely—by building a very high palazzo. A palazzo half a kilometer in height, like the contemporary our favorite Ostankino,[49] and on the top for theese palazzo to have the figure of a laaaaday—lifesize height, that is namely a casino in the breasts, and, in the head, itself a bit larger than a four-story house, the adminstrative offices of his (button-making) firm. The finger of that lady was ought to be pointed to the sky and on the finger a ring or, in essence, a round balcony along which our swindler had intentions to go for walks. Here's what kind of crime was being plotted against healthy thought and human good tastes. The funniest thing is that the project would have been realized, but revolution washed away the countless wealth of the prince and flung him personally beyond the borders of our world. Since then there has remained near Moscow a round, sinister foundation pit with some sort of stakes, lakelets of tainted water and bundles of birch trees which have grown up through the concrete.*

*Precisely here it was that Smelldishchev led our idol, Lyova Mala-khitov.*[50]

The depressing site appeared in front of Lyova. Like a lunar crater, only filled with snow and with bundles of rusty armatures of a sinister configuration jutting up here and there. New construction projects in the capital were already approaching fairly near to this bad place: no further away than one and a half kilometers there loomed the skeleton of nine-storey buildings, where occasional windows of weirdo nightowls and the neon signs of hairdressing salons were lit up. A warm, human world was very close, but here the wind howled with such convincing terror that Lyova understood there was no road back.

"What devil possessed me to agree to this rendezvous?" the despairing, belated thought flashed through his mind. "Indeed, how many times have I sworn not to agree to a rendezvous of this sort..."

"So the lady, it seems, didn't show up, Yuf?" he said with a nervous laugh. "Well, given the little lady's absence, we can split and go home, eh?"

Smelldishchev didn't answer. He stood exposed to the wind, stretched his hands out at his side in rapt concentration, like a rocket before take-off.

"Let's wait five minutes or so to cleanse the conscience and then scram," Lyova said with simulated courage as he jumped up and down and clapped his mittens together. "Otherwise, you know, old puddy, this freezing lambaster will drill its punches right through to the bones."

Smelldishchev rose up into the air. The stupefied Lyova watched as "old puddy Yuf" slowly but surely soared higher. At about thirty meters from the earth, Smelldishchev stopped his movement and, having spread wide his extremities, hung above Lyova like a helicopter. This, undoubtedly, was really a security-guard helicopter or, to speak more precisely, a tipster. Her tipster.

"So that then, I see, is what sort you are, Malakhitov the rather famous." Lyova heard behind him a voice not devoid of pleasantness. He turned slowly around and saw...

On a block of ferro-concrete sat Lady. In spite of the night's darkness, Lyova could discern all the features of this Lady absolutely clearly, and therefore we, too, will have to describe this person's external appearance and dress in detail.

She was rather large. An excellent boa of black fox-fur covered her voluminous bosom. One hand of the Lady, dry and disfigured, with sclerotic veins, was decorated with expensive rings and bracelets, the other, similar to the arm of a heavy-weight weightlifter, was corseted to the shoulder in a black glove. The Lady's stomach was covered by very thin chiffon through which there shone the most diverse tattoo designs, beginning with a primitive little heart pierced by an arrow and ending with a most intricately needled frigate. From the shoulders, in majestic folds, there fell a cloak of pile velvet. Lady had the heavy face of a free-style wrestler, but it set off beautifully the Cupid's bow shape of her crimson lips. Her hair was permed in pretty little ringlets and her head was crowned with a fashionable hat that looked like a propeller.

"Recognize me, Malakhitov?" Lady asked in a cordially patronizing tone.

"It stands to reason, I recognize you," Lyova answered in a quivering voice.

"Why then do you abhor me?" Lady asked in an emotional woman-like fashion. "Aren't I really a beauty?"

She stood up and drew closer, limping in the felt boot on her dry leg, but, by way of compensation, hoisting her other one—naked but for the pink garters—in a can-can step. She flapped her cloak and, with a suddenly stony face, assumed the pose of a powerful athlete. Then, evidently unable to endure the strain, she grasped her side and ooh-ed, but quickly regained her composure and gave Lyova a smile that promised lots.

"Why then do you abhor me?" she cooed tenderly.

"I don't abhor you at all," Lyova mumbled haltingly. "I don't abhor you, not one little drop."

"You abhor!" Lady bellowed, bared her good teeth and suddenly burst into sobs. "Do you really think of me, Lev? Did you actually remember me during that match with the Canadians? Why don't you refer to me in your poems? Ahh, I can't find any feeling for me in your violin and saxophone improvisations, but at times...,"—Lady suddenly frowned meanacingly, roared with a menacing voice—"at times you even spurn me, and I, after all, love you sincerely..." Having cast him a fleetingly crafty look, Lady lifted her little skirt a bit, as if to fix a garter on her healthy, full leg. And, as a result, a thigh was exposed from which there grew a wriggling little worm.

"Why oh why, my friend, lieber Freund, cher ami, do you shun your Lady?"

She hobbled forward still closer to Lyova, brought her Roman face near—the one now significantly more weighted down (if one doesn't) consider the lips), and held out her healthy arm in the black glove.

"Why?"

"Because you are Stinking Lady!" Lyova shouted with a tremble, but not without a small amount of courage, too.

He waited for a thunderous outburst, a deafening hiss, a blow, an eruption, whatever, but nothing followed. Lady, having lowered her arms, stood in a kind of helpless, almost doomed pose. Only in her face did certain changes take place: slowly, her mouth and eyes widened, and in them there appeared a yellow light.

"Understand," Lyova began speaking hastily and inconsistently, "I don't have anything against... I even... in my opinion, more than once... of course, you know... I expressed myself respectfully, but you request passionate love and this I... am not able... physically not fit... as for 'stinking' I take that back... it slipped off my tongue, forgive me, you simply... are not to my taste... partially... although I also acknowledge certain of your charms... you..."

The eyes and mouth had already dazzled him. He glanced upwards in horror—above him, extremities outstretched, hovered four Smelldish-chevs.

"Nope, I won't kiss you!" Lyova cried out furiously and fell on his back into soft, powdery, white snow, into the deep pit. "Go to 'Nash-sharabi'! There'll you find yourself a suitor..."

He will never, never kiss even the hems of this Lady's dress. She's not his Lady. This is a nashsharabian, underground, rotten, second-hand, delirious, under-the-counter, camphor-reeking spawn of the spider tribe which has strayed through the back streets of Moscow since ancient times. Let her promise you alcoholic, tumultuous fame and lure you with casks of soft-black caviar, the most delicate suede, and the least rustling of silk hats, with furs of otter and nutria skinned alive, but know!—you lay a finger on her and there's no getting away, she will suck from you everything, your mind, honor, youthful cleverness, talent, and your love. It's better to perish!

He no longer noticed that Lady, having lost all interest in him, was ooh-ing and ahh-ing as she hobbled away—grasping at the rusted armature. Nor did he see how the Smelldishchevs attached their hooks to a concrete slab and lowered it onto his powdery warm pit.

Morning was remarkable for its unexpected brilliance and ruddiness—"frost and sun, a marvelous day"[51] ... Lyova came to and spotted a narrow strip of sunlight which filtered like a needle through the concrete tombstone.

"Wow, I went and overdid it yesterday," Lyova frowned. "Shame, shame ... What the hell? Where in the devil have I ended up?"

He tried to raise the slab, but it stands to reason he was not so fortunate. He tried to dig out under the slab, but neither the snow nor the earth even stirred.

"Hey, what's with me, huh?" Lyova thought with fear. "What sort of foolishness is this? To tell the truth, can't feel the cold at all. Must shout, shout, notify fellow humans that Malakhitov's covered by a concrete slab ... after all, I've got practice today, got to be photographed in Stoleshnikov, and Nina ... O God!"

Suddenly, quite near, motors revved up and hoarse voices were heard to say "heave! ho! start it up, in reverse" and a lot of unprinted and unprintable expressions. Lyova watched as steel cables were attached under the slab and then an automatic crane revved up its motor and lifted the slab into the light-blue sky ... Lyova scrambled out of the pit and saw that the whole "crater" was full of bulldozers and cranes and workers moving sluggishly here and there. Apparently, the city authorities had taken measures to clean up the evil emptiness and to build on it something useful and pleasant to the eye.

"Thanks, guys, you rescued me!" Lyova shouted to the workers. "I overdid it a bit last night, who doesn't now and then ..."

The workers didn't pay the slightest bit of attention to this famous person. They stood at the edge of the pit and morosely looked downward. Lyova shrugged his shoulders and took off for the city. He walked with a lightness surprising even for him, as if he were swimming through the air. With pleasure he watched people rushing to the metro and the puffs of cigarette smoke in the crowd and the newspapers rustling in people's hands. It was pleasant for Lyova to see these faces so robust in the bitter frost, to feel himself a part of the crowd, and he promised himself to begin from this time forward a new life.

A strange thing happened in the metro. Lyova popped all his five-kopeck coins into the automat, but the go-sign just didn't flash. Behind him people were pressing forward, grumbling in bewilderment. Lyova shrugged his shoulders and walked through the turnstile freely—the machine didn't even register his passage.

In the train an elderly skier sat down on him. Lyova sensed no uncomfortableness because of this; he was merely taken aback at the skier's lack of propriety. There was something surprising in this—to come right up to a person and simply sit down on him.

"I didn't settle up"—the frightening thought suddenly flashed through Lyova's mind. "I didn't settle up yesterday at the 'Nashsharabi'." He rushed to the exit and, already in the doors, caught the reflection of the ill-mannered old man who was sitting in the very same pose, with his pear-nose on exhibit.

In spite of the early hour, the dreamers were already on patrol near the "Nashsharabi." Lyova gave a start from habit, but obviously the dreamers had totally turned to salt from their expectations—they didn't even crane their necks towards the nation's idol. Andrianych also didn't raise an eyebrow to answer Lyova's greeting.

Lyova entered the foyer and was amazed at the quiet and freshness which reigned there. All tables were arranged in long rows, covered with starched tablecloths, and set with a modest, clean-looking breakfast: smoking pots of coffee, crisp rolls, cream, jam. There was no hint of the rancid smell of yesterday's "seywha."

At the tables sat Lyova's friends and associates in complete silence: soccer and hockey players on the national teams—Maiorov brothers, Starshinov, Yashin, Chislenko; the poets Evtushenko, Voznesensky, and Rozhdestvensky; Tigran Petrosian, Spassky; Jean-Luc Goddard and Marina Vlady; John Updike, Arthur Miller; Dmitri Shostakovich, Academician Lavrentyev; Armstrong and Ella Fitzgerald; the cosmonauts Leonov and Armstrong-Aldrin; Sartre; Vysotsky and Konenkov; Vitsin, Nikulin, and Morgunov...and many other well-known and kind persons. [52]

Lyova stopped on the threshold, raised his hand unsurely in greeting, and his soul contracted—he had never experienced a more frightening moment.

And suddenly, far back at the rear of the dining room, a little door opened...

Someone tall, tan and feminine, with luminous dark-blue eyes and in a white dress—wasn't it the wife, Nina, saintly and inaccessible?—moved towards him and there was love in her eyes.

"Am I really saved?" thought Lyova. "Really saved, saved, saved?"

1968

# Notes

*This story was translated from the text published by the emigre firm "Silver Age" in 1981, which differs in several places from the original publication in the Soviet literary journal *Avrora* in May 1971. The *Avrora* version is shorter thanks to the cuts made by the censors. The segments of the work which were restored in the "Silver Age" publication are designated in our translation by the use of italics. However, some of these changes were minor and these differences can be summarized as follows: "Darling of the people" (p. 112) and "the people's darling" (p. 113) were both changed to "the darling of the public." "Although, it's true, under the rubric 'Their Morals' " (p. 114) read "although, it's true, with a misleading caption [v perevernutom vide]." The designation "active public figure [deiatel']" replaced "Komsomol member" (p. 115 of our translation); the inconclusive "but . . ." stood in for "but not with such voluntarism. mark my words, that's how it'll be" (p. 121). The phrase "Yehudi Menuhin's bow" (p. 121) was changed to "Oistrakh's bow" and the phrase "Girls of Russia!" (p. 129) to "Girls of Moscow!" Certain names were changed in the long list of cultural figures which comes towards the end of the story; these changes are explained in note 52.

1. Plants producing military equipment in the Soviet Union are commonly called P. O. Boxes. It is a state crime to reveal where such plants are located.

2. GAI (pronounced "guy-ee") is the acronym for the Traffic Control Department. The abbreviation is used so often that it has replaced the official name of this administrative department in colloquial speech.

3. Salieri was an Italian composer and friend of Wolfgang Amadeus Mozart. According to legend, Salieri poisoned Mozart out of envy for the latter's talent. In Russian culture this legend became well-known thanks to A. S. Pushkin's "little tragedy" *Mozart and Salieri,* written in 1830.

4. Gorky Street is one of the main roads in downtown Moscow; it runs north from Manezh and Red Squares and has many shops which attract local residents and tourists. (See note 9 to *Surplussed Barrelware*).

5. Maurice Richard, nicknamed "Rocket," was one of the most famous Canadian hockey players of the 1950s. He spent 18 years with the Montreal "Canadiens" and had 544 regular season goals. According to his contemporaries and peers, Richard's accomplishments came largely as a result of his sharp instincts and brute strength. Aksyonov's descriptions of Richard are corroborated by the recollections of Richard's playing by Gus Hall, a goalie with the Detroit and Chicago teams: "When he came flying towards you with the puck on his stick, his eyes flashing and gleaming like a pinball machine, it was terrifying."

6. The "Kelowna Packers" are a hockey team from Kelowna, British Columbia (population approx. 60,000), which has travelled to the USSR to play exhibition games with Soviet teams.

7. Konstantin Loktiev, Alexandr Almetov, Veniamin Alexandrov, Boris and Evgeny Maiorov, and Vyacheslav Starshinov were the most popular Soviet hockey players in the 1960s. The first three played for the team of the Central Sports Committee of the Red Army (TsSKA), the second threesome for the Moscow team "Spartak." These two teams were the main contenders for the Soviet national championship in the decade of the sixties. During the specially organized tournament in the late 1960s between Canadian and Soviet national hockey teams, the six players mentioned above made up the first and second line units at the position of forwards.

8. The *Jen min jih pao* is the newspaper of the Chinese Communist Party. The rubric "Their Morals" is a heading under which Soviet newspapers report all kinds of oddities and curiosities in Western bourgeois life.

9. The Russian Father Frost is an equivalent of the West's Santa Claus, Saint Nicholas, etc. Therefore, he is portrayed as being fat, red-nosed, and white-bearded in the Soviet Union, too. Nowadays, Father Frost appears at New Year's celebrations, not on the religious holiday commemorating the birth of Christ, and he is often accompanied by his daughter, Snowmaiden. For the New Year's parties Russian children often dress up in costumes and masks to look like forest animals, fairytale characters, or cultural heroes (the curious names in the text are fairytale characters who have become the subject of children's plays and cartoons).

10. Mikhail Tal and Tigran Petrosian are famous Soviet chess grandmasters. Each of them was a World Champion: Tal in 1960-61 and Petrosian in 1963-69. Bobby Fischer is the greatest American chessplayer. (See note 111 to *Surplussed Barrelware*).

11. "Stavrogin's Confession" is a chapter (sometimes titled "At Tikhon's") in Dostoevsky's novel *The Possessed*. Censors objected to inclusion of this chapter in the novel on the grounds that the subject matter (the atheist Stavrogin's complicity in the sordid death of a young girl named Matryosha) was unsuitable for the general public and Dostoevsky acquiesced. Thus, this section of the novel was not included in editions of *The Possessed* published during Dostoevsky's lifetime. Subsequently, some critics have considered this chapter central to the novel as a whole and essential for understanding the complexities and sordid aspects of Stavrogin's personality.

12. Lyova uses the word 'filin' (eagle owl) as an endearment for his wife Nina and this term implies that she wears glasses. *Bubo bubo* is the Latin term for this bird and we have used it since it sounds more like a nickname in English than does 'eagle owl'.

13. Viktor Shklovsky (1893-      ) is a Soviet Russian writer, philologist and literary critic. In the 1920s he was one of the leading figures of the Society for Studies of Poetic Language (known by its acronym OPOYAZ) and one of the founders of the Formalist school of literary criticism. Shklovsky considered literature to be the sum of certain literary devices and invented the term "ostranenie" (estrangement) to describe one literary device which he felt was particularly felicitous for reviving and revitalizing poetic language. In the 1930s both Shklovsky and the Formalists fell into disrepute in the Soviet Union and were heavily criticized for their approach to the study of literature. In the 1960s, however, Shklovsky became a father figure for young writers, like Aksyonov, and critics; his new-found popularity was one of the phenomena associated with the cultural and political "thaws" of this decade and, likewise, with the worldwide interest in the ideas of the French Structuralists, who advanced theories similar to and somewhat derivative of those advanced earlier by Russian Formalists.

14. David Fyodorovich Oistrakh (1908-74) and Igor Stravinsky (1882-1971) are world-famous musicians of Russian birth. Oistrakh was a noted violinist and Stravinsky a renowned composer.

15. Izmailovo is a district (*raion*) in the southwestern part of Moscow.

16. There is something peculiar about Lyova's purchase of a Soviet car in "Italy." Perhaps, the reader is to understand that he bought it for hard currency in order to avoid the usual three- to four-year waiting period if one purchases a car in the USSR in roubles. A second interpretation would be that Lyova bought one of the Italian Fiats which are produced in the Soviet Union under the brand name "Zhiguli."

17. Marfa Posadnitsa was a fifteenth-century patriot and 'posadnitsa' (governor) of the city-state of Novgorod who led her people in the unsuccessful resistance to efforts by the princes of Muscovy to bring Novgorod under their control. Modest Mussorgsky wrote an opera called *Marfa Posadnitsa* which is based on this historical figure.

18. This paragraph reconstructs Lyova's trek through the center of Moscow. The Central Telegraph Office is located on the corner of Gorky and Ogaryov Streets, four blocks from Red Square. There is no sentry box there. Manezh Square is situated just to the north of and adjacent to Red Square; it takes its name from the building on it which housed a show-ring for horse-riding before the Revolution and now functions as the Central Exhibition Hall. It was

in this building that the famous Exhibit of Young Moscow Artists took place in 1962 which began the chain of events that led to the row mentioned in notes 102 and 103 of *Surplussed Barrelware*. Bronnivitsky Gate is the fictional form for Borovitsky Gate, the public entrance to the Kremlin; it is situated right behind the Manezh building.

19. The quote is from Alexander Blok's play *The Rose and the Cross*, written in 1912 and published in 1918. Specifically, the lines translated here are the first five lines of the song sung by Gaetan in Act II, Scene III.

20. The Central Children's Theater is located near the Bolshoi Theater on Moscow's Theater Square. This theater specializes in productions for young audiences; its performances for the youngest children include adaptations of fairytales in which various animals are played by special actresses (*travesti*-Russ.) who act professionally in children's theater.

21. These words are the third line of Act I, Scene I in Alexander Blok's play *The Rose and the Cross*.

22. These words follow those annotated in the preceding footnote, i.e., as line 4 of Act I, Scene I of *The Rose and the Cross*.

23. The quote is from Sergei Esenin's poem "I neither pity, nor call, nor cry . . ." (See note 93 to *Surplussed Barrelware*.)

24. The word "voluntarism" is used incorrectly in Russian by the manager. In modern colloquial Russian this word is often mistakenly employed to mean "an act of independent will which goes beyond that which is necessary or expected" and is therefore considered to be "voluntary" action.

25. "The Tale of Tsar Saltan" is a poetic fairytale by A. S. Pushkin. In this tale the prince Gvidon shoots a buzzard which tries to kill the swan princess. Baba Yaga is the traditional witch and, often, a villain in Russian fairytales.

26. Pollitrovich and Zakusonsky are telling surnames. The first derives from the word for a "half-liter bottle" (i.e., of vodka) and the second from the noun for "snacks." Thus, Baba Yaga is saying that he works in order to get enough money for something to drink and a bite to eat.

27. The phrase "the best of our generation, take me for your trumpeter" is taken from Yevgeny Yevtushenko's poem of 1957 called "The Best of Our Generation" ("Luchshie iz pokoleniia"). "Fellows with upturned collars" is the title of a poem in Robert Rozhdestvensky's collection of verse *Radius deistviia (The Radius of Action*, Moscow, 1965).

28. Nikolai Ghiaurov is a famous Bulgarian opera singer with a deep bass voice. In 1960 he became a member of Milan's *La Scala* company. Yehudi Menuhin is a world famous violin player. Viktor Konovalenko is a popular Soviet hockey goalie who played on national and Olympic teams in the 1960s. Yevgeny Yevtushenko is one of the popular Soviet poets of the 1960s who has taken to writing prose and acting in recent years. Valery V. Popenchenko (1937-75) was a famous Soviet boxer; he won European titles in 1963 and 1965, an Olympic medal in 1964.

29. In the phrase "a trifle internally he gnashed his internal teeth," there is a suggestion that the Buzzard in some way is affiliated with the police agents of the Ministry of the Interior (MVD).

30. Maxim's (Paris; 3 rue Royale), Waldorf-Astoria (New York; Park Avenue), and Nashsharabi (fictional) are linked together as restaurants where people go in order to be seen more than to dine. Maxim's and the Waldorf-Astoria became fashionable haunts of the very wealthy at the turn of the century; Maxim's celebrated its 75th anniversary in 1968.

31. "Wild melody of the clarinet" is a line of verse from Nikolai Gumilyev's poem "You and I" ("Ja i vy"), which is one of the works in his collection *Campfire (Koster*, 1918).

32. Thor Heyerdahl is the Swedish scientist and explorer famous for his Kon-Tiki and Ra voyages. He was one of the few foreign scientists who became a well-known figure in the Soviet Union during the 1960s. A Soviet doctor named Yury Senkevich took part in Heyerdahl's second Ra expedition from Peru to the Pacific islands.

33. Jean-Luc Godard is a French film director who, during the 1960s, was a leading

representative of "cinéma vérité." Marina Vlady is a French movie actress of Russian descent who married the Soviet bard Vladimir Vysotsky, who died during the time of the 1980 Olympic Games in Moscow.

34. There is a Russian saying that a person with two crow's tails on the back of his head (or with two "crowns") will be very lucky in life. Malakhitov must be extraordinarily lucky since he has three such crowns.

35. Ortega y Gasset (1883-1955). The idea of reality mentioned here was developed by Ortega in the book *Neither Vitalism nor Rationalism* (1924). For this Spanish thinker, the true nature of human life is a "radical reality" (*realidad radical*) which is different from philosophical realism ("natural organic" reality) and philosophical idealism ("natural inorganic" reality). Ortega considered that cultural and physical environments give an individual's "I" its existence; he expressed this thought most cogently in the formulaic and famous expression "I am myself plus my circumstances" (*Yo so yo i mia circumstancia*).

36. Friedrich Engels (1820-95) was one of the founders of Marxism and a close friend of Karl Marx. The quote here is from Engel's work *Herr Eugen Duehring's Revolution in Science* (1878, also known as *Anti-Duehring*), which was directed against vulgar materialism.

37. These lines of verse by Vyacheslav Ivanov make up the third stanza of his frequently anthologized poem "Voices" ("Golosa," lines 9-12). Ivanov (1866-1949) was one of the leading Russian Symbolists: his philosophical, aesthetic and critical works expounded the idea that the poet's highest mission is to uncover the "symbol" at the heart of religious myths.

38. Yu. F. Smelldishchev sounds very much like an anglicized form of the surname Smerdishchev (which would mean, roughly, "stinker") and suggests that Aksyonov's character is a fictional "cousin" to Dostoevsky's Smerdyakov of *The Brothers Karamazov*. This correlation is noteworthy because it draws attention to yet another allusion to Dostoevsky's works in this story and because, as such, is a reference not easily perceived by English readers with no knowledge of Russian.

39. "Spearchucker" is our translation of the Russian word "ostroga," which designates a kind of spear used in Siberia to catch fish and, by extension, the soup made from the fish which are caught. It is noteworthy that the word for this type of spear is phonetically similar to the old Russian word for a prison ("ostrog").

40. Tiksi is a port in northern Siberia. There are a lot of secret plants (P.O. Boxes) in the area near Tiksi.

41. In Dostoevsky's *The Possessed*, Tikhon is the monk to whom Stavrogin shows his confession. Not all of Tikhon's advice to Stavrogin can be characterized as "humble words," but in general the monk answers Stavrogin's impudence and bravado with controlled and thoughtful responses. Tikhon is able to penetrate to the depths of Stavrogin's soul and discern his ulterior motives.

42. The quote is from the poem "Three Sisters" by Velimir (Viktor) Khlebnikov (1885-1922). Khlebnikov was a leading poet in the first decade of this century and a leading figure among the Russian Futurists. He published a number of works in which he developed his utopian ideas of completely reorganizing the world. Khlebnikov created a so-called "trans-rational language" and the theory of the "self-contained" word. His extraordinary talents in experimenting with and reforming Russian poetic language distinguished him in the history of Russian literature.

43. "Girls of Russia" is a phrase which did not appear in the first publication of this work in the May 1968 issue of the magazine *Avrora*. Instead, there appeared the phrase "Girls of Moscow." This small detail is indicative of how Malakhitov was reduced from a national to metropolitan figure in the *Avrora* version. The genre classification specified in the magazine publication can be seen, in retrospect, as clear evidence that Aksyonov's full text was not being published; it reads: "Novella, Magazine Version" ("Povest', Zhurnal'nyi variant").

44. Rkatsiteli is a dry Georgian white wine.

45. Alexander Blok is famous for his poems dedicated to the "Beautiful Lady"; Konstantin

Tsiolkovsky (1857-1935), in addition to being a famous inventor and scientist in the field of space-exploration technology, was a writer of science fiction fantasies; his preoccupation with the ideal interplanetary flight coincided with the activity of the Symbolists and Futurists (the latter often spoke of him in their poems). Blok and Tsiolkovsky shared a penchant for utopian ideas, whether the application was to romantic love or flights in space.

46. "The morals of a yellow devil" is an expression which means the power of the dollar. After Maxim Gorky returned from his trip to America in 1906 he wrote the story "The City of the Yellow Devil," castigating the evils of capitalism (specifically in New York City) and his book gave rise to the Russian euphemism used here.

47. Klukhorsky pass (el. 2781 meters) is a divide in the Caucasus mountains through which the Sukhumi Road passes.

48. The fact that there is a rumor that Lyova Malakhitov has exchanged four thousand roubles for hard currency is a hint that the exchange took place illegally, on the black market.

49. Ostankino is the area of Moscow which gave its name to the famous television and radio communications tower of the city.

50. This foundation pit may be an allusion to the project to build the Palace of Congresses in Moscow on the Kropotkinskaya Embankment on the site of the destroyed Church of the Redeemer. The project was conceived during Stalin's rule and called for construction of a huge building in the "wedding-cake" style with a giant figure of Lenin at the top. Lack of funds caused the project to be abandoned. Instead, in the 1960s the swimming pool "Moscow" was built on the site of the once unsightly foundation pit. There may likewise be a mild allusion to the rediscovery and partial rehabilitation of the writer Andrei Platonov in the 1960s and early 1970s (this is suggested by Aksyonov's word for the foundation pit—'kotlovan'—the same as the title of one of Platonov's novels and by the highly colorful speech recorded in the "document").

51. The quote is from A. S. Pushkin's poem "A Winter Morning."

52. Lev Yashin (b. 1929) may have the distinction of being the most popular and famous Soviet soccer player ever; for many years he was the goaltender for the Moscow "Dynamo" team and the national team. Chislenko is also a popular soccer player and a forward on the national team. Andrei Voznesensky and Robert Rozhdestvensky are Soviet poets who came to fame in the 1960s as representatives of "youth literature." Boris Spassky (b. 1937) is a Soviet chess grandmaster and World Champion (1969-72); he lost his title to Bobby Fischer. John Updike is an American author who visited the Soviet Union with a delegation of American writers in the 1960s. In the same decade Updike's book *The Centaur* was one of the most popular works translated into Russian; his popularity was particularly evident among members of the younger generations. In 1979 Updike made a "guest contribution" to the almanac *Metropole*. Arthur Miller is an American playwright who likewise travelled to the Soviet Union in the 1960s and met many literary figures in Moscow; his plays *A View from the Bridge* and *The Price* were produced in the Soviet Union and enjoyed great critical success. Dmitry Shostakovich (1906-75) was one of the Soviet Union's greatest composers. Academician (Mikhail A.) Lavrentyev is a Russian-Soviet mathematician and, since 1946, member of the USSR Academy of Sciences; he was the individual who assumed most of the responsibility for creating the scientific research community of Akademgorodok ( a "think tank" community located near Novosibirsk). Louis (Satchmo) Armstrong and Ella Fitzgerald—American jazz musicians known the world over who have a large group of fans in the USSR. Leonid Leonov is a Soviet cosmonaut, the first man to walk in space. Neil Armstrong was the first man on the moon and, with James Aldrin, one of the American astronauts to fly in the Apollo missions. Jean-Paul Sartre (1905-80) was a French philosopher and existentialist. He was a very popular figure among younger members of the Soviet intelligentsia in the 1960s, both as a philosopher and as a playwright. Vladimir Vysotsky, who died in 1980, was the most popular bard of the 1960s; the first of his songs to be published (the lyrics, that is) appeared in the 1979 almanac *Metropole,* organized and edited by Vassily

Aksyonov and his friends. S. T. Konenkov (1874-1971) was a prominent Soviet sculptor. Vitsin, Yu. V. Nikulin, and Morgunov are popular Soviet movie comedians; Nikulin began his career as a circus clown.

In the *Avrora* publication there appeared a different list of individuals. Following the mention of Chislenko are the [American] poets [W. H.] Auden, [Allen] Ginsburg, and [Lawrence] Ferlinghetti" instead of Yevtushenko, Voznesensky and Rozhdestvensky. John Updike and Arthur Miller are not mentioned, and instead of Dmitry Shostakovich there is the English composer Benjamin Britten and the Soviet highjumper Valery Brumel instead of Academician Lavrentyev. Of the American astronauts, only Neil Armstrong is mentioned and [Duke] Ellington replaced [Louis] Armstrong. No Soviet cosmonaut was included and neither were Vysotsky or Konenkov. Sartre was grouped rather incongruously with [Henry] Moore, the English sculptor.

# Super-Deluxe

Vladislav Ivanovich Vetryakov, the same guy who's Slava to his friends and Gibbon to his most intimate circle of friends . . . dot-dot-dot. You and I look around in confusion: the predicate must be either lost or not yet found, for we still don't know where to put our hero—on what dot of the map, in what circumstances and environment, or what action to offer him. So meanwhile, let's handle his nickname: Gibbon, that's a strange one, eh? It is, as we indeed all know, a species of monkey; yet I must tell you there's nothing monkey-like about Vladislav Ivanovich's appearance. Quite to the contrary, from the first moment of acquaintance people are struck by his admirable humanity, and we would also like to draw attention to the particular sparkle in his eyes. Such eyes are the mark of a person capable of admiring the objective world and seeing in it not just a heap of things, but also the fascination of various prospects. That's how I'd describe his eyes to the reader. As for the nickname Gibbon, it all began as a joke: he was in the sauna with his closest friends, or rather, they were having a good time drinking vast quantities of "Carlsberg,"[1] telling anecdotes and stories, and generally goofing around. Tarasian began to imitate an elephant, Lyova a dying swan, and Vladislav Ivanovich— dangling his arms down to the floor—started to hop up and down in front of the mirror and to shout "I'm a gibbon! I'm a gibbon!" And would you believe it, neither the elephant nor the swan stuck, but "gibbon" did— Slava, the Gibbon. To tell the truth, there were certain grounds for this nickname to stick to Vladislav Ivanovich: phylogenesis had for some reason meted out to him longish arms and an excessively hairy body, but these insignificant external characteristics didn't hit you in the eye. Especially if rather than fooling around in a Finnish sauna, you were riding in a taxi dressed in a really fine blue flannel suit, lightly tapping a product of the Italian shoemakers' art, peering through fantastic French glasses with an amiable and almost rapt expression as you view the world, Odessa's Seashore Boulevard, the statue of the Duc de Richelieu,[2] and the panorama of the harbor with large snow-white ships at its center. So, having found a place for our hero, let's forget about the nickname Gibbon in order to fill our hearts with admiration for this wonderful citizen, Vladislav Ivanovich Vetryakov, who looks like a theoretical physicist and, moreover, one who has travelled the world. "It's staggering!" said Vetryakov, "just staggering!"

"What's staggering?" asked the cab driver gloomily.

"Well, all this! Odessa, the port, the ship!"

The cab driver cast a suspicious glance from under his long hair, as though he were wondering if he had a nut for a fare.

They came to a stop right by the huge hull of the liner "Caravan." Vetryakov handed the cab driver a fifty-rouble bill. It was a crackling, new, rather large note, of a quite pleasant greenish color. Vladislav Ivanovich had decided long ago that if a person had a taste for money he should begin with fifty-rouble bills. Ten-rouble bills are just like slightly off-pink slices of veal; twenty-five-rouble notes are such an indecent size and have such a repulsive and faded color. One- and three-rouble bills?.. well, I'll tell you frankly, Vladislav Ivanovich didn't have a really clear idea what use it was for the Treasury to print those under-ten smallfry, all those rumpled wads of skin, little clods, dead sparrows... no, no, they all look so ridiculous! A man of taste ought to set his sights exclusively on the design of the half-hundreds.

"No change," the cab driver said and handed the bill back. "Don't earn that much money in two days even."

"Cheer up, friend! Keep the change!" said Vladislav Ivanovich.

"Now *that's* staggering!" muttered the stunned cab driver.

Having picked up his suitcase and "attache" briefcase, Vladislav Ivanovich began to walk up the gangway of the snow-white giant. He was bursting with song and so was everything around. On board the "Caravan" songstress Parkhomenko was singing "Oh, you nights, sailors' nights!"[3] And Vetryakov sang in his soul a song from his childhood days in the young pioneers: "In Capetown Port with cacao on board." The duty-officer was talking on the phone with someone when he took Vetryakov's ticket. However, once he'd glanced at it, he hung up the receiver and gave Vladislav Ivanovich a respectful and attentive look. It was, after all, a ticket for the 900-rouble super-deluxe cabin. This way, please! Be so kind! Please, here's the elevator! Lyuda, show the gentleman, please, to number 02! Lyuda—haughty, pink-cheeked and all acrackle, the embodiment of inaccessibility—opened the mahogany door beyond which a kind of miracle of comfort was immediately revealed. "Just a minute, Lyuda!" "Don't give me that 'minute' come-on, I'm on duty!" "No, no, you misunderstood me. This is just to celebrate our getting acquainted. Maybe you'll find it useful. I hope you won't be offended, it's just a trifle..." The passenger fussily snapped open his suitcase and in a second the cabin stewardess was holding a box of "Madame Rochas" perfume, a whole ounce. Oh, mother dear! On her trips abroad Lyuda hadn't even dared to glance at such things. "Well, well, Lyuda, well, I see you're happy, and I'm glad that you're happy, of course, because happiness is very becoming to you."

"My goodness, comrade, what are you... Oh, mother dear, you really shouldn't comrade..."

148

"Vladislav Ivanovich Vetryakov, a physicist. I'm a physicist, Lyuda, do you understand? It's really nothing for me."

Lyuda let the physicist into the super-deluxe cabin with a certain amount of caution and, standing a safe distance away, showed him the refrigerator (Italian!), bathroom (entirely Swedish!), color T.V. set (American!), stereo components (Japanese!), and telephone (our make, but on the level of European standards or maybe even higher). "It's really a wonderful ship! But Lyuda, where did they come up with such a strange name for her? The 'Caravan.' " "What's so strange about that? Don't we have the 'Azerbaidzhan' and the 'Kazakhstan'? Now there's the 'Caravan'. . ."[4] "Well, I'm glad, Lyuda, that we've become acquainted. I repeat once more that this trifle, this—you agree, don't you, it's not a bad design?—this bagatelle doesn't commit you to anything. On the contrary, if you need something, Lyuda dear, well I don't know, well, it might be anything, say, money, if you, my precious, need money, come to me at any time."

When he was left alone, Vladislav Ivanovich began to arrange all his things in the huge, two- or, perhaps, three-room suite, if you count the bathroom, and why not consider it a room—this blissfully spacious area laid with pink Dutch tile? The super-deluxe! He hung his brown and grey suits, his blazer and "Safari" blue jeans suit in the closet; arranged piles of English shirts and fine-wool sweaters on the shelves; put away his shoes with the design that "bordered on a work of art," as Gachik Tarasian said; took out the Parisian men's cologne and then cognac, whiskey, and gin. The temporarily careless arrangement of all this represented the most perfect design or, in other words, pop-art. Seized by the ecstasy of existence, Vetryakov begin to jump around on the cabin's fluffy carpet, to flip all the switches and push all the buttons, and with that the cabin came to life, began to sing and light up: a television set featured something heroic, a stereo system played something romantic, and enormous windows opened onto a blue sky dotted with seagulls and masts. Vladislav Ivanovich began gliding around with a crystal glass filled with exactly two fingers of Courvoisier cognac, as was *de rigeur,* and at precisely that moment the telephone rang, which aboard the "Caravan" did not mean you should expect bad news, but, on the contrary, a futher improvement in your life. That's exactly how it turned out: Vetryakov understood immediately by the tone of the voice that whoever was calling was his kind of guy:

"Welcome back, Slava! This is Marat and Edik calling. Perhaps, you don't know us, but we know you. Andrei Mikhailovich referred us to you; Lev called him yesterday. So, uh, everything's on schedule. We'll deliver the order right away."

In half an hour two fine fellows in jeans and leather arrived, real optimists. Without anybody's help they dragged several boxes of drinks and snacks into the cabin: Schweppes tonic water, Vladislav Ivanovich's favorite Carlsberg beer, Beefeater's gin, caviar, smoked sausage, toasted almonds—everything perfect to a tee. Looking at the order, Vladislav Ivanovich was filled with a warm, almost exuberant feeling. No, no matter what you say, the feeling of camaraderie still exists in this world; as soon as he had mentioned in passing that it would be a nice thing to have an order delivered on board the "Caravan" Lev immediately said "I'll be done." Vladislav Ivanovich could well imagine how Lev had gone through Rosko, and how Rosko made connections via Vadim Leshin because it wasn't wise for Rosko to go straight to the level of Andrei Mikhailovich, and so it was Vadim who called Serafima Ivanovna, and she informed Andrei Mikhailovich on the QT, and only then, after he had received the go-ahead, did Lyova call Andrei Mikhailovich directly. No, no matter what the skeptics say, there is still genuine friendship among men in this world. That's how it happens—sometimes just a glance at a person, and it's immediately clear whether you'll go "prospecting" with him or if you'd rather refrain.[5] That's how Slava himself was introduced to his circle of friends about ten years ago. Let's see, where was it exactly? While out fishing, in a sauna, or simply around a table? Some details have been erased from memory, but the most important one remains forever. Boris the race car driver had brought him there, and in half an hour Lyova or Gachik, or perhaps Stepan Akimovich himself had said, "Let's drink to Slava! We can go prospecting with him!" And life had confirmed this: nobody let anyone else down. That's real men for you!

On the sea the steamship "Caravan" was a noble sight! This wanderer, chartered the world over, usually took Swedes and Englishmen for a trip to the archipelagoes of Polynesia, or Columbians and Argentinians for a trip in the opposite direction, to the fjords of Norway, and sometimes also visited her native waters to gratify her compatriots. On those cruises, the gaming machines, those so-called "one-armed bandits" were sealed up (because the spirit of profit and the belief in blind fate are alien to our people); a certain something characteristic of them was replaced by something characteristic of us,[6] and "Caravan" set out on the route Odessa-Batumi-Odessa,[7] giving the entire Euksinian Pont and nearby shores the pleasure of observing her presence.

Thus, we have found a proper place in this marvelous, almost dazzling world for our hero and we have provided him with everything he needs. We could now let him out of his deluxe-suite onto the deck, for the peripeteia of the story, but before we do this we should perhaps touch upon one detail of his luggage—the "attache" case, that flat suitcase/briefcase which was brought into world-wide use by James Bond, Her Majesty's Secret Service Agent 007 with a license to kill.[8] However, is it worth it for us to make an attempt to peer into this case and stir up its contents? All the more since Vladislav Ivanovich never counts money himself or rearranges it? There's nothing about Vladislav Ivanovich to remind you of the Covetous Knight, [9] he doesn't really care much about money because, believe it or not, he's not a crook, not a greedy-fingers, not even an artful dodger. He is a friend, a reliable person, an unbiased and brave comrade-at-arms. He is the Prince Myshkin [10] of the contemporary partisan structure, a link in the notorious system of "elemental redistribution" [11] and he is, in the final analysis, just simply a theoretical physicist. His last name is not being kept secret; it genuinely exists: Slava, yes if you please, for friends, yes please; he is always open to friendship. We won't say a word about Gibbon and by no means because it is some kind of criminal nickname, but because it is just his own bad joke which turned out to be very sticky.

So, let's let our hero go up onto the deck and straightaway encounter the ballerina Sokolova. Being very sensitive to cold, she has a shawl draped around her shoulders. In her huge eyes one can see the hope of spending a few days alone. Alas, she's already been noticed by several adversaries of women's loneliness. One of them, definitely a physicist, approaches and blocks her way. What should she do? Well, anyway, at least he's not the worst of them.

"Good evening. Well, here it is, the cradle of humankind. Do you smoke? Winston or Kent? Please! Pardon, but wasn't it you I saw in the ballet program 'White Nights' [12] a few days ago? Oh, what luck, it's a great pleasure to meet you. My name is Vladislav Ivanovich Vetryakov, a physicist. Well, how do you like the cradle of humankind? Yes, yes, of course, I can be more specific. Your Leningrad, for example, is the cradle of the revolution, but the Mediterranean Sea is the cradle of humankind. Our Black Sea, this very sea, is part of the Mediterranean. Well, did you catch my joke? Excuse me, have you already had dinner, Olga-dash-Natalia? Of course I know you are Valentina, but since you've smiled it must mean that you understand humor. We will have dinner in an atmosphere of humor and good spirits, without once mentioning physics or ballet."

The prices in the restaurant turned out to be catastrophically low and the menu clearly humdrum. It seemed to be saying: eat, but don't stay too long. However, Vladislav Ivanovich absented himself for a minute to talk with the waiter Gera, whom he "charged up" to the point of the latter's complete amazement and the table was soon covered with food delivered directly from the hard-currency store. [13] Valentina Sokolova's head was spinning. She is so exquisite, Vetryakov thought as he noticed how the ballerina shut her eyes at the sight of eels and rock lobsters. Wow, am I going to gorge myself on all this, Sokolova thought with her eyes closed.

"What music do you like, Valentina?"

"I like baroque music," the ballerina opened her eyes: hope I didn't spread it on too thickly with the "baroque";[14] that it wasn't too much, the physicist won't simper.

But he was already walking in a vigorous manner towards the orchestra, towards the seven boys in the "Seven Wheels" group, those truly distinct optimists of life.

"Hit the baroque, guys!" he requested and "charged" them up so forcefully for the entire evening that the "seven wheels" began at first to spin off in different directions, but then quickly recovered and cut right in to what they were asked for—the rock-'n-roll tune "Memphis."[15]

"Oh, Valentina, Valentina," Vladislav Ivanovich was saying at the beginning of dinner. "I look at you, at your gentle movements, your oval face, your manner of drinking and eating and once more I confirm my credo—down with pessimism! What a grave mistake was committed in the past, in the Middle Ages when in ignorant minds the thought was born that 'there is no happiness in life'! A very unfortunate mistake, Valentina, which is now being corrected by the whole march of history. Well, tell me then, isn't it happiness to eat together? Well, look around: we sail together through the cradle of humankind, the orchestra is playing baroque music, we're eating delicious fish together..."

"And molluscs! Yes, molluscs..." Sokolova suddenly let out a rather strange whirling burst of laughter and held up a lobster by the tip of its claw with her spinning fingrs. Her neatly combed bird head was already spinning too.

"And moll-uscs!" Vladislav Ivanovich picked up the wonderful word in delight. "Yes, of course, molluscs!"

Suddenly, something unpleasant stung Vetryakov as he looked once again at the ballerina's spinning paw. Something was missing. A cold current penetrated that bouillon sea of Vladislav Ivanovich in a thin stream. What was missing? Suddenly it dawned upon him: the paw was minus a ring, a fetchingly beautiful ring. It was necessary as soon as possible to eliminate this injustice, to correct this defect. Vetryakov laughed even more happily: tomorrow in Yalta he'd go to a jewelry store! The anticipation of placing a ring on Valentina's paw even brought him a certain excess of happiness. There are people in this world whose nature it is to fear excessive happiness, who see in it some instablility, some elusiveness, but Vladislav Ivanovich was not one of them. He had his credo: man is born to happiness as a bird is to flying!

"Oh, ye gods!" giggled the ballerina.

"Gods of Olympus!" Vetryakov exclaimed as he looked around. They had already started a third bottle of champagne and it could now very well be that one of the passengers might turn out to be from the Olympian assembly.

"You run into acquaintances everywhere, here too," Valentina laughed irrepressibly and teased a group of people who had just arrived and were standing and looking around in the center of the hall. She teased them with her delicate tongue, with her paw which was still missing a ring, and with the lobster claw. "Oh, gods, it's as if I'd never got out of VTO . . ."[16]

"Representatives of Art!" exclaimed Vetryakov. "What a stroke of luck! We physicists very, very much like to eat with the people of art!"

He launched himself towards three men and two ladies, bowed and scraped, and dragged them along with him waving to Gerasha with one hand (Give me some advice, friend!) and gestured with the other towards the orchestra (Hit it with the baroque, guys!). He dragged them to his table without paying attention to their bewilderment or slight resistance. "Valyusha, greet your friends! Don't be shy, comrades! The union of science and art, and life itself, prompts us to get together!"

At this point we should stop and rack our brains a bit as to what, within acceptable limitations, is not forbidden even when you're writing a story. There may be a certain anxiety as to whether our situation may seem rather artificial: as soon as the suspicious rich man found his stride on the steamship, the author immediately palms off "art people" on him. Having made this apologetic body movement addressed to the readers, I can freely and calmly seat the newcomers, because within the limits of literary convention these "people of art" are somehow no longer people or even figures, but mere phantoms—literary clichés.

One of them, who looked like a lion, was quite old! However, an expression of eternal amazement made him look younger and livelier, because amazement is not a quality of old age or a stiff lion-mask and, therefore, although he looked like a lion, it wasn't much like one.

"Melonov!! He's very famous!"

The second was a typical faun with reddish curls which protruded in some places on his head as if under the pressure of horns. The corners of his sensual mouth were slightly raised, but he looked sad. Since the feeling of sadness is not very well developed in fauns, he resembled a certain sort of atypical faun.

"Razdvoilov!! He's very talented!"

The third one was quite sultry; the back of his head was straight and flat, the outlines of his face and figure were decisive and severe. He looked like some toreador. However, for some reason he very often closed his eyes (can you imagine such a habit in a toreador?) and made a lot of unnecessary movements with his hands: for example, he'd put the palms of his hands to his ears, lips and eyes; cross his fingers; or swing now his right, now his left arm. All this is probably not very typical for toreadors, so consequently it was only remotely that he resembled a toreador.

"Charov!! He's very witty!"

The fourth one was a lady who resembled a lioness born to be free (she was by no means the match for the surprised lion). Her age and experience on stage had helped her to accumulate in herself tremendous energy potential and, of course, a barely restrained aggressiveness. This really made her look like a lioness; the air of danger was all around her.

"Yazykatova!! A terror of a voice!"

The fifth was a nymph, not a mischievous one, but a dreamer. Her softly streaming hair and languishing eyes seemed to wander off somewhere or were perhaps concentrated on one thought—on a daydream of Attic groves—and they made her look like a true dreamer-nymph.

"Svezhakova!! The embodiment of femininity!"

It wasn't clear, precisely, who these celebrities were, either to us or to Vetryakov. But that isn't really essential. The main thing is that they were poets and artists!—It's such a pleasure to see you in person, just like that, in the flesh, and to eat together! Please, don't attempt to pay for yourselves, I beg you, please, don't be offended! Do you have quail on the menu? Gerasha, bring us three platters of quail hen! Garnish and decorate them! Flambé them like they do in France! Wait, wait, hang on ... let me send something to the kitchen, here, give the chef this greeting from our table, he deserves it, no two ways about it: he's a real professor of the Academy of Stomachs! Bravo! Bravo! What did you say? The feast of Lucullus?[17] That's really a great joke! Someone suggested a song, any objections? Let the days of our life flow like the waves, we know that happiness awaits us ahead![18] ...Let's drink to...to...let's drink, comrades, to...what should we drink to?...to friendship, comrades! To the friendship of men and women! Let's never part, never, eh? Never, never, okay? Let's meet in Moscow! I invite you all to the "Arkhangelskoe"! Or to the "Tower of the Seventh Heaven," agreed?[19]

"You'll never get in there, to that celebrated 'Seventh Heaven,'" Razdvoilov said.

"What did you say?" Vladislav Ivanovich was taken aback. "What do you mean won't get in? That's just not possible." At that moment he realized that perhaps Razdvoilov, being an artistic person, did not understand the little practical matters of life and, with a wide smile, Vetryakov made a common although somewhat familiar gesture, rubbing his thumb and index finger.

"Not really, bribes are not accepted everywhere," Razdvoilov winced, "nowadays there are foreigners, delegations, and tourists everywhere, but..." he coughed and added, "damn it..."

"It's when you don't offer enough that they don't accept," Vetryakov explained in an instructive tone. "For example, if I come upon some obstacle, I begin with a hundred. They don't take one hundred—I give 'em two hundred; they don't take two hundred—I give them three. Anybody will take three hundred. You don't believe me? Try it!"

154

For some reason Razdvoilov took in this practical advice as a joke and burst out laughing.

"So, you are a physicist?" asked Charov. "Theoretical?"

"Both theoretical and practical."

"He is an outstanding physicist!" sang Valentina Sokolova, reeling in her easy chair.

"Then, of course, you know Shalashnikov, Zakharchin, Gerd, and so on?" Charov continued.

"I know a lot, but I'm not allowed to talk about everything," bragged Vladislav Ivanovich with a studied air of importance. He nodded silently, staring straight into Charov's eyes.

"You mean the Problem? Are you assigned to the Problem?" asked Melonov, entering into the conversation.

Vladislav Ivanovich drooped slightly, although he knew that such lulls were unavoidable at parties like this, that there was nothing terrible about it, that in just two or three more steps they'd crest the ridge beyond which happiness would begin again.

"Enough of these stupid questions!" ordered Yazykatova. "Can't you see what a magnificent physicist Vladislav Ivanovich is?!"

The nymph Svezhakova held out her hand to Vetryakov in silence. There it was, that gesture, that Olympian gift! Yes, yes, of course, let's dance and let's offer each other the movements of our tantalizing bodies.

In the "Trade Winds" restaurant on the upper deck of the liner "Caravan," a dance had been storming in full swing for some time now. Below, in the "Albatross" restaurant, the dancing was also stormy. Still further below in the "Dolphin" restaurant, the dances were just as stormy and undoubtedly the dancing that went on in the open areas of the stern and the bow were just as stormy. It should be added that in hundreds if not thousands of restaurants all along the Black Sea the dances were indisputably and simultaneously storming in full swing. Moreover, I assume full responsibility for the claim that dances were storming in full swing at that hour all over that enormous region of the country from Dikson to Batumi.[20] The dancing was limited only by the corresponding meridians beyond which dances had already ended in the east and had not yet started up in the west. During recent years stormy restaurant dances have become an obvious phenomenon in our country and, therefore, I may allow myself a short digression. After all, I myself used to dance quite a bit and I remember it perfectly well. I even intend to describe the dances of the preceding decades at some future date. Therefore, I have the nerve to say that such body freedom as was found in dances of the late '70s had never been seen before in Russian society. Barriers of age and size were broken down. The seductive sounds of saxophones and guitars drew into the whirling circle huge ladies falling out of their crimpline dresses and modest men who, it would seem, should have been more disposed to playing dominoes and, in their turn, out-of-breath captains of our industry who danced alongside asexual longhairs in jeans. Chairs were knocked over and the problems of everyday life were forgotten.

What a soothing and exhilarating freedom of body movement! The rhythm of the rock-'n-roll shimmy is society's way to happiness! Everything is allowed in these frenzied and selfless dancing collectives. Nothing and nobody provokes suspicious glances. There's shouting, noise, laughter. Everybody joins in singing the chorus "Ah, Odessa, pearl of the sea!" It's the marvel of our lifetime—this spontaneous Soviet upsurge of dancing. They say that even foreigners are surprised.

Through the mass of dancers Yazykatova approached the orchestra, striding with the springy gait of a wild animal through a pre-dawn savannah.

"Now I'll rock them in the 'retro' style!" The lady in beige pants leapt onto the stage, leering at Vladislav Ivanovich with a dangerous, voluptuous smile.

While Vetryakov was jumping in the crazy "baroque" dance and following the ecstatic and sinuous body of the dreaming nymph with glistening eyes, he caught a few glimpses of a table at which a heavy-weight company of half-breed males from the Caucasus was sitting.[21] And each time he caught sight of this table, a little black trail of residual alcohol appeared in his soul under the dome of happiness, like the vapor of an invisible jet. Vladislav Ivanovich quickly determined that the focal point of the group was a thickset but certainly not fat man with the huge forehead of a Mao-Tse-Tung, the jetblack eyes of a Pugachev, and the bushy sidewhiskers of a Denis Davydov. [22] This man, just like a *bogdykhan* (a Chinese emperor), was stretched out in a Finnish armchair with his body quite relaxed. He was clad in a close-fitting lace shirt through which an undershirt was visible; a black "Sochi" tie with an ominous outerspace design worked in silver thread slashed downwards like a sword.[23] The others addressed their toasts and told their anecdotes precisely to him, to this dark-complexioned bogdykhan of mysterious, but related (for such it seemed to Vladislav Ivanovich) physiological structure; he heard them out attentively and solicitously, laughing and stretching his hand to each storyteller for the congratulatory handshake. As Vladislav Ivanovich determined, they were also optimists, of course, but not quite optimists of the same type, not quite from the same circle to which he and his friends belonged. These were rather heavy-set and somewhat antiquated optimists and, perhaps because of that, the thin vapor of residual alcohol afterburn appeared in Vetryakov's heavens every time he glanced into that corner. Especially that one brief moment when it seemed to him that the bogdykhan had winked at him almost imperceptibly! Oh no, no, all this didn't deserve his attention! His happiness wasn't disturbed, for his happiness was here, all around him: the "baroque" and "retro," with everything bubbling over!

"No need to be mournful!" Yazykatova sang in a low, knee-buckling roar, slapping herself on the thigh. "The time will pass for separations! For all previous sufferings! The reward will come!"

That's how everything kept going, how everything kept bubbling and boiling until Vetryakov discovered himself alone at a table which recalled the half-destroyed but still breathing Pompeii. The art people had sloughed off somewhere, and the entire "Trade Winds" was already empty. The lights had gone dim and the waiters and cleaning ladies, exhausted by the partying crowd's maddening pressure, wandered inertly among the tables as if they didn't know how to approach them.

"Gerasha, my precious, if you please—the bill, a cigar and a cognac."

That's what it means to charge up a person properly from the beginning, to awaken the friend in him. Without any haggling over whether, say, "the buffet is closed" or some such, Gerasha brought out a tray with a glass of "Martel," a cigar and a four-digit number on a slip of paper.

With the cigar in his teeth Vladislav Ivanovich came out onto the promenade deck which was bathed in moonlight and glanced around at his sea neighborhood floating at that hour in a cloud of abundance (as one would expect). It was a marvelous plain of deserted sea, ennobled by light from heaven and the "Caravan" moved across it as powerfully and confidently as the destiny of mankind. And something akin to that cloud of abundance illuminated by the slightly mournful, but infinitely noble light of the moon reigned at that moment in Vladislav Ivanovich's soul, and, at that moment, in this cloud of abundance he seemed to himself to be a powerful foreign ship which brings people the gift of goodness and happiness. It didn't matter that he had been stranded right now by Valentina, the nymph Svezhakova, and even by comrade Yazykatova: they had already received from him a certain "charge" of human warmth and were therefore no longer alien to him.

On the deck he caught sight of a lonely figure whose coat collar was upturned. It was Razdvoilov, gazing into the depths of the starry Pont.

"What are our thoughts about, friend?" Vetryakov asked him quietly.

"About Aristotle," was the answer.

"I'm enraptured," Vetryakov pronounced.

"There's something with which to be enraptured," grinned the sad faun. "Take for example his definition of happiness as the manifestation of a soul which acts in harmony with virtue. Do you see here a connection with the notion of freedom?"[24]

"I'm enraptured."

"There is something with which to be enraptured—to have said so much, so long ago."

"I'm enraptured with you," Vetryakov said. "Standing like that on deck with your collar upturned and thinking about Aristotle!"

The faun turned his wide smiling face towards him as if to say: who else is there to think about Aristotle here if not me, the classical goat-legged voluptuary? The faun's ears suddenly seemed to become pointed. What did he hear in that even rumble of the sea? Was it the tapping of a woman's heels breaking down under?

"Excuse me," he moved Vladislav Ivanovich aside and hurried off somewhere into a sparkling shade where there was a fleeting glimpse of something light and fragile.

"What happiness it is to serve art . . ." Vladislav Ivanovich was saying in the morning into a telephone receiver as he lay in his presidential super-deluxe bed. "You must always be happy, Valentina, because you bring to fruition a manifestation of the soul which acts in harmony with virtue."

"I'm deeply unhappy, Vladislav Ivanovich!" Sokolova sobbed from the depths of the ship. "My joints are growing old. I have never had an ear for music. I memorize my moves like a doll from the village sticks. I hide everything from everyone . . . except from you, dear Vladislav Ivanovich . . ."

"Take heart, Valentina, console yourself," he billed and cooed as he looked through the window at the stupendous blueness of the sky. "Up ahead we have Yalta. Just think about us having that yet to come—pearly Yalta!"

Right then and there some metal spring of wonderful anticipation really seemed to cast him upward. Detached from his marvelous mattress (having "taken off," that is, into the air), he caught a glimpse through the window of the undulating blue Crimean mountains and the houses scattered along the slopes, and then he spread out his hands and bounced down again onto his super-mattress just as there sprang to his eyes the clean and friendly face of the floor attendant Lyuda . . . —"oh, I've just dropped in to see you, Slava, run by for a little money. The girls are offering stocking-boots . . ."—followed by a new take-off (but this time with a flip head over heels), a dive into the refrigerator, the burning delight of Carlsberg beer, a quick go under the shower, under a "Braun" razor, under a Dior atomizer and into the "Safari", and . . . , and . . . once again all that physics and all that jazz started up.

"According to Artistotle's teachings, every form of matter derives from the unity of four elements: earth, air, fire and water. You find these four elements everywhere, no matter where you stick your nose. A diamond ring is no exception, either, oh no! Of course, it is nonsense to consider a nine-thousand rouble ring to be more beautiful than the human finger of a woman. You ennoble this material substance with your finger,

158

Valentina, and not vice versa! The four elements are mixed much more beautifully in a woman than in a diamond. I call on Razdvoilov as a witness. Do you agree, poet?"

"I'm stunned by your gesture," Sokolova said, "what sort of salary do you make?" Vladislav Ivanovich took her heart-touching human hand in his own, turned it over like a submissive little bird, and kissed her palm on the mount of Venus.[25] He immediately felt embarrassed by this possessive gesture. "If we must talk about money in light of Aristotle's teachings, then we have to say that there is nothing more primitive with respect to the very process of creation (if, of course, we don't go to the real source—that is, trees) from which money matter is known to be produced, at least according to our scientific circles. Having already moved on to trees, however, we can easily imagine the combination of the four elements in their gigantic trunks. Look how they tower above the waterfall! Well, here we are. We've docked..."

Having delicately outstripped his guests so as to enter the "Waterfall" establishment ahead of them, Vetryakov quickly charged up the entire personnel—for you! and you! and you! and you, too, my pretty one!—with such lightning-fast shots of optimisim that here, once again, we find ourselves in the midst of comfort and tranquility under the quietly rattling crystal mane of a rare phenomenon in nature and, again, we are philosophizing:

"So, you despise money, Slava?"

"No, I respect it, but not more than trees."

"You would've made a good philosopher," Charov cracks a joke.

"What do you prefer: sturgeon on a skewer or shishkebab? I'll make no secret of the fact, my friends, that I have always been attracted to dialectical materialism. I regret that I didn't get any special education in that area. I envy you poets. I deify you. I still cannot believe that we are eating together."

Everybody around the table was laughing and such a relaxed atmosphere was established that they all began to behave eccentrically, to return to the first principles of Aristotle. Let's say, there's a market place right before our eyes: earth, air, fire and water are mixed together here and become the embodiment of marvelous vegetable creations with their nutritive souls. We load our hands up with everything, in antique, unlimited quantities: strawberries, cherries, radishes, and, most importantly, flowers, flowers, flowers! The earth gives us its fruit as a gift and we give it our unlimited aspiration for happiness, for beauty. Slava releases flocks of green papers from his sleeve, like a magician. The super-deluxe—crammed full with gifts from the Mediterranean and, alternatively, with designs from the Common Market—is transformed for many hours into a hearth of happiness and artistic, intellectual communication. Trays of roasted meat are brought to the table: lambs and pigs—those possessing two types of souls, the nutritive and the sensory. "Nature is both demonic and divine. Isn't that right, Razdvoilov old buddy? Am I saying it right? Isn't that what Aristotle taught us? People possess three types of souls, my friends: the nutritive, the sensory, and the rational; I'm not mistaken, old man, am I?" "Ha-ha-ha, an extra soul gives us an opportunity to fill our stomachs with both flora and fauna," Charov cracks a joke. "Comrades, in all our passion for classical thought let's all the same reaffirm that we are materialists. We shouldn't forget what it is that's made us what we are—namely, work and struggle!" "What struggle could possibly be under your wing, Slava?" "Gentlemen, I am obliged to declare that I have already lost my rational element," said Melonov. "Let's blend with nature, become plants and animals." "I'm a dandelion." "And I'm a goat!" "And I, dear men, am a caress, a creature still unknown to anyone, I'm a caress—an enormous caress. I want to go to Greece, I want to go to a leafy grove..."

"Slava, why aren't we dancing, why aren't we singing? Suggest something for everyone to sing!"

> No matter what you say,
> There really is no way
> For a king to be wed,
> Even one king, through love!

roared Super-Deluxe No. 02. Vetryakov was whirling all over the fluffy carpeting, bumping all up and down his guests—the invited and the uninvited, the known and the unknown. "What marvelous creatures they are," he thought about them rapturously. "No, no, Vadik Razdvoilov and our teacher Aristotle are right a thousand times over: life is the aspiration of moral earthly creatures to realize the potential which lies within them."

"Vladislav Ivanovich, they say that you are a colossal swindler, is that true?" Yazykatova asked him at one point.

"No, of course, it's not true, Varvara, it is utter nonsense. Judge for yourself! What have we got to steal in physics—a handful of neutrons, a jug of plasma? Who needs it? Everyone already has it. You won't find 'goods in high demand' in physics today, that's all in the past. Of course, if you need anything from somewhere else—a sheepskin coat, say, jeans, a quartz watch—that wouldn't cause me any difficulty. Of course, that doesn't mean I'll steal those things somewhere, Varvara. Even if you wanted to, you couldn't steal such things, and I don't even want to. Stealing is repulsively primitive; it's the base impulsive move of a reptile. Yesterday at dinner or at breakfast or sometime in between Vadik was discoursing upon the upper limit of human feelings. He said that a feeling of friendship is located at the upper limit. I applaud this, Varvara. Friendship is my hobby. A friend is what I am. I work at the upper limit. I have a great number of friends, and I help them to recognize one another, to really get to know each other. By uniting strong characters I arrange the vital design, the pattern of life. Did you understand me, Varvara? The net of human relations had need of a modest unselfish spider and I sometimes play that role. Do you understand?"

"I would understand better if you explained it by means of an example," Yazykatova's exceptional face reflected the powerful work that thoughts do.

"Please, suggest your own example, Varvara."

"Well, here's an example for you," Yazykatova subtly smiled. "My book of memoirs, *Keeping Step with the Song,* is to celebrate my fortieth year as a creative artist and entertainer. Could you fix it up with a publisher?"

"That's not one of the easier tasks, but let me give it a try right now," Vetryakov answered quickly, leaned back in his chaise lounge, closed his eyes and began to whisper something.

In contrast, Varvara Yazykatova turned as tense as a spring on her chaise lounge as, with screwed-up eyes, she followed the movements of his lips and tried to guess where the thought was moving to behind them. An amazing woman, by the way, this vocalist Yazykatova! Vast experience in life helped her to adapt her appearance to any and every trend. Age no longer played even a minor role. In the morning at the edge of the swimming pool she was the very picture of youth—in a transparent robe and with flowers! In the evening, in a restaurant, she was an alluring lioness experienced at sweet battles. And should the conversation turn to questions of social status or to the rankings in art, there would appear before you a stern, asexual and ageless public figure.

So, what could one guess from the way Vladislav Ivanovich's lips stirred? What thought was at work?

"Felix... let's start with Felix... Felix plays on Saturdays with Volodya and Mikhail Yegorovich... we'll reinforce Felix with Seryozha, who will drop by together with Inessa... Inessa and Gordeyev's wife are friends... Mikhail Yegorovich has access to Gordeyev... Gordeyev has access to Storozhova, Svetlana Maximovna, and we'll reinforce her from the other side with Rezo, whom my Gachik will call... Storozhova, already, can handle it... can... already at... can handle it at the level of Kapis... and if Kapis himself withdraws, then..." That's how Vladislav Ivanovich moved, scarcely audibly, around the system, the network of his friendships, and it reminded Yazykatova of a certain pulsating and gelatinous-but-solid mass charged up with electricity. "Why there's where Tolya is!" he shouted suddenly at the top of his voice and gaped joyfully with his light-blue, nearsighted eyes wide open. "Varvara, consider the contract with you already signed!"

"Slava, how free you are with the money," said Melonov on one occasion.

"Want to know why? Because money is an anachronism! Of course, even now it provides for some things, and it's a joy to see how good feelings are revived in people when you give them these green designs, but believe me, friends, money is losing its meaning year by year in this epoch of high demand. I often live for months practically without money... No, no, that doesn't mean I don't spend it; it means that I don't earn any. I sort of forget about it, do you understand me?"

What fullness of life! As he looked from the summits of the Crimean mountains or from the slopes of the Caucasus at the foamy outlines of the land, at the blazing blueness of the sea, and at the "Caravan" waiting below with her ultra-modern inclined masts, smokestack that looked like a sea lion, and the mirror of a swimming pool on her upper deck, Vladislav Ivanovich could actually feel the sensation, as he gazed at all this, of that extraordinary trepidation which is the property of genuine life.

At this particular moment we ought to take note that this man's character was, indeed, such: he never considered bad weather, slush or penetrating cold to be typical for our planet; he always traversed those periods without retaining any memory of them. The memory of this creature called Vladislav Ivanovich Vetryakov was reminsicent of a kaleidoscope in which only that which is bright and friendly assumes various crystalline combinations;[26] when something amorphous and brownish-grey came to the surface from certain muddy depths, say, those from his childhood (for example, standing in line for flour during that post-war year of famine; the black-ink numbers on his frozen paws that were tormented by hangnails), well, right then and there the kaleidoscope shuddered and the carnival began anew.

"It'd be so nice if all my people, all my friends were to turn up beside me right now! After all, there are people well attuned to sitting at anyone's table and sharing anyone's company, people whom one might just as easily call physicists as lyricists:[27] say, for example, Lyova, or Gagik, or, hey, Stepan Nikolayevich. Now that's true super-happiness: to bring old friends together with the new ones."

Vladislav Ivanovich entered a telephone booth, dropped several 15-kopeck coins into the automat, and began to dial Moscow. Why couldn't Gagik, say, or Stepan, or any other friend fly to some nearby port today, come on board the "Caravan," and fling himself into Slava's welcome embrace and, moreover, into this generally joyful atmosphere—into this Mediterranean cradle of humankind permeated by wellsprings of contemporary views on the world and by Aristotle's philosophy? The telephones did not answer.

"No need to call, Gibbon," Vladislav Ivanovich suddenly heard a voice say very closely behind him. The one whom he had called "bogdykhan" behind his back during the whole trip stood in front of him; he had opened the door a bit and was leaning against the telephone booth.

"Beg your pardon," Vladislav Ivanovich expressed his surprise in a most polite manner. "You called me Gibbon, ha-ha-ha, and, that means this is all a joke..."

"There's no need to call either Levka, or Gagik, or Stepan." The swollen but not dull eyes on bogdykhan's face, almost black from suntan, studied Vladislav Ivanovich's physiognomy. "Let's go for a walk, Gibbon."

They started to walk along the shore embankment. Bogdykhan walked a little bit in front of Vladislav Ivanovich, and one could detect in the way this bogdykhan walked that exceptional trait of being used to commanding: not looking back at the person he had invited in the firm belief that the individual he'd invited would undoubtedly follow him (was simply incapable of not following).

"I've been watching you," the bogdykhan spoke as he walked. "You are having a good time in the nicest possible way. I approve. Did you spend a lot?"

"Excuse me... but I... in a certain respect I'm... even...," answered Vladislav Ivanovich.

The bogdykhan suddenly stopped, took his companion by the crown button on his blazer and raised his index finger, as black and powerful as an ancient Asiatic symbol, to Vladislav Ivanovich's nose.

"Never have regrets about what you have spent on food and pleasure! If you do, no good will come of it for you! Do you understand me?"

"But I don't have any regrets whatsoever..." babbled Vladislav Ivanovich, "... how can one have regrets? What for? Rather, I'm happy, although I would like, nevertheless, to ask you something. You know about our joke, so does that mean you know...?"

"I know everyone."

Once again, the bogdykhan was walking along without looking back at Vladislav Ivanovich, with his powerful belly in front of him as if it were being taken for a stroll.

"All my friends?"

"Everyone," said the bogdykhan.

"But for some reason I don't know you."

"There was no reason for you to know me. Let's go drink some beer together."

They ducked under the canopy of a local cafeteria and sat down at a table to the side. A waiter gave them an attentive look as he ran past.

"Tell him to bring some good beer," the bogdykhan ordered. Maneuvering between the tables Vladislav Ivanovich dashed after the waiter, quickly "charged" him up and there soon stood before them two mugs of fine, not ordinary, beer.

"You remember the French 'pletfurm' shoes?" asked the bogdykhan. Vladislav Ivanovich gasped.

163

"You remember the Scandinavian chendeliers? That Italian lacey-shmacey? The Swiss wig-shmyg?"

Of course, alas! alas!, Vladislav Ivanovich remembered these "goods in high demand," and he also remembered how they were delivered from the South to various warehouses (whether the warehouses stored vegetables or sanitation equipment was of no consequence); he also remembered and even knew approximately where all these luxuries were manufactured and...and with each new word from this "bogdykhan," some black-ink bubbles burst in his kaleidoscope, and he even had to shake his head in order to restore the radiance in it.

"Do you have your passport with you right now, Gibbon?" the bogdykhan suddenly asked.

"What?" Vladislav Ivanovich responded, as if he'd just awakened. "Passport? Yes, yes, of course, it's here, in my pocket."

"Go to the airport and take a flight somewhere. Perhaps to the Baltic seashore or to Tashkent.[28] But don't go to Moscow. I wouldn't advise your returning to the ship, either. Have you understood me?"

The bogdykhan had already got up from the table when Vladislav Ivanovich managed to collect himself somewhat and to grab this unknown but most important friend by the elbow.

"But how can this be? It's impossible. Just to up and fly away?!"

"That's my advice, you understand? I took a liking to you—you were making such a good time of it. So I'm giving you a piece of advice. Whether you stay or fly away, that's up to you."

"But everything I have was left there!" exclaimed Vladislav Ivanovich.

"Don't have any regrets about that!" Once again that rocking Oriental symbol of a brown finger arose before Vetryakov's nose. "Never regret what you've spent having a good time!"

"Oh, I have something different in mind, not those material things!" Vladislav Ivanovich gestured hopelessly with his hand. "I am talking about people, about spiritual matters, about the intimacy of relations, friendship, happiness..."

"Aristotle?" grinned the bogdykhan. "By the way, for three years he taught a boy who grew up to become a bandit..."

"Who?" exclaimed the stunned Vladislav Ivanovich.

"Alexander the Great, don't you remember?"

These were the bogdykhan's last words, and with these words he disappeared from Vladislav Ivanovich's life; he walked out of the cafeteria and confidently conducted his stomach into the dense crowd milling under the royal palms.

After he left, Vladislav Ivanovich sat for a long time in the damp and drafty cafeteria, stubbing a Winston into a saucer while the establishment became noisier and noisier and the beer more and more repulsive although, as before, it still wasn't the ordinary kind. Vladislav Ivanovich laughed dramatically at himself, "the chicken's fried, but the lace was French, the platform shoes Scandinavian, and the great Alexander a Macedonian . . ."

The cafeteria's red-striped tarpaulin drapes were flopping in the wind, a subtropical darkness was bulging up on the horizon, and the white hull of the "Caravan" stood out more and more distinctly in the pre-storm twilight. The electric excitement was intensifying in the crowd along the shore embankment and in the flock of birds in the sky.

Thus, we make preparations so as to introduce gradually the next literary cliché into the action of our story: an intensification of the drama accompanied by threatening atmospheric phenomena. Gigantic bolts of lightning appear one after another like eucalyptus trees in the black sky before the inert, stolid face of Sukhumi.[29]

On board the "Caravan" there flicker fleeting glimpses of merrily frightened people—in the windows of cocktail bars and cabins, from the bridges on the promenade decks. Nothing threatens them there, inside the womb of this ocean giant, and their fears are merely a continuation of the game. Vladislav Ivanovich is standing behind a corner of the harbor control tower, very close to the ship's gangway, which had been desirable and inviting an hour ago but now concealed within itself the uncertainty, alarm, and collapse of his life. The first drops of rain—heavy, like grapes— fell onto his blazer . . . One must not scorn the advice of a man such as the bogdykhan, if you want to save yourself. Two taxi cabs slowly make a U-turn on the still dry pavement of the shore embankment. Quick—to the hubbub of the airport, into the swarm of boarding and deboarding masses. But Vladislav Ivanovich is motionless. His gaze moves slowly across the decks of the "Caravan." What will he see there? Maybe, in the next bushy bolt of lightning, a reflection of the diamond on Valentina's swollen, pitiful finger will flash out for a microsecond or, maybe, there will be a flutter of her shoulders sensitive to the cold or of her earlobes—so touching and tiny in the midst of the universe? Maybe, that Flemish opulence of the table and the faces of all his clever and kind friends awaiting his return from the shore will suddenly flash, dreamlike, through the side of the ship, through its steel hulk. Maybe, a lonely figure will appear suddenly to him—someone burdened with life, wrapped in a statuesque tunic that all the same billows in the wind on the launching deck which is as distant and soulless as a cliff: what loneliness, what bitterness—his contemporaries hadn't understood him, he was driven away from Chalcis,[30] for three years he had taught a boy and the boy grew up to become a bandit . . .

Right then the stormy downpour began to pelt down furiously. As if taking no notice of the sheets of water pouring onto him, Vladislav Ivanovich slowly climbed the gangway to board the "Caravan."

Having used this tempting cliché, we could have finished the entire story just like that, for it is now absolutely clear what lies ahead for him in the future. Nevertheless, he proceeds to his super-deluxe and we have to follow him, whether we want to or not.

In his cabin there fluttered (this verb is not very precise, of course, with respect to how it characterizes movement, but its metaphorical sense is quite precise), yes, so there fluttered a splendid rosy soul—the floor attendant Lyuda.

"Slava, doll, I dropped in again for some money. I took two hundred, okey-dokey? Oo-oo, you are all wet, Slava, my pet! Well, come here, taik a baf, a bat.., bas...damn, I've forgotten again where you're supposed to stick your tongue in that damned English language."

Nimble, womanly fingers; the heated breathing of a woman's care. "Excuse me, Lyuda, I'm rather in an ambiguous situation, always, when I'm with you. On the other hand, I don't want to offend you because you might think that I'm somehow indifferent towards your attributes, but that's not so at all, I'm not at all indifferent, as you can observe, Lyuda dear, my darling, but on the other hand . . . you may think that I somehow lay claim to you on account of . . . well, on account of this nonsense, this stupid money and there again I'm afraid of offending you . . ." "How could you possibly offend me, Slava, my dearest!" "And you, Lyuda, you are so dear to me!"

Washed, dried and ennobled by the woman's joyous and fast service, Vladislav Ivanovich walked out into the ship's twilight depths which were already buzzing with music. Everything was open: all the cafes, bars, restaurants, dancing halls, and souvenir shops. One could catch fleeting glimpses of people everywhere. The "Caravan" was already coursing through the open sea. She had passed the hurricane zone and the West now glittered with a phantasmagorical sunset extending half way up the height of the horizon. From the opposite side there approached the enchanting East—no less solid or thick than the West. Through a window he saw the backs of his friends on the promenade deck: all the magicians of the arts were present; probably, everybody was expecting his or her faithful Slava, and everyone was contemplating the sunset. Razdvoilov's touchingly short-fingered paw was travelling quietly along Sokolova's spine. With piercing melancholy, the thought occurred to Vladislav Ivanovich that for him the coming night might be the last opportunity in his life when he could make manifest the acts of his soul in harmony with virture that's so closely linked with the notion of freedom. Now he will disappear and buy gifts for them all, for all those spiritually close to him. A transistor for Razdvoilov, an Orenburg shawl for Svezhakova, a lacquered Palekh box for Melonov, some turquoise cufflinks for Charov, a Dagestan necklace for Yazykatova, and for Valechka Sokolova he'd need to add earrings identical to the rings described above.[31] Oh, how they will be ennobled by the flesh of her earlobes—skin translucent in a Mediterranean, Venetian or Genovese

166

sunset. What a design that will make![32]

Everything was done as planned, and the reader can imagine Vladislav Ivanovich's last night aboard the "Caravan" without the slightest difficulty—all those pre-finale ecstasies. But before us there now looms the problem of a finale, and again my pen tries to avoid existentialist labyrinths, to set off running along the beaten tracks of literary clichés.

Cliché number one. On an early but already dazzling morning the "Caravan" has moored at a dock in the port of Batumi. In among the people on the dock who are meeting friends and relatives on the ship and those who've come out of sheer curiosity are two men on business— OBKhSS officials.[33] Just off to one side is a van with bars on its windows. Vladislav Ivanovich descends the gangway modestly and quietly to face justice. He carries his attache-case in one hand, and in the attache-case are a sweater and toilet articles. The former contents of the chic suitcase no longer concern either our hero or us.[34]

Now he is in the van. There follows a mis-en-scène behind bars. Behind the bar grating are faces and nearby doves swarm. It is remotely reminiscent of the Russian realistic painting *Life is Everywhere.*[35] Probably, it's not only we, but the hero as well, who make such associations and, therefore, he gently whispers as he glances at the birds,

"Life is everywhere . . ."

He raises his eyes in order to bid farewell to the "Caravan" and he sees three whirling couples on the dancing stage of the ship's stern. Sokolova with Razdvoilov, Yazykatova with Charov, and Svezhakova with Melonov all perform the morning waltz with inspiration, color and selflessness.

"Everywhere there is chic life . . ." Vladislav Ivanovich thinks quietly, almost philosophically, but no longer says anything.

Cliché number two.

. . . Vladislav Ivanovich modestly and quietly descends the gangway to face justice. Silence and morning drowsiness reign aboard the "Caravan." There's routine activity on the docks. The collapse of illusions goes unnoticed. It happens quite often, you must agree: amid the swarming masses of people who move along routinely, there is often present one person inside whom something thunders sacrificially and desperately, but silently. And suddenly, some powerful, unanticipated sound swells behind the scene of capitulation. It is precisely "The Song of a Singer Off Stage"; it suddenly breaks across the Batumi docks in gigantic decibels. Either a drunken sound technician has cut in with it or the energy of the literary cliché has simply materialized by itself:

> With passion and languor,
> The flame of desires
> Stormily throbs
> In seething blood!

167

At that exact moment Vladislav Ivanovich sees his friends running towards him, he sees their beautiful eyes, their hands outstretched to him, their palms turned outward in a gesture of desperate compassion... "Slava, Slava, we love you, you are honest, you are good...an appeal...the jurisdiction...."

"No, no, my friends, don't worry," smiles the happy Vladislav Ivanovich, "I'm actually somewhat...of a substantial crook...." Diamond tears glisten on the women's cheeks; Valentina Sokolova—that small, fragile and forever dear creature—sensitive to the cold and suffering from polyarthritis—clings to his chest in a farewell embrace.

"Slava, I will wait for you...."

Cliché number three: the rebellion of individualism—march to the beat of your own drummer![36] The "Caravan" was not successful in escaping the storm; moreover, she fell right into its eye, where she was spun around by terrible and uncontrolled centrifugal forces and, after that, the currents of individualistic intention dragged her stern into the Bosphorous and further—into the Dardanelles—and cast her for a long time amid the countless islands of the Aegean archipelago until she could overcome the raging elements and restore herself on an inflexible course for Batumi.

Contemporary technology triumphed. The liner made its exit—slicing the stormy waves—not having lost, as a matter of fact, a single atom, a drop, a tiny bit...except for one of her passengers whom nobody needed anymore, as a matter of fact, because he now represented the type of individuum who's mutinied.

Meanwhile, as he wiped his glasses and soared in the waves of the Aegean Sea, the proud and gloomy Vladislav Ivanovich thoughtfully meditated on a commune-inimical meditation.

"There are no longer individuals in our world; there are only human systems. By supplying people goods in high demand I am, in essence, a scoundrel bucking the system. The path of humankind is predestined by the laws of nature. I will not reform, no matter what the epoch. Let me be judged here, in the cradle of humankind. Let any social order, even that of the most primeval age, judge me."

Towards morning the storm calmed down and the water became warmer. Vladislav Ivanovich managed to doze off a little bit on his back as he lay on a quietly powerful but soft wave. When he woke up he saw that he was approaching an island with reddish-brown cliffs which displayed all of their folds beneath the rays of the rising sun. Here and there in these geological folds there stood white figures who looked like statues; some were standing near the water and some higher up. They were a dozen strong men dressed in white and seemingly sculpturesque clothing that stirred in the gentle breeze: the trial by jury, the philosophers of the Lyceum School...[37]

With this, having tired of literary compromises, we finish the story.

168

# Notes

1. Carlsberg is a foreign beer not easily purchased in the Soviet Union. The fact that Vetryakov and his friends drink this Danish beer illustrates that they have access to goods in the restricted food stores where people can make purchases only by means of hard (i.e., foreign) currency or special "rouble certificates" available to foreign diplomats and certain privileged Russians.

2. Duc de Richelieu gained prominence for his furthering of the growth of the town of Odessa. In 1826 a bronze statue of the duke was erected which depicts the Russian provincial governor in Roman costume; the statue stands on the square which is situated at the top of the famous granite steps that descend to the city's harbor.

3. Lyudmila Parkhomenko is a Soviet singer who was a very popular performer in the 1960s.

4. It is common practice in the Soviet Union to name ships for one of the fifteen republics, e.g., Azerbaidzhan or Kazakhstan. The designation "Caravan" has nothing to do with this practice but the correlation seems plausible to Lyuda since all three words end in "-an." Vladislav Ivanovich's somewhat more romantic view of the ship's name calls to mind the nostalgic longing for "nomadic" wandering which was expressed in many of the city romances sung by bards popular in the 1960s. Novella Matveyeva, for example, popularized a song entitled "My Caravan."

5. The Russian term for "to go prospecting" (*idti v razvedku*) can mean both foraging or looking for something in an adventurous way and scouting out or spying on someone. In this instance, there is an ambiguity in the Russian which finds no exact parallel in English. This is the same expression which Volodya Teleskopov uses to speak of Vadim Afanasevich when they have bonded their friendship with crony/ Nastya's expensive homebrew.

6. There are state lotteries in the USSR and it is legal to place bets on horseraces, but one does not find Las Vegas type casinos or slot machines in the Soviet Union because they are outlawed. Video games operated by coins have made an inroad into the USSR in the very recent past, but on a limited basis and in small quantities. This does not mean that gambling is no longer a Russian vice (as it was for many during the nineteenth century), but rather that it is not legal in most instances.

7. Odessa-Batumi-Odessa is a holiday cruise across the Black Sea. Odessa is located to the Northwest of the Crimean peninsula and Batumi is on the southeastern shore of the Black Sea not too far from the Turkish-USSR border. Batumi is the capital of the Adzhar Autonomous Soviet Socialist Republic.

8. The series of James Bond movies produced largely in the 1960s were an integral part of pop-culture in the West. This phenomenon found a curious echo in the Soviet Union, where Aksyonov and two other writers (O. Gorchakov and G. Pozhenian) published a novel entitled *Gene Green the Untouchable: The Career of CIA Agent No. 014* under the pseudonym/acronym "Grivady li Gorpozhaks."

9. In A. S. Pushkin's little tragedy entitled *The Covetous Knight* (1830) the main character is a miserly baron. In Russian culture "Covetous Knight" is an epithet analogous in meaning to the names "Midas" or "Scrooge."

10. Prince Myshkin is the hero of Dostoevsky's novel *The Idiot*; he is a person noted for his humility and gentleness as well as for his eccentricity. The first two of these qualities are suggested by the prince's surname, Myshkin, which derives from the Russian word for "mouse."

11. "Elemental redistribution" serves a very vital need in the life of all Soviet citizens. Distribution of goods by the state is cumbersome, wasteful, and inefficient; it is one of the worst failings of the economy and centralized planning. "Elemental redistribution" is

sometimes a risky affair since it is quasi-legal at best and illegal if it becomes large-scale blackmarketeering. Aksyonov's term is more precise and neutral than the rather misleading phrase "unofficial economy" and speaks of a phenomenon which is both more comprehensive and organized than the more individualistic way of coping with shortages and deficits known as 'blat'.

12. The "White Nights" is a concert program performed in Leningrad during the period from the end of May to the end of June. This period when the sun shines long into the "night" is also referred to in Russian as "white nights." The festival program consists of ballet performances, concerts of classical music and performances by famous vocalists.

13. Hard currency stores stock high quality merchandise produced in the Soviet Union and goods imported from abroad. These stores are closed to ordinary Soviet citizens. (See note 1.)

14. The Russian word for "baroque" (*barokko*), which has a stress on the second syllable, is used by Valentina as a euphemism for "rock" music since the word itself suggests that association.

15. "Memphis" was a popular rock-'n-roll tune composed by Chuck Berry in 1959; it became a hit record in 1963. Soviet rock groups, such as the fictional "Seven Wheels" mentioned here, often imitate, perform and even re-record Western music.

16. VTO is an abbreviation for Vsesoiuznoe Teatral'noe Obshchestvo (All Union Theater Association). The VTO headquarters are located on Moscow's Gorky St. There is a very fine restaurant in the VTO building; it has a western-type bar to which only the members of the VTO ("the people of art") are admitted.

17. Lucius Licinius Lucullus (circa 117-56 B.C.) was a Roman general and statesman. He achieved spectacular success in the war against Mithrodates VI and, as a politician, was noted for his actions against Pompey. After 59 B.C. Lucullus found his sole pleasure in living luxuriously and this gave rise to the saying "the feast of Lucullus."

18. "Let the days of our life flow like the waves, we know that happiness awaits us ahead" are lyrics from a popular Soviet song.

19. Arkhangelskoe is an old estate of the Yusupov family. It is located near Moscow and has been converted into a museum. A restaurant was built near the museum which became very popular because of its traditional Russian cuisine. "The Seventh Heaven" is a restaurant located in the Ostankino Television Tower in Moscow. The restaurant attracts Muscovites chiefly because of its architectural novelties (for example, it has a rotating floor) and because it offers a marvelous panoramic view of the city.

20. Dikson is a northeastern Siberian port located on the Karsky Sea and just to the east of the gulf between this sea and the mouth of the Enisei River. Dikson is located at 80 degrees longtitude, 75 degrees latitude and Batumi is at approximately 42 degrees longitude, 41 degrees latitude. An imaginary line drawn from Dikson to Batumi would set off "European" Russia from all that east of the Urals.

21. By the phrase "half-breed males from the Caucasus" one should understand Georgian or Armenian men who have Turkish or Mongol blood in their ancestral lineage and/or who have been raised culturally as Russians. There is an apparent allusion here to Georgians who emulate Stalin. The original speaks of "half-Caucasians" or "semi-Causcasians"—terms which have the sound of ethnic slurs when rendered literally into English because of the association of "Caucasian" with "WASP."

22. Mao Tse-Tung was former Chairman of the Chinese Communist Party; Yemelyan Pugachev led a peasant uprising in eighteenth-century Russia; Denis Davydov was a hussar soldier who became a hero in the 1812 war against Napoleon, especially because he organized a partisan movement against the French. Davydov also wrote poetry in which he glorified hussar life, drinking and love. He also penned the lyrics for the "folksong" about Lake Baikal which Aksyonov used in constructing the "circle" of *Surplussed Barrelware* (see note 90 for that work).

170

23. A Sochi tie is a narrow black tie with silver or red streaks. This kind of tie was very fashionable in the 1960s. The trend was set by Georgians who travelled to the cities in the North to sell oranges or flowers at the markets and for whom the tie was a sort of trade mark.

24. The source for Aristotle's ideas presented in this story is the philosopher's treatise known best by its Latin title *De Anima*.

25. The term is taken from palmistry, where the "Mount of Venus" designates the part of the palm below the thumb.

26. The association of ¡Vladislav Ivanovich's outlook on life with a kaleidoscope identifies him as a kind of "fictional cousin" to Volodya Teleskopov of *Surplussed Barrelware*. The surname "Vetryakov" (*veter*—wind) speaks to this character's involvement in the system of "elemental redistribution" and to his chameleon-like adaptability in appropriating the ideas of his friends and in adjusting to a variety of social occasions. However, at heart, Vladislav Ivanovich is an optimist and, what's more, one who genuinely loves life.

27. The expression "physicists and lyricists" was coined by the poet Boris Slutsky and used as the title for a poem he wrote in 1959. Subsequent to the publication of this poem Slutsky's expression became a euphemism for "the sciences and the humanities"; his ideas spurred an extensive and sometimes acerbic debate about the merits and accomplishments of technologists and humanists, and found widespread reverberation as a literary theme in the decade of the sixties.

28. In suggesting that Vladislav Ivanovich go to the Baltic Seashore or to Tashkent the bogdykhan is being genuinely lenient in dealing with the likeable physicist. Within the Soviet Union the three Baltic republics of Latvia, Lithuania and Estonia are noted for their relatively high standard of living and for their tolerance towards individuals who are living on the fringe of Soviet society. Tashkent, the capital of the Uzbek Republic and the fourth largest city in the USSR, does not share this reputation, but it is in the heart of Central Asia and therefore a place where "elemental redistribution" is a more time-honored and accepted *modus vivendi* than in the large Russian cities.

29. Sukhumi is a port and a sea resort on the Black Sea in Soviet Georgia.

30. The Macedonian king Phillip II invited Aristotle in 343/342 B.C. to educate his son Alexander. Literature and politics were probably the main subjects of instruction. Aristotle's tutorship ended in 340, when Alexander became a regent for his father. Thus, there is a certain discrepancy here between fact and fiction. Aristotle lived in Athens, not Calchis, from 335 B.C. He left Athens for Calchis only in 323 B.C., after being accused of impiety; he died the following year.

31. Orenburg is a town in Eastern Siberia which is famous for its products made of wool; the village of Palekh is located 200 miles northeast of Moscow—it is a center for the folkcraft of making black lacquer boxes that are hand painted, decorated with gold and feature subjects from Russian folklore; Dagestan is a region in the Caucasus mountains—the necklace referred to here is probably made of embossed metal (in Russian the word "chekanka" is used to speak both of a method of embossing metal and of the artifacts which an artisan produces).

32. The word "design" was one of the catchwords widely used in the 1960s by speakers of Russian. The art of design was believed to be a new mode of expression, a sign of new times. Soon, "design" came to be used not only in connection with a form of art or a theory of communication, but also in place of such words as "picture," "construction," "combination," "outline," etc.

33. OBKhSS is the abbreviation of Otdel bor'by s khishcheniiami sotsialisticheskoi sobstvennosti (Sector to Combat against Theft of Socialist Property). It is a government bureau which exerts control over the bookkeeping, financing, expenditures, etc. of various factories, stores, etc. owned by the state.

34. The contents of the attache-case are a clue that Vladislav has prepared himself for going to prison or to a forced labor camp.

35. *Life is Everywhere* is a famous painting by Nikolai Alexandrovich Yaroshenko (1846-

98) an artist who belonged to the school called the "Wanderers" (Peredvizhniki). Yaroshenko's canvas, finished in 1888, depicts a car of a prison train that is hauling prisoners to Siberia. The train car has a window with bars on it and prisoners are looking outside at the free world, where a child is feeding bread to some pigeons.

36. "March to the beat of your own drummer" in the original is the Russian saying "one's hand is the master," which means "one does what and how he/she feels like doing."

37. The Lyceum School (or, simply, the Lyceum) was founded by Aristotle in 335/334 B.C. at a sacred grove of Apollo Lyceus and the Muses in Athens. The school took its name from the epithet of the god; it later became known as the Peripatetic School. In Aristotle's time and under his immediate successor, Theophrastus, scholarly activities at this school flourished, especially in the fields of mathematics, music, botany, politics, medicine, history, metaphysics and ethics.

# Destruction of Pompeii
## (A Story for Bella)

Every time you approach Pompeii you think: "Now here's a little corner of paradise." The platitude is inescapable, for prior to plunging down into Pompeii from a high point on the road above the city, you catch sight of the marvelously chiselled shoreline and white houses rising from the bay in terraces interspersed with the eternally verdant flora. The eye is captivated: greenery swirls above the city with abandon and climbs the steep gray-white wall of the mountain range that shelters the town and the shore from the north winds. And each time "all these things" (as modern idiom would have it) loom before you, you sense a powerful uplifting of the soul, some half-forgotten moment of ecstasy, and the expediency of your own presence here. And inside the car, in the space between the windshield and your own forehead that little platitude flashes by: "now here's a little corner of paradise."

In early spring that year I set out for Pompeii with the most serious of intentions. I had made detailed preparations to spend no less than a month here, far from the frantic noise and dirty slush of Rome, in the hope of bringing a three-year project to completion, that of polishing off a major opus in my specialty. I had meticulously selected books and manuscripts and loaded them into the trunk, which also contained the clothes necessary for the "sundry occasions in Pompeiian social life." Now with respect to these "sundry occasions in Pompeiian social life," well, I must confess that I was jerking my own knee a bit there, for as I packed the suitcase, I kept saying to myself sternly—now none of those "social occasions in Pompeii." Only a jog in the mornings, work in the afternoons, a walk in the evenings and a bit of listening to the radio before going to sleep. Track shoes with thick soles, a typewriter, and the transistor. Oh, the times I'd become entangled in the so-called romance of that seaside resort! The number of totally scandalous escapades had been so huge that I tossed into the suitcase most of my classy threads (the distinctive hallmark of our circle) for the "sundry occasions in Pompeiian social life."

In our circle the thing to do in those years was to be taken for a foreigner at first glance, but absolutely not at second glance. You were supposed to be slightly scornful of both your own (those long since recognized not to be foreigners) and of foreigners (those who were obviously not your own).

So, as I was tossing various kinds of silk shirts and sweaters from London into the suitcase, I was tacitly allowing the idea that Pompeii nonetheless would "suck me in" to slip through the net of all my strictures about serious intentions. However, since I was tossing all the stuff in haphazardly without sorting it out, I was more or less telling myself that if I should get sucked in it wouldn't be for long and that it would just be for a momentary diversion from my righteous labor.

I booked a room in the old Intourist hotel "Oreanda"[1] which faced onto a row of palm trees. In among the palms, almost obscured from the view along Shoreline Road, stood a plaster of paris statue of Historic Titan[2] painted bronze. By some strange fluke he had been dragged here to the inner courtyard of the hotel, where the masses could take no pleasure in contemplating him. To tell the truth, even if you could detach yourself from thoughts of what he represented, the figure itself still looked rather strange: a fake bronze patrician in a thick coat who stood under the shade of palms, in the midst of magnolia leaves and the purple flowers of a Judas tree; he held his right hand outstretched, palm upwards, as if he were weighing a small watermelon or bolstering up some dairy maid's tit.

It's funny that I was in no way annoyed by having it for a neighbor! Quite to the contrary, this figure hidden from everyone except me and several other patrons of the "Oreanda" suddenly struck me as being a rather likeable and, to a certain extent, even congenial fellow. I made a distinction between this Historic Titan of mine and all his other millions of replicas, and I pretended that he was a hypothetical consultant, adversary, and evaluator for my righteous labor.

The "Oreanda" is situated on Shoreline Road, directly above the sea. Having stashed my suitcase in the room, off I went to acclimatize myself in the way creative types have traditionally "acclimatized themselves" in Pompeii: you sit on the pebbles three meters from the Mediterranean Sea with a manuscript of your cherished opus in hand, gaze at a page on which something has been inscribed, like "one can also reach this conclusion, based on the theory of disturbances, from yet another point of view once focus has been centered upon the collapse of the system which takes place under the influence of certain disturbances, when the system's energy level is expressed as Eo and there is a total disregard of any possibility of the system's collapse." You repeat these expressive, carefully coined lines and, at the same time, attune yourself to your primeval and primordial homeland as you listen to the waves reshuffling the pebbles and deeply inhale the smells of boundless courage and joy.

Try to steer clear of Shoreline Road with its idle crowd of vacationing barbarians, the facade of the hotel covered with a scaffolding where devil-may-care painters are idling about. Don't be tempted to drop in at the cafe, either, where that familiar company of Romans convenes by the window on the second floor.

It went without saying that there were two or three Georgians in this company, too, who oversaw and paid for everyone, proposing toast after

174

toast to Arabella.

"Ara-bella!" one Georgian would say, holding his wineglass high above the table.

And everyone gazed at the glass as if it were a fortune-teller's hypnotic crystal ball and repeated: "Ara-bella!"

It's funny that in the Georgian tongue "ara" is a negative particle and that Georgians, in toasting our famous Arabella, almost seemed to be consecrating their drinks to a sort of mysterious Non-Bella.

Arabella rose up from one of the small cafe tables and extended her glass of wine to me. She and I had been slightly acquainted, so she was holding this beverage out to me, the one luxury which she possessed, in a kind of mute gesture of welcome. Her hand had stretched through the glass, and, exposed to the wrist, was now offering me something pleasant.

Should any speculative talk arise as a consequence of this, I will certainly explain that at that moment it was simply impossible for me to have had either Arabella or, what's more, the wineglass in my line of sight due to the obstructions in my plane of vision caused by my position.

Meanwhile, a painter had calmly climbed down the scaffolding to the cafe window, taken the glass from her hand and bowed spryly to thank her. He had just about positioned his little pinkie on the glass stem so that he could partake nobly of this noble beverage when he suddenly interrupted his enchanting ritual and hollered at someone in a powerful voice: "Nikolai! Lie the brick down! I order you, lie the brick down! Lie the brick back or I'll shoot!"[3]

There was absolutely nothing around from which he could have fired a shot. In discussions later, this fact was echoed far and wide along Shoreline Road. Why would he shout "I'll shoot" when there wasn't a weapon to fire?! He bellowed "I'll shoot," you understand, but what did he have to shoot with?! These people are really something: they shout "I'll shoot," with no firearm at hand, but what can you do about it, they're such braggarts?!

Passersby looked to see whom this painter was shouting at so loudly and they all spotted another painter in splotchy overalls who was standing on the scaffolding and painting a third-floor balcony. He was painting away to his heart's content, sluggishly and sloppily; he blew his nose on his sleeve, not suspecting a thing. Above him, the second painter; there likewise stood on the balcony a third painter, who had a brick in his hand aimed at the crown of his co-worker's head.

A long, drawn-out second:
1) The first painter was still holding the glass of fine wine. The second

175

painter was holding a brick aimed at the third one's head. The third painter was holding his brush with a shaky, drunken hand.

2) The second painter smashed the brick against the third painter's head. The third fell from the scaffolding onto the asphalt, where he lay sprawled out. The first painter drank down the glass of wine.

3) The painter with the empty glass in his hand dashed off somewhere—either to save the victim or nab the criminal. The second painter, his face bathed in a dazzling smile, finished off the third painter with a second brick. And the third one, with a violent twitch, flopped onto his back and once more sprawled out, spread-eagled and motionless.

A dark puddle began to collect.

Shoreline Road burst into a babble of shouts: "He did it for his broad, his broad, his own wife."

Some brave individuals tore through the door leading to the balcony. The murderer, still bathed in a dazzling smile, scrambled across the railing, and his body flew head over heels, struck against the second-floor balcony, and plummeted like a sack down to the asphalt right beside the first victim; immediately a second dark puddle began to collect.

As in Bizet's opera, over a woman, a whore—the hairdresser Svetka—and out of jealousy, two skilled workmen perished in broad daylight.[4] They hadn't even had a lot to drink.

From the crowd of vacationers under the surveillance of the voluntary militia came a steady hum of voices. The appropriate vehicle drove up and individuals designated for such tasks removed the corpses. Slowly, the vehicle moved away.

The person responsible for what had happened dashed out of the hairdressing salon on Shoreline Road. The dazzling bright polyester-clad body under her white work-smock, now flung wide open, glistened with the delightful chimera of unruly flesh.

It's been reported that they had even had two kids, and some people used the past tense in reference to them because they assumed that Svetka's kids vanished together with their fathers.

The hairdresser lunged at the ambulance car with her hands; shocks of tufted red hair seemed to bounce across the roof of the vehicle. Her hands left black marks. And it's with hands like this that they shave us!

Later, I had the impression that the destruction of Pompeii began precisely from this moment. It was as if that fatal incident initiated the collapse of the resort town and all its sanatoriums, restaurants, and monuments to workers and to Historic Titan. As if the painter with the brick had given a signal to the volcano. As if only then the whiffs of smoke had begun to appear above the rocky spur suspended in the golden sky.

In actual fact, however, if there was any link between the two occurrences, it was more likely to have been the other way around: puffs of smoke began to appear much earlier. No one noticed it for a long time because, strange though it seems, the residents and tourists in Pompeii were not in the habit of observing nature closely. Generally, they observed only one another, for it was exclusively in the collection of individuals that they saw the source of their pleasures or, as it's fashionable to say now, *kaif,* their version of "la dolce vita."[5]

To be precise, the puffs of smoke were noticed only when they had turned into really thick smoke. However, the vacationers supposed that it was just a local tourist attraction and the natives thought it was just a case of some experiments or other being conducted in the mountains which had to do with nothing more or less, putting it as simply and bluntly as possible, than our armed forces. The military strength of our republic was such that the possibility of any natural disaster occurring could just be dismissed.

The thought didn't even enter anybody's head, of course, to search for a link between the pink smoke in the mountains and the wave of strange acts which, like a deluge, rushed ashore. The sudden flare-up of passion in the painters' guild was just one of the many ensuing episodes.

Stories like these began to circulate:

Early one morning a highway patrol inspector was supposedly seen at one of the major intersections. He was shaving, sitting on the roof of a patrol car in front of a huge round mirror installed there to facilitate traffic safety, but certainly not for the convenience of shavers.

Rumor has it that in the "Carthage" bar one evening black marketeering voluntary militia men sort of beat up a Dutch tourist. They were listening, you see, to some old songs and he, you understand, was disturbing them—either by trying to peddle some piece of merchandise or by asking them to fix him up with a girl. Yet if one takes into account the special relationship between the Dutch and the People's Voluntary Militia of Pompeii,[6] this is probably the least credible detail in all of the many strange events which were reported.

And something else, too. One couple at a dance held in the Club at the Woodworking Plant shed all their clothes and gave a public exhibition of the act of coitus. What's more, they not only escaped being beaten up, but even enjoyed the loud applause of the other dancing youths. And, in addition, the club's director appeared before the City Council with a bouquet of wild poppies[7] when he was summoned to undergo disciplinary criticism. What's amazing is that they accepted the bouquet.

The director of a film crew from Rome placed a call to the very same City Council and proposed, in conjunction with the film he was shooting in

Pompeii about life abroad, that the whole town be converted into a film studio, that is, to restore capitalism, for all practical purposes, in Pompeii.

Also, some criminal types bashed a zinc bucket over the head of the pensioner Karandashkin[8] who, as a free service to his country, was selling state lottery tickets on Shoreline Road. Of the hundred thousand tickets which the muggers took from him not one was a winning number. Subsequently, Karandashkin sent an open letter addressed to all honest people of the planet, only to have the letter published in the newspaper "The Furnace of Health."[9] This led to a very absurd polemic which came to a halt only after the Ideological Commission issued a direct order.

Yet the record for mindless cruelty in those days turned out to be the attack on the circus tigers by some deadbeat tramps. They chased the beasts, frightened to death, out of their cages with fire extinguishers. These tigers had performed as circus entertainers for ten generations, so they now jumped through hoops simply because of genetic traits, not in response to any training. Once they had scattered through the town and come into contact with the strange lifestyle of the resort's inhabitants and tourists, they quite naturally ran wild again. The thunderous roars of these ill-fated creatures could be heard in Pompeii right up to the last day of its existence.

However, there were also occurrences of some questionably-perspicuous acts of virtue. Once, late at night, a threesome grabbed Matvei Tryapkin,[10] the chef at the sanatorium "Homeland," by his coat lapels and demanded: "You have 50 roubles?" Now where would a drunken cook get a hold of such a sum of money? The robbers frisked the poor fellow and, once they'd convinced themselves that he wasn't lying, gave him a gift of a fifty-rouble note.

What is the link between people's behavior and the action of fiery lava from the underworld—one of cause and effect or the opposite, a direct or indirect connection? No one knows, so everyone stays confused. The pink cap on top of the volcano grew larger with each passing day.

But oh how successfully my work progressed at the time! In the morning I would leave the hotel in my springy track shoes and begin to run up the asphalt-covered grade which led from the lower to upper level of the park. During the minutes just before dawn, when the dark-blue crest of the horizon in the East charts its domain with special clarity because the sun is about to burst out from behind it at any moment, my brains were teeming with all sorts of good ideas. I saw page after page of my opus, "Repercussions at the Quasi-Discrete Level," dance before my eyes.[11] And my whole steam engine all warmed up quickly, skillfully and synchronically—the lactic acid in my muscles oxydized and broke down, oxygenated hemoglobin stretched my fallen alveolae, and my aesthetic gland, not to be caught napping in this burst of energy, gladly awoke and took in everything ecstatically: the tea-rose bushes which secretly and lovingly beckoned from under the stone walls where they had cornered a bit of light, the secret and slightly wanton swaying of the billowing Persian lilac, and the naively euphoric smell of the dew-drenched wistaria. What lines I managed to write then, what marvelous lines! "The system inclined towards collapse does not possess, strictly speaking, a discrete spectrum of energy. Particles which fly off during its collapse travel into infinity!" What lines!

I took breakfast right at my work table; I would eat a couple of cold, boiled eggs prepared in advance, drink some instant coffee, and read my new sentences through the window to Historic Titan. He would usually screw up his tiny barbaric eyes (a strange mixture of genes from a steppe nomad and a Swiss clerk)[12] and stare at me in a thoroughly indecisive manner. Nonetheless, it was my impression that he condescendingly approved: write, I say, write on. What is there, huh, to keep you from writing with your swanky gold Mont Blanc pen[13] on the pristine page? Write, but don't forget about the people who compensated for their passion to write with prison bread and water.

The countless replicas of Historic Titan can be divided into two basic types: majestic images and lifelike images. Yet that Historic Titan of mine, secreted among Pompeii's blooming flora, was neither one nor the other. Some nameless sculptor had captured him in this emigre pose, it seems, while he was strolling casually and mindlessly. He'd probably had his quota of such empty days when he was making history: times when the movement falters and splits into stupid factions, the greengrocer's and butcher's bills pile up, but a ray of light, however slim, still glimmers in the kingdom of darkness—the "Knopf" publishers have promised an advance and in Rome the colonel of the centurions has been shot and wounded.[14] A small matter, but all the same good news. At any rate, he could enjoy a quiet stroll with his neighbor, the tooth-extractor Gruber,[15] and say, illustrating with his characteristically Volga palm turned upwards: well, well, Herr Gruber, you won't believe it, but it's a perfect archetypically round breast, such a compact and solid little watermelon . . . This HT of mine was really no titan at all, just a slightly perlexed and unhealthy patrician who bathed infrequently and talked a lot. A neighbor like any other neighbor, a regular *citoyen.*

I recited to him: "—. . . as a result of the effects of relativity the level represented by the variables L and S splits up into a series of levels represented by the new quantity J . . ."[16]

He heard me out with no particular show of enthusiasm, but also with no strong reaction—as if he were making use of the pause to get a word in about his little watermelon.

On one paradisic morning (judge this epithet by what was said earlier), I noticed a thin crystal glass containing good wine on the palm of my Historic Titan. On the pedestal below, curled up like a pretzel, slept Arabella, her head on the historic shoes. My gaze woke her up.

"Good morning!" she said, "do you know that Pompeii is threatened with destruction?"

"When?" I asked.

"Will three days from now suit you?" she inquired.

I thought a bit and replied, "Three days? That's a long time."

"Maybe it'll be less. Make haste."

"How did you happen to turn up here, Arabella?"

"I stumbled onto his lordship here in the bushes quite by chance. He startled me, this poor abandoned child of history. He spent a long time telling me about Astrakhan watermelons and, as always, was grossly exaggerating. However, I listened to him the whole night through. After all, he's been unfortunate and isn't understood by anyone except his poor wife. If you trace the lineage of Polovtsian aristocrats,[17] he and I even turn out to be distant relatives. It's sad that the European branch of our ancestors split off so long long ago. Their bough withered, but ours has borne fruit right up to the present. And who's to blame for that? I offered him all that I possess. The glass in his palm, you see? He's noble, you see, 'cause he hasn't touched it. He left it for me to have this morning. How sweet of him! No, no doubt about it—his private life was definitely misunderstood."

She stood up and stretched. Her white slacks and blouse were covered with bronze colored dust. The Titan was beginning to flake here and there.

O Rome's darling, mythical Arabella! Every time you encounter her you think it's just some trick of television photography or that newly invented holography. She scampered up the statue of Historic Titan like a monkey, securing her bare feet cleverly in the sculpture's defective spots, and took the glass.

"Good morning!"

Head tossed back. Large gulps. A huge neck muscle was adeptly pumping down the moisture which had stood out overnight under the starry fermenting sky.

"What's that? Something transmitted via enemy radio stations?" I asked.

"Oh, no! I myself put it in his palm," the pretender Arabella reacted in fright, "this is my wine, I swear."

"I'm not talking about wine."

"What about, then?"

180

"The news. Pompeii's destruction."

"Oh, that!" she remarked, dangling her legs gaily as she hung from HT's arms. "Yes, yes. It's either the song of an angel or blatant lies from the radio."

I began to put on my track shoes.

"How's the writing coming?" Arabella asked. "Read me a few lines from 'Repercussions'."

I obliged.

"Bravo!" she exclaimed.

"And how's your singing doing?" I inquired.

"I'm fed up with it," she said with a laugh. "You've got it easy—you sit there like a lump and write. Performing songs on TV is desperately boring."

"But your fans..." I started to say.

"I know, I know," she said, dismissing the comment with a wave of her hand. "I'm trying to find a different way to get them to prop up their existence. Are you actually getting ready to jog? Take me with you."

We started off running together—evenly and rhythmically, with the intoxicating smell of wine from her puffs of breath. But when I later glanced to my side, I no longer found her next to me. I turned completely around and, in the distance which was growing more blurry with each step, caught sight of a truck vending beer. Painters and film people had gathered around it. Arabella, with her palms extended outwards, was encouraging our dopey citizens to prop up their existence.[18]

That evening ash began to fall on Pompeii. A lacklustre moon lit up the crest of the mountain range, above which there floated a rose-pink luminescence. Here and there, serpentines of fire crept along the wooded slopes.

Foreign radio stations were reporting Pompeii's destruction loud and clear. Our capital calmly but forcefully denied the rumors as slander.

That night I finished work on my monograph and set off for the hairdressing salon. For some reason I had a sudden urge to alter my appearance radically: maybe, to have them trim a bit off the temples or give my moustache a new twirl. In short, willy nilly, my legs carried me off to the hairdresser's.

Picture me that evening: an enormous strapping red-head with a glint in his eyes! Good intentions forgotten. Forgotten, too, and thoroughly ventilated from my mind—the well-turned phrases in "Repercussions." Clearly realizing that Pompeii had "sucked me in" this time, I moved cheerfully towards the vortex of the "suction"—the hairdresser's.[19] Flakes of ash flittered gracefully, swooped towards the lamplights of early evening and fell on the crowd of barbarians who, as always, were yearning for kaif.

A Greek liner had docked hard along Shoreline Road. Music drifted from that direction. They were playing the new hit record "Love Machine" over and over again. A teeming crowd milled around at dockside. Everyone except the most arrant lazybones was trafficking on the black market: young pioneers, pensioners, musicians, and even centurions in uniform. And just between us, there were even centurions in civilian clothes. It even seemed that the ultimate purpose of black marketeering had already been lost sight of; the primary goal of making money had been forgotten. Now it was merely a chaotic and greedy exchange: a hunt for clothes, drinks, various types of Japanese baubles, and tobacco.

Here I am at the hairdresser's: over the entry pre-revolutionary naiads hold aloft a wreath; on the left side of the door is a memorial plaque honoring the underground meetings of the Pompeii cell of our bee-hive; on the right a memorial plaque honoring the visit of the "great chronicler of the twilight era when public consciousness began to fade."[20] There remains some question as to whether he spent a long time here and what he did during his visit, whether he ever had his moustache curled or the hair on his temples trimmed.

However, it seems that during the twilight epoch there wasn't a hairdressing salon on this site, but rather a sanitary house of ill repute. Of course, perhaps this, too, was nonsense—just a city legend told with a faint jeer. Uncouth boors usually spread only spiteful and bawdy stories about the chroniclers and it's impossible now to reconstruct the truth—archives have been destroyed and the historical record has been completely distorted through propaganda.

Anyway, I walk into the reception room and right away I see my reflection in two dozen mirrors. Quite an imposing sight: the arrival at the hairdresser's of a whole crowd of enormous, red-headed gargantuans. Two dozen armchairs and an equal number of hairdressers, too—pudgy, skinny, busty, tushy ones, in creased and soiled smocks, and all of them in the same state of intoxication. A full load of customers. One is cackling insanely, twitching in the armchair with his arms and legs; another has bent his flabby body over and is moving his hands idly back and forth above the floor as if in search of underwater treasures; a third, having grabbed the chief hairdresser by the buttocks, is swirling around on his armchair and serenading her with the waltz song "He's shy—not bold." The rest are shaving, more or less.

What's the first impulse of the red-headed giant who's just entered? Why, he'd like to drive all this rubbish out of the broadway barber's temple with a whip and at one fell swoop plop down on all twenty-four chairs, because for some reason he is insanely pleased with all two dozen of the women. A most shameful impulse, of course.

Cut-down-to-size, I notice: here, it turns out, even the waiting line—

five to seven other musclemen—has to hang around idling; in what way am I better than them?

There's nothing that can be done about that. This is the drunken rubbish you have to live with: a community of people stuttering and slurring words and poisoned by cheap disgusting port wines, that one-rouble swill with a slimy chemical sediment, the so-called "Mumbo Jumbo."[21] With rubbish like us, not only Pompeii but, in a year or two, even Rome will topple. But we somehow have to live together with them, that is, with ourselves, and to face destruction with them. Emigration? No, that's just smoldering embers, both inside and out.[22]

The line rocked back and forth, drunken and pot-bellied, with mindlessly smiling eyes and faces smeared with volcanic soot. No one in the present company suspected that a short distance away, on the far shore of the dark, oil-slicked sea in the "lands of Capital," hundreds of hairdressers spend their time in charitable quietude, with the reserved assurance that they can expect only upstanding customers. On the other hand, I said to myself as I joined my comrades on line, in a certain sense there is the same—if not worse—rotten smell everywhere.

"The same—if not worse—rotten smell is everywhere," I said out loud to boost the courage of my comrades.

"It's worse in our metallurgical district," said one smiling fellow.

"Why are you looking?" a second smiling fellow asked.

" 'Cause. I'm just looking," said a third smiling fellow.

"He waunts to look," uttered a fourth smiling fellow.

"Lat'm look," the fifth smiling fellow said.

"Look, if you waunt," the sixth smiling fellow said.

"Look, does no difference to me," said the seventh smiling fellow.

The red-headed giant looked at the group of port winos, not without a certain sense of horror. One of the smiling degenerates stood out from the others and made a definite impression on him: the powerful mould of a foolish old face—a retired colonel of the legion of honor. At least all these heirs of Caesarism have preserved something in their features, I thought, it may be the stability of an ungifted but majestic epoch. Should I stick with them, the last piers of society?

A peal of thunder slowly rolled over Pompeii. For a second the stormy sea was lit up. The floor of the hairdressing salon heaved violently. The pre-revolutionary Dutch tile cracked and shattered.[23]

Perhaps all that's left is to join ranks with Caesarism, the red-headed giant thought. Theirs may be the only pillars which haven't begun to rot from the inside out. He offered the colonel a Marlboro cigarette.

"On television they're saying the overseas lands are putrifying," the colonel said, inhaling the pale blue smoke. "But actually, we've got the cesspool here and they've got the economic achievements. And what's the

183

reason?"

"What?" the red-head asked.

"Ain't no decent organization," the colonel explained willingly. "They criticized Marshal Tarakankin[24] and that criticism was right, I agree. However, they forgot that the Marshal had a brain. The kind of orders he gave? Why, to delay demobilization of all personnel with demerits for the same number of days as they had black marks on their record."

"Why is there no latrine here?" one smiling fellow asked in surprise. "The comrade here's pissing without the presence of a latrine."

"Every pencil wants to piss, but they hold their lead in silence," said another smiling fellow.

"Marshal Tarakankin arrived at our trireme," the colonel continued, "in time for demobilization. They saw the personnel off with an orchestra, but detained seaman Pushinkin[25] for 105 days because in his three years of service he had chalked up 105 days in the brig. Everyone else returned to their productive civilian jobs, but Pushinkin roamed aimlessly through all compartments of the trireme and became disgustingly louse-ridden."

"Pardon me, but what link is there between this situation and the economics lag?" the red-headed giant asked.

"They've forgotten how to organize things right," the colonel explained. "Moreover, the campaigners fighting against cosmopolitanism seriously damaged the quality of our science. Just look around—no self-respecting tomcat will eat today's sausages."

"You've got sour aspic for brains," the red-headed giant mumbled as he moved away from under the pseudo life-jacket colonnades of Caesarism, not without some dismay.

Then, yet another blow. In one terrific burst, a gust of hot wind blew down all the palms on Shoreline Road. One of the pre-revolutionary naiads toppled off the frieze and cracked into pieces. The glass door to the hairdresser's shattered with a loud bang. Flakes of ash and the vile trash of this public resort flew into the salon itself. Filthy smocks clung to the extremely enticing bodies of the 24 frightful tarts.

A second or two later and there was only the barren waste of catastrophe before our eyes: crimson flashes of sheet-lightning, palms bowed over by the wind's iron broom, a bloated sea with our naval fleet clumsily sliding down into its gluttonous mouth—had that poor fellow Pushinkin not served on one of those triremes?—and the torso of the naiad flung onto the street. Remember at least this, if all else is forgotten, remember at least this!

A group of youths walked past, guffawing and singing the song "Love Machine."[26] In the process of stepping over the naiad, one of them propped his leg on her in order to lace his shoes. All's normal; life flows past, empty of memories; the organizations responsible cope with the ravages of natural disasters; the prognosis is good; Rome stands firm, unshaken.

Suddenly, all at once seven closely shaven and neatly cut citizens came out of the beauty salon.

"Next!" boomed the voice of the chief hairdresser on the loudspeaker. The PA system, it turned out, was still working there.

The red-headed giant fell onto a chair, right into a woman's eager hands. How can they condone such filth when their guild's service is public beauty? Fingers with broken nails and chipped polish darted nimbly across the red-headed client's chest, belly, and groin. A gigantic and eager mouth, smeared with lipstick, laughed above him. Tits were falling out of the unbridled polyester blouse. The wet hem of a skirt stuck to the protruding lower abdomen, and everything below brought to mind that deep-water Agave known for its passion for lurking, sucking in, and swallowing innocent fish.[27] So, that's who's got the red-headed giant: Svetka, the disgrace of the city, the widow of the two painters.

"So, that's who's got me!" the obscene mouth laughed. "The red-headed one, red one, saucy one, shameless one! Let's get out of here, Red, let's get the hell out of here! I'll give you a shave on the beach! Take all this stuff! I'll do it to you 'deluxe' style on the beach!"

"Excuse me, but it seems to me that's against all the rules," babbled the red-headed giant. Nevertheless, he stuffed his pockets with boxes of powder, creams, and a rubber atomizer containing "Shipr" cologne, and helped Svetka to take down from the wall an ancient mirror with a special golden frame.[28]

"Tomorrow, Senkina, you will be fired for laying the customers," said the chief hairdresser.

"Watch out or you'll be sacked yourself, Shmyrkina," Svetka shouted back. "It's not a private operation we've got here, it's a guild. You yourself fuck behind the partition and the customers aren't satisfied."

A bushy crack opened up in the ceiling. A volcanic wind whirled through the salon, lifting up a tornado of cut hair. Face to face, the two women rapidly snarled at one another, something completely offensive and incomprehensible.

The red-headed giant began dragging the mirror to the beach. Behind him Svetka was dragging spotted bed-sheets.

"Oh, momma dear! What a customer I've hooked, oh-ah-oh," moaned Svetka.

The red-headed giant gripped her thighs in his hands, but turned his head so as not to see her terrible face.

Waves of gray pebbles lay on the beach and in all their troughs there

185

was grunting and squealing. Sin was being committed everywhere, and ashes fell onto all this carnal bestiality.

In our case the sin was aggravated by the stupid mirror. it stood at the heads of the copulating pair, and everytime the red-headed giant raised his head he could see in it his strangely undisturbed face.

Behind him, in the mirror, the crimson sea was becoming more and more luminous, the volcano was burning brighter and brighter over Pompeii.

Then two chicks in hip-hugging jeans appeared in the mirror. They stood with their horsey faces downcast, swaying back and forth. One of them held her hand on her friend's pubis, while the other squeezed her friend's breast.

"Here, Galka! Look how the pros work!" one of them said, sort of hiccuping in our direction. "But we are still trying to find our kaif."

Right then and there they tumbled down into some pit, where they expressed their ecstasy in real bawdy language: oh, I got banged sweet, ah, I'm all wet, oh, Galka, oh, Tomka, look how starry the sky is, look a star is falling a star is falling...

What they took for stars were falling volcanic bombs. The torturous and jolting eruption began reducing the carnal bestiality's bellowing to an exhausted lowing.

"I tell you, Client, you made me rustle," Svetka uttered. "Since Nikolai and Tolya killed each other I haven't had a feast like that."

The soot was smeared all over her face; her eyes shone thankfully.

I looked at myself in the mirror. Where had the red-headed giant disappeared to? My balding head was melting away like a candle, my body was swelling up like yeasty-beasty, sour dough.

A scorching stone crashed onto the beach, cast up a fountain of pebbles, spun like a top, and rolled into the sea, where, with a hiss, it sank in a cloud of steam.

I got up and walked away, hardly moving my elephantine feet. Buttons on my shirt popped off and my hairy black stomach hung down, suddenly unbelievably swollen.

Roofs of the houses along Shoreline Road cracked under the pounding of boulders. Broken windows were raining down. Neon letters which survived here and there spelled out abracadabra. A powerful flame was raging inside of a little store with the coquettish name of "Sweet Tooth." However, next to it, people who had gathered in the morning were quietly standing on line at the neighboring grocery store. They were waiting for the delivery of some fantastic boiled salt pork, although there could be no chance of a delivery since all the passes above Pompeii were enveloped with smoke and covered in flames.

186

Orchestras were playing everywhere. The "Love Machine" thundered from basements, from under the canopies of open-air restaurants. People of all ages danced in a frenzy. It was freedom of movement unthinkable in the times of Caesarism: eyes bulging and mouths lusting; the eerie Pompeiian shimmy.[29] Socialism which imitates capitalism is socialistic to the point of tears.

Of all the people who had it good in the burning Pompeii, the gloomy fat guy with dirty dark locks hanging down on both sides of his balding forehead had it worst of all. The arrogant elephantine fat guy was meandering feebly and mindlessly through the crowd until he saw a telephone booth for long distance calls. From that booth he could immediately plug into the capital's telephone system, but, strangely enough, it was empty: apparently, nobody had any need at all to call Rome. The fat guy stepped into the booth.

"Do you know that we are burning?" he asked his colleague at the institute, the first person whom he managed to reach by phone.

"Old man, it's too late for philosophical questions!" playfully laughed his colleague—in principle, an okay fellow, who, as a matter of fact, was no different than me: the same kind of crafty slave of the communal system which swallowed us all up.

"No, not in the philosophical sense at all," said the fat guy. "Pompeii is perishing. The volcano has gone mad."

"Well, that's no topic for a telephone conversation," his colleague uttered angrily.

Everything is clear. Now they will put me down as a provocateur. I hung up the receiver and through the glass I saw Arabella who, dancing and waving her hands, headed up a very merry company. A calm herbivorous snake was lying softly coiled around Arabella's shoulders.

"Hey, come out of there!" Arabella shouted to me. "Why are you swelling up over there in the telephone booth? Look, gentlemen, how this character has swollen up!"

A couple of merry Georgians pulled the fat guy out of the telephone booth and offered him a bottle of wonderful wine.

"Where do you get such wine?" I was surprised. "And where, in general, do you find all these nice things?" I asked simpleheartedly. "How is it that you Georgians manage to live rather sumptuously in the midst of all this wretchedness?"

"No problem," the Georgians answered merrily.

A scorching piece of rock hit the telephone booth and instantly wiped it off the face of the earth. The face of the earth, in turn, slid apart under our feet and formed a crack half a meter wide. We jumped over the crack and walked along Shoreline Road passing lines of people craving kaif and those having a good time inside of burning cafes.

A small clever boy, a "young naturalist," was following on Arabella's heels and whining: "Lady, give me back my yellow-belly. I took it on loan from the zoological lab for some research."

"Child!" Arabella clasped her hands. "Do you really mean to separate us? Can't you see how your yellow-belly likes hanging around my neck? Child, the snake and I love each other!" She took the head of the yellow-belly in her palms and kissed it on the mouth. "Child, I confess that I myself am quite a yellow-belly and if you are truly a young naturalist, you must study both of us."

Something like a ball of lightning flew over Shoreline Road and hung over the main square of Pompeii, over the City Council building and over the most powerful and majestic sculpture of Historic Titan.

"We are all yellow-bellies!" enthusiastically shouted our entire company: Oh, that magnetic Arabella!

What was hanging in the distance over the square did not hang for a long time. It struck and scattered in a zillion sparks. Then, for a second, a phosphorescent light appeared and illuminated the main square. One could see the statues of various epochs falling: a border guard, a woman tractor-driver, a tank driver, an astronaut..., —and how the principal, most powerful statue began to fall down. It became frozen in my memory just like that—in the state of leaning and falling—because the phosophorous disappeared and the crash of the statue's fall was muffled by the swelling uproar in Pompeii: orchestras, shouts, laughter, and the crackling of fires. A thought flashed through my mind—and how is mine, my personal HT doing there, what has happened to him?

"No victims!" exclaimed one of Arabella's retinue.

"An extraordinary phenomenon of nature, comrades! A volcanic eruption with no loss of life. It is the counterpart to the neutron bomb: material goods are destroyed, people remain whole. That's precisely what I reported to Rome on the hot line: no losses of human life; courage is making a stand against the elements!"

By his entire appearance, this man, dressed in an official two-piece suit, with our bee-hive pin in his buttonhole, was supposed to personify the stability of our all-embracing administration, but a small muscle was twitching in his face, and a bottle of cognac was sticking out of his jacket pocket.

Arabella encouraged him with her soft palm, caressing his neatly combed hair from one side of his head to another.

"Poor child, deserted in the midst of the fiery elements! This morning you were still reigning in your City Council office, and now you are all alone! We won't leave you! Take heart!"

"I am taking heart," the secretary looked trustingly at Arabella.

"That's exactly what I reported, I managed to say on the hot line: courage is making a stand against the elements..."

"Lady, give me back my yellow-belly!" begged the young naturalist. "It's time for it to eat."

Someone who appeared to have once had and lost some secret power approached, holding in his hands a bottle of Pepsi-cola and a glass.

"Your reptile, does it eat Pepsi-cola?" he asked the young naturalist, looking at him with his still penetrating eyes.

"It hasn't tried it yet," the young naturalist mumbled," but I...I, personally, Comrade Colonel, eat Pepsi-cola with pleasure."

The colonel in civilian clothes, chief of the local department of centurions in civilian clothes, began to pour the bubbling Pepsi-cola into a glass and to treat the young naturalist and his snake to it. The boy swallowed the foreign drink greedily, while the yellow-belly hanging down from Arabella's shoulders only delicately sipped the brown moisture.

Our company was growing. It had turned into a crowd. The men and women and the young and old were walking; children and dogs were jumping up and down; cats were scurrying back and forth; and tigers from the local circus dragged along like sheep. The whole crowd was following the darling of all our people, the metropolitan area, and the barbaric regions: the television mirage, Arabella.

She once sang in an expressive voice in the attics and basements of Rome and was famous only among the attic-basement elite. Then, suddenly, this strange creature with the hypnotic voice appeared on TV in among all the mug-ugly pedlars, and all of our preposterously savage people, tired of hearing about their achievements, did not boo her; they fell in love with her. What miracle brought her into the tele-communication system? Wasn't it the first symptom of the present seismological storm?

Where were we going? For some reason, uphill—closer to the fire. Along the steep narrow streets of Pompeii, past the burning houses and closer to the scorching heat, we were ascending the Hill of Glory. In the houses, homemade vodka-distilling machinery was exploding, television tubes were bursting, and mirrors were melting, but the inhabitants for some reason didn't seem to take notice of the destruction of their property. Everybody was in a rush to get whatever kaif there was left and to join up with us.

"You've become younger again, pal," Arabella told me. "Where's your hairy belly? Where's your muddled look?"

Indeed, I felt a kind of strange youthful lightness. More and more easily, happier and happier, I was jumping over the streams of scorching lava which spread over the cobblestone road. Once, among dozens of other faces in a piece of broken glass, my reflection flashed out at me—this, it seems, is how I looked about twenty-five years ago, in my student days.

Strange transformations in age kept occurring during our entire procession: the young naturalist, for example, in his shorts was now resembling a very boring senior lecturer, and the chief of the secret service—a masturbating schoolboy, one of those who always hang about in school restrooms.

"Stop!" the secretary of the City Council suddenly shouted. "Here's the special-supplies warehouse!"

In front of us were the smoldering ruins of quite an ordinary house. A black "Tiber"[30] limousine was ablaze next to it.

"Five minutes before the destruction of the City Council building I gave an order to Ananaskin[31] to do a complete inventory," the secretary of the City Council explained worriedly. "Oh, no, Arabella, I assure you, I, personally, don't need anything: I'm just curious what the results were."

The gas tank in the "Tiber" exploded: a pastorale for the fire storm in the background. The door to the special-supplies warehouse fell off and Ananaskin appeared on the porch, hunched over from the weight of a huge smoked sturgeon that he was carrying on his back.

"Here's all I managed to save," he wheezed.

"Dear Ananaskin!" exclaimed Arabella. "Humble secret supplier! Gentle distributor with respect to labor! Are you shaking, Ananaskin? Take heart! Kiss the yellow-belly and join us."

Moaning, Ananaskin put his mouth to the snake's lips. Someone immediately came to his assistance, then an second and a third; they put their shoulders voluntarily under the beam of sturgeon, its weighty hulk.

We were drawing near to the top of the Hill of Glory where, among the destroyed bas-reliefs, there flickered a little ribbon of the Eternal Fire. So touching, in the raging of that Non-eternal Fire!

"It wasn't for us that this fish swam, and it wasn't for us that they smoked it, either," Ananaskin groaned. "They were expecting an important person. But now there's no point in keeping their secret—it was the Pro-Consul himself! Fortunately, he did not arrive..."

"What do you mean didn't arrive?" asked a man standing behind Ananaskin's back. "Who do you think is volunteering his help with transporting this beam of sturgeon?"

The little guy turned out to be the one who had been expected with such trepidation by the entire Pompeiian administration for two weeks already—the Pro-Consul from Rome. It turned out that his plane landed right in a puddle of lava and stuck there like a fly. No car was provided and the guards ran off in different directions to the barber shops. Now the Pro-Consul was walking among the people, trying to be inconspicuous.

Behind him, under the beam, the pensioner Karandashkin was

190

walking with a zinc pail on his head. The procession of the four volunteers was brought up in the rear by my plaster-with-pitiful-remnants-of-gilt Historic Titan from the "Oreanda."

"Are you up to our sturgeon, comrades?" questioned Ananaskin.

"It's precisely labor like this that liberates peoples from those forms of exploitation which have become standard for them," Historic Titan spoke out.

"Just where is it we're going?" Karandashkin asked from under his pail. "Where will we eat this fish?"

"Don't you understand?" a Georgian dancer expressed his surprise. "Ara-bella will now sing to us from on top of the hill!"

"What a blast!" the pensioner shouted loudly.

"What a blast!" echoed the entire procession.[32]

"How could I abandon them, these dear scarecrows?" Arabella thought with a quiet smile. "How could I deprive them of myself? What will they have without me? Sappho, George Sand?"[33]

At the top of the Hill we all took our places. All around dry grass was burning, alabaster was melting, and the bas-reliefs of heroic deeds were tumbling down. Down below, to the thunder of its own jazz, Pompeii was collapsing.

> Flaring up higher, growing more crude,
> The feast is raging, the talk is rude...
> My dear little girl, oh, Pompeii,
> Child of Caesarina and of slave...[34]

Arabella sang out and then cleared her throat a bit.

"I haven't sung for a long time, but now I will sing everything for you—from the beginning to the end, or from the end to the beginning, or from the middle in both directions."

The volcano was roaring like all the radio jammers of Caesarist times and of our days put together, but the feeble voice of the singer was heard all the same.

"Whazz she singing?" asked Karandashkin, knocked off his rocker by the sturgeon, which he had never before seen or eaten in his entire life.

"She's singing her own stuff, not ours," explained the Pro-Consul sluggishly, giving rare fish its customary tribute.

"It's amazing music, not human," croaked the Historic Titan pensively, quoting his own thoughts on classical music (Collected Works, Volume XII).[35]

Flowing around the Hill of Glory, the streams of lava poured down onto Pompeii. From the top it seemed that everything was finished, but more new crowds of people still kept ascending the Hill.

There came our workers and vacationers, the crowd fishing for contemporary kaif, the advocates of maximum satisfaction of their own constantly growing needs. Everybody was sure that it was a live broadcast of Arabella's performance, so therefore nobody thought of the destruction of Pompeii. Television and the government know what they are doing; in this world there are no miracles.

Thus, with this faith in faithlessness, we all fell asleep on the Hill of Glory. Each of us was forgetting everything blissfully and irrevocably. For example, as my brain began to go to sleep, it was forgetting stanzas from "Repercussions," my proud work designed to win the minds of humankind, and a thought about the vanity of vanities flashed through my head,[36] but was immediately forgotten.

Nobody woke up, even when it started to rain. Streams of water descended from the merciful heavens on high and pacified the volcano. We were sleeping in clouds of hot steam, and then under the constantly increasing gushes of a pure north wind. The wind blew away the steam and cooled off the settling lava, but we were still sleeping.

When we woke up, a cool and bright new day had arrived. Thousands of light, clean creatures were sitting on the Hill of Glory and didn't remember anything. A quiet and unfamiliar landscape stretched all around us. We were all looking at each other—author of "Repercussions," tamed tigers, cats, dogs, painters, film people, musicians, Arabella, Georgians, Svetka the hairdresser, the chief hairdresser, the retired colonel, the colonel of the secret police, the young naturalist, the secretary of the City Council, Karandashkin, Ananaskin, the Pro-Consul, the lesbians, Historic Titan, and all of yesterday's troglodytes of materialism. We were all looking at one another, not recognizing anybody, but loving everyone. Thousands of eyes were looking around with the hope of grasping the purpose of our awakening.

Finally, we saw a small tongue of fire at the top of the Hill and next to it there was a hot loaf of bread, a wheel of cheese and a pitcher of water. That was our breakfaast. Then we saw a narrow path which ducked in between the cliffs and rose towards a pass in the mountains. That was our way. A second later and on the steep spur of the volcano appeared a snow-white, long-haired goat. She was our guide.

That's what happened in Pompeii that year at the beginning of spring. Later on during the excavations, scientists were surprised that no traces of human bodies were found in the destroyed buildings. In only one building, something resembling a school, they found a slithering emptiness in the lava which pointed to the fact that, probably, some time ago it was filled with the body of a small harmless snake. This allowed archeologists to make the suggestion that the inhabitants of Pompeii kept in their houses tame herbivorous snakes called "yellow-bellies."

VI—VII.    '79

Written in the notebook which was Bella's gift in the spring of the Metropol year.[37]

# Notes

1. Before the Revolution, the name "Oreanda" was associated with the imperial estate located about 4 miles southwest of the Crimean port of Yalta. Known for its picturesque ruins of a Roman castelleum and a chateau (burnt down in 1882) and the beautiful "Oreanda" church in the Byzantine style, this estate played a prominent role in A. P. Chekhov's story "A Lady with a Dog."

2. "Historical Titan" is an allusion to V. I. Lenin or, perhaps, a fictional titan who represents a loose amalgamation of both Lenin and Stalin. Countless statues of Lenin are erected all over the Soviet Union; some of them are made of bronze (especially in the large cities), but the majority of them are replicas cast from the most famous sculptures. Certain types of poses are prescribed for these statues: Lenin as a leader of the Soviet people, with his hand outstretched to symbolize the way to the bright future ahead; Lenin as a pillar of the Soviet state, with his hands clutched behind his back and his eyes set in an intent appraisal of the distance ahead; Lenin as a thinker, sitting in a chair with a look of deep thought expressed on his face, etc.

3. In the original the worker uses a corrupted form of the Russian verb "to lay." To render his colorful speech, we chose to make use of the confusion on the part of many speakers of English between the verbs "to lie" and "to lay."

4. The opera alluded to here is Georges Bizet's *Carmen* (Paris, 1875).

5. The Russian word "kaif" was probably derived from the American slang "kef," which means a drowsy, dreamy condition that is produced by smoking narcotics. "Kef," in turn, derived from the Arabic word "kaif," which denotes "well-being." As the Russian word "kaif" was used by young people in the Soviet Union during the 1960s it came to have several basic connotations: from a verb meaning "to get high" to exclamations such as "swell," "great," etc.

6. The special relationship between the Dutch and the People's Voluntary Militia of Pompeii is, of course, an anachronism, but it does find a modern parallel in the way Soviet police treat and use some foreigners from such neutral countries as Finland.

7. The inference here is that the poppy is an opium-producing species. In the original the plant is called a "mountain poppy"; we substituted the adjective "wild" because we were not able to substantiate the existence of any opium-producing plant called a "mountain poppy."

8. The surname "Karandashkin" derives from the Russian for "pencil" (karandash).

9. "Furnace of Health" has a more euphonious sound in English as the name for a newspaper than "Forge of health" or "The Smithy of Health," which is what is found in the original (Kuznitsa zdorov'ja). This is not the name of an actual Soviet newspaper, but the phrase "forge of health" is used in colloquial Russian to refer to sports camps or resorts oriented towards sports and body building.

10. Matvei Tryapkin is a name with a Gogolian sound to it. Translated the name means "Matthew Milksop." Phonetically, the surname recalls that of the judge in Nikolai Gogol's play *The Inspector General*: Lyapkin-Tyapkin.

11. "Repercussions at the Quasi-Discrete Level" is a title that suggests the author is a "physicist" turned "lyricist," to use terms hotly debated in the Soviet Union during the 1960s. (See note 27 to "Super Deluxe".)

12. The allusion here is to Lenin's origin, specifically to the mixture of German (Volga) and Tartar blood in his ancestral lineage.

13. "Mont Blanc" is a very expensive and elegant fountain pen of Swiss make. Since mention of this type of fountain pen is attributed in a roundabout way to the Historic Titan, it is worthwhile noting that Lenin spent a number of years in Switzerland during his exile abroad. The narrator alludes to this fact, too, in the reference just above in the text to a Swiss clerk.

14. There is no allusion to a historical circumstance in the mentioning here of the American publishing firm "Knopf." A plausible reason for referring to this particular publisher is that the firm has an international reputation and the surname "Knopf" is Germanic so it blends well with fictionalized Swiss and Austrian setting in this part of the story.

15. In the original, Gruber is called a dentist (dantist), but the more professional term struck us as being too mild an English equivalent for this neighbor (surely, Austrian) of the Historic Titan whose surname calls to mind Adolf Hitler's other name, Schicklgruber.

16. The variables L and S may well be thinly disguised allusions to Lenin and Stalin. In view of the leader-disciple relationship which develops throughout this story between Arabella and the people who come into contact with her, it is possible that the variable J may be symbolic of Christianity (i.e., alludes to Jesus). In keeping with the way scientists write mathematical formulae in Russian, these variables all appear in Roman letters in the original.

17. The term "Polovtsian aristocrats" is an allusion to the Tartar origin which Bella and HT have in common. Bella, in turn, is an allusion to the contemporary poet Bella Akhmadulina, the prototype for Aksyonov's heroine in this story. In the introduction to her long poem "My Genealogy," Akhmadulina wrote, "My father's grandfather, who endured a bitter orphanage in Kazan living in hellishly difficult poverty, explains—by his surname alone—the simple. secret of my Tartar surname." This work was published in Moscow in 1977 with the title *Svecha*.

18. There is a playfully metaphysical idea behind the Russian term for "to prop up [their] existence": obodriat' k dal'neishemu sushchestvovaniiu (literally, "to encourage [them] to a further, or future, existence"). In practical everyday life, Arabella is striving to help people realize that a certain amount of kaif is accessible to and needed by them. On a higher plane, she uses her artistic talents as a means to "charge people up" rather than the lavish gifts and money which Vladislav Ivanovich Vetryakov employs in the story "Super Deluxe."

19. In the Soviet Union barber shops or, as they are often called, "salons of public beauty" serve many purposes other than the styling or cutting of hair. They may function as centers of information where everything which has not made its way into the offical media can be disseminated. Also, one might set up a date here with a local prostitute, especially if the barber shop is located in one of the sea resorts in the South. Finally, for men these places may serve as a kind of clubhouse, where males discuss various domestic and world problems as they wait in line for a haircut.

20. "Great chronicler of the twilight era when public consciousness began to fade" is a phrase which has the sound of Communist jargon meant to allude to V. I. Lenin.

21. The term for this beverage ("Mumbo Jumbo") in Russian is "bormotukha." Bormotukha is a cheap port wine which is often drunk by alcoholics as a vodka chaser. The origin of the wine's name is the verb "bormotat'," "to mumble." Chasing vodka with bormotukha has but one purpose: to get so drunk that you cannot say two words straight.

22. Russians often speak of two kinds of emigrants: those who actually leave the homeland to settle abroad and those who remain in the Soviet Union but disassociate themselves with the government in meaningful ways. Both these options are disregarded by the narrator here

194

when he refers to the possibility of emigration as being "just smoldering embers, both inside and out."

23. The mention of Dutch tile at this point in the story may well be an allusion to the mosaic tile floors in Pompeii which have been uncovered by archaeologists. In a Russian context, "Dutch tile" are usually associated with stoves, not floors, and with the reign of Peter the Great.

24. Marshal Tarakankin's surname derives from the Russian word for cockroach (tarakan).

25. The detention and, evidently, subsequent demise of seamen Pushinkin in this story has an allegorical quality to it which suggests a veiled allusion to the imprisonment and resultant death of someone in a prison camp. Perhaps, on the other hand, Pushinkin's fate is only to be understood in a broad sense as that suffered by many under the whimsically cruel orders of Marshal Stalin.

26. If there has never been a rock-'n-roll song called "Love Machine," there ought to be.

27. Agave was the daughter of Cadmus and mother of Pentheus; according to classical mythology, she tore her own son to pieces while he was spying on a Bacchic orgy at Dionysus' instigation (with the aim of stopping these celebrations).

28. "Shipr" is a men's cologne with a heavily alcoholic base. (See note 124 to *Surplussed Barrelware*.)

29. The Russian word for this dance is 'triasuchka' (shake, shimmy) and suggests in a way that no name for an analogous dance can in English the earthquakes and volcanic eruptions which took place when Pompeii was destroyed in August 79 A. D. by the violent upheavals of Mount Vesuvius.

30. The Soviet equivalent for the black "Tiber" automobile is the car called "Volga." This is the automobile usually used by party officials.

31. Ananaskin's surname derives from the Russian word for pineapple (ananas).

32. These two exclamations in the original mean literally "What kaif!" Our translation into more idiomatic English is based on the information provided in note 5.

33. Sappho and George Sand are linked here because they are famous women writers for whom the theme of love played a major role in their literary endeavors. Sappho (7th to 6th centuries B.C.) is renowned as a poetess who lived in a community of women on the island of Lesbos. George Sand (pseudonym of Amandine Aurore Dupin, 1804-76) was a French novelist and a major figure in the cultural life of her time.

34. These verses are lines 17-20 (fifth stanza) of Bella Akhmadulina's poem entitled "Volcanoes." For Russian text see Bella Akhmadulina, "Vulkany," in *Sny o Gruzii* (Tbilisi: Merani, 1977), pp. 18-19, where the lines lack the punctuation marks of triple dots.

35. The Historic Titan's remark about Arabella's singing finds an analogue in V. I. Lenin's assessment of Ludwig von Beethoven's music. Russian readers would recognize the source of the Historic Titan's remarks, so the author expanded this paragraph slightly from the original in order to ascribe to HT a multi-volume collected works.

36. "Vanity of vanities" is the pessimistic phrase which is repeated throughout the book of Solomon in the Bible to characterize life on earth.

37. The almanac *Metropole* was published and circulated privately in the Soviet Union in 1979. Vassily Aksyonov, Andrei Bitov, Viktor Erofeev, Fazil Iskander, and Evgeny Popov were the editors of this almanac which was subsequently published by Ardis and, in an English translation by W. W. Norton in 1983. Bella Akhmadulina was one of the major contributors to the almanac and it is to her that this note refers.